FOR MY PEOPLE

AWACHA NAY

BOOK 1

HEIDI ENNIS

For My People
By Heidi Ennis

Copyright © 2014 by Heidi Ennis
All rights reserved.

This is a work of fiction. While the author has done her very best to present the ways, speech and relations of the indigenous peoples of the Pacific Northwest, some of that information has been lost, and some is kept to themselves by the modern tribes. That is their right. Where gaps exist, the author has made her best effort to fill them with fictional material that seems consistent with other ways and outlooks which are more general knowledge, or at least more generally available.

Cover Copyright © Katie W. Stewart Magic Owl Design

ISBN: 9780692423974

First paperback edition: 4/2015

Also available in eBook publication.

PRINTED IN THE UNITED STATES OF AMERICA

For my dad.

Author's Note

First of all, I have to thank the greatest editor that I could have asked for. I had no idea I needed you so much. J.K. Kelley, thank you for demanding that I take my shoes off, put my toes in the sand above that spot along the River and listen to the voices. *Kw'ałá, siks.*

Thank you to Virginia Beavert and Sharon Hargus. You do not know it, but your belief in and dedication to the preservation of the Sahaptin language has taught me much about the courage and strength that still exists today in the hearts of indigenous people all over this country. Also, I could not have completed my work, nor would I be as excited about the work that I do, had it not been for two men who made it their lives' work to understand and preserve the indigenous languages in the Pacific Northwest: Father Charles Pandosy (1824-1891) and George Gibbs (1815-1873). May your work live on.

Thank you to an inspiring writer and mentor, Shawn Inmon. I'm still not sure why you took on a newbie like me but thank you. To Katie Stewart at Magic Owl Design, thank you for the beautiful artwork on the cover and maps. You continue to amaze me. And to Debra Ann Galvan, thank you for the quick and painless proofreading. I appreciate your time more than you know.

Thank you to my mom and sister, who will always be my loudest cheerleaders. And to Desi, thank you for encouraging me from the very beginning. I honestly could not have done it without you, my friend.

Finally, to Mike, Camryn and Collin, thank you for always acting interested when I told you something that fascinated me about cave drawings, or giant prehistoric bears, or all the ways to cook salmon. Thank you for enduring those long car rides so that I could see something with my own eyes. But most importantly, thank you for sharing me with the voices in my head. *Átawishamash.*

Author's Suggested Readings:

A Dictionary of the Chinook Jargon, or, Trade Language of Oregon by George Gibbs, Cramoisy Press, 1863.

Alphabetical Vocabulary of the Chinook Language by George Gibbs, Cramoisy Press, 1863.

Grammar and Dictionary of the Yakama Language by Rev. Pandosy, Cramoisy Press, 1862.

Ichishkíin Sínwit Yakama/Yakima Sahaptin Dictionary by Virginia Beavert & Sharon Hargus, Heritage University, 2009.

Prologue

In the beginning...

The days are getting colder, the sky darker. The Sapsikw'ałá says a time is coming when we will no longer see the great Aanyáy at all. I fear that day. I was trying to remember the story of old when the Great Spirit was so bright in the sky and the unending coldness so far away, but I can no longer remember. I must focus on the task given to me now, though my fear is great. Did my father's father feel the same fear as I? I find comfort in this thought. I must continue on, for them...my people.

Time cannot be determined, at least not in conventional ways. Mother Earth was constantly changing, and the sun had abandoned her. Yet in this cold, desolate, pitiless environment there wandered a proud and determined people intent upon one thing—survival.

With death in the form of starvation and an endless winter at their heels, they walked on. Heads down and hoods pulled low, they followed him. They would follow him anywhere, as they always had, as they always would. He would not fail to protect them, to provide for them. He was their strength...their hope, and their chief.

He walked ahead, one sure foot in front of the other. He would let none sense his anxiousness. His strong hands trembled from the extreme cold, his fingers clenching into fists and stretching out again. Yet he carried his shoulders proud under the old bison skin cloak, the great beast's head at the back of his neck comforting him—as much as comfort could be found.

He knew the people followed him, but he could no longer hear the soft crunch of hide-covered feet, nor the occasional whimper of a chilled little one. He only heard the eerie cry in the wind, the one that haunted him, that made sleep impossible. He took a deep breath. The frigid aid stung his nose and burned the back of his throat, but fill his chest and infused his muscles with strength. And by breathing, with every breath in his lungs, he found the will to keep going. His burden was a great honor and a great responsibility.

Time passed, although he did not know how long. Each moment seemed an eternity. Then a glimmer of hope lay ahead in a vast snow-covered mountain range. They waited, huddled together for warmth and safety. He went on ahead, alone. The people watched the spot where they had seen him last, and they prayed.

The wind screamed and the cold bit as he climbed the rocky incline, the entrance high enough for safety, low enough for daily sustenance needs. Could it be? He refused to hope. Once inside, the darkness was engulfing and suffocating until he remembered to breathe.

He closed his eyes to listen: a soft drip of water, an echo in his footsteps, his heart pounding in his chest. He controlled his breathing. He wanted to fall to his knees, to weep, to cry out in thanks to the Great Spirit—no, there would be time. He stepped to the very edge of the cliff overhang, took a deep, penetrating breath and called them to him.

He called them home.

Asku let the memory overtake him. By now, he knew better than to fight it. For far too long, he had feared what was happening to him, and as long as no one else knew about it, it was fine—or so he told himself. Would any others of his people, the Patisapatisháma, understand it? The Teacher, perhaps. The Chief—his father—just maybe.

In his mind he could see the cave clearly. He could feel the cold silence all around him, in spite of the stuffy heat of his room in the present. He could see the small boy, could see the Chief and the old *chalámat* pipe at his lips.

Asku felt like he was floating, blowing on a cool breeze. He let the vision wash over him...

The harsh elements continued outside the cave, but inside was light, warmth, and life.

Kaga, Saigwan's father and Chief, puffed on the small chalámat. A fire crackled loudly in front of him, the reindeer bone making more noise than wood, but burning more slowly, and more plentiful to find. The burning-bone smell filled the cavern anew each morning, a reminder of harder times.

The name, Saigwan, still worried Kaga. The child had been born the night of their arrival in this very spot five winters earlier. Some had called it an omen. Then they had waited three moons for the Spirits to name him. The name meant strength, power, and integrity. And also, change.

Kaga feared for the child's path, and that which must lay ahead for the people.

Saigwan looked once over his shoulder before slipping away from his father, who did not tell him to come back. He wandered to the back of the cave, to the tunnel that had held his curiosity as long as he could walk. He knew the voices came from this way. Saigwan had to know more about them, why they called to him. He was too little to guess why.

With each step he took, he heard them calling. They called him by name.

Saigwan peeked around a corner. The torchlight no longer touched the walls, but he could sense the expanse of the inner ritual chamber. He heard the change in the sound of his footsteps, felt the movement of air around him.

He heard his name, an echo. He heard singing, shouting and chanting. He could feel strong emotions emanating off the walls: fear, pain, death.

He held the torch up to the nearest wall, his fear climbing higher in his throat, threatening to suffocate him. On the walls were pictures of animals and men, the work of Yiska. This elder, who had been a mighty hunter in his youth, had suffered a crippling injury and now was an artist and storyteller. Yiska's paintings and tales spoke of and to the soul of the people. Saigwan recognized the Chief by the bison cloak, the great beast's head resting at the back of his neck.

The chaos of music and song, ritual and celebration, fear and shouting pounded through his head. He ran to the next wall and the next, trying desperately to make sense of it all. What was this place?

Saigwan backed away from the pictures toward the center of the room. His legs hit a solid, rough object, the ancient altar. It tore at his bare skin as he fell.

He got up and ran, fast as his little legs would carry him, scraping his arms and hands along the walls to find his way in the darkness. The chanting and the beat of an invisible drum followed him, the voices growing louder and louder the faster he ran, calling him back into the chamber.

He hit something solid, not a rock. He tried in panic to run the other way. When he felt a strong grip on his upper arms, he lost control and fell to the ground, holding his ears to escape the echoes of his fear.

Soon the sounds faded as the distant voice of his father grew closer. Kaga's strong arms cradled little Saigwan against his broad chest.

When the light of the main chamber cleared the shadows, the Chief put Saigwan down and knelt before him. "One day you will understand, my son...my títa, you cannot not run from them."

Saigwan did not understand. Why did the voices haunt him? He could hear them sometimes at night even, calling his name.

>———→

Eight winters later, the inner ritual chamber still haunted Saigwan. When he entered, his heart quickened with fear and awe. The noises around him, the song, the drums, the fire and the shadows were terrifying, yet intoxicating. He closed his eyes, fighting down the urge to panic.

The song was the same. The voices were the same. He could feel his people all around him, in body and in spirit, voices resonating in his very soul.

Niyol, Saigwan's best friend since his earliest memories, sat across the fire from him. Niyol lifted his chin slightly, a silent beckoning that conveyed: Náy, yawtíi...are you all right?

But Saigwan could not even acknowledge Niyol's concern. He tried to remember his father's words from that morning...

"I am proud of you, Saigwan," the Chief had said as he untied the necklace of bear teeth and claws. Saigwan noticed long, deep scars on his father's chest that the necklace had always covered.

"This was my father's and my grandfather's and his fathers before him, always passed down on this special day. Someday you will pass it down to my grandson. It will protect you and give you courage…táaminwa, always." The Chief fastened the necklace about his son's neck.

"Thank you, túta," Saigwan whispered.

"There is strength and there is honor that comes from bearing that necklace, tita," the Chief had continued. "Great men have worn it, men that have given all for this people. They will guide you, speak to you, and teach you…if you listen, my tita."

The Chief stepped closer to him, moved the necklace aside, and laid a warm hand over Saigwan's heart. "But truly, they are here already." At that moment, Saigwan had felt that he could do anything.

He was not so sure now.

Strong arms were under his, lifting him off the ground, many hands carrying him around the circle. Then he felt the cool stone as the hands laid him upon the altar that he had once tripped over, all that time ago. The Teacher stood at his side. Others held his arms immobile.

He willed himself to breathe through his nose as he had been taught, seeking to calm himself.

Saigwan knew his father was close. He hoped to make his father proud.

A new song started, softly at first, building in volume.

The Teacher sprinkled something across Saigwan's body, then rubbed it hard into his chest and arms. Each of the Teacher's fingers wore a sharp claw, once belonging to a great bear. Saigwan watched the claws sparkle in the glowing firelight.

The old man raised his hands high and screamed unintelligible words as he stabbed the claws into Saigwan's chest. Saigwan felt flesh tearing, opening, and stinging pain as the claws ripped across and down his side. He clenched his fists to keep from screaming, and did not make a sound, not even as it happened again.

Then the room was quiet.

These were the wounds, scars to be, that branded a future Chief of the tribe. The pain was Saigwan's pride. He felt blood running down his sides. Only when the Teacher poured something over his chest, something that burned like flame, did a brief cry escape Saigwan's lips.

Hands lifted Saigwan to his feet before Kaga, the man who was to him both father and chief. Kaga nodded.

Saigwan understood he was a man now, and everything had changed. The deep stinging in his chest left no doubt.

Chapter 1

Asku looked up from his feet and realized it was happening again. All eyes were upon him. His mind raced through the previous words he had only vaguely heard. *Where did the old man lose me this time?*

His grandmother clicked her tongue from somewhere behind him, the usual prelude to a cuffing for inattention. "Um," Asku stuttered. "Hmm, well…" He looked at the ceiling, then at his best friends Hawɨlish and Kitchi sitting next to him, then back at the floor.

The Teacher's eyes clouded with sadness.

"Áwacha náy." The old man kept his eyes on Asku. "That is the way it was," he finished, as all the children shouted in unison, *"Íi…*yes!" Story time was over.

The Teacher waved the others out. The small group of older women and children stood up, stretched their legs and backs, took young ones by the hand, and walked out of the smoky cedar longhouse.

Asku picked up his hide mat and began to shake the dust from it, standing up to his full rangy height. Wiry rather than bulky, already taller than some adult men, he had a runner's deceptively strong frame and graceful stride. Like many Patisapatisháma men, he wore his hair in a single long braid down his back. He had spare features with high cheekbones and bright, intelligent eyes.

He felt a quick, painful rap to the backs of his ankles. He turned around but saw only the small elderly figure waddling away. *How does she do that? If I hurry, I can beat her home. Mother will understand; she always does. Grandmother is—*

The Teacher waited at the door, looking disappointed, blocking his exit. "Asku?"

"Sapsikw'ałá, I am sorry. I—"

The old man raised a hand to quiet Asku, leaning heavily on the teaching stick. "What is in your heart, *myánash*...my child?"

"What do you mean, *Sapsikw'atá?*" *Not another lecture.*

Asku was not about to tell the truth: that visions of an ancient relative were playing out in his head, stories of old come alive. He could even smell the memories at times, feel them, bringing him to tears or leaving him sweating in fear, as if he had lived them himself.

"Askuwa'tu, what do you feel when you hear the stories? What does your heart tell you?"

Asku began edging toward the door. "I'm sorry for not paying attention, *Sapsikw'atá*. I did not mean to be rude. Besides, I have heard the story before, and I am sure the Great Spirits would be trying to teach me the same thing as last time. Persistence, right?" He slipped past the Teacher. "Have a good day, *Sapsikw'atá*," Asku called over his shoulder.

"You too, my *tita*," he heard the old man sigh.

Asku knew the Teacher had stalled him just long enough that he would never beat his grandmother home. So Asku ran.

With the great river called Nch'i-Wána at his back, and Pahto in front of him, Asku began to feel free of his elders' burdens, but not completely. Even as he took lungfuls of the clean, fresh air, he imagined or felt adult disapproval behind him. "Grow up," "take your place," "chosen" ...*responsibility, character, wisdom, courage.* But also: *weakness, disappointment, coward...*

He ran, and he tried to let it all go.

Far ahead of Asku stood mighty Pahto, nearest of the three Smoking Fire Mountains of the Great Mountain Range. Wy-east, with his sharp-tipped snowy peak, stood tall and proud Beyond Nch'i-Wána and Toward the Setting Sun. Lawilat-ła stood in all her regal, distant, round-capped beauty Toward the Setting Sun. Way off in the distance Toward the Great Mountains, Taxùma's distinct snow-covered peak and smaller adjoining summit glimmered brightly.

Asku revered them all, but Pahto was his mountain, under whom Asku had lived for all his life. When Asku had sought solitude, peace and forgiveness, he had found these in Pahto's presence. At times Pahto hid beneath thick cloud blankets, or in ominous thunder clouds. Sometimes Pahto wore clouds as a thin white headgear about his snowy summit, resembling an enormous version of the shells found at the Great Sea where the sun passed beyond sight of any person.

All was clear and warm today as Asku looked up at Pahto, his base and peak vivid and glowing in the sunlight. Asku heard the sharp piercing cry of an eagle soaring high above the tall evergreens off in the distance.

Taking one more deep breath, he continued on his journey—away.

The end, his final destination, was a small waterfall along a tributary of Łátaxat Wána where it cascaded over a cliff. An agile boy like Asku, who knew how to reach the spot with the fewest gully descents and climbs, could reach it and return in less than half a day's light. This, his sanctuary, Asku had named *Yixa Xápaawish* after the beaver family that occupied a large space downstream. The deep pool at the waterfall's base glistened and sparkled in the bright sunlight. The water rippled quietly down to the old beaver dam. Just below the tranquil pile of sticks and engineered debris, a small trickle escaped to create a stream that eventually made its way to Nch'i-Wána near its narrows, Toward the Setting Sun from Asku's home, and downriver from the great falls of Wayám.

Asku pulled the sling and bow from his shoulder, sheathed the long, black *chúksh* blade that he always carried, kicked off his moccasins, undid his clothing, and let it all fall to the ground there before Yixa Xápaawish: clothes, worries, insecurities. He dove headfirst into the pool.

The icy water hit his body with a chill that cleansed away care and doubt. He swam under water as long as he could, letting the voices and whispers and worried looks flow out of his skin and into that cool water. He floated on his back, staring up into the beautiful blue sky.

I can do this. I will do this.

Some time passed before Asku swam back toward his clothes. Just as he reached his hand over the mossy rock at the water's edge, he saw movement. A large black bear meandered from the dense underbrush, one big, hairy paw at a time. The bear grunted as he walked, as if talking to someone.

Boy and bear saw each other at the same time and stopped. The bear's nose lifted slightly, sniffing the air. Bears were rare near the Patisapatisháma village, but the tribe often hunted and gathered toward Pahto, which was bear territory. Following his training, Asku dropped his eyes to avoid confrontation and swam behind the waterfall. While the bear could easily swim out to him, the slow retreat made it unlikely that the bear would consider him a threat.

The bear kept his eyes on Asku and moved toward the water, stepping over the strewn clothes. Something about this bear's face looked familiar, yet unlike other bears Asku had seen. Standing directly over Asku's moccasins, the bear bent his head to drink from the pool.

For some reason, I am not afraid. "And neither are you, *anahúy*," Asku said aloud.

The bear blinked his dark eyes and snorted, shaking his big head. Asku chuckled with amusement as the bear turned around once, twice, three times, knocking one of his moccasins into the water. Then he disappeared the way he had come.

Asku waited a few moments just to be safe, keeping an eye on the floating moccasin, but he was starting to get cold. He looked to both sides, which he had never quite done from that spot. Something caught his eye to the right.

It was a rock, protruding from the muddy side along the falls just above the pool's surface, light in color. There was no way to guess its ultimate size, but it did not seem to fit in. For one thing, it looked flat on top.

First, my moccasin, or it will end up in Nch'i-Wána one day. Once he had fished it out and tossed it safely ashore, he swam back to the odd stone and splashed some water onto it to rinse off the mud. It was flat on top and seemed to be in layers. Only an area about the size of a new baby was sticking out.

Asku grabbed the rock, braced as best he could and pulled. No movement. There had to be more of it buried in the soil along the waterfall. He rinsed off a little more of the mud on the side, took a close look, and his eyes grew wide.

Embedded in the rock was the shape of a small seashell, like those that came up Nch'i-Wána in trade from the peoples at the Great Sea. And not far below it was something blue and gray.

I have been told that the flint we usually trade for at Wayám comes from rocks like this. Is this flint? If so, this is very special and rare. I have almost never seen it this color.

Asku swam to shore, found a rock of suitable size, dug something of a foothold in the pool's side near the rock, and banged. It wasn't easy, and his position did not allow for the best striking angle, but chip by chip the light stone broke off. It was brittle enough. One more good shot, and he marveled.

He had laid bare a stretch of the bluish-gray stone. Asku pulled a smaller rock from its eroded entombment in the muddy bank, adjusted his angle, and tapped at the most exposed part of the beautiful stone. He held his other hand where, if a chip flew loose, he could stop it before it landed in the water. Asku struck, just so. He heard and felt the piece break, hitting his palm. He closed it gently on the fresh flint flake, examined its edge. It was not as sharp as *chúksh*, but what was? *I could cut deerhide with this, no problem. This is a treasure.*

He emerged from the water exhilarated, once again in control.

"Now to face reality," he sighed. "My mother and grandmother are probably waiting for me."

➝

The hills above and around Asku's village rolled Toward the Great Mountain Range, carven by valleys and gullies. Thick grasses, bushes and short trees covered the rocky shrub-steppe landscape. Asku heard the river long before he saw it.

His village lay on a plateau just back from the steep bluffs overlooking the swift, wide Nch'i-Wána. If one canoed with the current, Toward the Setting Sun, one wound up at the Great Sea: endless water tasting of salt, where other peoples combined fishing and hunting to catch fish the size of longhouses. If one canoed against the current for a few days, one came to mountains, though none like Pahto. There, Nch'i-Wána curved left through a steep canyon, into dry country with great prairies and other peoples both hospitable and suspicious, narrowing as one went. It was the greatest river his people knew, and they had always been here.

As Asku entered the village, his little brother Susannawa stepped into his path. "*Ála* is looking for you," Susannawa whispered, looking back over his shoulder. "She's mad."

"Do not worry, *nika*." He ruffled the little boy's hair. "Where is Mother?"

Asku knew the answer already. Asku's mother and sisters would be where they always were this time of day, at the firepit preparing the family's evening meal.

"At the fire. You should hurry, though. Father is on his way. Scout came back just…"

"*Kúu mísh*." Asku pushed past the boy. The Chief, their father, could not be far behind the scout. Time to face his grandmother's anger and punishment before his father returned.

"*Pa'iwáxim*…wait for me! You promised to take me fishing!"

"Another time. Sorry Sus."

The rich, satisfying smell of smoked salmon emanated from the firepit area. Nis'hani and Mininaywah, his little sisters, played near the flap of the family's home tent. His elder sister, a pretty teenager named Nayhali, was cutting vegetables while Chitsa, his mother, leaned over the smoky pit sprinkling dried herbs onto the salmon steaks skewered over the fire. She looked up from her work.

"Askuwa'tu, I have been worried, *isha*."

"*Íla*," he began, "*Sapsikw'alá* …the story. Grandmother—" he stammered, nothing like the speech he had planned on his walk home.

"*Chú'*…hush," she snapped. "Help me with this, please. Your father will be here soon." She passed him the small water bowl and antler ladle.

Asku began dipping water from the bowl and ladling it onto the hot rocks, trying to keep his face out of the steam and smoke. "*Íla*, I am sorry," he began again. "My mind wanders. It's so hot in there, and the old man drones on and on sometimes. Most of the time," he added under his breath. Nayhali snorted.

"I understand, *isha*. I am not angry with you. Your grandmother is, though, and wants a word with you."

"*Íla*, please–"

Chitsa cut him off. "Askuwa'tu, you are the son of the Chief of this people. Your grandfather is chief of the people I grew up with, the Wawyukyáma. You cannot be a careless boy forever. Listen to them, for one day they may speak no more. Your path is to lead this tribe, whether you want to or not." Chitsa's tone softened. "Stop running, *myánash*, because you cannot outrun the future. *Míshnam pamshtk'úksha'*…do you understand me?" Asku knew of no kinder sight than his mother's smile.

"Yes, *íta*."

Just then, a large form appeared behind his mother. She gasped as his father's strong arms lifted her off her feet and into his embrace. "Napayshni," she said, burying her face in his neck. "I have missed you so."

"So have I, *átawit*…my sweetheart," the Chief whispered into Chitsa's ear. When he put her down, he turned his attention to his eldest son. "How goes it, my *títa*?"

"I saw a bear today, *Wyánch'i*." His mother gave him a look, glanced at the Chief, and returned to her work. "How was the hunt?"

"Two bull elk and a handful of goats," answered his father, laying his hunting gear on the half log seat behind him. "Walk with me, *títa*," he said to Asku. "I would like to hear about this *anahúy*."

The Chief walked around the back of their home and out onto the trail that circled the village's perimeter. The trail connected Asku's father—chief of this tribe, the Patisapatisháma, *the people like branches of a tree*—to every family in the village. Although the tribe spent most of the year at this spot, within a short walk of the bluffs that overlooked Nch'i-Wána, their basic homes remained temporary and easy to move. Once or twice a year, the villagers packed up and headed into the hills below Pahto for the *wák'amu,* the flowers whose nutritious bulbs were an important part of the diet, and the delicious huckleberries and blackberries that played roles in both diet and food preservation. Individuals or families might come and go as they pleased, often to visit or trade with the many tribes of the river country. The Patisapatisháma had good relations with most of their neighbor tribes, some of whom were more like family, and sought to remain at least on polite terms with all. The bluff and fishing grounds on the village's side of Nch'i-Wána, Toward the Rising Sun from the falls of Wayám, were sacred to Asku's people. Since the beginning of legends, this steep bluff overlooking a broad curve of Nch'i-Wána had been the home of the Patisapatisháma.

Wayám was a series of cascading waterfalls. Many traveled there to fish, to trade and to build relationships. It was a short canoe trip from the Patisapatisháma fishing area downstream to Wayám, which had villages clustered on both sides of the river. The Tlakluit, across the river from Wayám, were allies and friends of the Patisapatisháma. During high traffic fishing and trading seasons, one could find upwards of a thousand people at Wayám, most of them *wanawiłá,* faraway visitors.

The Chief often went down to Wayám to meet with other chiefs and *Nch'ínch'ima,* and when possible, he brought Asku and Susannawa along. Wayám was the thrumming economic pulse of the region, a meeting and trading center where people traded tools, oils and furs for *ch'láy* (salmon flour), baskets, jewelry, and other prized crafts or raw materials. The Patisapatisháma women learned as girls to coil baskets of all different sizes and shapes, using earthen pigments and berry juices to decorate the exteriors with elegant reddish geometric designs.

As Asku and his father walked, they came first to the home of the Grandfather, the tribe's healer. Only his fellow elders called him Kiyiya, his given name. Just past the Grandfather's home stood the old, weathered Totem and the ceremonial firepit, where the people gathered for important events. Across from the Totem was the vividly decorated Story House and home of the Teacher. As they approached, the Teacher stepped from the door followed closely by Asku's grandmother. Asku jumped behind the Chief, hoping they had not seen him.

"Ah, Napayshni," the old man smiled, "how goes the hunt?"

"Very well, Haymawihiu, very well," the Chief replied.

The Teacher held his hands up in blessing, palms toward the Chief. "*Kw'ałá*...thank you, Great Spirits," he chanted, "for returning our son safely to us. *Watwáa naknúwim*...protect and take care of us."

"Thank you, *Sapsikw'ałá,*" the Chief replied.

The old man walked away, winking at Asku as he passed.

When Asku looked up again, she was there, a small elderly woman with arms folded, glaring at him with unnatural malice. Asku made a habit of avoiding her.

"Napayshni," she began, "we must talk, now."

"Hello, *iła,*" said the Chief in a respectful tone.

"Your son—"

"*Íła,* we will talk soon," he said. "Asku and I must check on the meat." Asku hurried along behind his father, glad for a reprieve. When they were good and clear of the small, angry presence, the Chief slowed his stride. "Now, tell me about this *anahúy*."

Asku related the experience as they meandered through the village. The Chief listened, now and then asking a question. They walked together from one end of the village to the other, then began circling around the outside. Asku's curiosity finally got the best of him.

"*Wyánch'i*, what's wrong? Is everything okay?"

"Well, I have been gone a long time, *tita*." His voice was rich and strong, the way Asku wished his own voice sounded. "I have not been here to walk the village, as I normally do each morning. So, I need to see how our people have fared in my absence. Observe as we walk. I make sure longhouses are stable, tent homes are standing strong, and that there is no evidence of anything falling down, predators, or other problems. Then I must look in on some people. For example, do you remember Sunsaa, the elder who fell during the Spirit Hunter ceremony before we left?"

Asku remembered the ceremony, one of his favorites. He nodded. Sunsaa, a pleasant old man with outstanding crafting skills, had broken some ribs and was not doing well.

"I must check on him and see how he recovers. I hope he is better. If people who have had misfortune never see me, they may doubt whether they matter to me, and a chief cannot give people that doubt. If I should need their support in a difficult time of my own, I might not have it."

Just then, Asku flinched as something flew down from the longhouse roof above. The Chief did not flinch but held out his hands to catch the slight frame of Susannawa, as if he knew the little boy had been there all along.

"Well, hello there, little one," the Chief laughed in delight, swinging his son up over his head.

"I missed you," Susannawa squealed as large fingers tickled under his arms. One of Asku's favorite people in the world, little Sus was a kindhearted, silly boy who was never where he was supposed to be. The best places to seek him out were tree branches, or on roofs of longhouses. Asku seemed to spend a good portion of his life obeying their mother's directives to go look for Susannawa.

"Let us get you both home to your mother," the Chief said. "I will finish my walk later."

▸——→

That night, Asku lay on his bed of animal skins thinking of his adventurous day, especially about his bear. Oblivious to spiritual visions, angry grandmothers or tribal duties, Susannawa lay warm and still and at peace next to his big brother.

Grandmother had come in late that evening. He gazed over to her sleeping spot across the room. Tomorrow, or soon at any rate, he would have to face her.

He could hear the soft rustle as his parents did the thing that parents did at night. He glanced over at them in the dark. He tried not to listen, but it was not easy. All he understood about that thing was that no one was being harmed, and that it was normal and good for parents. It put them in a better mood, so it was good for him as well.

Asku closed his eyes and sighed. *I will never understand it all.*

With that, he drifted into sleep.

Chapter 2

Asku awoke sometime in the night, on edge. He listened but heard only his sleeping family's soft breathing.

What was that?

The hairs on the back of his neck were standing up. He felt like he had just stepped out of Yɨ̲xa X̲ápaawish. A more patient listen brought sounds of wind blowing, the firepit hissing. His mother's coals needed to remain hot overnight, and they usually did unless there was heavy rain. There was none, and he heard nothing else.

Even so, something was drawing him from his bed. Something was calling to him.

He stepped out of the animal coverings and slipped his elkskin wrap over his shoulders. As he opened the door flap, the moonlight gave him a glimpse of his parents. His mother nestled against his father's bare chest. He quickly shut the flap behind him, slipped his moccasins on and began to walk. Where, he did not know.

Something had definitely called to him.

Asku walked along the trail toward the center of the village, past the Grandfather's tent and into the ceremonial circle around the big firepit. There, he turned to face the Totem.

It was well that he had a fine wrap, for the night was cold. The sun had not even begun its trek into the sky, although he could see a slight brightening Toward the Rising Sun. Light and warmth were some time away. Asku sat down on the outside of the circle, pulled the wrap around his legs, and tucked it under his knees and feet.

I am supposed to be here. But why? What is going on? Am I going crazy?

He closed his eyes and breathed, in and out, in and out…

"I cannot see him," the young chief-to-be whispered.

"Look closer, títa. Close your eyes. What do you hear?"

Saigwan closed his eyes and absorbed. Birds…leaves rustling, hooves crunching. Breathing, hearts beating…

"I can hear him," he whispered excitedly.

"What do you smell?" the Chief asked.

Cedar…fir…water…fur…antler…bone…blood pulsing through veins…

"I smell him too," Saigwan whispered. *"It is shwúyi."*

A dozen or more stag-moose cows, one bull—twelve hands at least with long, thin legs and massive, intricate antlers—could not yet be seen with the eyes. But with the heart of a hunter, they could be felt.

Saigwan clenched his atlatl and spear.

"Áwnam wá wishúwani?" the Chief asked. *"Are you ready now?"*

"Íi," Saigwan replied. He turned away from the Chief and crept alone through the thick bracken fern.

The breathing and quiet thumping hearts grew louder. He positioned the spear-butt in his atlatl, holding it in the poised position hanging behind his shoulder. Saigwan felt as if he floated closer and closer to the large bull, until his eyes could see the game.

He prepared his throw, prepared to take the bull's spirit into the next world. He stood on the balls of his feet, his father somewhere right behind.

With one large, silent step out into the open, he brought his right arm back as far as it would go—

A feral snarl came from his left, sending a terrible chill down his spine.

Danger, Father, danger!

The cat leaped from the thicket and sunk his long incisors into the bull stag-moose's neck. Its legs buckled from the combination of the wound and the cat's weight, scattering its harem in a moment's time. The sight awed Saigwan as the animal fell without a glance in any direction, meeting its fate unknowing.

Saigwan tried to remember his teaching despite the urge to flee. The speartooth, in adulthood, had the weight of three or four strong hunters. It was as fierce as it was aggressive.

It also never hunted alone.

Before he could see or smell it, Saigwan heard the other cat.

"Túta, pináwaachik!" he cried out. "Father, watch out!"

The cat's powerful paws, as large as a man's outstretched fingers, landed against Saigwan's back, throwing him forward and over a small bluff. The animal's great weight came down on top of him. He felt bones cracking, flesh tearing, and hot searing pain. Due to the animal's weight, he could not reach his long knife. He hoped his father was far enough away to be safe.

And then it was over.

When Saigwan came to, moments or ages later, his first awareness was great pain. He looked around and saw first the great speartooth, blood still leaking from a spear in or near the heart.

Saigwan could move, barely and with great pain. Every breath hurt.

"Túta...Wyánch'i! Where are you?" He guessed at the answer, felt tears begin to mix with the blood on his face. Where is he? He was so close before.

Saigwan fought through body-wide pain to stand up. Looking around, he counted....cat...cat...bull; all dead.

Then he saw what he never would forget, not in all his life: his father, his protector, his strength, his Chief.

The Chief had hurled the spear that had saved his son's life, leaving him to battle a speartooth with only a knife. He had done even that with skill and valor, taking the great cat with him. Now he lay with eyes open but seeing nothing, chest neither rising nor falling.

Kaga, Saigwan's father, the great and mighty Chief, was gone.

And Saigwan was alone.

He knelt, the pain of injuries as nothing compared to that of searing loss. He buried his face into his father's chest, embracing the man who had at once been a great Chief and a stern yet loving father. Saigwan neither knew nor cared how long he remained in that final embrace.

Finally, he took a breath. The clean, cool air cleared his lungs, filled his heart and opened his eyes. What came next was not optional.

The blood and animal carcasses would attract even more ominous creatures. Moving quickly, Saigwan freed each of the animals' trapped spirits. He placed the warm hearts upon a small stone that would serve as an altar, gathered a bit of wood, made fire, and chanted the words he had heard so many times before.

He felt his strength leaving him, but could not succumb, not yet.

He hoisted the Chief's body over his shoulder, the pain and weight almost unbearable. He had to return his father's body home, could not leave him in this spot. How he would manage it, he did not know or consider.

>———

Saigwan would later remember little of the trek to the place they had left the other hunters, and then home. He would remember hearing the cry from the mouth of the cave once they were spotted, then the beginning of grief-wailing. He would remember the whispers, the cries, the moaning. But he remembered no pain as the Grandmother removed rocks and dirt from his wounds, not even from the sewing to close the large gashes across his back.

He would remember their whispers, though.

"Fourteen winters is too young…"

"But he carried him, alone, a great distance."

"Strength, determination, character…"

"But is he ready?"

Asku awoke, eyes filled with tears, his heart filled with a profound sense of loss that was not his own. He felt at his back, no pain. A relief, to return to his modern reality in which his father was alive, the only giant cats were the much smaller cougars, and no game animal looked quite like the one Saigwan and Kaga had hunted.

He looked up at the Totem, strained his neck to see the very top. "Is it you?" he asked. "Are you speaking to me?"

"The Spirits of the Totem speak much but are heard by few."

The answer came from behind him. Still adjusting, Asku quickly threw off his wrap and jumped to his feet. He drew a deep calming breath when he saw who it was.

"I did not mean to frighten you, *myánash*," the Teacher said softly. "Please relax."

"You did not frighten me, *Sapsikw'ałá,*" Asku stammered. "I was just…was just—"

And how do I explain what just happened to me, especially when I'm not sure myself? And do I even want to? Asku sat back down and pulled the elkskin around his shoulders. The Teacher walked toward the Totem, bowed his head and leaned against his gnarled walking stick.

"May I join you, Askuwa'tu?" he asked.

This was a strange thing, an abnormal honor. Weighing his options, Asku split the difference with an annoyed, nodded grunt. The old man smiled and sat down.

Asku adjusted his wrap and looked more closely than usual at the Teacher. The old man always wore his fresh-snow hair tied back in an intricate plait that reached to his waist. He wore two long strands of tiny, colorful beads around his neck, with white shell tassels hanging from his earlobes. He sat with shoulders hunched, covered with a heavy, ornate blanket.

I wonder what all that means: the beads, the blanket designs. No one else in our tribe wears ear decorations like those. And I want to know what in Spirit's name is happening to me. But how do I bring it up?

Glancing back at the Totem, weathered and strong, Asku found his courage. His voice cracked a bit as he spoke. "*Sapsikw'ałá?*"

"Yes, *myánash?*"

"I am sorry for falling asleep during story time yesterday." Asku's heart lifted slightly. "Well, I was not really asleep. I just have a lot on my mind, I guess."

The old man remained still, but Asku thought he saw a slight movement at the corner of his mouth. He knew the old man loved him; had always done so, but sometimes he had a strange way of showing it.

The Teacher was harder on Asku than on the other boys, always calling on him, often disappointed with his responses. Somehow, whenever Asku was in trouble, the Teacher was never far away.

Just as the sun's first light hit the top of the Totem, Asku saw something he had not noticed there before. *What is that?*

Heavy footsteps from behind them broke Asku's train of thought. His father sat down between them, crossed his legs and closed his eyes to the sunrise. The trio breathed the new day together for a short time, and then the moment was over. *And I have no more answers. I return empty-handed from that hunt.* Asku looked at the silent, majestic Totem and thanked the Great Spirits for speaking to him, although still unsure what they were trying to say.

"Haymawihiu," his father began, "there is a matter I wish to discuss with you. Do you have a moment this morning?"

The old man nodded and motioned to the longhouse. The Chief turned to Asku. "Your mother needs your help with the young ones, *tita*. It is washing day."

"Oh man, I forgot." Asku stood quickly and ran in the opposite direction, forgetting all courtesy.

His mother depended on him during washing day. She would have risen some time ago, which explained why his father had come looking for him. His first mistake of the day, and before even doing anything at all.

The village was waking around him as he ran. Children old enough to do so safely would stoke up the fires, while the women would care for the very young. The older girls and boys would go with large, tightly woven baskets to fetch water. Nayhali was surely doing this already.

He sprinted past the family home at the beginning of the trail to his own, where a fluffy little head peeked from a doorway. The head's owner, Sus's friend and frequent wrestling and climbing challenger Matahnu, took a flying leap into Asku's arms. "Asku, Asku!"

I was supposed to take them fishing yesterday, thought Asku. *Instead, I ran off.* "I am sorry, Mat. I lost track of time yesterday. Where is your mother?"

"At the river, Asku. It's our washing day. And I am going to help!"

"How are you gonna help? You are just the size of a chipmunk," Asku exclaimed, poking Matahnu in the ribs. "But guess what? It is our wash day too. I will meet you down there and we will catch us some fish. And today, we will do it for sure. I promise."

The little boy's face lit up. He ran back into his home, demanding that his grandmother help him find his moccasins, as Asku headed up the path wondering how his own grandmother would react to such a bossy little boy. He nearly collided with Nayhali, carrying a large but empty water basket on her head. "Sorry, *nána*," he exclaimed.

She rolled her eyes and adjusted the basket. "Watch where you are going, *nipa*," she said, giving way to a smile. Sus and the little sisters came bounding down behind her with other, much smaller, baskets of their own, and the little group began the long walk to the river.

Turning back toward Asku, Nayhali motioned up the path with her free hand and mouthed a warning: "Grandmother." Without waiting for another word, Asku jumped off the path and turned around behind the family's tent in hopes of coming out the other side unnoticed.

But she was waiting for him there.

"Askuwa'tu Haylaku," the old woman spat, eyes again past anger and in the realm of malice. "You are a disgrace to this family."

"*Ála*, I am sorry." He took a step back from her and raised his hand in the respectful greeting. "I didn't mean to—"

She kept moving toward him.

I have never seen her quite this mad. When I was younger, I had to put up with anything she handed out. She yelled at me, said terrible things to me, hit me with her stick, switched me, and I had to take it.

I am finished taking it, but my father would want me to do it respectfully.

Asku stepped back with instinctive caution, for he was in front of the family firepit. From his earliest memories, his mother had impressed upon him the invisible circle of safety around that pit. "*Ála*, please, if you would just let me explain—"

"You bring shame on this family," she hissed. "The *Nch'inch'ima* have agreed with me, that you will amount to nothing. We will make your father send you away."

That hurt, but Asku resolved not to show it. He took a deep breath. "*Ála*, please let me explain—"

Before Asku could continue, Grandmother swung her walking stick at his head. By reflex, he grabbed the end just before it came in contact with the side of his face, and as he knocked the stick away, he took one careless step backward. His foot caught on a large rock.

Asku tried to roll sideways as he fell, lest he fall directly into the firepit. It worked...mostly. His left shoulder hit first, and he heard the sweat sizzle on his skin as it touched the hot rocks. Before the pain hit him, he smelled the leftover scents of roasting salmon and elk meat, of vegetables and *wák'amu* cakes. Then came the distinct smell of searing flesh and singed hair.

Asku rolled safely clear of the rocks bounding from the pit, but the burning pain came with him, the worst hurt he could ever remember. Grandmother stood over him, her twisted walking stick back at her side. Dust and dirt circled around him as he struggled on the ground at her feet, the burning sensation getting worse.

He heard a gasp, then his mother's voice. "What have you done?"

"He has—"

Asku could not see the look his mother directed at his grandmother, but it would have made any sane person back away. "Amitola, get away. Now!" snarled Chitsa. "I will deal with you later, but don't ever touch my son again, ever. You have an evil heart."

Asku heard tottery footsteps leaving the area. He breathed through his nose, trying not to cry. "My back is on fire," he moaned, rolling from side to side.

"Askuwa'tu, hold still and let me see." Chitsa knelt beside him.

"My shoulder," he hissed through the pain, "I stepped back, almost fell into the firepit." He turned onto his side and tried to hold still as a cool breeze blew him a moment of minor relief.

Chitsa looked around for the water baskets, which were gone, and reached for the water bowl from yesterday's handwashing. She began pouring what remained of yesterday's water carefully down her son's shoulder, a little at a time. Asku sucked air in through his nose and gritted his teeth. Although the liquid stung, it offered momentary relief while it lasted. When it was gone, the burning came back even worse than before.

Chitsa stood up. "That is all there is, Asku. Stay right here." He watched her scurry toward Matahnu's family's longhouse, then sat up and laid his head and arms across his knees.

Chitsa was back in record time with fresh water.

"Well," Chitsa continued, after bathing and examining the burn for awhile, "I think you will survive. Your shoulder is burned pretty badly, a spot about the size of my hand or a little bigger. The skin is already peeling off in spots and blistering. It will hurt for a while, but I think you are lucky. It could have been much worse."

Neither of them heard the Chief approach. "Chitsa," he said, formally, "what has happened here?"

Asku could not turn far enough to see his father. "I fell into the fire," he groaned, as his mother poured more of the cool river water over the burn.

"Yes, I can see that. And since you do not normally fall into firepits, I am still wondering what has happened."

Asku started to shift all the way around, preparing for a full explanation. Before he could, Chitsa hissed one infuriated word: "Amitola."

The Chief's eyes flashed briefly with anger.

"*Túta*," Asku spoke up, "I fell into the fire. I grabbed her stick before she hit me, she did not mean for me to fall in."

"Hmmm." He looked at Asku, then at Chitsa, then up at the sky. "I will see the Grandfather and ask him to prepare something, *títa*. I will see you both this afternoon."

Chitsa nodded, stood and leaned down to help Asku to his feet. "Come, Asku. You can rest while I finish preparing the washing. The little ones are already down there, but we can head down when you are ready."

"*Íta*, did you hear what she said about me? Is she right? Do others think that also?"

"*Chú', myánash*," she soothed. "Hush, child. It is no concern of yours. Your father will see to this."

Asku sat down on the nearest bed while his mother bustled about the tent. He tried to shut out his grandmother's verbal and physical violence. *As if I could ever forget. But Mother is wrong, even if she just wants me to feel better. It is a concern of mine, without any doubt.*

He tried to breathe to calm himself, to shut out the pain. He searched his mind for peaceful things: Pahto, the great eagle, the cool breath of Yɨxa Xápaawish on his skin, and the bear that had knocked his moccasin into the water. Then he thought of Saigwan, the ancient chief of this tribe, and his agonizing journey back home with his father's body.

Thoughts of his ancestor's pain and strength somehow made it easier to bear his grandmother's abuse and the resulting burn.

As Chitsa began to load up for her washing day labors, the question burst from him again. *" Íła?* Am I what Grandmother said?"

Her jaw tightened. Dark eyes flashed, then she cupped his chin and leaned in to look her son directly in the eyes where he sat. Chitsa enunciated every word: "You are not a disgrace, nor are you a disappointment. You are Askuwa'tu Haylaku. You are the first son of Napayshni Hianayi and Chitsa Hihiwuti, daughter of the great Wawyukyáma *Wyánch'i* Kalataka Wahchinksapa, and you will be chief of this tribe someday. And if anyone is going away, it will not be you."

He breathed deeply and ran his fingers through his snarly hair. Chitsa stood up before continuing. "You will need to be careful of your shoulder. Grandfather will prepare a poultice that should prevent it from becoming poisoned, which is a danger with bad burns. Until then, Nch'i-Wána will do you good. The Great River is mighty and healing. Your grandmother will not be returning home tonight, so do not worry."

"How can you know that *íła*?"

Chitsa leaned in and whispered. "Because *isha*, and keep this to yourself, if it should come down to it, I will bar her at knifepoint. I do not need anyone's permission, not even your father's, to keep out of my home a bitter person who does my children harm. It is like chasing away a starving old *kw'ayawí*." Her voice went back to normal. "Now, let's get ready to go. Remember that gossip spreads faster than a fire in dry grass. You are their chief's son, with nothing to be ashamed of. You must stand proud. Think of the future, and the time when you will lead them. They wonder if you will be a strong leader in your time, if you will be ready when it comes, and they hope you will be. Show them your character, and how wrong Amitola is."

Memories of Saigwan, rippled through Asku's mind. *That is like what they wondered of him. How can she know it?* He took a deep breath and stood up. *I will be fine. I will show my grandmother, and everyone.*

Asku picked up the basket by the door, feeling the burn pull painfully across his shoulder, and walked outside.

Chapter 3

Asku found his physical injury easier to handle than its emotional aspects. *Is Grandmother right about me? Am I strong enough?* He followed his mother down to the washing area downstream from where the tribe fished. She was dressed for washing day, hair tied back in one long braid, a shorter dress designed for a day to be spent standing in water—but still beaded with attentive care. Not so long ago, he had caught her in height, then passed her up. *I remember when she noticed it. She pulled my head down to kiss my forehead, then started crying.*

I do not think I will ever understand girls, even my mother. Wasn't I supposed to grow taller than her? Well, she might be smaller than me now, but she is strong. Stronger than me. Especially in her spirit.

Asku looked up ahead, where the trail crested a steep bluff lined with prickly sagebrush. As a toddler, he had tried to run ahead, and had detoured through the sagebrush. His mother had not chastised him as she smoothed the dried medicine leaves and clay on the scratches and cuts, but he had learned a valuable lesson that day. *I learned not to push rudely past mothers and grandmothers heading to the river, because the bushes bite.*

At the crest, archers stood watch to the left and right of the trail. While most river traffic meant no harm, the Patisapatisháma found it prudent to know who came and went. Asku nodded at the watchers, who greeted him before resuming the river watch. It was a duty he had done in his turn, many times. Chitsa raised both of her arms and unfolded her hands to the sky, fingers outstretched. Asku closed his eyes.

"*Kw'ałá*...thank you, Great Mother," she said, "for providing."

Asku breathed the fresh, gusty winds of Nch'i-Wána, tasting the air as it refreshed his lungs and heart. It was almost as good as his trip to Yíxa Xápaawish, with the eagle and the cool swim under the quiet breath of Pahto. As far as he could see Toward the Rising Sun, the mighty river came with rolling thunder through its giant canyon, farther across than any bow could shoot. Beyond Nch'i-Wána were steep cliffs, then grasslands and rivers and high forests. And as far as he could see Toward the Setting Sun, the eternal Nch'i-Wána made its way toward the Great Sea. He looked below the sharply zigzagging trail to the edge of the river, heard children playing, saw mothers washing, young women hauling and fetching and hanging. As Asku and his mother made their careful way down the trail's last switchback, Nayhali came running toward them.

"What took you two so long?" she snapped. "Aanyáy's face is high in the sky. We will never get it all done."

"It is good to see you too," said Chitsa, "as you are so cheerful and patient."

Asku snorted. He knew why she was in a hurry today. He had promised Nayhali not to tell their parents that she was in love with Chaytan, the Chief's adopted younger brother and right-hand man. Neither was sure how the Chief would respond.

Nayhali smacked Asku hard in the stomach as she reached for the heavy basket in his arms. Asku shook her hands away.

"I have got it, Nayhali." *Knowing these two, I may have to pick it up again because I chose the wrong spot.* "Where do you want it?"

She pointed toward an empty drying rack to the left of Matahnu's mother. Only as Asku passed her did she see his shoulder. "*Nípa?*" she gasped. "What happened?"

"*Chú',*" snapped Chitsa. *That's fine*, thought Asku. *Nayhali needs to be told to shut up more often, and I do not want to talk about this burn. I will have to soon enough.* He placed the heavy basket at the edge of the river and dipped his hand into the cool water, bringing it up to trickle down his shoulder. It stung yet refreshed.

"Where are they?" he turned back to Nayhali.

She pointed toward the rocks Toward the Rising Sun of the washing area, where their small siblings frolicked with many other small children.

"Asku, look!" belted out Matahnu, from somewhere.

After a glance about, Asku spotted the little boy crouched next to Susannawa, who was poking a short stumpy stick into a crack between two rocks. Nisy watched from behind him, nervous about something.

Mini, whose full name of Mininaywah meant *Little Whirlwind* in a language from the south, was jumping from rock to rock while singing loudly. He had learned never to turn his back on that one.

"How goes it, *nika*? Are we gonna fish or what?" Asku squatted next to Sus, picked up Nisy, then changed his mind as he felt the pull against his blistered shoulder.

Nisy whimpered into his chest. "*Wáxpush*, Asku!"

A rattlesnake? What are these idiots doing playing with a rattlesnake? Just then, the snake struck at Susannawa's stick. It was indeed a rattler, and a rather large one. "*Pináwaachik!*" Asku shouted as he jumped back, "watch out!" He pushed Nisy and the boys behind him. They all tumbled on top of each other in the sand.

"Give me that stick now," Asku demanded. "And get Mini down off those rocks! Rattlesnakes are not toys! They're as dangerous as the fire! Now stay back, and don't be between me and the snake!"

The kids will be down here all day. We cannot have a rattler so close. And with all the stuff that has happened this morning, I forgot my knife. Of all the days.

Asku looked over his shoulder to see who was around. Kitchi, one of his best friends, was coming his way. "What's got you all agitated, man?" Then: "What happened to your shoulder? That looks nasty."

"Tell you later. Right now, do you have your knife? I forgot mine. They were playing with a *wáxpush*. We can't let it run loose around here today."

"No way! Hawilish's got his, though. Hey, come give us a hand." Kitchi called out to the third of their usual trio of adventurers, currently boyhandling a heavy basket of clothing for the women. Hawilish was nearly Asku's height and of similar build, much appreciated by the girls of the Patisapatisháma for his handsome features and careful grooming. Kitchi was shorter, broad in the shoulders and hips, built like a young bull, and usually wore a teasing expression on his round face. As usual, he hadn't bothered to braid his hair or change out of yesterday's clothes. Over came Hawilish, asking what was going on.

"If you take a look at those rocks, you will get some idea," said Kitchi.

"Susannawa has trapped a rattler between those two rocks," said Asku, motioning toward a spot some twenty-five steps away. "So, he decided to play with it, and it's really angry, of course. I haven't a spear or knife or anything with me."

"Will this work?" Hawilish pulled a knife from his belt, a short, flint fishing blade with a smooth antler handle.

"It should if we lash it to a stick." Kitchi followed this up by looking among the young ones, where possession of some sort of stick was a certainty. "Susannawa, this is your chance to help the warriors. Wouldn't that be fun? All you have to do is let me borrow that stick. And stay back. A *waxpush* is dangerous. If he bites you, you can die." The child was glad to hand over his toy.

Asku pointed out the snake's exact location, although the trapped rattler was already announcing its location. Hawilish tied his knife to the end of Sus's stick, then handed it to Asku. "You sure you feel up to this with that shoulder? What happened to you, anyway?"

"I'm fine. Tell you later." Another little boy tried to edge forward, then ran into Kitchi's firm palm. Asku advanced on the rattlesnake, extended the makeshift polearm, and waited for the snake to strike at it. It did, missed, then recoiled with a hiss and a warning rattle. After several jabs, Asku's thrust caught the rattler in the spine some four inches below the spadelike head. It thrashed but died quickly as the boys kept the small children back. When he was sure it was dead, Asku finished severing the head from the body at a safe distance, then motioned the little ones over to check it out.

The snake was beautiful, one of the biggest Asku had ever seen. The rattle itself was at least a finger in length, followed by brown and white stripes that met in the middle with intricate patterns. Asku unlashed Hawilish's knife, then used it to reveal the large, sheathed fangs. It was time for the lesson. "All you little squirrels, get over here, now, and come look at this. It is safe now."

Matahnu tried to back away, but Hawilish propelled him back. "See these?" Asku began, indicating the fangs. "*Waxpush* uses them to find his food. He bites something, and it dies. Then he can swallow it and crush it with his body, which is stronger than you might think. The fangs are also how he defends himself from little children who bother him. If you leave him alone, though, he will usually not bother you. He cannot eat you, so he wants you to go away. We would not have killed him if we had just been traveling through. He eats mice and other small rodents, which does us good. Look at his pattern so you know him. Most snakes don't have fangs with poison."

Kitchi and Hawilish gave their best stern adult glares.

"And especially you, Susannawa," Asku rumbled, warming to his subject. "Do you realize how far we are from home? If that snake bit you, as small as you are, even if you lived long enough to reach the Grandfather, you would probably not survive. And what about your little sisters? How could you put the sisters in that danger?"

Susannawa looked miserable.

"When you see a rattler, you must always think of who else might step on him. Anyone younger than you is your job to watch out for, like I watch out for you. You did not do that. How would you feel if Mini died?"

Susannawa began to cry. Matahnu looked like he wanted to crawl into the hole with the rattler. Nisy was still whimpering and barely hanging onto Mini as she squealed and squirmed to be free from her sister's terrified clutch.

Okay, that's enough. He grabbed Susannawa by the shoulders, kneeling to his level and shaking him slightly, and quieted his tone. "You scared me, *nika*. I do not know what I would do without you." He turned toward Matahnu, "You either." And he pulled both boys into his arms. "Now, tell me you understand about a *wáxpush*, and won't do anything this dumb again."

Both nodded. "I'm sorry, Asku," said Susannawa.

Kitchi picked up the greater portion of the snake. "This is the part you get, Sus. Now you have to skin it. The meat is good, too. If a certain young *wyánch'i* is done being *sapsikw'atá*, and Hawilish here will let us use his fish-knife, I'll teach you how. The head is for the Grandfather."

"What does he do with it?" asked Matahnu.

"Do I look like a Grandfather? I don't know. Maybe he makes medicines with it. And yeah, you can watch, Mat. But keep an eye out for the other kids."

"*Wáxpush* is usually by himself," added Asku, "but do not take that for granted."

When the snake was skinned and butchered out, Asku shooed the children away. "Now, man, tell us," demanded Kitchi. "What happened to your back, *pásiks*?"

Asku sat down under a low juniper tree, keeping an eye on the children but especially Mini, and told the story. It felt good to talk about it, although he left out the part about his grandmother's hurtful words.

"Tough break," Kitchi slapped Asku's arm.

"That's harsh, though," commented Hawilish. "*Nch'inch'ima* are grouchy sometimes, but I can't believe she meant for you to fall on the firepit rocks."

"I wish I were that sure," said Asku.

"Grandfather's going to want to look at that," said Kitchi.

"No doubt," said Hawilish. "So, where'd you go yesterday?"

Asku filled them in. After some more lazy conversation and babysitting, he went down to check on his mother and Nayhali, taking little Whirlwind with him. The women were soaked, tired, and crabby. *I promised to fish with the boys, so this can work. We will get them all some food.* Asku offered, and his mother gave a curt acceptance. Making sure the little sisters were occupied with a large cluster of buttercups and daisies, and after a rattlesnake sweep, Asku led the little boys to the fishing hole.

The morning fishermen had already emptied the village's weirs, called *nixanásh*. The young men checked and re-set the large wickerwork traps in the swift-moving spot along the river. Kitchi and Hawilish stood out on the *twaluutpamá* or fishing platform, watching as fish began to trap themselves in the cages. Once within a trap, the different varieties of salmon could not swim out again. Instead, they seemed to continue swimming upstream without getting anywhere.

Asku left the little boys in the care of Hawilish and Kitchi, took a glance at the girls, and went to the small riverside firepit to get that phase started. Before long, they had twenty beautiful salmon halves roasting over the crackling fire. The wind must have blown the smell downstream, for the women were drying off and walking his way. Some of the older girls shooed Asku away from the cooking, lest he ruin it through some act of masculine incompetence. He sat on a half cedar log bench with Kitchi and Hawilish.

A small feminine figure approached Asku, her large expressive eyes lowered in shyness. It was Hatayah, who of all the girls of the tribe most often found reason to catch his eyes. Her hair was loose and windblown today, just as he best liked it. *And I've never told anyone, but somehow she seems to have figured out that I like it. How do they do that?*

Hatayah presented him with a bowl of cool, fresh water straight from the river. Her eyes had that intoxicating sparkle.

"*Kw'alá.*" He took the bowl from her hands and drank his fill before passing it back to her. "Thank you."

Watching Hatayah walk away had much more appeal than thoughts of grandmothers and burns and responsibilities.

—→

Without much to do for a time, Asku watched the children and ran his eyes over the portion of Nch'i-Wána that was home to the Patisapatisháma. While Nch'i-Wána was a provider of things of life, no one but a fool took the river lightly. It was always rougher and swifter than it looked from high above, or from a distance.

No canoes were passing today, but they were unremarkable sights. Many traveled from far away to barter at Wayám, with its plentiful fishing and great wide waterfall close by. The distance from its source, scarcity, specialization of crafting, and danger of obtaining an item would all affect its value in trade. For example, most shells from the sand of the Great Sea were not dear but were fragile and had to be carried well up Nch'i-Wána; in fine condition, they fetched reasonable value. While ravens weren't rare, their jet-black feathers were rare to find laying about from natural molting, and many coastal tribes revered the legends of Xuxuxyáy with his mysterious ways. This made raven feathers relatively scarce and dear, when they were even available.

As the sun moved past its midpoint and toward setting, the exhausted women began packing up for the day. Asku herded the little ones back toward their mothers, then went down to the river's edge with Kitchi and Hawilish. They would help the women get themselves and their work safely out of the water.

As Asku looked out across the river, Hatayah's mother began to hoist her heavy basket onto her head. She lost her footing, slipped, and fell toward the current from thigh-deep water to where the riverbed started to descend. Hawɨlish saw it happening first and ran to the river's edge to help as she disappeared under the deep water, her family's belongings rapidly drifting downstream and out into the faster current. Hatayah pulled up the ends of her skirt and ran into the water. She had her mother's head above water and was helping her to stand again as Hawɨlish splashed past them both, diving out into the current.

Fortunately for Hatayah's family, Hawɨlish was a superb swimmer. His mother had nicknamed him *Nuksháy*, because she said he could swim like a river otter. Asku splashed into the water to help Hatayah and her mother, glad for the water's chill after its initial sting. The two easily pulled Hatayah's mother to the shallows and helped her up. Hawɨlish took several strong strokes into the current to catch the basket, then made his way shoreward with sidestrokes. Her mother safe, Hatayah and Asku ran downstream to where Hawɨlish struggled with the heavy basket and his waterlogged trousers.

"*Kw'ałá*," said Hatayah, without looking up at either boy. She squeezed the excess water from the ends of her short skirt—a fascinating sight for both boys—then settled the heavy basket on her head and went back to her mother.

Once he was able to peel his eyes from her, Asku looked around. He did not remember ever standing in this spot before. Behind him, the bluff was so close to sheer as to be impassable. He scanned the cliffs Beyond Nch'i-Wána just as Kitchi joined them. Kitchi pointed at some spot across the river. "Hey, do you see that?"

Hawɨlish and Asku both shielded their eyes and looked. Asku noticed nothing. "Is that a cave?" Hawɨlish asked.

"*Minán*…where?" Asku asked. "I don't see anything."

Hawɨlish moved closer to him, pointed Beyond Nch'i-Wána, and Asku a small dark spot that stood out from the rocky cliffs: definitely the mouth of a cave.

"Feel like hiking, *pásiks*?" Asku asked. An uneasy feeling roiled his insides. *There is something familiar about that. I don't know what. It makes no sense, because I've never been there before.*

"*Kúu mish,*" Kitchi teased. "Can you make it that far?"
"I don't see why not."

>——

Back at the village, having convinced himself that it was his responsibility to check in on Hatayah, Asku found himself walking past her family's tent. She was outside with her mother, Laytiah, and her aunt, laying clothes out to dry.

"*Kw'ałá,* Askuwa'tu," Laytiah began. "That was a nervous moment."

"Hawilish did the hard part, *lamyáy*. I just came to see that you were both okay," he said, lamely.

"We are well, thank you again." Laytiah turned back to her work. Asku met Hatayah's eyes briefly before she looked down.

"*Kw'ałá,* Asku," she said. Her mother hissed at the familiarity. "I mean, Askuwa'tu Haylaku."

Asku nodded, rounded the corner to leave, but glanced back over his shoulder. His heart flipped as he caught her watching him, smiling. She looked away in haste, dropping a set of clean trousers on the dusty ground. He did not see her mother look sharply at her, then at his retreating back.

Asku then checked to see that Matahnu had made it home. He had and was taking a nap. He accepted thanks for killing the snake, then headed for his family's tent. On the way there, he met his father.

"How goes it, my *tita?*" he said, smiling.

"I am well, *túta*." Asku began to tell him about the day: the snake, the fishing, Hawilish saving the basket for Hatayah's mother, and about the cave. This last piqued the Chief's interest.

"Do you plan to explore it?" he asked.

"Yes, we do."

His father nodded. "First see to that burn, though. I am glad you will not go by yourself. Caves may hold many things, and this one could hold some you cannot see."

Asku nodded back. *That's an odd thing to say. What does he mean by that?*

When Asku got home, he found Susannawa clamoring about the uses for his snakeskin. "The best thing would be a satchel, a *talápas*. But first you have to cure it, or it will rot and smell disgusting. Come to the *twáytash*, where we keep the supplies, and I'll teach you." He took Sus to the smokehouse, which reeked of blood and dead animal parts from the recent hunt and showed him how to cure the skin with a paste of bear grease, liver and bone marrow. Once it was properly stretched on the drying rack, both were in a hurry to be out of the suffocating *twáytash*. "It will be dry in a couple of days at the most. Take it to Nayhali and ask her to teach you how to sew it properly. Now, come and help me clean up around our firepit, and get it going. Mother expects this of us. Someday it will be your job, which you will have to do without being told."

Napayshni had brought home a hunk of fresh elk meat, a nice change from their usual salmon. While watching his mother prepare it for cooking, Asku picked up a small chiseling knife and the piece of wood he was carving into his bear, meant as a gift for Nisy.

"Asku," Chitsa interrupted, "not now. The Grandfather sent over the healing poultice just a while ago. Go prepare, *isha*, while dinner cooks. I know you don't like it, but if that burn isn't cared for, it will become poisonous."

"Yes, *ila*," he grunted, laying his bear aside. Nayhali ushered him to his bed. The day's activities had distracted him from the pain, and now it returned full strength.

Nayhali sat down at the little bedside table and mixed water into the Grandfather's concoction of willow bark, sweetgrass and ginger. For a time, he just endured as his sister spread the herb mixture on his burn. By the time Nayhali affixed the clean hide covering the burn, he could smell elk steaks even over the poultice's pungency. His shoulder was numb, an improvement. "Now let's go eat," said his sister, and they went outside.

He found his mother bustling around the fire, while his father and Sus were taking a close look at Asku's bear.

"How do you feel, Asku?" asked his father.

"Still kind of sore. I can handle it. I see you found my carving."

"This is coming along," the Chief said. "Is this the creature you met yesterday at your waterfall?"

"Yes, at least what I remember of him. I would like to see him again. He seemed to know me, though it's hard to explain."

Napayshni smiled. "Asku, I think you may have a *Pawaat-łá*...a Spirit Guide."

"Really? How do you know?"

"Well, *anahúy* in these parts run from us. Unless, of course, you get between a mother and her young one," he said, with a smile over at Chitsa. "Now, that does not mean that I want you to go looking for him again, *tita*. It is too dangerous alone. You understand?"

"Yes, *Wyánch'i*, I understand."

Dinner passed much as any other family dinner, with laughter and chatting about the day. Just as mealtime was winding to a close, Asku heard soft, shuffling footsteps behind him, and looked around as one might upon hearing a snake's rattle. Her walking stick in hand, his grandmother surveyed the scene.

"Blessings, *lamyáy*," said Asku's mother. While she lowered her eyes respectfully to the ground, her tone contained a hint of something else. Nayhali did the same. There might or might not have been a rude grunt of acceptance in reply.

The Chief stood. "*Íła*, a word." It was not a question.

Amitola followed him back down the path, but Asku could only hear bits and pieces of the conversation.

"I asked you not to return here. You are no longer welcome at my fire."

"Disrespect, defiance, disgrace..."

"He is my son. You may not speak that way of him."

"Your responsibility, then."

"Yes. And not yours. *Áwna náwnak'i*...we are finished now!" *I know that tone*, thought Asku. *That's when he doesn't want to hear any more backtalk.*

The Chief returned to the fire alone. He was silent for the rest of the meal. For the rest of the evening, Asku and Nayhali made a point of keeping the little ones from disturbing him. The only official business he tended to was a walk with Asku and his friends to study the cave at a distance. After some questioning, the Chief gave them guidelines: a day there, a day to explore, a day to return. They should return by sunset on the third day. All in agreement, each boy had spent the evening preparing his equipment.

Chapter 4

Asku rose before the sun, excited for the day.

Before he departed, his mother gave him another dosing with the Grandfather's remedy and tried to send more along with him for his friends to apply each day, but he insisted that he would be fine. She in turn insisted on a cloth wrap to keep his arm immobile and the salve on the burn, and on that they reached compromise.

The Chief and Teacher stood under the Totem waiting for them. The three approached with respectfully bowed heads. The Teacher raised his arms high above his head, fingers outstretched, and eyes closed.

"*Watwáa naknúwim,*" he repeated three times as he turned once toward Nch'i-Wána, once toward Pahto and once toward the Totem. "Great Spirits protect our sons, teach them and return them to us."

Asku met the Chief's eyes. He held up three fingers, unfolding them one at a time. *Three days, no more.* Asku nodded his understanding, and the young adventurers set off down the trail.

They reached the edge of Nch'i-Wána without incident, and Kitchi tossed Asku his gear. "Since you are going to be so much help, little *wyánch'i,*" Kitchi said, "hold this stuff." Hawɨlish and Kitchi went over to the small flat plain where the tribe stored its canoes, picked up a small birchbark craft, and lifted it onto their shoulders. Most of the tribe's canoes came through trade, made by a coastal tribe and traded for *yixa* pelts or *ch'láy* at the Wayámpam. They were awkward, but not heavy, and were versatile enough to carry people or goods through calm water or rapids. It would have been pointless to bring one of the great dugouts, which would have been a problem for three young men to lift, launch, or maneuver.

"The cripple is going to slow us down a lot, eh, Hawɨlish?" jibed Kitchi as they set the craft into the shallows.

"If we have to break through any rocks, I'm sure your head is harder than them," cracked Asku. But he unwrapped and stowed the bandage. *It is better to deal with my mother's anger when I get home than to put up with three days of heckling. Plus, I can put it on again just before we land back here.*

Asku's father had suggested a likely landing spot below the cave, but with three passengers, the current took them somewhat downstream of the spot "Well, either we paddle back up," Hawilish began, "or we can carry—"

"No way, man," said Kitchi. "I am not carrying this thing all that way!"

Asku took a look around. "Well, if you're too weak to carry it, then I will just have to figure out something else." He jumped into the water and grabbed the braided leather rope tied to the front of the canoe. It was only thigh deep, though cool and swift, and a few steps told him that he was still on the underwater part of the sandbar. Taking careful steps, he towed the canoe upstream to a spot nearer their original landing area. They beached the canoe, unloaded their gear and caught a couple of salmon for later. Kitchi hooked the fish to the end of his pole and hung it over his shoulder. "What's the plan?" asked Hawilish.

Asku looked up at the rising hills. He could no longer see the cave opening, but he knew they were directly below it. "We go up there. It's there. I'm sure of it." He pointed up toward the rocky basalt cliffside. "Let's get climbing."

Kitchi snorted. "Do you think we are mountain sheep?"

"No, because mountain sheep do not complain nearly as much as you," said Asku. "If you think it's too steep, or that you are not strong enough, you can stay down here and watch the canoe, like a child."

"Knock it off, you two. Let's find the base of a deer trail. If they can find a way up, so can we, right?" said Hawilish. Kitchi grunted, and he and Asku began to follow.

After working their way a distance up the beach, Hawilish found a narrow animal trail and led the way up. Asku's shoulder stung occasionally, especially when he reached in front of or above himself, but it felt a lot better than it had during the night. He had been unable to get comfortable and had barely slept.

The sun hovered just above the horizon when they finally reached the base of the next tier of basalts. From across Nch'i-Wána, the cave entrance had not seemed so high above the ground. Also, from that distance, they had been unable to see the loose rock below the entrance. The climb promised difficulty and danger.

They set up camp in a sheltered dip walled by large basalt columns, a safe place so long as there were no clouds in the sky, affording temporary relief from the relentless river wind. Asku built a small fire, while Kitchi whittled freshly cut cedar branches for cooking stakes, and Hawilish cleaned and sliced the salmon. They thanked the mountain and the salmon that gave their lives to feed them.

Asku went to stand atop a rock that afforded him a different view of his world. He was now Beyond Nch'i-Wána, of course. Toward the Setting Sun, Wy-east's proud peak stood out with its snowy cap. Toward the Great Mountains, he could see Pahto far off in the distance. He had the urge to close his eyes and obeyed.

A vision appeared in his mind: people huddled together off in the distance, all watching a certain spot. It was either dusk, or very overcast. Asku heard a distinct cry from somewhere above him, calling them home.

That voice was mine, and not mine. Someone, something, is guiding me.

Why? Is there a way I can know?

We will see soon, maybe.

Asku opened his eyes, nodded at Pahto and returned to the campsite. After dinner, they sat around the fire, wraps pulled tight, weapons close by. "No wonder we live on the other side," Kitchi complained. "This wind is freezing my balls off."

"There is a cry in the wind," said Hawilish. "It's weird."

Asku told the boys what he had seen earlier, and what the Totem had told him the day before involving the speartooths. "I think Pahto is speaking to me," Asku finished.

Both boys nodded, staring into the fire. Such were not matters for teasing.

They had grown up together. Kitchi and Hawilish would go anywhere, or do anything, for Asku, however hard a time they might give him about it. They were *pásiks,* his best friends—as close as brothers.

Whether or not they understood the visions he might see, or the burden his lineage might carry, they were dedicated to him.

"So, man," Kitchi said, changing the subject. "How about that Hatayah, huh? She is sweet." Asku smiled into the fire. "I sure would like to—"

"*Chú'*," Asku growled. Hawilish giggled nervously. Kitchi ignored both of them.

"Did you see her legs when she pulled her skirt up? I thought I saw between her legs, man. Makes me all—"

"Enough, Kitchi. I mean it. *Chchúu txának.*"

Kitchi glanced over, smirked a bit. "Okay. I get it now. Sorry, *pásiks.*"

That night, Asku fell asleep thinking about Hatayah. He remembered her lifting her skirt to squeeze out the water but did not remember seeing between her legs. The only thing he remembered seeing was her mother going under the water and the family's washing basket heading out into the current.

>——→

Asku awoke well before dawn, as if something had prodded him, but nothing seemed to have done so. In fact, the dawn stillness was rather a warm relief from the wind-whipped night. He rose quietly, relieved himself behind a nearby tree, then sat down to take in the view. The sky was a palette of changing colors, with the early light casting golden oranges and yellows on the mountains and their misty peaks.

What will we find? Who is speaking to me in that cave? And what are they trying to say? He flexed his shoulder. It still hurt, but less than yesterday.

He could bear the anticipation no longer and dug a toe into Kitchi's rib cage. "*Áwna wínasha*...let's get moving."

Kitchi rubbed his eyes. "You're not wasting any time, I see. Okay, give me a moment." They got Hawilish up, snacked on the smoked salmon they had brought, loaded some coals into the fire-carrier, then packed their things and eyed the final ascent. The path to the cave-mouth led over small talus slopes, rockslides and boulders. To Asku's eye, getting back down might be the hard part. It took time and caution, but they finally reached the rock face directly below the cave-mouth. As they stood before the open darkness, Asku tried to spot the village. "Well," Kitchi panted, "that was easy."

Both Asku and Hawilish laughed, pointing out Kitchi's skinned elbow and shoulder. Kitchi replied with a rude gesture. All three drew *chúksh* blades, just in case. Kitchi, who had the best hearing, put a hand to his ear. The others froze in complete silence born of long habit.

"What do you hear?" Asku whispered, after a few moments.

"Nothing. Maybe water," said Kitchi. "You?"

"It is a moonless night in there," Hawilish said. "I have no idea what's inside. Can't hear anything either." He stepped back, took out his fire-carrier, waited for the other two to shield his work from wind gusts, and lit a torch he had brought.

The mouth was large enough for the three of them to enter shoulder to shoulder. By Hawilish's light, Kitchi took a step into the tunnel, one hand on the wall to his left and the other on his knife. "Whoa!" he said, taking a step back. "Check this out." Kitchi held what looked like a very, very old torch.

"Was that on the wall?" Asku asked, examining it.

"Yeah, it was just there near my shoulder," Kitchi turned it over in his hands. "It just came off."

The end was charred, and the wood below the charring looked like it had once been soaked with something. "Probably some sort of oil used to keep it burning?" suggested Asku.

"I dunno, man. But I have a feeling it stunk." Kitchi peered into the darkness. "This place seems old, doesn't it?"

"And a bit creepy," Hawilish added. Asku started to go into the cave, then hesitated.

"What's up, *pásiks*?" Hawilish.

"Not sure." *And I wish I was. I'm afraid I'm about to find out.*

"Well, that's reassuring, little *wyánch'i*," Kitchi snarked, prodding him in the ribs. "What are you not telling us?"

"I have told you everything, man. I have weird feelings about this cave. But let's go." Asku took a deep breath and stepped inside, navigating by Hawilish's torchlight. Their steps gave off the faint echo typical of caves, no matter how cautious force of habit made their step. It was part of every boy's training: *the more noise you make, the more sounds you drown out. Silence is your friend.*

Asku took a deep but quiet breath, then led the way deeper into the cave. After a moderate distance, the walls started to widen. Asku halted. Kitchi and Hawilish did likewise.

"What?" hissed Kitchi.

"I hear water dripping in the distance," Asku whispered. "There is a breeze. There must be another tunnel somewhere." He was beginning to feel lightheaded and a little nauseous. Kitchi looked at Asku, nodded, and they continued deeper into the darkness.

The tunnel eventually opened up into a large room, too big for one torch to illuminate. Asku looked to his left and right and saw similar old-looking torches on walls. Some still had tatters of old grass hanging from them. Hawilish lit the one nearest him and handed his to Kitchi.

"Smells like the Grandfather, doesn't it?" complained Kitchi. He lit another one on the wall. The air was cool and musty, though not stagnant.

"Looks like no one has been here in a long time," Hawilish said. "I don't see any footprints. And these torches have not been lit since long ago."

They circled the room with Hawilish's torch until they confirmed that it was empty, other than some ancient firepits. Asku poked around a particularly large pit with his knife and hit something hard below the thick ash layer. A little digging revealed several huge bones and fragments. He wrenched one out and passed it to Kitchi. "Do you think whoever lived here burned animal bones?"

"What is that? A deer?" asked Hawilish.

"That's way too big to be deer," Kitchi said. "It's bigger than my thigh. Look!" He held it against his leg to prove his point.

Asku walked toward the wall directly behind the largest firepit. The dim light seemed to show some drawings. The Teacher had mentioned that some old caves contained drawings from long ago. "Hey, come over here with that torch. I think the bones came from what this drawing shows."

They complied. "What is that?" asked Hawilish. "A bison? A really big, weird looking one?"

"That is not a bison," Asku explained. "At least, I don't think so. The horns are wrong, but they remind me of some animals from the Teacher's stories. Something is familiar about it. Look at this one, though." He pointed to another animal form, catlike with long teeth like rattlesnake fangs. "Nothing like that lives around here." *But I think it used to.*

Kitchi looked at the bone in his hand, then at the picture. He whistled in awe.

"This place must be really old," Hawilish said, nervously. "We don't have animals like that around here. Could they be from the time our people fled the Ice Spirits and first came here? The Teacher told that story just two days ago, right? You fell asleep, Asku," he needled.

"I heard the story, okay?" said Asku, nettled.

Closer inspection with better light showed that the walls were covered with pictures. They seemed to tell the story of a people. Asku could not have described what he sought, but he would know it when he saw it.

And then he found it. Him.

He was only a stick figure, but he wore the bison skin with the head still attached, resting at the back of his neck. It had to be him.

Kitchi walked up. "Who do you think that is? I would love that wrap in the winter, wow."

"That's the *wyánch'i.*"

"The chief?" Hawilish asked. "You think these were our people? So that would be like your ancestor?"

"I think so. This is the cave."

The boys explored for a while, taking souvenirs to show the Teacher. "If this is the cave," Asku said, "then the other tunnel should be somewhere over there." He pointed toward the back of the large room. *Where the little boy ran away from the spirits to the safety of the chief's arms. What if those spirits are still here? Am I strong enough to endure my ancestors in this cave too?* The slight movement of cool air made the tunnel easy enough to find, though that was not the only reason.

"Smells like rotten piss," Kitchi whispered.

"Not like the Grandfather anymore?" Asku teased. "Cuz I am sure he would like to hear that he smells like rotten piss."

"Knock it off. Let's see what's in there." Hawilish said.

They began to pick their way down the narrow tunnel. At times the ceiling was low enough that they had to hunch down. After twists and turns, ups and downs, the tunnel opened up again and they stopped to stretch. Hawilish sat down to dump pebbles out of his moccasin. Kitchi snickered, but it rang nervous rather than calm and smug.

Asku closed his eyes to listen. *My head does not feel right*, he thought, straining to hear. And hear he did.

The drumbeat echoed toward them from the distance ahead, echoing off the walls to pound in Asku's ears. He covered them, with no way to know that he was feeling as much as hearing.

The drums gave way to chanting, then to screaming, louder and louder.

He tried to back away from the noise. He stumbled backwards, over rocks, and smashed hard against the rough tunnel wall. Asku fell to the ground, covering his ears and head with his arms, a desperate effort to escape what he heard and felt.

When Asku came to, the sounds and feelings had ceased. He found himself in a seated cower with his back to the cave wall, knees pulled to his chest. A voice, Kitchi's: "Asku. What's happening?" Asku opened his eyes to see Kitchi crouched in front of him, his knife ready.

Hawilish shook him slightly, grabbing the wrong shoulder. The sudden pain helped boost him back to normal awareness. "Hey man, come out of it. Asku, look at me."

His eyes began to clear. "Did you guys hear that?"

Kitchi stood up but kept his knife out. "A gust of wind came from that way," he whispered, pointing into the darkness. "Pretty strong."

Hawilish looked shaken. "There was a voice in that wind, an evil voice. We've looked around here enough. There are spirits here, for real. Let's turn back."

"No way, man," said Kitchi. "We need to find out what this is."

Asku stood up, trying to smile. "I don't think it's evil, Hawilish. But I am glad that I'm not the only one hearing things. Did you hear the drums and chanting?"

"No, just a moaning breeze," said Kitchi. "Pretty weird."

"If we were not *pásiks*, there is no way I would go any further," said Hawilish. "But we are." Asku nodded, let Kitchi haul him to his feet, and went forward.

As the tunnel opened up into a small chamber, the air became hotter, damper, and more stagnant. "It's hard to breathe in here," Hawilish coughed.

"There's the altar," Asku pointed to the center of the room, his breath growing short. "That's where the manhood ceremony took place. I remember seeing it in my head. The young chief lay there."

Hawilish hollered for the others and pointed to a drawing. The painting was expert work, perfectly preserved. Asku shivered to see its depiction. "Look, there he is lying on the altar. See the bear claws on the ends of the Teacher's fingers? They are stuck in his chest; see that?"

"Look at the blood spurting," Kitchi said in awe. "Do you think that really happened?"

"If it did, he wasn't having any fun," Hawilish muttered.

"I think it did, Kitchi, because I saw it before I saw this. Look, there he is again," he added, pointing to a second drawing.

The pictures had impressive detail, better than those in the main chamber. Asku could discern touches like skin color, faces, even the teeth and claw necklace. The boy and the chief looked so alike standing side by side. The boy wore the necklace, with blood running down his sides and his stomach. The chief had long, white scars on his chest, just at the place the necklace had been.

Asku heard the drums again. He sat on the rocky floor, raised his hands, wearily welcoming the Spirits to him. *At least this time I won't slam myself into the wall.*

The drums beat and the ceremony became clear. Asku was there.

Strong arms lifted the boy onto the altar. Men on each side held his arms outstretched. The Teacher chanted something Asku could not understand, though it had a few familiar sounds. The boy's chest rose and fell in quiet gasps of anticipation and fear. He looked about Asku's age, perhaps a year or two younger.

Asku flinched as the claws dug deep into the boy's flesh and across his entire chest. The boy was immobile, but every muscle in his body tightened. Another man poured liquid over the wounds, and it mingled with the blood to rill down his sides and onto the cave floor.

Asku's last sensation was the smell of blood and whatever decoction the man had poured. Then the vision was gone, and his head hurt. He felt his awareness fade. "*Áwna winasha*, something is not right here," said Hawɨlish's voice, sounding far away.

⊱——➤

He had a nightmare, one of large animals he had only heard of with teeth the length of his arm; of Susannawa and his sisters being too close, but not being able to get to them; and of being lost in a cave in the dark, hearing yells behind him, which might have been Kitchi and Hawɨlish's voices. Asku dreamed of his mother being dragged away by a huge bear, and of carrying his father's dead body back to the tribe on his shoulders. Then it all went dark.

When Asku opened his eyes, he could see the bright daylight shining into the cave entrance. His head hurt in a groggy, heavy sort of way. "What happened?"

"Glad you are awake, *pásiks*," said Hawɨlish.

"You pick the strangest times to take a nap," said Kitchi. "If you don't want to walk on your own, just say so next time."

Asku made a feeble but clear gesture of mild rudeness. "That's fine. Now how about you tell me how I got here? My head feels like something hit it, but I didn't feel that happen."

"You started to pass out," Kitchi began. "There was a breeze, and it smelled pretty bad. You weren't making any sense. The torch started to get weak. We remembered what the Teacher said sometimes about caves, that spirits would smother a torch if they did not want you around, so we figured we had better get you out here. We didn't feel too great either, but at least the light lasted long enough to get us all back to the firepits with the giant bones. I wasn't sure any of us were getting out of there alive."

Asku coughed and spat to one side. Hawɨlish looked at it. "No blood, at least."

"*Náy*…are you sure you're all right, little *wyánch'i*?" Kitchi asked.

"Yes,"

"I think we are done exploring for the day," said Hawilish. "When you're feeling better, let's climb down and make camp."

"That was strange. That scene, on the wall, it became real in my mind. I saw them rake the claws over the guy laying there."

"The Teacher will want to know about it," said Hawilish. "I'm glad it wasn't me." Asku said nothing more about it, nor did they ask. After about an hour, Asku felt a bit better, and they started down.

As they made their way down the cliffside, Asku could not shake the pounding in his head. Every painful beat made the drums echo throughout his mind. He tried to concentrate on the way Kitchi's bow bounced across his back as they walked, but soon even that became fuzzy. At the campsite, he sat down and closed his eyes, trying to take in as much good air as possible, but the drums became louder and the visions clearer.

Kitchi looked over at Hawilish. "It's kind of late, but maybe we should just get him home tonight rather than stay out here again." Asku heard it at a distance.

"Yeah, I don't like the way he's looking. If we don't get him down the slope now, tomorrow it may be a bigger problem."

"Then let's not waste any time." Kitchi did a deep knee bend, pulled Asku's arm over his shoulders, and stood up with him. "Come on, little *wyánch'i*. Watch your step and put your weight on me." It worked, thanks mainly to Kitchi's husky frame and strong legs, and they began the trek downward.

They did not make good time back to Nch'i-Wána. Asku was moving slower and slower, eventually having to lean on both for support. By the time they reached the water's edge, Hawilish and Kitchi were carrying him.

"He's hot, Kitchi, it could be the fever," Hawilish said.

"Must be something in the cave." Kitchi tucked his sling carefully under Asku's head in the canoe. "He will be fine."

The sounds of canoeing lulled Asku to sleep. It was very dark when they reached the other side. They hoisted the canoe as far as they could up the beach, leaving Asku inside.

"You're faster," said Kitchi. "*Kitu…*hurry!"

Hawilish took off up the trail with his antelope stride. Kitchi sat next to the canoe, his hand on Asku's head. "Asku, can you hear me?"

Asku tried to reply, but his night faded out.

>——→

Asku heard voices, tried to open his eyes.

"It's gonna be okay, man," Kitchi whispered. "The Chief's coming."

Asku turned his head slightly toward the oncoming sound and opened his eyes a little. His father was there, and others. "My son," the Chief said in his command voice, "awaken now." He shook Asku's shoulder, "You must awaken, my *tita*."

"Yes, *Wyánch'i*," Asku replied in a faraway voice. "I'm okay, I think. It's hard to breathe, and my head hurts bad. I don't know what happened."

Strong arms lifted Asku from the canoe and laid him onto something firm. His father's hand was still upon his shoulder as they ascended the trail. As they walked, Kitchi and Hawilish told the Chief the story. After that, Asku heard only bits and pieces of conversations around him:

"…only time will tell…"

"…it may be an oncoming fever, or it may be a Spirit Journey, Askuwa'tu must learn for himself."

"…the Great Spirits will heal him and return him to us, or they will not…"

He felt hands upon him, soft chanting or singing nearby. He was in a tent or longhouse, saw shadows dancing around outside. The Grandfather or his mother would wipe a cool rag across his face and squeeze drops of water into his mouth.

He awoke again later to quiet. Opening his eyes slightly, he saw the Grandfather making something with his hands. The old man came over to him.

"How do you feel, *tita*?"

Asku's voice failed him. The Grandfather smiled and held a cup to Asku's lips. He drank, felt his throat burn and gagged a bit, then fell back asleep or unconscious.

>——→

When Asku next regained awareness, his head hurt less. He tried to sit up but fell back onto the furs with a grunt. The Chief and Grandfather came over.

"Asku, my *tita?*"

The Grandfather laid a hand on Asku's forehead, looked into his eyes and sighed. "He is out of danger, Napayshni. The Spirits have returned him."

Life regained some semblance of normal the next day. He was well enough to return to his family's home. To Chitsa's encouragement, he ate a little. A number of well-wishers stopped by, eventually getting on the Chief's nerves enough for him that he made an excuse about going to speak with the Teacher. Hawilish stopped by, a pleasant distraction from Nayhali's fussing. "Man, am I glad you are okay," said Hawilish. "People were worried."

Asku grunted a reply as he tried to find a comfortable spot on his side. "Well, I appreciate it, but I hope they will stop worrying now. All this attention is embarrassing."

"The Chief sent your grandmother away," Hawilish said in a low voice.

"What?"

"Um, yeah. They had a big argument. Everyone was trying to give them space, but your grandmother went a little crazy, man. She threatened your life. Something about doing more than knocking you into the fire next time."

That hurt. *How could her heart be so bad toward me? I always treated her with respect.* "What?"

"Sorry, Asku," Hawilish continued. "I don't understand everything that happened. All I know is he had Chaytan take her away."

"Oh." Asku felt a rush of melancholy. "And everyone heard this?"

"Naw." Hawilish shifted uncomfortably. "Well...yeah, everyone heard."

There was a quiet rustle as someone approached. Nayhali poked her head in.

"*Nipa,*" she interrupted, "you have a visitor."

It was the Teacher, wearing the beautifully decorated blanket over his shoulders. The long necklace of beads swung back and forth as he walked. The boys dropped their eyes in respect.

"Blessings, my sons," the Teacher said, raising his free hand.

"Blessings today, *Sapsikw'ałá.*"

Hawilish excused himself with a slap to Asku's chest. "See ya later, man."

I'm happy about this. I'm also nervous. But it must happen, whatever I feel. The old man scooted the stool next to Asku's bed and sat down. Both hands on his walking stick, he leaned forward and looked at Asku for a long time. "How goes it, *myánash?*" he asked, at last.

So much to tell and ask. No idea where to start. "I am well."

The old man just looked at Asku and waited.

"*Sapsikw'ałá,* can I tell you something?"

The old man nodded, and out it all poured. The Teacher leaned on his stick in the patient, immobile attentiveness of the elderly.

Asku talked about his bear, his grandmother's anger, the Totem speaking to him, the cave and Saigwan's stories, the paintings, and even about his dreams. He laughed about Kitchi and Hawilish debating over the animal bone and kept as calm as possible when he spoke of his grandmother's exile. When Asku spoke of the ceremony in the inner cavern of the cave, the old man just nodded. Finally, Asku said what he least wished to admit, but must. "*Sapsikw'ałá,* I do not think I am strong enough." Asku closed his eyes in exhaustion.

The Teacher laid a gentle hand on his shoulder. "My *tita,* the Great Spirits do not choose the weak."

Asku slept peacefully that night, without dreams.

Chapter 5

Asku ventured out to the firepit the next morning, where he enjoyed a quiet morning with his family. He finished the bear and presented it to Nisy, who danced around and around the firepit singing happily to her bear. Mini and Sus felt left out, one more vocally than the other, so he began two more projects.

Chaytan had come by after the morning meal and had gone somewhere with the Chief. His mother said it was none of his business, but it surely had to do with his grandmother. He missed her, and he did not miss her.

Around midday, the Grandfather came to check on Asku's burn and sickness, pronounced his progress satisfactory, and left. Not long after that, the Chief returned, quiet and weary. There were more visitors as the day wore on, but still not the one Asku was looking forward to most of all.

Until she was.

Hatayah's family approached, with her mother in the lead and two younger siblings behind her carrying one large basket of *chcháya*. The quantity suggested that they might have spent much of the day gathering them.

Hatayah's mother dropped her eyes respectfully to his father. "Blessings today, *Wyánch'i.*"

"Blessings, *x̲ítway*…friend," the Chief replied. "Thank you for your visit."

Hatayah presented the basket to Asku. "*Kw'ałá,*" he said with a smile, motioning to the seat next to him. "Can you sit for a while?"

Hatayah looked at her mother, who looked to the Chief. He nodded, and Hatayah sat down on the log nearest Asku. Hatayah's mother had some ideas concerning the village garden and began a further discussion with Asku's parents. Even then, he knew they were keeping one eye on him.

"Are you better?" she asked. "I've been worried about you." Her small hands twirled the fabric of her skirt.

Asku tried to puff up a bit, but it hurt. He settled for stifling a wince of pain. "I am fine. Better now than I was."

She was the most beautiful thing he had ever seen. Her long dark hair flowed free, with strands straying across her eyes. He wanted to reach up and tuck them behind her ear, but that would have been quite forward. Her eyes were big, dark as the night sky, eyes in which he could get lost.

Hatayah motioned to his current carving. "What are you making?"

"What? Oh, this. *Yixa*...for Mini."

"It's nice, Asku." That began a discussion and comparison of crafts, in which Asku tried not to become an idiot every time Hatayah smiled. After she left with her family, he could not stop replaying it in his mind. *And there is nothing my parents can do about that, so there.*

Chaytan returned not long before their evening meal. After a quick nod from the Chief, Nayhali invited him to stay. Asku had always liked Chaytan, who was tall, strong, loyal, and reliable. Asku had once asked the Chief why Chaytan admired him so. "Chaytan is my Matahnu, Askuwa'tu," his father had said. "You will understand someday." *He's not quite right about that*, Asku had thought. *That's what older people always tell me about many things, but I already understand it. I will grow up, and so will Mat, and we will always remember how it was when he was tiny and looked at me like some great warrior. Maybe Chaytan remembers my father teaching him not to provoke rattlesnakes.*

In bed that night, he whiled away the last wakeful moments thinking of Hatayah. What his parents were doing was not helping him to think of anything else. He decided to see her again tomorrow.

➤

Asku awoke the next morning with a start. All was quiet with his family, each in his or her place. The sky held just a purple hint of the dawning day. Asku got up, knowing where he must go.

The Teacher was already there, with closed eyes and folded hands. Asku sat down near enough to him for three other people to sit between, had there been any. He pulled the wrap tightly around his shoulders and closed his eyes.

"Teach me, Great Spirits," he whispered. "I will listen." He breathed until his breath assumed a slow, steady rhythm, and he floated through time…

Saigwan looked longingly from the cliff edge at the mouth of the cave. The memory was still so strong. Yiska painted the scene not long after on the back wall of the cave near the other tunnel. It was a memorial—to him.

Saigwan's back had healed, though he knew the scars would be with him for life. His heart had not healed, however. A season passed, although the people did not experience seasons much. All seasons were just cold and dark now.

It would soon be time to hunt again.

Today would be different from other days, for today Saigwan had to choose a mate. After he had returned with the dead chief, he had been offered daughter after daughter after daughter. He knew the tribe only wished to console him, or make a man out of him, or both. And he had tried, but the pain and loss left no room in his heart for anything else.

He would need a family. It was his understood responsibility. But Saigwan felt alone. After the Chief's death, his mother had seen him through recovery, then had yielded to her own grief. The fever took her off swiftly. Saigwan did not cry, not for either of them. He was now responsible for his younger sister, Kasa, and for his people. He would not let them down.

The cave was already filled with the day's excitement. Saigwan began his rounds from family to family, starting with his own. His sister looked up upon his arrival and smiled. "You must clean up, yáya. Do you need help?"

Saigwan waved her comment away, not in the mood for teasing. He walked the circle, doing as the Chief had.

Other families looked up upon his arrival. The men would nod:
"Blessings today, Wyánch'i." The women and children would lower their
eyes. But today was a little different, for the women and older girls all
seemed to have a glimmer of something in their eyes.

I am so not ready for this.

He stopped at the Teacher's fire. "Blessings, Sapsikw'ałá."

"Blessings today, títa," the Teacher smiled. "How goes it today,
Wyánch'i?"

He sat by the fire and sighed. "I think we will need to hunt again
soon." Is that the best I can do? Come on, Saigwan.

The Teacher laid a hand on Saigwan's shoulder and smiled.
"Every mother and father are wishing you will choose their daughter, and
every daughter is praying to the Spirits now for the same."

"That is what I am afraid of," he mumbled.

The old man laughed, not unkindly. "Niyol will place his stone?"

"He agreed, without hesitation. I believe that asking anyone else
would have wounded him in the heart." And there is no one else I would
trust as much to look after my family if something happens to me.

"That is very good. And I believe, a wise choice in other ways,
Wyánch'i."

"Thank you, Sapsikw'ałá. Now, if you will please excuse me, I must
go and prepare."

Saigwan bathed and dressed, donning the bear claw necklace and
the bone bracelet his father had given his mother some time ago. He
wrapped himself in the bison cloak that had belonged to his great-
grandfather. It was too big for him, but his to wear, nonetheless.

He then went to the inner ritual chamber, where he could think and
prepare his mind in peace, until he felt calm enough for the events to
come.

Túta, be with me today, *he finished, and returned to the main*
chamber.

>——→

Saigwan sat in the chief's chair at the head of the ceremonial fire in the main chamber. The tribe sat around the perimeter. What he did today would affect their whole future.

The Teacher stood. A young man in back began a slow, soft drumbeat: one stroke, silence for as long as it took to exhale, two strokes, silence, then repeated the sequence. The Teacher began: "Wyánch'i, blessings today, and to all our people. As you know, we have gathered here so that you may choose a mate to join your firepit and family. Since ancient times, the custom has been that a man wishing a mate must have a friend, a Stone-Bringer, who will promise before the people to care for his friend's mate and children in case he can no longer provide. The Wyánch'i is as subject to the custom as anyone else."

The Teacher let that soak in, then continued. "The Spirits will witness the commitments given today. Let them be well-considered."

For a breath or two, all were silent. When the Teacher broke the silence this time, his voice carried farther, radiated formal gravity. "Wyánch'i!"

Here we go. "Blessings, Sapsikw'ałá."

"And to you as well, on this day when you take a mate. Please call for your Stone-Bringer now."

Saigwan raised his voice a bit. "Niyol!"

A strong, rangy young man in his later teens got to his feet. "Wyánch'i."

"Will you bring a stone to my firepit?"

Niyol knelt, picked up a stone that weighed about as much as a child. Heads turned to examine the stone and its bringer's bearing, noting with approval that Niyol did not affect to notice its weight. It was a neatly broken portion of columnar basalt, two hand-lengths wide and one length high. Niyol came before Saigwan, holding the basalt before him.

Now the Teacher stepped over to the two men. Saigwan stood up and extended his left hand, which the Teacher took. "Niyol, when you place this stone at the firepit of the Wyánch'i, you will accept responsibility for the well-being of his family should he become unable to care for them. You understand fully?"

"Íi, Sapsikw'ałá. He is my Wyánch'i, but he is also Saigwan, my pásiks. I am honored to have the responsibility." The ritual had no strict

standard response here, for the words were to be the Stone-Bringer's own. Quiet murmurs of approval buzzed through the assembly. Niyol's father watched stolidly, but his dark eyes glinted paternal pride.

"*May you not need to, but should you, may you do it well,*" *said the Teacher. He took Saigwan's left arm and dragged an obsidian flake across it, just deep enough for a flow of blood that would not clot immediately. Then he nodded to Saigwan.*

He had seen it a dozen times, and now he was a participant. Saigwan wiped up some blood with an index finger, then painted a small stick-figure family on Niyol's stone. A man, a woman, miniature versions of those—and last, a second man, watching from nearby. It is a good thing I am Chief, not Artist, *thought Saigwan, but what counted was the intention.* "Niyol. Please take that stone to my firepit, then return."

Niyol nodded. As he turned, following long custom, he managed to make sure the tribe could see Saigwan's painted family. There came a faint satisfied hum, with a few near-stifled sobs from women who found themselves deeply moved. Everyone remained in place except Niyol, who set down the stone in a suitable spot at Saigwan's firepit where passersby could examine it until the heat cooked off the dried blood. This done, he returned to stand behind and to Saigwan's right. The Teacher nodded, then addressed the gathering and thumped the floor with his walking stick. "Let the young women come forward."

The Chief had rights to any woman, but responsibility to all. He could even take another man's mate if he wished, though that was discouraged. Saigwan had no intention of doing so.

Mothers or aunts brought forward each young woman of a certain age, in her turn. Una was one of the first, and while Saigwan sat through the entire process, he had a difficult time concentrating on the rest. No one missed the cues, of course, but it would have been disrespectful to the remaining young women for Saigwan to betray his presumptive choice. "If you lose the respect of the women," *his father had taught him,* "that of the men will not last much longer, and your authority will fail. Their work and lives are hard. They must know you understand their minds. They must know that you will listen to them." *He redoubled his effort to avoid giving any of the young women short shrift.*

When it was done, and the Teacher held up his walking stick to signal Saigwan to choose, he walked toward her. She dropped her eyes to the ground.

"Blessings, Una," he said, privately infuriated to hear his voice cracking at this of all times. He slid his mother's bone bracelet over her hand and above her elbow. His heart raced.

"Blessings, Wyánch'i," she whispered. She looked up into his eyes, and in hers he found hope and light. She had chosen him too.

He led her to the temporary tent behind the fire. The tent was plain and simple and filled with animal skins, one from every family in the tribe, just for this special occasion. The Teacher held open the door flap and closed it behind them. All was quiet and would remain so until their union was consummated.

The girl was soft and sweet and smelled nice. His desire for her was great, but his fear of hurting her was greater. He had no idea what he was doing, and although at first he found it hard to concentrate with the people just outside the tent, the two of them figured it out together. Then, more than anything else, he closed his eyes and enjoyed the blessing of holding someone close.

Asku opened his eyes. The sun was up now, the colors bright and glorious in the sky. The Teacher stirred beside him.

"Sapsikw'ałá?"

"Yes, Askuwa'tu?" The old man wore his usual kind smile.

"What happened to Saigwan and the people in the cave? Did they fare well?"

The old man nodded and smiled, "Are you feeling well enough for story time today, my *tita*?"

"*Íi*...yes."

"Good," the old man said, standing and stretching. "I have something special planned with you in mind."

Asku took the long way home, or so he told himself, as he made his way toward Hatayah's home. He had to stop several times to rest. *Is it my imagination, or are people looking at me in a strange way?* He even thought he saw one young woman change her path to avoid him.

The village was alive with the usual morning bustle: the fresh catch, water chores, and cooking preparations. Hatayah's home was no exception, and he stepped around the corner.

"Blessings today, *lamyáy,*" he said. Hatayah's mother returned his greeting. "I am sorry if I startled you." Hatayah was not there.

"No, not at all, Asku. Please sit down. How do you feel, *myánash?*"

"Oh, a little better each day, *kw'ałá,*" he said, pulling his wrap tighter against the chill. Hatayah was probably at the river getting water.

"Would you like something to eat?" Laytiah asked.

"No, thank you. My mother will be annoyed if she prepares a morning meal and I do not eat it, I am sure."

"So am I," Laytiah said with a smile, and turned back to her cooking.

A few moments later, Hatayah and the little ones arrived, and she almost dropped her water basket in surprise. Her smile flooded his chest with warmth. "Blessings today, Askuwa'tu," she said, stumbling a bit on the formal words. As Asku prepared the expected reply, he heard heavy footsteps, and a very familiar face appeared around the corner.

"Blessings on this beautiful day," said Napayshni, nodding to Laytiah. "I am looking for my wayward son, who insists on worrying his mother each morning by disappearing before anyone rises. Have you seen him, by chance?"

Hatayah giggled. Asku rolled his eyes.

"Well, look here, it's him!" the Chief exulted, pointing in Asku's direction. "Come, *tita,* let's get you home." Father began to herd son homeward, but Asku spared one look back at Hatayah. She smiled and waved. His heart fluttered. *She is definitely the most beautiful girl in our tribe.*

"Sorry, *Wyánch'i,*" Asku began. "I thought I would make it back in time."

"Hmmm." His father's most frustrating maneuver: the indefinite answer that revealed nothing. A few moments passed, then: "Asku, I must leave for a couple of days."

"When?" Asku never liked it when his father left the village.

"Chaytan and I will leave in the morning." They were nearing the family home. "I am leaving you in charge, Askuwa'tu Haylaku."

"*Kúu mísh*," he said, after a moment's hesitation.

His father said nothing more. At the firepit, Chitsa and Nayhali felt no such constraint. "Where have you been, young man?" demanded his mother. "I should tie you to that stool."

"We will talk later," said Napayshni, then left again. Asku sat down heavily on the nearest bench, whereupon Nisy climbed into his lap with her bear.

"Where you been, Asku?" she asked. "Do you want to be tied to a stool?"

He was certain he heard his mother and sister snicker. "I was visiting the Totem, *lítsa*," he whispered. "It calls to me, you see. So, I go talk with the Spirits there, and with the Teacher." *And it feels good to tell that to someone who will not ask me questions I would rather not answer. But that reminds me...* "Oh, *íła*, there is story time today."

"That is good news, Asku." Chitsa did not look up from the *wák'amu* cakes she and Nayhali were making. "Nayhali and I will be gathering *wawachí* today," she said, waving toward the mountains and their regular acorn-gathering spot. "You can look after the young ones and take them to the Story House with you."

"Okay. *Íła*, where is the Chief going?"

She put down the wooden bowl. "He needs to go visit his sister's tribe, the Wanuukshiłáma. It is a couple days journey from here, at the Great Sea. He must get your grandmother settled. He will leave tomorrow morning."

"Oh. Yes." He tried to keep a neutral tone. His mother sighed, wiped her hands on her apron and sat next to him.

"This is not your fault. A long time ago...actually, Asku, you need to ask your father about it." She bustled around the firepit again.

Nayhali looked back and forth, realized she was not going to learn anything more just then, and picked up an old cedar bow and a quiver of arrows. "We better get going, *íła*. It is a long walk." The family had baskets big enough to fit Susannawa inside, some with straps on one side to be worn across the back. Nayhali loaded one of the baskets onto her back, then held the other basket up for her mother to slip her arms through. Both women donned their wide-brimmed cedar hats, which kept the sun out of their eyes. His sister might not be the shot Hawɨlish was, but she was good enough.

Shortly after the women departed, Susannawa and Matahnu returned, Hawɨlish close behind. The little boys cheered at the news that they had been excused from acorn-gathering. As Asku and Hawɨlish herded the children toward the Story House, Napayshni fell in with them and swung both little girls up onto his shoulders. As they walked, Asku quietly retold the Totem's story to Hawɨlish, hoping the Chief could hear as well.

"Oh, wow." Hawɨlish shook his head and ran a hand through his hair.

"I know," said Asku. "Try seeing it all happen in your head, man."

The Story House was already full, and a bit stuffy. All the village's children seemed to be present. He soon remembered why, and that Hatayah would not be there.

Kitchi jumped up and pulled a stool over for Asku. Nisy climbed into his lap; the others sat around his feet. He heard the longhouse door close as the Teacher took his place in front of the ceremonial altar. A smudge stick burned in the center of a small table, filling the Story House with the trademark lavender/lemongrass/sage smell that Asku had always liked. The smoke from a small fire between the Teacher and the rows of children drifted through the ceiling vent.

"*Áwacha náy*," the old man began, as he always did. "This is the way it was."

"*Íi!*" the young people replied in unison.

"Long have our people looked up into the face of the majestic Pahto. Long have our people lived within the protective arms of the mighty Nch'i-Wána. Long have our people warmed their backs beneath the gracious Aanyáy, but not that long…"

Pulling Nisy closer under his wrap and checking that Mini had not absconded, Asku closed his eyes to listen.

The Teacher spoke of a time when Aanyáy was missing. She had abandoned them…

In the time of the Uyt-łáma, the First People, the beautiful and mighty Aanyáy looked down upon the lands. She saw the mountains with their cool streams, short, thick evergreen trees and snowfields aplenty.

She saw the rivers flowing freely with thousands of salmon in their final journey toward their spawning grounds.

She saw the mammoth, as he and his family travelled along the wide open plains.

She saw the bison in a herd as abundant as the grass of the fields.

She smiled down upon the majestic eagle, as she returned with fish for her younglings high atop an old evergreen tree.

She laughed at the beaver with his teeth full of tree bark, at the otter cracking an abalone shell in his hands and at the chipmunk sitting on a log and shoving acorns into his mouth.

She watched proudly as the speartooth, the bear and the wolf methodically hunted their food. And she closed her eyes in respect when another gave its life as prey.

All is balanced, *Aanyáy thought to herself.* All is good.

But in looking around, something was missing. Where was the one called man? Aanyáy looked in the mountain, she looked in the river and she looked in the cave. The man was nowhere to be found. She was worried.

Finally, growing weary in her search, she found him lying under an apple tree. His head rested against a root; his hands folded across his chest. He snored loudly.

"Man," she called from above, "what are you doing?"

The man opened one eye. "Go away, Aanyáy, it is hot, and I am tired." He rolled to one side and resumed snoring.

Aanyáy steamed brightly. "Have you put your toes in the cool mountain stream today, man?"

The man did not answer.

"Have you sat at the banks of the mighty river today, man?" She hoped.

The man did not answer.

"Have you felt the musty drops from the inner chamber of the cave today, man?"

Yet still, no answer.

Aanyáy's anger burned fiercely now. "Have you watched the beaver, the otter and the chipmunk today, man? Have you seen the bison herd in the fields? Have you seen the mammoth family on the plains, the eagle in her nest? Have you felt the sand between your toes at the sea today, man?"

The man still did not answer.

Tears began to fall from Aanyáy's eyes. "Man, did you see the predator and the prey today? Did you honor those who gave their lives to feed others today, man?" Her tears fell as cool drops on the man's skin.

"Leave me be, Aanyáy," the man raised his fist to the sky. "I will do all those things tomorrow." He took cover under the apple tree as her tears fell steadily to the ground.

"What more must I do for you, man?" she cried out loud. "I can do no more!"

Aanyáy hid her face in her hands, and as she cried, a dark cloud covered her. The tears began as puddles on the ground, which soon became streams and rivers. The clouds covered Aanyáy fully as she cried in her anguish.

Darkness overtook the man, and he became afraid. The rivers of tears were cold and began to freeze. The man ran for cover, to his family's cave close by.

He ran past the mammoth as it struggled to free itself of the tears and the ice, its family washing away.

He ran past the bison as the ice froze the herd where they stood on the plains.

He ran past the frozen river, the beaver and otter lost below.

He ran past the speartooth, the wolf and the bear as they ran for caves of their own.

The man entered his cave at last. He turned toward Aanyáy one last time, his face to hers as the last sliver of her beauty disappeared.

"Man," said a booming, deep voice from behind the darkness, "all of this was for you."

The man fell to his knees in fear, as the darkness and creeping ice overtook all the land.

The Story House was quiet. Mini stirred at Asku's feet, asleep again, her head in Susannawa's lap. Nisy dozed in Asku's arms.

All may not have been well for Aanyáy in the story, but it is for me.

"Children," the old man whispered, "what do the Great Spirits teach us in this story of old?"

He looked around, watching children avoid his gaze, hoping not to be called upon. Kitchi shifted and found some fascination in Nisy's hair. Hawilish cleared his throat in anticipation. The Teacher looked at each child before stopping at Asku.

"Askuwa'tu?"

"Yes, *Sapsikw'atá*." Asku sat up a little straighter, moving Nisy to his other arm. "Aanyáy represents the Great Spirit."

The Teacher nodded, waited.

"The Great Spirit created everything for us, from the mountains to the sea, the mammoth of old, to the pesky little chipmunk. But it is not a free gift, I do not think."

Asku paused for a moment, contemplating his response.

"We are responsible for all things, as they were a gift to us." Without knowing why, this moved him deep inside. Hopefully, Kitchi was not looking, or he would hear about it. "If we start forgetting our place, and no longer respect the circle of life, we run the chance of losing all things we hold dear," he finished.

"Yes, Asku. Very much so." The old man raised his voice. "*Áwacha náy!*" he shouted, shaking his teaching rattle.

"*Íi!*" the children replied.

They stood, picked up the hide mats and piled them in the corner. The Teacher met each at the door.

"*Watwáa naknúwim,*" he said to each. "May the Great Mother protect you and grow you this day and each day forward."

The children all dispersed homeward, or playward, or wherever. Asku stretched, feeling better, ready for whatever the next few days held for him. He reached down and took his little sisters' small hands for the short walk home.

Chapter 6

Early in the morning, yet again, Asku heard the Totem's call. He arose and went to sit before the tall sculpture before the sun even began to rise. As the wind picked up, he listened to the voices…

Saigwan had been born to a great chief and grew up seeing how people followed his father, mostly out of respect and love. They now followed Saigwan because that was how it had always been done, and because through him the Great Spirits protected them all. Every day Saigwan awoke, he hoped to earn the same the same respect and love. His sister had not recovered well from their father's death, but life had to move forward.

He took her to walk, for no stated reason other than the brief appearance of Aanyáy, to one of the most compelling viewing spots he knew. They could see as far as a man could carry a load in a day, over carven valleys and to bluish mountain peaks. Watching the wind fling her hair about, more like a woman than a girl, Saigwan knew there would not be a better time to do his duty.

"Kasa," he said, "Niyol has asked for you."

She said nothing.

"When your time comes, will you go with him? He told me that he has admired you for a long time but wishes me to present the question. As yáya, not as Wyánch'i. He wanted me to make clear that if you were not willing, he would not bring it up again, nor resent you. His words made my heart feel good."

She still did not move or speak.

"As you know, he is my *pásiks*. I know he would treat you well, and provide well, and help you to raise a family you would be proud of. But if you do not wish it, I also will accept this."

Still not a word.

"Please say something."

"Niyol is good," she said, looking into the great distance. "I will go with Niyol."

Saigwan relaxed. "This is wise. Niyol will have you and care for you as long as he lives. I swear it."

Saigwan saw Kasa wed to Niyol at the changing of the seasons, and then time passed, and he enjoyed watching his sister's belly grow. Niyol and Saigwan often sat together at the mouth of the cave talking of hunting, of women, and of becoming fathers. The young Chief wanted a son, but he was very much looking forward to Niyol's child-to-come.

Kasa grew more and more tired as time went on, but Saigwan and Niyol enjoyed taking care of her. Even Una, although saddened by her own barrenness, joined in.

The day came at last. "Niyol," Kasa cried out in surprise as water gushed to the ground at her feet, "get the Grandmother! Right away!"

Saigwan laughed as he tripped and fell on the way. "*Yáya*, I am afraid," she said, swaying on her feet.

"Great Spirits be with you, *lítsa*. I will take you. Remember the many experiences that have given wisdom to the Grandmother to help you." He lifted her into his arms and carried her inside the nearby birthing tent. It was filled with all sorts of womanly things, from burning sage to piles of furs and wraps.

A woman inside pointed to the birthing-bed, where Saigwan set Kasa down gently. "Blessings, *Wyánch'i*," said another, older woman. "Now, with respect, please get out." She ushered him outside.

Soon the firepit outside the tent was busy with young mothers and children. "Do not worry, *Wyánch'i*," an old woman said, as she patted Saigwan on the arm. "The first one can take a long time."

"*Kw'ałá, lamyáy*," he answered. Then Saigwan took Niyol by the shoulders to make his rounds.

They walked around the perimeter of the cave, the same circle Saigwan had walked each morning for the last three winters, and many times prior to that with his father. They stopped and sat with the Teacher for a moment.

"How goes it, my sons?" the old man asked. They heard a long cry from the birthing tent. Niyol dropped his face into his hands. "Oh, I see."

After a short silence, Niyol spoke. "I have heard the sounds before. It always sounds as if the mother has fallen into a firepit. It is different for me this time because I can do nothing. When I hunt, I have a chance to influence the result. If I am stalked by a speartooth, I can have influence; I can be alert enough to foil the ambush. Now I am like a baby left alone on a rock."

"It is the circle of life, tita. Kasa and the child are in the hands of the Great Spirits."

Saigwan nodded, scowled. The hands of the Great Spirits had taken too many things from him in recent memory, and he was ready for them to stop.

"Kw'ałá, Sapsikw'ałá," Saigwan said, standing to go. He left Niyol staring into the small fire.

"Blessings today, young Wyánch'i," the Teacher replied as he disappeared around the corner.

The torches lining the main chamber wall of the cave were positioned to illuminate Yiska's artwork, memorializing important scenes of the tribe's history. The one nearest him at the moment was very familiar, and Saigwan stopped to admire the beautiful picture of his father standing at the mouth of the cave with his bison cloak on, arms raised in thanksgiving. The people were below. Saigwan saw his mother, her belly swollen, and he breathed deeply. How anyone could make such images with colors and chewed twigs, he did not know, but Yiska made the past live on.

The torches led Saigwan further around the perimeter of the cave. He stopped at each firepit, examining tents, firepits, clothing, mothers, fathers, children. Were they safe, healthy? Did they need anything? Was there enough fuel for the fires? Were the tents in need of repair? Were the little ones properly cared for? Had he not done this, they would have concluded that he did not care.

When Niyol came running toward him, Saigwan's heart skipped.

"My son is here," Niyol exulted, eyes alight. *"Kasa calls for the blessing. Will you come, Wyánch'i?"*

Saigwan slapped him on the back. *"It is a great day. Yawtíi, I would be honored."*

The Teacher held the tent flap open for Saigwan. His sister glowed like his dreams of Aanyáy: hair a tangled mess, face exhausted and aglow. The baby boy suckled noisily at her breast, her arms encircling him.

She disengaged the baby and placed him in his uncle's outstretched arms. Saigwan kissed the infant on the forehead, then turned and placed him in the arms of the Teacher.

The Teacher stepped from the tent and held the child out in front of him in blessing and thanksgiving to the Great Spirits. He sang:

"Watwáa naknúwim,

"May you always have strong shoulders,

"May your spear always fly straight and true,

"May your song always be long,

"May your heart always be filled with courage, and may you walk softly and respectfully with the Great Spirits."

The sky was still dark, though one like Asku who saw Pahto most of the days of his life could notice the first light striking its side Toward the Rising Sun.

Asku pointed to the Totem. "Sapsikw'ałá, what is that at the very top?"

"That is the mammoth bear, títa," the Teacher replied.

"Oh." It looked nothing like a bear, or at least nothing like his bear. "What is a mammoth bear?"

"Ask the Totem, myánash. Ask Saigwan."

Asku repressed a snort of irritation. *I hate it when he won't answer my questions. But I know that the top of a Totem is the most important part of the entire piece, always reserved for the Great Spirits. So, whatever that is, mammoth bear or whatever, is an important part of our past.*

Heavy footsteps behind him signaled his father's approach. Today the Chief and Chaytan would leave for the Wanuukshiłáma village. The

Chief's sister Huyana lived with her family there, and would take Amitola in.

"Blessings today, *Sapsikw'alá*," the Chief said.

"And to you, my *tita*."

"Are you ready, Askuwa'tu?"

Asku nodded and stood, stretching his back and shoulders. The burn felt a little better each day. *Maybe I can plan a trip out to Yixa* *Xápaawish with Kitchi and Hawilish, or maybe take a walk with Hatayah somewhere alone. I wonder how I could do that. I wonder whether I should.*

"How goes it this morning, my *tita*?"

"I am well, *Wyánch'i*," he said as they walked behind the Story House. He couldn't stand it. "*Túta*, what is a mammoth bear?"

"A mammoth bear?" The Chief stopped to face Asku, looking at him as if he had just denied filching berries. "How do you know of that creature?"

"Um, it is at the top of the Totem...right?"

"Yes, there is a bear there, that's right." The Chief sighed and turned back toward the trail. "*Tita*, that bear is an animal that never returned after Aanyáy's reappearance. She returned some animals to us but kept others. No one knows for sure why."

"Oh, like the story from yesterday. Did the mammoth bear look like a bear?"

"Yes and no," said the Chief as he squatted to inspect the base of a nearby tent. He lifted the hide slightly and found a missing stake, then continued as he pounded the stake in place with a nearby rock. "This bear was said to be the size of a man when standing on four feet, its legs longer than our bear, its nose shorter, ears bigger."

Asku bent down to help pull the hide out as far as possible and hook it over the edge of the stake. "Was it as unpredictable as our bear?"

The Chief stood up; the repair complete. "According to legends, the mammoth bear was said to be even more dangerous and aggressive than the great speartooth." He walked toward the front door of the Grandfather's tent and entered. "Blessings today, Grandfather."

"Ah, Napayshni. Blessings to you too, and also to you, Askuwa'tu. How do you feel?"

"I feel better every day," Asku said, smiling, "thanks to you, Grandfather."

The old man smiled. "The Great Spirits provide us with the materials and the learning. It is up to us how we use those."

After some small talk, Asku and the Chief were on the trail again. "Do you stop at every home every day, *Wyánch'i?*"

"I do." The Chief walked a few man-heights off the trail, outside the circle, and bent to the ground. "It is important for our people to see me and expect me. That way, I know what's going on and they know they can depend upon me. If I did not, they might begin to think I did not care about them. It is not that they could not notice or fix small problems themselves; what matters is that I will. Does that make sense, my *tita?*"

"Yes, *Wyánch'i.*" Asku went over to look at the spot the Chief was searching. Tracks and scat. Asku lifted a piece with a nearby leaf and smelled it. "A *xálish.*" After a pause, when it became evident his father would say no more: "But just one, I think. When the pack throws out an old *xálish*, he has no more chief but himself. He may be very hungry, and a little bit crazy."

"Now you see why I walk the trail each day."

"I do. And this means we have to act, right?"

"Why would we have to?"

His father seemed to love answering questions with questions. "Because a wolf scouting out the village must be hunted and killed. There are always little children running around, and a hungry wolf could make one vanish. We have hunted them before. I will go," Asku finished, puffing up a bit in readiness for a hunt.

"Normally, yes, but not this time. You must continue recovering, and I need you here." Asku slumped, but knew the words were true. "We will stop and talk with Nayati."

The morning passed quickly as father and son stopped at each family home, asking about conditions and offering help with small fixes. At the home of Sunsaa, an old widower who had been injured in a fall more than a moon ago, Napayshni and Asku lingered for awhile. The Chief consulted Sunsaa about the wolf sign, behaving as if he had come mainly to seek advice and knowledge. Asku promised to come and visit the elder over the next couple of days during the Chief's absence. As they left the tent, and the Chief silently blessed the man and his home, the lesson sank in. *Everyone wants to feel important. My father knows how to make them feel important. They will do as he says because of this. Now I am excited to come back in the morning. This elder is also a very capable carver. If I brought the turtle I'm working on for Sus, I would learn something, and he would feel cared about.*

They soon came upon a messy sight: Kitchi and his father Nayati skinning a beaver. The Chief and Nayati talked at length about hunting the wolf. Decisions and plans made, and Kitchi would go along.

"Well, crippled little *wyánch'i,*" Kitchi cracked, "while we are out hunting a x̱álish, you can stay behind and guard the women, nurse babies, prepare for your *Małáwitash,* talk with the Spirits, that sort of thing."

"*Chchúu tx̱ának*...be quiet," Asku said, lobbing a dirt clod toward Kitchi's head. "Besides, if your aim has not improved, you will just be carrying the bags."

Asku and the Chief said their goodbyes and blessings and continued on. They walked toward the bluff to look down at Nch'i-Wána below, and the women and children washing there.

"Asku, my *tita,*" the Chief began. It was the *do not interrupt me* voice, but it might also mean an explanation. Asku waited in silence, gazing toward Saigwan's cave.

"There is something you must understand," his father continued. "A long time ago, the Chief of this tribe, your grandfather, had three sons. Two of these sons were from the grandmother that you know, Amitola. One of these sons was from a mother not known much to us. The Chief only spoke of her once that I can remember. He spoke of grace and beauty, cunningness and spirit wisdom. The Chief found this woman...well, no one knows for sure where he found her, but he desired this woman. She vanished immediately after, returning thirty winters ago, with a son in her arms."

Asku risked a glance at the Chief. His eyes were closed and his shoulders heavy. "She came and went as if a Spirit herself. And she walked with the spirit of a bear; a great bear, the mammoth bear." The Chief opened his eyes and looked at Asku.

Asku's heart raced.

"The tribe was afraid, especially your grandmother, but the Chief wasn't. He took the child from her arms and accepted him. Then she and the great bear vanished. As seasons went by, everyone could see the child was in fact his son."

Some time passed as they stood in silence.

"Asku," the Chief continued, turning to face him, "the child was me."

Asku nodded. Now things made more sense.

"My father took good care of his family and our people. There was no love between him and your grandmother, though he took care of her as his own. Over time, to your grandmother's great anger, he chose me as his successor. She had sons older than me that should have been chosen, had it not been for *T'at'aliya*, the Witch Woman, or so she called my mother. My mother, whomever she was, never returned. Your grandmother was the only mother I have ever known."

Patience, Asku told himself, waiting out his father's pause.

"Some in this tribe believe—although I hope it is not fireside discussion anymore—that your grandmother's blood could not be chosen for the chief of this people because her line was cursed in some way. Our tribe has stood for many thousands of winters, Asku. We know not how long, exactly. The great chief Saigwan's blood is mine, as it is yours, my *tita*. And that blood is pure and strong and eternal."

Again, Asku waited.

"Do you understand, Askuwa'tu, about your grandmother? Do you understand her anger, Asku? It is not at you, my *tita*…it is at me. It is jealousy and resentment, boiled in a stew of a bad heart."

"I do, *Wyánch'i*," Asku nodded. "I understand."

Whether I will have any idea what I should do about it, or not do, that I don't yet understand.

Chapter 7

The Chief and Chaytan left for Wayám shortly after that, when Aanyáy
was still well at their backs. Amitola waited for them at the home of a
relative there. They would get her and make their way down river by
canoe, the quickest and easiest way to the Wanuukshiłáma. Asku's aunt,
the Chief's older sister, was mated to the chief of the tribe at the Great
Sea. All Asku knew of his grandmother's exile to the Wanuukshiłáma was
that Chaytan had taken her to wait at the Wayám, and that Hawilish had
said she went peacefully—albeit with great anger toward the Chief, who
would now do his duty by seeing her settled and cared for, despite her
hatred.

But what of T'at'alíya, *my real grandmother? Will I ever know
anything about her or her tribe, or why she came? And what of the
mammoth bear that walked beside her?*

Maybe I should be careful what I wish for.

After seeing Chaytan and his father off, Asku joined his family for
their mid-morning meal around the fire, but soon excused himself by
grunting about needing to check on something. 'Something,' of course, was
Hatayah.

Every time he thought of her, he felt strong feelings inside, a kind
he had never felt before. Not that long ago, Hatayah's father had died in a
terrible hunting accident. Asku had a vivid memory of the hunters carrying
his body home, wrapped in a freshly skinned elk hide, and Hatayah's grief.
Now the tribe cared for Hatayah's mother and children. They always
received a share of the hunt, despite not having a hunter in the party.
Hatayah's younger brother was only about Susannawa's age. It would be
many years before he was ready to care for his family.

Asku approached the tent quietly, having second thoughts. Before he could change his mind, there was Hatayah, poking at something in the firepit. No one else was around.

"Blessings today, Hatayah," Asku said, trying to sound natural.

She jumped up with a start, dropping the stick into the firepit. For a moment it appeared she might fall in, but she recovered. "I am sorry," Asku said. "I did not mean to frighten you."

"Asku, hello. No, you did not frighten me. Sorry. Blessings," she added, manners remembered.

"Let's get this out." Asku retrieved the stick from the firepit and handed it back to her.

"Kw'ałá, Asku," she said. "Please, will you sit?"

He contained his excitement only with a supreme effort. "Only if you join me," he answered, smiling back.

"Are you feeling better?" she asked.

"I am well, *kw'ałá.*" *I don't see how she cannot hear my heart pounding.* "I feel much better."

Hatayah nodded. "That is good news. I was really scared for you. Everyone was."

She was worried about me! Get control of yourself! His voice broke a bit, humiliatingly, as he attempted speech. "Hatayah, I was wondering…well, if you were not doing anything important…not that what you were doing wasn't important…" *Oh man, I am going to blow this.*

She touched his arm. He felt a flutter ripple through his body. "Yes," she said, flashing that smile that was like Aanyáy on a spring morning.

Asku gave her his arm, then led her to the outside trail of the village. They walked around the village for a long time, talking about many things and about nothing at all, sometimes laughing. At one point, she stumbled and tightened her grip on his arm; he pulled her closer.

After walking with her about as long as he felt he could get away with, Asku escorted Hatayah home, then walked to his own home in something of a dreamy daze. He found Susannawa and Matahnu play-fighting with sticks by the drying tree. His mother and Nayhali were busy pounding *wawachí* cakes, and the little sisters were napping in the tent.

Nayhali looked up from the mortar and pestle, then didn't look back down. "What are you so happy about?" she taunted. A drop of sweat rolled down her face. Pounding acorn flour was hard work. After they were shelled and dried in the sun, they were boiled and then roasted, sometimes a couple of times, until the rancid yellow oil floated to the top. His mother and Nayhali would work all day on this batch: chopping, pounding and grinding, then sifting, again and again. They were always in some rotation of acorn flour production.

And something similar would need to be done with the nearby wák'amu pile too, he noticed. "Just took a walk," he said, as if it were a minor thing.

Nayhali stood up and put a hand on her hip. "With whom?" she demanded.

"With Hatayah, *nána*, if you must know," he responded.

"How do you feel, *myánash*?" his mother asked, without looking up from her kneading. There was some cycle to their work, which he had never understood, except that they spent a lot of time, and he was grateful.

"Good, *íła*. May I help you?"

Nayhali handed him a basket of freshly picked acorns. "You can sit down while you sort these," she said. It was tedious work but needed doing.

Within the first few dozen acorns, he uncovered a large black spider, its plump body dwarfed by the length of its many legs. As the spider tried to scurry up the side of the basket, Asku tapped the basket's outside. He caught a glimpse of the dreaded red paint on the spider's belly and grabbed a nearby woven lid—in the process, spilling a batch of freshly picked huckleberries all over the place—and slapped it over the acorn basket before the spider could get back out. "Get back! *Tíshpun!*" he yelled.

In Asku's relatively brief experience, there was no word more certain to inspire girls or women to rapid action. "Where?" said Chitsa, backing away a bit along with Nayhali.

"I believe I trapped it in the acorn basket. I am sorry about spilling the berries," he added, as if they would care under the circumstances.

Chitsa circled over and swept Mat and Sus off the ground. Nayhali gathered up her skirt ends and climbed onto a log, knowing the little girls were safely stowed away in the tent. "Everyone is accounted for, Asku," said his mother. "You can take that basket away now and get rid of the spider."

Keeping the lid down tight, Asku carried the large basket and set it down next to the drying tree. He stepped back and lifted the lid partway. No spider. If he dumped the basket, they would have both a mess and a loose black widow spider running around. Picking up a rock, he pulled the lid off completely.

Inside it was the *tíshpun,* hanging on for dear life.

Asku jumped, dropping the lid at his feet. Expletives escaped his mouth as he brought his rock down on the spider, still in the lid. After a moment, and a breath, he lifted the rock and peered underneath.

"*Kúu mísh,*" he breathed out. "It's all right. I got it."

Asku and the little boys gathered around to identify it. Even his mother came over to check it out. "Oooh," said Chitsa, pointing with a stick to show the little ones. "Look, it's a mother spider. See how she carries her babies on her back? This is a *tíshpun,* a very dangerous spider. You cannot even see her teeth, but her bite is as dangerous as a *wáxpush.* And since she makes no noise at all, you must watch more closely for her. Understand?" Everyone claimed to.

Chitsa turned to her eldest son. "Asku, you must take this to the Grandfather." She stood up, wiped her hands and returned to her work. Nayhali began to pick up and blow dust off those huckleberries which no one had trampled in the commotion. Asku helped the little boys scoop the dead spider onto a piece of wood, then led them to show it to the Grandfather.

A short time later, Asku left them behind with the Grandfather and returned to his home firepit. "Man, that was a big *tíshpun, ila,*" Asku held his hand up, fingers outstretched, in comparison. "You and Nayhali better be careful when you're picking up acorns next time." He shook the basket around a few times before bringing it back to his spot at the firepit.

"Tell me about your walk with Hatayah, Asku," his mother said, conversationally.

Asku glanced at Nayhali, who was stifling a snicker. "It was nice, *ila.* I really like her." He talked for a while about Hatayah and their time together, about seeing the Grandfather this morning, and about his plans to visit Sunsaa tomorrow. At length, uneasily, he remembered the wolf scout.

"*Íla*, where are Nisy and Mini?" She motioned to the tent. He did not feel any better.

I knew that.

"We found <u>xá</u>lish scat on the outside trail this morning. Kitchi and his father will hunt the wolf today." Now his throat felt dry. *Something is wrong.*

How long has it been since I saw those two little chipmunks?
Too long for my comfort.

He suddenly realized some time had passed and the little boys had not returned.

"*Íla*, I will go and drag them home." While Asku did his best to keep worry out of his voice, he couldn't conceal the act of grabbing his knife and sling. He threw the wrap from his shoulders and moved out. Out of the corner of his eye, he saw his mother wave a hand toward the sky beckoning the Spirits for protection.

He double-timed it toward the Grandfather's home, stopping for breath, then tapped softly on the door. "Grandfather?"

"Come in," the old man replied. Asku found the Grandfather sitting around a small fire. A pot hung in the center, smelling of lavender and something else.

"Blessings again today, Grandfather," he said, remembering his etiquette. "Please excuse my abruptness, but have Susannawa and Matahnu left?"

"Yes, *myánash*," the old man said, stirring his concoction while mumbling something Asku could not make out. "They were quite pleased with the rather large specimen you brought them to show me. They left just a few moments before your arrival."

"Did they say where they were off to, Grandfather?"

It took the Grandfather a few moments to answer. "Yes, something about burying the *tíshpun* down in the draw Toward the Setting Sun, near the place they found that old <u>xát</u>xat." The old man looked up at last. "Is everything all right, Askuwa'tu?"

"I hope so, Grandfather. Excuse me."

Asku sprinted around the corner on the side of the village nearest Nch'i-Wána and met Hawilish. "Hey, man, what's the big hurry? I am going out to test some new arrows."

Asku took off. "*Wyanúukim íchin*," he hollered. "Come this way!"

The runoff draw was dry nearly all the time, except when it rained or a lot of snow melted. It had many smaller side draws along its gradual path to Nch'i-Wána. As had Asku and Hawilish and Kitchi at their age, the boys considered it their playground.

They approached the last bowshot-length in stealth, listening to the sounds of children's voices. Asku felt an overpowering sense of danger and drew his knife. Crouching, he listened in the way he had been taught, to all that was there, and what was not but ought to be. The boys arguing; a slight breeze. No animal sounds. *No birds.*

Asku's skin crawled. He lifted his hand in warning to Hawilish, gestured to get ready.

Then he heard a rustle from the side draw to his left. Asku glanced at Hawilish, who nocked an arrow as silently as possible. One well-placed step at a time, they began to advance.

"No Sus, that's not right," Matahnu's voice drifted from nearby. Susannawa said something unintelligible in response.

There. Asku saw the gray fur he was dreading and froze. The wolf was also hunting, unaware of the older boys' presence, their scent near enough and like enough to the children that it did not alert the loner. Asku nodded in the wolf's direction, watched for Hawilish's nod of acknowledgment from the corner of his eye. He could only hope that the old wolf was a little deaf and signed: *shoot him. I'll finish him.*

Hawilish answered with a slow draw of his bow. Asku could see the boys now, still unaware of the danger down in the main draw and readied his next action.

The arrow whizzed through the air and pierced the wolf's neck. It lurched forward with a loud yelp but did not fall, not a mortal wound, at least not soon enough. That left a starving lone wolf, one of the most dangerous creatures known. The wolf stuck to its hunt, continuing toward the little ones.

"Run home!" Asku yelled at the little boys, who jumped and yelped in surprise. They scrambled up the draw past the older boys, then took off for the village. The wolf also started but did not flee. "Me," Asku yelled at the predator. "Come try for me, _xálish_! I am more your size!"

The animal stopped in its tracks and looked back toward Asku. It stood above his hip in height, the largest either of them had ever seen, surely an elder who had once been a chief among its kind. Its tattered fur bristled on its back as eyes radiated desperation. Blood dripped from the arrow hanging from its neck. The wolf bared its teeth and gave Asku a low growl. He kept his knife foremost, hoping to slash and roll clear.

The wolf began its leap just as Hawilish's bowstring hissed. The second arrow sank deep into the wolf's chest. Its leap became a sort of truncated flop, but the wolf struggled to its feet as it began to lose the final battle for life. Asku began to advance, but Hawilish grabbed his arm. "_Pináwaachik!_ Watch out. There may be no need for the risk. Don't be stupid."

Wise advice. I will take it. Asku maintained his stance, braced as the wolf tried to summon the strength to leap, then saw one hind leg buckle. Then the other, and then the ancient creature toppled onto its side. "It won't be long," said Asku. Hawilish and Asku stood ready for a sudden surge of life but observed its ebbing with the respect due an elder.

After about the length of time a man could hold his breath under water, the wolf's movement ceased. It died with its dark eyes still open. Asku and Hawilish approached, taking care, knives ready. Hawilish nudged the wolf with a stick. "Wow," he whispered. "That is the biggest _xálish_ I have ever seen."

"Nice shots, man," Asku said, quietly. "Thanks."

Shouts came down the trail as several hunters arrived with spears and bows in hand. Asku crouched over the wolf's body, peering into the lifeless dark eyes. "What's up?" he whispered to the magnificent creature. "Why so desperate?"

There was no answer.

"We should get started," Hawilish said, after giving Asku a moment.

Asku nodded, and they rolled the animal onto its back. It bore many scars. _Probably from a long stint as wyánch'i and defending his people, just old and lonely now._ Asku pulled the _chúksh_ blade from his belt and sank it deep into the animal's chest next to Hawilish's arrow. He turned it around once, then twice, then removed the first arrow. It was undamaged. So was the second, and Asku cleaned his knife, then sheathed it. He looked up.

Hawɨlish shook his head. "It's all yours. I think his Spirit called to you to set it free."

"No way, *pásiks*. Anyone can see that this was your kill."

Nodding, Hawɨlish reached inside the chest cavity and pulled hard, freeing the animal's heart—and with it, its Spirit. Another hunter had started a small fire.

Hawɨlish held the warm dripping heart high in the air and chanted. "*Kw'ałá, síks*. May you be free at last, my friend." He threw the heart onto the fire and squatted down next to Asku, watching the flames dance around the warm flesh.

A group of men moved in to carry the wolf's body back to the village, where it would be skinned. If every piece were not used or preserved in some way, the sacrifice of the x̱*álish* would be dishonored, which could lead to serious consequences. Asku took a deep breath and looked down at his bloodstained hands. He laughed out loud with relief and wonder at what had just befallen them.

Soon his mother came running down the path, two little boys on her heels. She had Nayhali's bow nocked. She came to a sudden stop at the sight of Asku—whole, but with hands covered in blood—a man, a Chief's son, her son. She raised her right hand in blessing and dropped her eyes in respect. As she turned to go, she slung the bow across her back and grabbed two little arms, not so gently.

Asku smiled at the sight, thanking the Great Spirits for their safety.

His shoulder hurt, but far greater hurts had been avoided.

Chapter 8

The hunting party scoured the hills and valleys for traces of a wolf pack but found nothing. The only tracks around the village were those of the lonely, gray wolf. Kitchi found himself in the unaccustomed position of taking a heckling from both Asku and Hawilish, but not for long in Asku's case. He had other business.

Asku knocked softly on the Teacher's door, announced himself, and entered. He found the old man sitting cross-legged before the small altar, his back to the doorway.

"I am sorry to bother you, *Sapsikw'alá*. I was wondering if I could speak with you?"

A smudge stick burned in the center of the altar. The bundle of dried herbs and leaves smelled strong and sweet, Asku recognized the familiar concoction. "Please sit down, Askuwa'tu, and tell me what is on your mind."

Asku sat, hesitated a moment, then began. "The <u>x</u>álish called to me." Asku watched the swirling stream of smoke. "Or at least, I think it was him. I felt something, a knowledge of great danger. Something called to me. I was afraid, but of what, I did not know."

The Teacher listened in silence.

Or... "Although, the more I think about it, *Sapsikw'alá*, I know the animal's spirit called to me...to send him home. Or to help send him home, since Hawilish made the kill."

There was silence, broken only by the crackling burn of the incense. Asku felt his head clearing. "The Totem also calls to me...and the cave. And Saigwan speaks to me through these things. I know it's him, but why?"

"Asku," the old man said, his eyes still closed. "You are nearly right. But your spirit is calling to them, my son: to the <u>x</u>álish, to the *anahúy* you met at the waterfall, to the Totem, and to the cave. And your spirit calls out to Saigwan. His own spirit answers the call."

Asku let the words sink into his heart. "My spirit calls to them?" he whispered.

The Teacher opened his eyes, looked at Asku without expression. "Askuwa'tu, you will do great things. Much will be asked of you—and you will give all you have. Of this, I am certain."

That does not sound good. "*Sapsikw'ałá,* I don't think I can." Asku felt tears threatening, embarrassment, weakness. "I am not great. What if I am called to these great things and cannot do them?" He wrapped his arms around his legs and buried his face beneath them.

"My *tita,*" the Teacher said, "you already are."

▶——

That night, Asku, Kitchi, and Hawilish sat with others their age around the outskirts of the ceremonial fire while the tribal elders, *Nch'inch'ima,* passed the *chalámat* and told stories. They called upon Asku to tell the story of the great gray *xálish.*

Asku stood, the chilly evening breeze above the heat of the fire refreshing his senses. He began with the aftermath of the *tíshpun* encounter. When he got to the part of spotting the lonely *xálish,* he stopped and gestured to his best friend.

"And here is where Hawilish must take over. He saved all of us: me, my little brother, and Matahnu. This is his story to tell." Several pairs of elderly eyes lifted a bit and seemed to be pleased.

Though suffering from a bit of public speaking anxiety, Hawilish managed to get through the rest of the tale. While he did, Asku glanced at the Teacher. The old man gave Hawilish the full attention that was due the new, softer-spoken narrator.

When the celebration ended, Asku headed home, tired and still distracted by the day's events. He tried to climb through the tent door quietly, but tripped, sprawling across the floor with a loud grunt and a muffled expletive.

"*Náy, isha,*" Chitsa whispered, "are you all right?" Asku heard a muffled giggle from Nayhali's sleeping area and tossed a moccasin in her direction.

"Yes, *iła,*" he whispered. "I am fine. Nayhali tripped me is all."

Nayhali sat bolt upright and hurled the moccasin back. "No, I did not!"

"*Amash wáchuk,*" Chitsa sighed. "Everyone hush now and go to sleep."

Asku crawled in next to Susannawa and fell asleep thinking about Hatayah. But his dreams soon turned to images of wolves and the little ones, then to a bear the size of a man, and to his mauled father trying to protect him, then bleeding to death.

>——→

Asku slept poorly and got up with the sun. He had wanted to get up earlier to visit the Totem but had first awoken with a bad headache. Sometimes the kinnikinnick mix that the elders used in the *chalámat* had that effect on him. He stooped over the family firepit and blew softly on the hot rocks and tiny smoking embers. Small sparks jumped as the rocks glowed orange and red from the moving air. He stoked up the fire and sat to enjoy its warmth in the dawn.

After the morning meal, with the last of his headache fading, Asku grabbed the turtle carving and began to walk the trail around the village. He stopped at old Sunsaa's home, asked to enter, and greeted the elder with formal respect. Sunsaa was sore and a bit frail that morning, but no less glad to see Asku, and welcomed him to sit down.

Sunsaa had not felt well enough to attend the celebration and was glad to hear the wolf story for the first time. Asku showed him the turtle carving, and in turn the elder handed Asku a similar wood carving. Its detail was amazingly intricate. "What kind of animal is this?" asked Asku.

"That is a speartooth," Sunsaa responded, coughing as he bent to point out the long front teeth. "A giant cat, he was also called."

"Oh, yes. I know this animal. I saw pictures of it on the cave walls. There are stories—"

"The cave?" The old man looked startled but recovered quickly and laid back down.

"Yes, *púsha*." Asku helped pull the animal skins up again. "Kitchi, Hawⱥlish and I explored this cave across Nch'i-Wána and up into the mountains. Something happened to me in that cave. I don't really know what, but I couldn't breathe, and everything went black. The place was full of drawings and ancient things. Not to mention, voices and memories and such. Do you know it?"

Sunsaa sighed. "I know it. However, right now I am very weary and would like to take a nap. Will you come visit again tomorrow, *myánash*?"

"Of course, *púsha*." Asku gently patted the old man's arm. "Blessings, and thank you for showing me that amazing carving," he said, as he slipped out.

He thought he heard a mumbled, "*Kw'ałá, Askuwa'tu.*"

The rest of his rounds were uneventful, with little children in particular wanting to hear the wolf story again. He got home not long before the midday meal. While Chitsa bent to her work, Sus and Nisy were crawling all over someone. Before long, he realized it was the Grandfather and laughed.

"Let me help you with those," said Asku, lifting both children off the Grandfather's back, tickling as he did so. They squealed with delight. He tucked Nisy under his arm and dumped Sus onto his back in a nearby pile of camas. The Grandfather laughed a deep, guttural laugh, the kind that warms the heart and draws everyone else to laugh as well.

"Asku, how do you feel?" asked the Grandfather.

"Much better, Grandfather. Even when running with Hawⱥlish, the burn did not hurt much."

"And the headaches?"

"Gone. I really do feel fine."

The Grandfather stood to go, patting Asku's shoulder. "Well, I guess you will survive, then."

>—→

Nayhali and Asku spent the rest of the morning relaxing in the sun at the village's small garden. After some small talk, Nayhali brought up Chaytan. They had taken a walk before he left with the Chief and had 'snuck into the bushes.'

"And what does it involve to sneak into the bushes?" teased Asku.

"That's all you need to know about that part, Asku," she snapped.

"There is no need to be crabby. You brought it up. How am I supposed to know?"

"At the rate you are going, I think Hatayah will teach you. But this is serious, *yáya*. If I wanted to talk to a child, I would have brought Sus. Please don't be like that."

"Okay, okay. So, where is this going?"

She paused for a few moments. "He promised to talk with Father while they are away, Asku," she whispered.

Asku turned to look Nayhali directly in the eyes. "Will you have him, *nána*?"

She looked up at the sky. "I will, with all of my heart."

"Well, Father should approve. He places great trust in Chaytan, who is a strong hunter. After all, you will be mated someday, and it should be to someone he respects, like Chaytan. And if it helps you, I think it is good."

Nayhali threw an arm around his shoulders and hugged him. "Thank you, Askuwa'tu. For your faults, you are a good brother, and you will be a pretty good *wyánch'i*."

I think that is meant to be a warm compliment. I was only speaking the truth. She must have a mate, one day, obviously, and Chaytan will be important to both of us for all our lives.

"Now," she continued, "we had better gather the things that Mother asked us to get."

The Patisapatisháma lived at this spot all year, with no need to move as some tribes did. When the fish did not run Nch'i-Wána, they could eat what had been preserved. The one exception was a few days in the summer when most went Toward the Great Mountains to harvest the *wák'amu* in a well-know meadow, sacred to many local tribes. The journey there for the *Wák'amu Ká'uyt*, the Celebration of First Camas, meant an exciting rendezvous with friends and family, celebrating the seasons and playing lots of games. The rest of the year, the tribe depended upon the village's garden.

To keep out deer, who would otherwise eat the garden bare every night, someone had long ago come up with the idea to surround it with tumbleweeds and brush impaled upon long stakes in the ground. Near the doorway, and part of its structure, stood a cedar shelter that could afford a bit of protection in case of a sudden rainstorm, or just to rest in the shade after working in hot weather. The garden had rows upon rows of the Three Sisters, a fruitful combination of crops they had gained from the Great Plains not all that long ago. The Plains traders told Asku's people how to plant them, and that the Three Sisters cared for each other regardless of Aanyáy's presence. The bean wound tightly and carefully around the thick maize stalk; the dark green squash covered the ground at her feet. The maize gave the squash shade, while she in turn fed the ground of her much taller sisters. The women had invested many days cultivating the Sisters for two or three winters before they bore edible food, a calculated risk that had paid off. Thanks to their hard work, and the tribe's sacrifice of growing space with attendant shortages, the crops provided a fresh and nutritious change to the Patisapatisháma diet. Birds still raided the garden, but nothing could be done about that at night.

The garden also housed the Grandfather and the Teacher's medicinal plants and herbs, important both for health and ceremonial purposes. There were stories about where and when the first seeds came to the Patisapatisháma; mostly through trade down river at Wayám or Toward the Great Mountains and the Rising Sun along the plains. *Ch'láy*—salmon flour—and *yixa*, beaver pelts, could fetch all kinds of interesting trades. But not everything would grow just anywhere, so tribal agriculture grew on the basis of trade, experimentation and accumulated understanding of each plant's ecology.

Asku and Nayhali walked each row, weeding as they went, then set to gathering their mother's list of items wanted. After some forgetting, some chastisement of Asku by his sister for inability to remember details, and remembering at last, they delivered the produce to Chitsa as requested. Nayhali got to work. If Asku remained nearby, he would soon be assigned something boring.

"It's a beautiful day, *iła*," he began. "I had an idea to take Sus and Mat, and maybe Hatayah's little brother Huwahkan fishing today. I think they would get along, and we should get some trout."

"Trout sounds great," said his mother without looking up.

"Okay. I will go see if Kitchi and Hawiłish can come along. Can someone holler for Sus?" he asked, heading out in search of his friends. After making plans with Kitchi and Hawiłish, he made his way toward Hatayah's home. He found them at their firepit.

"Blessings today, *lamyáy,*" he said to Laytiah.

"And to you, Askuwa'tu," said Hatayah's mother with a kind smile. "What brings you by?" Hatayah looked up at him with those twinkling eyes. *I must not become an idiot.*

"Well," he began, "I was planning an afternoon fishing trip with Susannawa and Matahnu. But I am just not sure how we will carry it all. We are going to catch many trout. How will I ever get all those fish home?" Asku said, catching Laytiah's eyes and then glancing down at little Huwahkan, absorbed in drawing in the dirt with a stick.

"Hatayah and I cannot go today, Asku, or we would be glad to help. And Huwahkan is far too young to go."

That was the necessary spark. "I am not too young, *iła*!" Huwahkan bounded to his feet. "I can help! Why can't I go?" he demanded.

Laytiah scowled, only half seriously. "Remember your manners, *isha*. We have company and you are being very childish. I will leave this up to Askuwa'tu, who knows what he and his men need. If you ask him with respect, maybe he will consider it."

Huwahkan drew himself up with dignity so comic that Hatayah had to clamp a hand over her mouth to repress laughter. "Blessings today, *káka*. If you are going fishing today, may I please come with you to help carry the fish?"

Asku gave the boy a gruff, mock-skeptical look. "I do not know, *píti*. You are no bigger than a muskrat. How much can you carry?"

Huwahkan stretched both arms out to the sides. "I can carry a rock this big, Asku!"

Laytiah seemed overtaken by a fit of coughing.

Asku pretended to mull it over. "Well, in that case, and since your mother approves, and since you are respectful, I guess it would be okay. Now, do you have a pole?"

Huwahkan disappeared in an instant, returning with one much too big for him. *His father's.* Asku smiled. "That one is perfect. Now let's go. We are in a hurry and there is no time to fool around."

The women maintained control until Asku got Huwahkan about a bowshot away. To Asku's great satisfaction, he could hear Hatayah gasping in mirth behind him. After some child-herding and gathering of equipment, the six set forth: Asku, his best friends, three excited little boys, four fishing baskets, and six fishing poles. They turned Toward the Great Mountains and the Setting Sun and meandered up a trail leading to a small tributary, where trout ran in plenty.

The older boys all had the same destination in mind: a spot where the river pooled, creating a nice little swimming and fishing hole particularly known for short, stumpy trout. The little boys scurried around the water's edge, climbing on rocks. Kitchi went to one of the usual spots and dug up worms while Hawilish began checking the fishing equipment.

"You three, go hunt us some more bait," directed Asku. "All right, *pásiks*, let's catch us some fish."

The little boys ran off, hunting worms along the marshy edge where the water did not seem to move much at all. They flipped rocks over and used sticks to dig in the muck and yelled about water skippers and even a frog or two. Hawilish tried, with moderate success, to get them to keep their voices down. Asku and Kitchi argued about the best spot to cast from, and in the end, each stuck with his own preference. The boys sat back to talk and enjoy the late afternoon sun together, guiding the little ones within the limits of their attention spans, reeling in two dozen trout.

Upon return to the village, the party stopped first at the youngest fisherman's home. His mother was not inside. Hatayah picked him up and planted a big-sister-kiss on his cheek. "How was it, *nipa*?"

"Put me down," Huwahkan demanded, trying to wriggle free.

After a moment, she complied. "You didn't answer me, Howa."

"We got lots of fish, *nána*," said the child, with vast self-importance.

"Mother will be very pleased. Thank you, Asku...and the rest of you, too."

Asku motioned to the other boys to distribute the rest of the catch and shepherd the other little ones home. Kitchi smirked but went.

"Here is the first fish that the little brother caught today. Make sure he gets to eat that one." Hatayah produced a wooden bowl. Asku dropped a fish into it the size of his hand, then two more. "You can have these, as well."

"Kw'ałá," she replied.

Asku set the basket down. They were alone; Huwahkan must have followed the other boys down the trail.

Without thinking, he moved closer, then a little more. She smelled of the garden, of sunflowers and herbs. His heart beat faster.

He brushed her cheek with the back of his hand, traced his fingers along her jaw to her chin, then brushed his lips across hers. As his stomach did a backflip, he heard her release a soft sigh. Asku reached his arm around her waist and pulled her close, so that he could feel her body against his, her lips brushing his, her breath on his face.

And then there were footsteps behind them, and it was over.

Asku backed away just as Huwahkan spoke up. "Thank you for taking me fishing, Asku. Can we go again tomorrow?"

Asku laughed. "Thank you for helping us with the fish. I will take you again soon." Huwahkan bounced around them, singing happily to himself. Asku smiled at Hatayah and turned to go, feeling as if he could fly.

Chapter 9

Saigwan awoke with his heart racing. He could not remember what had scared him so badly. He carefully climbed out from under the wrap he shared with Una, tucking it back around her. He dressed, grabbed his bison cloak, and stepped outside.

All was still dark, except for the night guard's small fire at the cave entrance. "Blessings, Wyánch'i," *the man mumbled sleepily.*

"How goes the watch tonight, yawtíi?"

"Quiet night, Wyánch'i. Nothing out of the ordinary."

Saigwan sighed. I am becoming an old woman. "Go to bed, yawtíi. Sleep has left me. I will finish the watch."

"Yes, Wyánch'i, thank you," *the man replied as he turned to go.*

Saigwan pulled his wrap tightly around his crossed legs. The fire warmed his face, but the chill at the back of his neck reminded him of the conversation that had produced his unrest.

"You must have an heir, Saigwan," the Teacher had said.

"I understand that, but I will not do that to Una." Saigwan had stood up and stalked out.

"You will do what is right," said the elder, into his chief's wake.

"I will do what is right," Saigwan mumbled to himself in the darkness.

Una was beautiful, kind, and took good care of him. But late at night, he heard her crying in the night for want of the child for which she so yearned. He would often pretend to roll over in his sleep and encircle her in his arms, which only made her cry harder.

"Please, Great Spirits. Please grant us a son." The clouds broke slightly, and a sliver of Mother Moon touched his face.

"I will do what is right," he sighed. "I will not abandon her, my mate, my partner." I will wait. If a son does not appear, I will announce

my sister's son as heir. I am their chief, and they will listen to me. I do not like the Teacher's nagging, especially saying that I will 'bring ruin on the tribe,' and the part about us being 'no more without my seed.' If my seed is so important and good, then why does it not take root in Una's belly?

Saigwan returned home to find a warm fire blazing. Una sat cross-legged in front of it, gazing vacantly, hair tangled. He knelt next to her. "How goes it this morning, átawit?"

She did not respond.

With both hands he took her face, forcing her to look into his eyes. "My dear, are you ill?"

"They are talking again, Saigwan," she said, pulling away and gazing again into the fire.

"They will always talk," he said, sitting down. "They are like a flock of magpies."

She looked up. "I have failed you, Saigwan. I am so sorry."

Saigwan's blood boiled. How dare they talk to her about this? It is none of their business. *He took a deep breath before replying, so as not to take his anger out on her.*

"No, you have not." He saw tears in the corners of her eyes "You are good to me, and I would have no other."

"Saigwan, you chose me, and I have failed you." He tried to brush her tears away, but she grabbed both his hands. "You must take another. Please. It is the only way to bring me peace and bring a child to our home."

Saigwan was not absolutely sure how a baby was made, but he was certain that it was not all her responsibility. He knew that when a man lay with a woman, sometimes her belly would swell with new life. He was certain the man played a role in the matter, although the Grandmother and other women disagreed. They were probably feeding her all kinds of nonsense about why she had not yet carried a child.

"No, Una," Saigwan pronounced. "I will not. You are my choice, my mate and my friend. I will not dishonor you. Maybe you will carry my child, maybe you will not. But you will be my mate until the Great Spirits take us home!"

The last part came out too loudly. He had not meant to yell at her, and he regretted it.

Saigwan felt a sudden need to love his wife. He made love to her with defiance, and in plain sight under his bison wrap. Then, he held her tightly as he pulled the wrap over them both to keep the chill out. And if they heard, or saw, I do not care. Let them see how good she is to me.

"Una, átawishamash…I love you," he whispered to her. "Until the end of my life."

"Me too," Una smiled through her pain and tears, "until the end…and beyond." She softly touched his face, sadness still in her eyes.

>—→

Some time passed. Her mood did not improve, and she spent more and more time sitting in silence or disappearing altogether. On more than one occasion, Saigwan and Niyol went looking for her when she did not return with the others from gathering. Once they found her sitting next to a small stream, her bare feet dangling in the icy waters below. Another time, they found her sitting at the edge of a cliff in a way that gave Saigwan a bad feeling. He had scolded her for it, letting his fear master his sense. She had not responded to him then; not to his anger, nor to his fear for her.

He was afraid to leave her, but the tribe needed to hunt. He kissed her forehead and told her how much he loved her, but she made no response.

The hunt went so well that they returned a day later than expected, the travois laden down with two heavy elk carcasses. The women of the tribe came out to prepare the meat.

Kasa was there, her young son tethered to her back, cozy in his wrap. But she walked right past Niyol's outstretched arms to face Saigwan, looking worried. "We cannot find her, yáya," she said, sadly. "She left in the night, just after you did. We have looked everywhere we can think she might be, without any success."

"Una has been gone three nights?" Saigwan felt something terrible deep inside. Kasa nodded in response, her eyes on the ground.

Saigwan dropped his wrap and equipment. In his heart, he knew where she was, and he ached for her.

He ran faster than he had run since he was a child. He heard soft footsteps behind him and knew Niyol followed. He always followed, and at this moment, Saigwan wanted no other with him.

Stopping just short of the cliff edge, he looked up into the sky. Aanyáy was shining briefly, and her warmth filled his emptiness. Niyol waited quietly next to him.

Motioning for Niyol to stay, Saigwan approached the cliff edge and looked down.

She was there, as he knew she would be.

He dropped to his knees and screamed in agony, a long howl of misery that shook the core of their existence, the tribe hearing from afar. His head in his hands, Saigwan cried in pain and anger; at her, at the tribe, at his life, his chosen life. Niyol knelt next to him.

Time passed, a long time perhaps, until Saigwan stood.

"I must go get her," he declared, wiping his face with the back of his hand.

"Let me go," said Niyol. "Please, let me."

Saigwan ignored him and began the treacherous climb down. They would have to walk the long way around to get back up, but Saigwan did not care.

She had been there for days, and her body was beginning to smell, to attract scavenging birds. The thick taste of death stung his nose from the top of the cliff. Once at the bottom, he ran to where she lay. In fury, he hurled a rock the size of his fist at the black birds, then dropped to his knees next to her.

She was pale and stiff, her body beginning to bloat, yet her eyes were open. The birds had not yet gotten to those. They were bright and beautiful, even when lifeless. He laid a hand across them. His thumb and forefinger caressed the soft tender skin and gently closed them forever. Her body was broken. Saigwan's heart felt not far behind.

"I am so sorry, Una," he said as he laid a hand on her chest and bowed his head. "You are broken because of me, because of who I am. I am so sorry."

Saigwan wept for a long time. Niyol stood in silence behind him, one strong hand on his best friend's shoulder.

"*Kw'ałá,*" he finally whispered, breathing deeply. "*Thank you for your sacrifice.*"

They wrapped her body tightly in Niyol's wrap. Then Saigwan picked her up and began to walk, refusing Niyol's assistance. As they approached the cave, the mourning song began. After he saw to the freeing and honoring of her spirit, he sat in silence by his fire. Some sent their daughters to him, but he paid no attention. Nothing could ease his despair—nothing.

The Teacher was shaking him. "Asku, *myánash,* are you all right?"

Asku looked up into the elder's thoughtful eyes. He felt the tears on his face and tried to regain composure. The loss and grief felt so fresh and real.

The sun was coming up just beyond the Totem. Asku could see the colors changing, pink and red, to gold and yellow rimmed in bright blue. The breeze was drying the tears.

"Did she do the right thing, *Sapsikw'ałá*? Did Una have to die?"

The old man sat back down and pulled his wrap around his shoulders. "She did what she thought was right, Askuwa'tu. The right answer is for her and the Great Spirits to know. Much was asked of her, too."

Asku cringed. "And she gave all," he whispered.

"She did," the old man sighed. "Some believe her spirit returned not long ago to fulfill her vow to this tribe. Many believe that Una's spirit never rested after her death, that she could never find peace for not carrying Saigwan's child."

That sounds like what my father told me. "She returned? When?"

Silence.

"*Sapsikw'ałá?*" Asku pressed.

Long moments passed. He gave Asku a look that seemed to burn clear through him. "Yes, she returned. About thirty winters ago, she came here."

Could it be true? My grandmother, the mysterious woman, could she be the spirit of Saigwan's mate?

"*Sapsikw'atá*, do you believe she found peace, then?" He wanted nothing more than to know that she did, at last. That it was possible to give all and come through the other side of things with peace in the Spirit World.

"I know she did, *myánash*," the old man said with his broad smile. "She carries much pride for her son, and for her grandson."

>———

Asku wandered where he knew he would find Hatayah, somewhere along the path used for hauling water. He walked her back to her home. "Can I see you later today, Asku?" Her voice was like a beautiful song in his ears. "After my chores, I mean?"

He smiled and nodded, feeling a little weird and dazed.

"Meet me at the garden at midday then," she said, with a soft touch of his forearm.

When she tried to pull her hand back, he grabbed it and pulled her closer. He drew his hand across her hip and around to the small of her back, spread his fingers wide to feel and hold more of her in his arms. He bent to kiss her, a long, warm kiss that made her lips part and brought a soft sigh. She seemed to melt inside of his arms. He tasted the sweetness of her lips.

"I will see you later today." He took a step back, but not too far back.

"*Íi,*" she whispered.

Asku talked with Sunsaa for a long time that morning. When he brought up the cave and Saigwan, the elder revealed that he had been there as well. "As a boy, a couple of times, with your grandfather."

"You knew my grandfather?"

The man coughed as he spoke. "My *pásiks, myánash*. There wasn't anything I would not have done for him...and him for me. That cave scared us to death once when we were young, not unlike the story you told me of your experience there. Your grandfather never wanted to go back there again."

"I guess I know how he must have felt. That place made me sick."

Sunsaa smiled. "He and I hiked up there once. We were younger than you are now. We saw the paintings, dug through some very old firepits. Did you see the paintings?"

Asku nodded. "We did. Pretty amazing."

"Yes. We found a back tunnel that twisted and turned a while, then opened up into an ancient cavern."

Asku shivered. "Yeah, so did we."

The old man nodded. "We did not stay long, because your grandfather heard voices in there. Singing and chanting, old lingering rituals maybe. He became afraid, and he was brave even when we were children, so I knew it was serious. We left and never went back."

"Can you tell me about the voices?"

"Yes, he talked about it for a long time after. It was something that I did not understand, but we were *pásiks,* so it was important to me too."

Asku had heard stories of the old chief's death, yet he still had so many questions. "What happened to my grandfather?"

Sunsaa tried to sit up, partly succeeding. "It was when your father was about your age, I think. There was a raid. Two of your uncles were killed by a band of Pyúsh P'ushtáayama that live somewhere along Pikú-nen down in the Blue Mountains. The river tribes try to avoid the Pyúsh; they are unpredictable at best. Although not all are evil; some are reasonable. But there is a small group that lives not that far from us, and it has an evil history. They came only to kill and to steal, as is their way."

Asku listened. "They came in the night and killed some hunters, hurt some of our women and young girls. They carried away your father's sister."

A coughing fit wracked Sunsaa for a few painful moments. Asku offered him water from the little bedside table, and a few sips helped to clear his throat.

"They killed your grandfather, there under the Totem. He died right there in my arms. We were very angry. Your father and I and a few others followed them, caught up, and killed them in the night. We rescued your father's sister."

"What a terrible time."

"It was," said Sunsaa, seeming far away. "Your father became chief. He made alliances with the two nearest tribes. The people at the

Great Sea, the Wanuukshiłáma, to them he gave his sister. Among the Elk Plains people, the Wawyukyáma, there he found Chitsa, your mother." He smiled again and patted Asku's arm. "He was your age, I think."

They talked a while longer about the Wanuukshiłáma, but Asku could not stop thinking about his grandfather and the old man. *Kitchi and Hawilish are to me as this man were to my grandfather, and Niyol to Saigwan. I feel things they must have felt, long ago.* When the elder began to fatigue, Asku took respectful leave.

Finishing his rounds, Asku found Matahnu and Susannawa sitting on a rock at the base of the trail. The two sat side by side licking the same piece of honeycomb, their fingers dripping with stickiness.

"You two are even more of a mess than usual. Did you get that yourselves?" Asku asked.

"Hawilish brought it," said Sus, licking his lips. "He left one for the little sisters too."

"You are lucky. That looks good." He walked up the trail to find the little girls sucking away on the other piece of honeycomb. His mother and Nayhali were busy, as always, and he offered to help.

>———

Asku snuck off not long after the meal. The morning breeze had yielded to a punishing heat, which lay heavy on his back as he walked down the little trail to the garden.

They sat next to each other under the shade of the cedar shelter, talking of their lives, or of nothing at all. She chattered on about her brother and little sisters, about her mother and about missing her father. She told of how her mother had been so proud of Huwahkan upon her return, had made some excuse and gone off and cried a little, and still at times wept at night for her mate. He reached for her hand and squeezed.

As the sun began to drop in the sky, it came time for both of them to go home. Chitsa and Laytiah would be preparing evening meals, and in the latter case, Hatayah had better be present to help or be prepared to explain why she had not been. Napayshni should return this evening, if his travels with Chaytan had gone well. Asku walked Hatayah home, hand in hand, and then bent to kiss her softly on the cheek. He let his lips rest there momentarily as he breathed the sweet smell of her skin. "I will see you soon," he whispered in her ear.

As he walked home, he ached to turn back and see her, to feel her, to smell her and never let her go. She consumed his thoughts. He wanted to listen to her talk about the things on her mind and to watch her twirl her hair around her fingers in that adorable way he found so feminine. With a twinge in his heart, he remembered Saigwan's story.

The Chief returned later that evening, looking very tired. *And not just his muscles. His heart is tired. Whatever he had to do, he does not feel very good about. This is a very bad night to tell him about everything that has happened here. All of it will still have happened if I tell him later.* "I walked the rounds, *túta*. Everything is fine. Sunsaa is at least not any worse, and he was happy to see me. I believe I should continue to visit him."

The Chief looked oddly at Asku. *Oops. He suspects what we talked about.* If so, Napayshni did not bring it up. "Very good, Asku. As he may have told you, he and my father were close, and I do not have the time to spend with Sunsaa that he deserves of me. I feel better about it. And now, my sister's family has sent us all some gifts."

There was something for everyone. A small wrap of soft sea animal fur, a large turtle-shell bowl, and two jars of oolichan oil for Chitsa. Nayhali got a long two-stranded necklace of shells, and Susannawa a rawhide sling with long sinew thongs and a bag full of shiny, clear rocks. The little sisters each got a bag of delicate shells and small starfish from the beach.

Then the Chief handed Asku an elaborately carved whalebone bow. "The Wanuukshiłáma chief carved it himself, *tita*. Take a look at the stories in it." The carving depicted a hunting expedition, down to the finest detail. There were six men in a long canoe, waves splashing up and over the sides. Three large animals swam near the canoe. One blew water and air from its head, shooting straight up into a flock of birds flying above it.

Asku turned the piece over and over in his hands. "That is a *sut'xwłá* hunt, *tita*. One gray whale will feed and provide for a tribe for an entire season. The hunt is the heart of the Wanuukshiłáma way of life."

"I do not know what to say, *túta*, except...wow."

The Chief smiled. "Apenimon will be glad to know that you like it."

But something was out of place. A bow was a sacred gift, and a rare one. Bow makers were few, for it took special skill and a long time. Most young men carried hand-me-downs from their fathers, grandfathers or uncles. His father had a beautiful bow, given to him when he became chief of this tribe.

And therefore, there is a message in this bow. "Why did he make this for me?"

The Chief answered only by giving Chitsa a small sad smile.

After the meal, Asku and his father walked together toward the trail. The Chief was in a better mood. "So, a little bird tells me you had quite an exciting few days. Tell me about it."

Asku told his father about the old gray wolf. He talked about Sunsaa, his visit with the Totem, and Saigwan's story. He did not hold back about Hatayah.

At that point, the Chief said nothing for a moment. Then: "Askuwa'tu Haylaku, we must talk."

Uh-oh.

"Your grandmother is settled, my *tita*," he began. "The Wanuukshiłáma chief is a good man and will provide for her. Of this, I am grateful. What I am going to tell you next, though, may be hard for you to understand." His father stopped and turned to face Asku. His face said that Asku would not like what came next.

"The chief has a daughter from his first mate. She is just a little older than you. In a little while, she will be ready, and she will be your mate."

Asku started. His stomach felt like doom. He took a step backward, speechless.

"*Míshnam pamshtk'úksha'*...do you understand me, Asku?"

Asku opened his mouth but could not find coherent words.

"When her sacred *Małáwitash* begins, which my sister thinks will be soon, they will bring her here and she will be your mate. I have met her, and she is sweet and kind. She can cook, and she will care for you. You will grow to love her as I did Chitsa."

Asku was no longer even hearing him.

"This is what is right for our people, Asku. Your grandmother will live there now, and because of that, we secure and build upon our good relationship with the Wanuukshiłáma. They are family now and will be even more so after your union is complete."

"No, *túta*," he choked out, crossing a line. "I do not want this."

"'Want' is not a luxury you have. Someday you will be chief of this tribe. It means less liberty, not more. I am the least free of all our people, and I think you know it, just as you have long known this could be your future."

"*Túta*," Asku continued, forcing coherency, "yes, I admit that I have. But I love Hatayah, I think. I could tell you 'no,' now that I have found someone else. Right?"

Napayshni, *wyánch'i* of the Patisapatisháma, placed both hands on his beloved son's shoulders. He looked deep into Asku's eyes, his own firm yet not without sympathy.

"Askuwa'tu Haylaku, you will do what is right.

"Your grandmother would have complained all the way to the Great Sea had I not told her to shut up. I got angry. I also told her that she was a tremendous fool, a very unkind grandmother, and entirely mistaken about you. I told her that she would see soon enough.

"I knew this was true when I said it, and I know it is true now."

Chapter 10

Asku grabbed his wrap, his sling, his knife and the new bow—but only after picking it up and putting it down a couple of times, his hands shaking with anger. Seeing what he was up to, and without a word, his mother hurriedly packed a bag of jerky, dried berries and acorn cakes, and tucked them into his sling.

"*Yáya,*" Susannawa asked, "*Máalnam wínata*…how long will you be away? Can I come?"

Asku grumbled something resentful and inarticulate, pushed past his little brother, and ran from the village without looking back.

He turned his eyes toward Pahto and just ran.

He stopped when he broke through the thick underbrush around Yi̱xa X̱ápaawish. It looked the same as it had on his last visit, when he had come to escape his grandmother's harshness, only to find it awaiting him upon his return. So much had happened since then. He had felt stronger, like he understood more, and freer than ever before.

Until his father's announcement.

What am I doing? What am I supposed to do? He found himself pacing in circles in front of the little stream, as angry as he had ever been: at his father, at life, at himself, at everyone and everything he could think of. Even, somehow, at Hatayah.

It took Asku some time to calm down enough for a good look at his surroundings. The waterfall looked the same, though it seemed to flow a little more heavily. Then he saw the tracks, and an excited chill ran down his spine. *It's my bear. My* Pawaat-ła, *as my father called it.* He examined the sign, but none was recent.

"Come visit," he called out. "I will be right here."

Asku sprawled out on the thick green moss, crossed his feet at the ankles, tucked his hands behind his head and closed his eyes. The sun, warm and calming on his bare chest, began to clear his mind. He drifted off to sleep.

His dreams came in inconsistent, mottled snippets. He saw Hatayah, then a young girl with an otter pelt covering her face and head, then a mammoth bear, then a family of beavers trying to drag a large tree around the spot where he was sleeping.

Some time later, he awoke to noises.

He opened his eyes, but the sounds were so close that any other movement could be very dangerous. He slipped the knife from his belt, gripping the antler handle tightly, remaining silent and nearly motionless.

The quiet rustling moved closer and closer. Something had detected him. He jumped quickly into a crouch; the long black blade ready in his hand.

"How goes it, *pásiks*?" said Hawɨlish, stepping into the clearing.

"Great watch you keep," snarked Kitchi. "A herd of *shwúyi* could have snuck up on you. At a run."

Asku stood up, sheathed the knife, and tried to look casual. "What are you two doing here?"

"The Chief said to go find you," Kitchi began. "He didn't say why, but—"

Hawɨlish finished for him. "We knew where you would be, and, well, we are best friends, after all."

They did not ask what had happened. For a while Asku forgot about his heartache. They followed the bear tracks up into the mountains, swam in the pool, and when the sun began to set, they hunted.

They worked their way up into the foothills, where the evergreens and undergrowth became much thicker. They stalked geese and squirrels, even a small black-tailed deer. A flock of mallards overflew them, and Kitchi lost two arrows trying to bring one down. It was Asku's turn to razz him for a general lack of good sense and marksmanship. In the end, Hawɨlish brought down two rabbits with his bow, and they returned to the waterfall.

"Look at those bear tracks," said Hawɨlish. "Only an idiot would camp down here. Let's climb up and camp above the waterfall." They did, and Asku made a small firepit with dry river stones. While he got the fire going, Kitchi and Hawɨlish prepared to honor the rabbits' spirits, then began skinning and cleaning them for cooking. The cool evening came alive with forest animal sounds.

"*Túnmash wá táymun?*" Kitchi asked. "What's up, man?"

Asku shook his head. "I don't want to talk about it."

"That doesn't work with us," Hawilish scratched his nose with the back of his hand, his small carving knife dripping with animal blood.

Asku blew carefully on the spark and added bits of dried grass until he had a small flame. When he had it going well, Hawilish performed the small ceremony, then went back to skinning and butchering. Asku sat down and stared into the fire.

The weight of his conversation with his father was back. It had been nice to be distracted for a while. Now he felt angry again, even more than before.

None of them said anything. Other than the fire, only the messy sounds of rabbit-skinning broke the silence.

"The Chief," Asku said, his inflection disrespectful, "orders me to mate with the daughter of the Wanuukshiláma chief. And it will happen soon, or so he said."

His friends kept working but listened.

"He said she is sweet and kind and can cook," he said, actually mimicking his father's voice, "and something about how I will learn to love her, like he did my mother."

Asku searched both of their faces and waited. Neither responded.

"See this?" Asku held up his new bow. "A present from the Wanuukshiláma chief." He tossed it to the ground as if it meant nothing, hard enough that he regretted it before it hit. Both his friends looked up in surprise, then stared at the magnificent gift lying in the grass.

"*Áwna wínasha, pásiks,*" Kitchi growled. "Let's go. We will go up into the mountains tomorrow morning. We can take care of ourselves."

"That doesn't make sense, Kitchi," Hawilish said, sharply. "How would that put him with Hatayah, in your view? Calm down. We are not going anywhere."

"Well, then we will just go back and tell him no," Kitchi turned to Asku. "We will be with you, man. We will tell him there's no way, right?"

"Shut up. That's not helping." Hawɨlish waved his hands, full of dead rabbit and blood, back and forth in Kitchi's face. Then he turned back to Asku. "What do you want to do?"

"I don't know." Asku felt sick to his stomach again. "I love Hatayah...I think I love Hatayah. I cannot hurt her."

They sat in silence for a long time, roasting the meat on pointed sticks. Dusk came on, bringing bats to flutter around overhead. Asku stared into the fire. *Looking at it now, I am glad they came. It was better that I am not all by myself.*

"Do you think you can refuse?" Hawɨlish asked, poking at the fire.

"No. He said that I would 'do what is right.' That is Chief-ish for 'you have no choice.'"

"*Ḵ'a'áay...*" hissed Kitchi, "and a guilt trip, if I have ever heard one."

"Yes, maybe, but that doesn't mean I don't have to obey. He also said, 'you will be chief of this tribe someday, Askuwa'tu Haylaku.'" His imitation of his father came out condescending and sarcastic.

"What if she's ugly, man?" Kitchi asked.

Hawɨlish rolled his eyes and threw a handful of dirt in that direction. "Kitchi, you are at it again. This is serious."

"What? I am just saying...that would be bad, right?" Kitchi said, faltering. "Or not. I suppose it doesn't really matter."

And Asku laughed, despite himself.

◆—→

Asku woke in the dead of night to Kitchi shaking him, a finger at lips for quiet. He pulled the knife from his belt and followed.

They crawled to the waterfall's edge for a careful look. At the pool's edge, where Asku had fallen asleep earlier in the day, was his bear. The animal looked up and directly at them, then bent to drink. The moonlight laid silver streaks on the bear's dark fur.

"That's him," Asku whispered. "My *Pawaat-lá*. See the white spot between his eyes."

When the animal finished drinking, he backed away from the waterfall, circled, swung his head left to right, then seemed to look up at the boys one more time. He nodded once, turned, and walked away.

"Wow," Kitchi said in a low voice. "You are sure that is the same bear?"

"Certain," Asku whispered. "Go to sleep. I will keep watch, since I probably can't sleep again. Oh, and don't wake Hawilish. He will freak out."

"True," Kitchi snorted. He stopped to add a log to the fire before curling up on the other side.

Asku sat with his back to the fire and his wrap pulled tight. Sometimes he would stand, walk to the edge of the waterfall and look down. The bear did not return that night.

Around daybreak, Asku walked away from the little camp to a spot where he could see the foothills and Pahto. From here, the majestic mountain seemed closer than he knew it to be. He sat and watched as light shone from his right, illuminating the mountain in silver and pinks and flashes of the whitest white on Pahto's snow fields.

"Is this my path, Great One?" he asked, into the slight breeze. "Is this the trail I must take?"

Asku closed his eyes just as the light touched his face and he was taken back again.

Niyol quickly took Saigwan away. For a couple of days, they walked Toward the Setting Sun through the foothills and high up into a mountain range. He had not spoken much. They hunted in the evening when they got hungry, and they slept when it was dark. The rest of the time, they just walked. Somewhere during the third day, as they were walking along a steep cliff edge, Saigwan just stopped.

"Who am I, Niyol?" he asked.

"You are chief of this tribe, and my pásiks."

"Am I?" Saigwan sat down on the cliff edge. He gazed into the distance but did not see the scenery.

In his mind, he saw Una again: alive, laughing and smiling. It had been a long time since he had seen her smile. Her hair blowing in a breeze, her burdens lifted, her pain gone.

She is not suffering, but she is still with me. Because I refuse to let go of her. This is not a kindness to her.

This is me thinking of my own pain, not hers. Hers is over. By refusing to release her, I tie her to my pain. I have no right or wish to do that.

And there, on that cliff edge with Niyol by his side, he let her spirit go.

"Be free, my *átawit…my sweetheart,*" he said, just above a whisper. "*You blessed us all with your life and in your death. Please be at peace.*"

A few moments passed and Saigwan stood again. "I am ready, yawtíi. Áwna túxsha…let's go home now."

Upon their return, Saigwan made his rounds through the cave. All seemed well, but his fire was lonely. The noises of families settling down together for the evening made his heart heavy, a feeling that deepened in coming days. He kept it inside, but he was angry: at them, at Una, and mostly at himself.

He continued living, he hunted, he walked his rounds, he attended meetings with the Nch'inch'ima. He sat at the mouth of the cave every night after sunset. Sometimes Niyol joined him, but most often he sat there alone. Sometimes he prayed, sometimes he wondered, sometimes he despaired, and sometimes he simply watched.

After returning to his fire on one particular evening, something happened. That was the night she visited him for the first time.

He heard her approach before he saw her.

"Blessings, *Wyánch'i,*" she said. It was Moema, a woman of the tribe, and he knew her story. Her voice was sweet and kind.

She was tall and slight, her hair long and plaited behind her, and quite a few winters older than he. She had lines near her eyes and around her mouth. She had been given to an old man, a situation he knew well; he had advised against it, but her father had allowed it, nonetheless. While Saigwan sensed that she had been unhappy for a long time, she had loyally cared for the old man until his death a couple of moons prior.

Sitting at Saigwan's feet, she pulled a small wooden bowl from her basket and arranged a mixture of bright red and orange berries, two long strips of elk jerky and a handful of chopped roots and bulbs. Then she pulled out a small bladder of water and looked up at Saigwan.

He met her eyes and melted inside their dark depths. How had he never noticed her eyes before?

"Will you eat, Wyánch'i?" Her voice was like a healing song to his ears.

"Thank you, Moema," he smiled at her. "Call me Saigwan, please."

Moema returned every night, bringing him food and drink. Sometimes she would eat with him; sometimes she would stay a while to talk about the day's happenings.

A moon passed before Saigwan felt his inner strength returning. When Moema came to his fire that night, he knew he was ready.

"Thank you." He reached for the proffered bowl as usual, but this time he placed one hand on each of hers. "Stay with me this night?" It came out like a plea, but he did not care how it sounded.

She smiled and dropped her eyes back to the ground. Saigwan watched her as he ate, feeling the return of longings that had leaped from a cliff to what seemed like their death as well.

They talked and laughed into the night, a happy time that intoxicated Saigwan. When he could not stand it any longer, he reached for her. For a while, he just held her close and enjoyed the warmth of her next to him. He pulled her wrap from her shoulders and encircled her with his own. She leaned back into his lap, and he breathed her scent deeply.

His longing overtaking him, he carried her into his tent.

It was not long before Moema glowed with child, for she was not past those days of a woman's life, and not long before she blessed Saigwan with a daughter and then a son.

Asku opened his eyes. He always felt a wave of sadness when the visions subsided.

"*Kúu mísh*," he whispered. His heart resolved to his fate, he returned to his friends. "I am ready to go home."

"What will you do, Asku?" Hawɨlish asked, beginning to bury the fire's embers.

"I will do the right thing. Won't we all?"

"Yes," Hawɨlish nodded, "we all have a path that we must follow, easy or hard, makes no difference. It is our path."

"But, man," Kitchi interrupted once again, "what if she is ugly?"

By now, Kitchi was ready to duck the dirt clods.

Chapter 11

They returned to find the village bustling with the news. The looks were different. When Asku walked past, some conversations stopped, yet resumed after he passed. Kitchi glared at a few of the gossips. Hawilish patted his back in encouragement.

She would already know, then. It must be causing her much pain. How many people will I hurt because of who I am? But he found strength in Saigwan's story: hope amidst pain.

The Chief and the Teacher were at the Totem, where Asku knew they would be. He sat down between the two men and wrapped his arms around his legs.

"I am sorry, my *tita*," said the Chief. "I know this is the right thing to do, but I am sorry for the pain it causes you nonetheless."

They sat in silence for some time.

"Blessings today, *Sapsikw'ałá*." The Chief stood to go. Asku followed.

"Blessings to you both," said the elder, with a little sadness in his eyes.

Father led son along the trail in the opposite direction from home. Then Asku realized where they were going. His insides felt like impending tragedy. He stopped. "*Túta*, must we, right now?"

"Yes, my *tita*," the Chief answered as he kept walking. "You owe her an explanation, as do I. The longer we drag out the hard parts, the longer we extend the pain, like a splinter under the skin that never gets removed until it swells up and causes sickness."

Asku lagged behind his father as they approached the small home. "Blessings today, *lamyáy*," he said to Laytiah.

"Blessings today, *Wyánch'i,*" she said, with the kind smile that showed where Hatayah had inherited her own.

Hatayah did not look up, and tried to act normal, but Asku saw her strained body language. All of a sudden, he wanted to change his mind. He could not hurt her, nor could he deny his feelings for her.

"Please, Laytiah," the Chief said, "can we have a moment of both your time?"

"Of course, *Wyánch'i*. Please sit down if you would like."

Her mother sat Hatayah down next to her on a bench near the fire, an arm around her. The Chief sat in front of them both. Though he would rather have knelt in a firepit, Asku reluctantly followed. Hatayah's eyes, which showed signs of recent crying, refused to meet his.

"I do not know if you have heard yet," the Chief began. "I have chosen a mate for my son, the daughter of the chief at the Great Sea. This will reunite our tribes once again, as they have been in the past. They are the most powerful tribe on the coast, for they control the mouth of the great Nch'i-Wána. They are good allies to have. Hatayah, you are too young, but Laytiah remembers what happened back when we neglected such tribal relationships. It was to our detriment."

He reached out a hand and placed it on Hatayah's, folded in her lap. "Hatayah, this is against Askuwa'tu's will. I am sorry that what must be is hurtful to you, just as I am sorry for the way it hurts my son. It is unfair to you, and not your fault."

A silent tear fell from the end of her nose. Asku sat on the ground with a grunt, wrapped his arms around his legs and hid as much of his face as he could.

Napayshni turned to Laytiah. "Will you show me that plan you had for the garden? It sounded as though it might improve our yield. We might test it to see." She nodded, patted her daughter's back, and got up to lead the Chief back down the trail.

When Asku finally looked up, he looked directly into her eyes. They were full of strength and courage, yet her chin quivered. He sat on the bench next to her and wrapped his arms around her. She let him hold her for a moment.

"I am sorry, Askuwa'tu," she said.

"You are sorry? I am sorry, Hatayah."

"You did not know, did you?"

He looked down at his own hands. "Not even a hint. Otherwise...no, wait!" He threw his hands up into the air. "Screw it! Let's run away together. I can take care of you. I will take care of you. *Atawishamash*, Hatayah." He grabbed her arms and tried to pull her to her feet.

She would not stand up. "No. No, Asku. That cannot be. We could not leave our people like that. We cannot be mated here. No, Askuwa'tu, you will take the chief's daughter as the *wyánch'i* says. It is the right thing to do. You are a good man, and you will be a good mate for her, and a good chief someday."

His heart sank. He squeezed her tightly one more time, wrapping his arms around her and breathing the smell of her loose hair.

"Hatayah, you will be a mate and mother that a man will be proud of, and you will always have a place in my heart." He kissed her hair, then turned and walked away.

Saigwan sat in silence, unsure how to comfort Moema. She rocked back and forth, back and forth, as if the child were still alive. Around them, the tribe mourned.

Saigwan's heart felt hard. He had loved and lost so many times that he no longer felt the twist in his heart. The little one had not even been named. He had been blessed; the Teacher and Saigwan had seen that done immediately. But from then on, he did not eat, he did not cry, and soon he did not breathe.

"Moema," Saigwan whispered, though she did not look up, "Moema, átawit?"

She was silent.

"We must say the words, and then we must let him go."

Saigwan gently pulled the infant from her grasp. She resisted, kept reaching, but he was firm. He took her around the shoulders and led her to the ceremonial fire. The tribe saw them and began to follow.

Asku looked up at the weathered Totem, the colors faded by time. He wondered who made it, and when. The mammoth bear at the top still perplexed him.

The clouds glowing with the rising sun looked ominous in bright pinks and reds. It looked and smelled like rain, and he muttered this.

"Yes, *myánash*," the Teacher said from somewhere behind him, "looks like rain."

After the exchange of greetings, Asku turned to go, then stopped. "*Sapsikw'alá,* how old is this Totem?"

"It has been here a long time, my son. They weather and pass on like anything does. But this one—" he walked over and rested a hand on one section, as if gaining energy from it—"has been here a long time."

"Who made it?"

"Your great-grandfather, chief of this tribe, a long time ago."

"My great-grandfather made this?" Asku looked at the Totem with a new appreciation. Animals, shapes and designs covered every surface.

"Yes, he was a master woodworker, as well as a mighty chief. I hear you may have some of his talents."

"I am not sure," Asku said. "Well…I do like making things with wood. I made a bear for Nis'hani, and I am working on a turtle for Susannawa and a beaver for Mini."

He heard well-known footsteps. "Blessings today," said the Chief.

"And to you." The Teacher turned to go. "If you will excuse me, I have some things to see to."

Asku smiled at his father. "*Shíx máytski*…good morning, *Wyánch'i*. Shall we head out?"

"My thoughts exactly, *tita. Míshnam wá,* Askuwa'tu?"

Asku thought about lying, about changing the subject, about yelling at the Chief again. "I am okay, I guess," was all he could come up with.

"Hmmm." The Chief paused for a moment. "I lost my father before I met your mother. Did you know that?"

"Yes, I did. Actually, Sunsaa reminded me of that while you were away. He said that grandfather was his best friend."

"Yes," the Chief said, looking ahead, "his *pásiks*." He was quiet for a moment, then cleared his throat and continued. "Your grandfather was killed, and the *Nch'ínch'ima*, the elders, named me *wyánch'i*." Asku saw sadness in his eyes. "They asked me many hard questions, and at one point, I was so mad I wanted to snap at them and tell them to choose a different chief, but that would have been wrong. I was young. I was no longer Napayshni to most people. I was now just *Wyánch'i*. I will not hold back from you, Askuwa'tu; more than once, my heart said, 'I just want to be Napayshni again.' But it was impossible."

The Chief stopped and sat down on a log near the trail. "We lost men in that raid, and that left us vulnerable. I was very lucky to have my father's *pásiks* by my side. I could not have done it without him. What was most important was to tighten our alliances in case things continued to get worse for our people. You know I gave my sister to the Wanuukshiɫáma Chief, Apenimon. He had recently lost his mate in childbirth."

"Apenimon controls the mouth of Nch'i-Wána. That makes him a very powerful man. To our good fortune, he is also a man we can respect, who deals honestly. There is not much that we have, that he does not have, but we control the river trade Toward the Rising Sun from him. He needs us as a friendly link to the Elk Plains, the Dark Mountains and beyond. Not much of note can come to his people from Toward the Rising Sun without our knowing of it. But we need him as well."

He took a deep breath. "But back to the history. After I gave my sister to Apenimon, I travelled to the Elk Plains, near Aputaput, to meet with your grandfather, Kalataka, and the Wawyukyáma of which he remains *wyánch'i*. We are also fortunate there, for Kalataka is a great leader whose people recognize his kindness and wisdom. He blessed me with his daughter, Chitsa."

The Chief smiled. "She did not come just then, but I did get to meet her. I was so nervous, it all happened so fast, but she was beautiful and sweet, and it was the right thing to do; for me, and for our people. Oh, it took us a long time after her arrival to even be able to talk to each other. We were so young and clumsy." He laughed out loud.

"But you know, Asku," he said, meeting his son's eyes, "she left her home and came to me. She came because she had to. It was her path."

If I still do not like it, I am beginning to understand.

"Chitsa was to be my mate, to give me daughters and sons. She represented an alliance between her father's tribe and mine. Your grandfather's tribe on the Elk Plains links us to other tribes through trade and security relationships. The Great Spirits have blessed us in this spot; we have all we need to survive, right here. But there are people who would seek to do us harm because of it. You may not realize it yet, but others are not so lucky. And still others are angry about it. We need relationships, allies, all about the lands that drain to Nch'i-Wána."

Asku gave some thought to how a marauding force might attack the village, and how to repel that force. *What protection is better than advance notice of trouble to begin with? If we had been forewarned back then, when my father was not yet chief, might we have taken less harm?*

"Anyway, back to your mother," continued Napayshni. "She is much more to me now, Askuwa'tu, than trade and a link to her father. She is my friend, and my advisor, especially on matters most important to a woman. And she keeps me warm at night."

Asku had a thought of Hatayah doing that and banished it.

"Do you understand what I am trying to tell you?" the Chief asked, in a leadership tone.

"Yes, I think so," Asku said, nodding. "What is her name?"

He smiled at Asku, "Her name is Kaliskah, my *tita*."

——

Asku had not seen Hatayah since the night of the celebration of the Chief's return. She had sat quietly with her family then, avoiding his eyes. Asku asked Hawilish to go check on her a couple of times, and he would return with news of the little family.

"But how is she?" Asku demanded.

"She's sad, man. What else do you expect?" said Hawilish. "I think she feels just like you do, *pásiks*."

He tried to think of Kaliskah when he was sad, but then his nerves would turn into a stomachache. Sometimes his mind would even wander to Saigwan and his mating ceremony. *Will it be like that for me? I have no idea what to do. And I hope our whole people will not be right outside listening.*

Asku did wonder about Kaliskah. The Chief had said good things about her, and he doubted his father would embellish. He could sometimes hear Kitchi's voice in his head: *but what if she's ugly, man?* But he had already decided that it didn't matter.

Later that day, when the little ones were napping, Asku sat down to work on Susannawa's turtle. The Chief was nearby sharpening his metal hunting knife on a speckled egg-shaped whetstone. Sometimes he would take a handful of sand from a nearby satchel, rub it back and forth on the blade, blow the sharp edge off and start over. A blade of metal was a rare treasure. Asku did not know how they were made; they came in trade, fetching high prices, or given as very special gifts.

Chitsa and Nayhali had just sat down to sew when Chaytan trotted up, panting. "We have visitors, *Wyánch'i*," he said.

"Who are they, *nika*?"

"They look to come from Toward the Rising Sun. They are darker," Chaytan stated. "Pyúsh maybe."

The tribe always posted lookouts on all four sides of the village, without fail; it was a perfect job for young people with good vision. The bluff overlooking Nch'i-Wána was the easiest. But because Nch'i-Wána was a busy thoroughfare for many tribes, a couple of men usually watched from above and below, some hidden, some out in the open hailing visitors. They rotated throughout the day, reporting comings and goings, who was on the move and who was trading where. This information sometimes provided good trade opportunities for the Patisapatisháma, who might set up a quick trip to Wayám with surplus goods.

Toward the Great Mountains and the Setting Sun, the watcher's job was to climb and keep lookout atop a monstrous rock. Another child, typically a friend, sat below, in case there was a need to send word to the hunter whose turn it was to supervise the watching. They were allowed to switch off, talk, as long as they didn't nap. It was all right, except when it was very cold. If it was too cold to put a child on top of a big rock, it was too cold to need a watch that far out.

Toward upper K'mił, in the direction of the Rising Sun, the watcher sat in an old and ratty pine tree, with a friend at the base. This Watch Tree was the favorite post of every kid in the tribe. A limber child could climb almost to the top. Asku had always loved his turns on the

Watch Tree. Chaytan was in charge of the watch today, so he would be the first to get news from any direction. When it was a man's turn, but he had other urgent responsibilities, Chaytan typically took charge. Now and then, Napayshni would do so instead. He had explained to Asku that this was good for morale, giving someone a break.

The Chief and Chaytan conferred in low voices. Asku could only hear a few words: "send scouts out to look around" and "set the archers along the back trail but tell them to stay hidden." The Chief motioned Asku to join them.

"Your knife, *tita*," he said under his breath, as he slid his own into the sheath on his belt.

Chaytan ran off. Napayshni and Asku went to the Totem to wait. "Here is where we will welcome our visitors," said the Chief. "We hope they are friendly, but if not, we can handle that as well. Be alert, be quiet, and follow my lead even if you know my words do not match my thinking."

Visitors were not rare, especially during peak salmon runs. Men and women came from tribes all over the area to fish down at the river; many had relatives among the Patisapatisháma, who took pride in their reputation as hosts. Most visitors were friendly and polite, and some came to trade; rarely did Napayshni order a defensive posture. *So why is he so concerned now? And why did Chaytan look so concerned? That didn't sound like they were expecting someone's cousins, or traders wanting a better deal on baskets than at Wayám.*

Soon the answer became clear.

Coming to meet them at the Totem were three men, darker than most Patisapatisháma. They looked ready for war, both in dress and countenance. All three had long plaits down the middle of their backs; the rest of their hair had been shaved or plucked. Their faces were painted red and black. Men painted their faces for celebrations, for hunting, for raiding. *They do not look like they came to celebrate anything. They bring no women, and everyone knows that a woman is a symbol of peaceful intent. They walk shrouded in a cloud of bad attitude.*

One of the men had tassels of beads and bone in his ears. Another had a similar piece hanging from his lower lip and through the center of his nose. All three had tomahawks in their belts.

Asku and the Teacher flanked the Chief, who stepped forward and raised his right hand in peace.

"Blessings, *wyanawiłá*...welcome, visitors," he said, in a voice meant to be welcoming yet formidable.

One suspicious-eyed man, the one with the ear tassels, took a step toward the Chief. He raised his hand in the peace response and spoke in a language that Asku did not understand. Napayshni motioned for the man to join him around the fire, where they sat awkwardly passing the *chalámat* and trying to communicate. The other two just looked around in an investigatory way Asku did not like.

"Where do you come from, *shíkhs*?" asked the Chief in the Chinuk Wawa, the trade language of Nch'i-Wána. It was a mix of many languages, and not a complicated one. Asku understood only a little, but enough to recognize it. *And no doubt I had better pay attention because I will need to use it one day.*

The leader patted his chest and pointed Toward the Rising Sun and Beyond Nch'i-Wána, shaking his hand as if a long way off.

"What can we do for you, *shíkhs*?" the Chief asked.

Moments passed. Then the man reached inside his wrap and pulled out a string of *áxsh'axsh* and a long, white animal tusk. He spoke in the Wawa, though with an odd accent to Asku's ear, and made motions with hands.

The Chief nodded and continued in the Wawa, "Ah, you have been to the Great Sea."

The man nodded, grumbled something.

The Chief smiled and spoke to Asku in rapid-fire Chiskin, the Patisapatisháma language. He did not turn his head, he left out words, and he used a lot of slang. His tone was that of a leader announcing great news deserving celebration, though his words were not. "Askuwa'tu, tell your mother food for six, you bring it alone, women stay back, big smile."

Aha! My father is as clever as Spilyáy in the Teacher's stories. Asku got to his feet with a happy smile and deferential manner. "Immediately, Wyánch'i. I will bring a fine feast. Blessings, *shíkhs*," he said to the visitor, as if charmed by the news. Asku walked briskly toward home, hoping he had not overdone it.

He returned awhile later balancing plates of dried salmon, fruit, nuts, and acorn cakes, which was difficult. Asku presented the food, and all three men ate, although the other two still remained on their feet. With effort, he mastered his outrage. *They are disrespectful to us, and especially to my father. He is an important man and is hospitable to them. They act as though we were slaves and should fear them. If they try anything dangerous, they can expect a surprise they will not enjoy.*

When he was done eating, the leader stood and nodded at the Chief. He then brushed off his backside and walked out of the village Toward the Rising Sun. The others followed him without a word or a glance back. They walked slowly at first, looking to the right and the left, searching, then moved faster once they got outside the village. And then they were gone, down the trail Toward the Rising Sun.

Archers stepped out behind and watched them as they walked away. The Chief and the Teacher also watched them go. For a long time, they stood there without speaking.

"Pyúsh P'ushtáayama?" the Chief finally asked.

"Yes," the Teacher replied.

"We had better prepare. Chaytan will return soon, with news. Then we will call the *Nch'ínch'íma* together."

"What is going on?" Asku asked.

"I am not sure, my *títa*. But we had better be prepared for whatever may come. And you handled that very well, by the way. I did not know what would happen, but I did not want to make my distrust obvious, or give away information, since they were clearly scouting us. What you did was important."

It was the first time he had really felt good since the news about his arranged mating-to-be.

❧⟶

"Túnmash wá táymun, níka?" the Chief prompted Chaytan. "What news do you have, brother?"

"They crossed at the ford past K̲'mił. There were canoes waiting there, two of them. Across Nch'i-Wána was a camp, maybe five or six more men. They are Pyúsh, for sure, *Wyánch'i.*"

"Hmmm," the Chief said, rubbing his chin. "He had gifts from the Wanuukshiłáma. The three of them must have scouted to the Sea and are returning now to meet their party."

"Will they raid?" Chaytan sounded calm about the prospect. *As for me*, thought Asku, *I wish I were so calm. The idea of war chills my spine. But if we must fight, we will.*

"No," the Teacher replied. "They are not raiding, at least not yet."

"Then, *Sapsikw'ałá*, why do they carry weapons for close fighting?" Chaytan asked.

"That is their way," the Teacher explained. "All Pyúsh carry the *k'iplach* always, probably to intimidate people."

"They were scouting, looking for something," the Chief added. "Or for someone."

"Yes," the Teacher added. "You, *Wyánch'i*. They are seeing what they might be up against, whether you are still a strong leader they cannot take lightly, or perhaps an easier target. You are right, we had better prepare."

The three were silent for a while. The Chief continued to rub his chin, contemplating. The others waited patiently.

"Asku." the Chief said, startling his son. "Go get Kitchi and Hawiłish. Prepare for a journey. Pack preserved food."

"Yes, *Wyánch'i*," Asku said, excited yet nervous. "For how many nights?"

"No more than ten days, to the Blue Mountains and back."

Kitchi and Hawiłish met the news with excitement. They packed quickly, bade their families goodbye, and made their way to the Totem for instructions and the blessing.

The Chief began. "Asku, you know the way, as you have been there. Canoe up Nch'i-Wána just past K͟'mił, then cross at the calm water. Chaytan has scouted their campsite, which is further Toward the Rising Sun on the heights. Do not be seen; if they are still camped up there, wait, and remember that they can see far from the heights, just as we can. So, climb up and move cautiously until you spot their campsite. They will either have left or be preparing to leave. Follow them, my *tita*, as you would track a bear that might turn on you.

"Since obviously you must not light a fire, make sure you have enough preserved food to sustain you. It should be easy to find and follow their trail. We think it very likely they will head toward the Blue Mountains and the Rising Sun. The most logical way is for them to leave Nch'i-Wána Toward the Rising Sun at the river Walawála, just past the Two Sisters; follow them that way. The normal trade route turns away toward the Elk Plains along Tu-se, then goes Toward the Rising Sun until it forks. Your goal is to follow them to the fork, and see whether they go into the Blue Mountains, or continue Toward the Rising Sun. Return quickly with news of which direction they go."

All three nodded. "We will, *Wyánch'i*."

"If the Pyúsh go some other way, follow them there and return to report, unless they go someplace it would be foolishly dangerous to follow. If that occurs, turn back sooner. Once you are headed along Tu-se, if there is an emergency and it makes sense, go to your mother's family, our Wawyukyáma allies on the Elk Plains. Do not, for any reason, follow your quarry into the Blue Mountains. You go no further than the trail fork. Is that clear?"

They all chorused that it was.

"Near Two Sisters, watch out for hunting parties from Kw'sɨs, which is a short distance further along Nch'i-Wána where Pikú-nen pours in. As you know, we have middling relations around Kw'sís. More likely though, you may meet Waluulapam, though I doubt it. I did not seek alliance with them because we did not have a connection, and they are so exposed to the Pyúsh that I am not sure it would be wise for us. Just remember your manners, and that your behavior could affect relations. You are my son and people might take your words as coming from me. Do not involve us in new problems. We have enough of those."

The boys laughed and nodded.

"It is a long trip, but you all are more than ready. Take care of each other, and do not make the mistake of trying to follow them too closely. If you can see them, they might see you, and you must not be seen."

"Yes, *Wyánch'i*," Asku replied.

"Then after your blessings, be on your way. *Sapsikw'ałá*, please?"

The Teacher gently touched each boy on the top of the head. *"Watwáa nakníwim,"* he chanted. "May the Great Spirits protect this son and return him safely to us.

Chapter 12

When Asku turned toward home one last time, he saw his father standing at the bluff, watching him as long as the canoe remained in sight.

"*Shín pawá piiník?*" Hawɨlish asked as they paddled. "But who are they? Are they the same ones that raided our village a long time ago?"

"Maybe, but maybe not. My father had heard that the band that attacked us was wiped out by a Mountain Tribe a long time ago, but sometimes tribes break up, or come together. The Teacher says that not all Pyúsh are like those, but I have heard others say they have an evil history, that the Spirits are angry with them."

"Does the Teacher think that they are coming back again?" Kitchi asked.

"I don't know," replied Asku. "But they came and left so quickly, asking for nothing and knowing full well the tribe's chief would present himself. The Teacher thinks they wanted a look at him."

"But what for, man?" Kitchi asked.

"If it is the band whose chief he killed a long time ago, they probably wanted to see what kind of threat he is, how strongly we would defend ourselves."

"Is that why the *wyánch'i* did not bring more of us to see them?" asked Hawɨlish.

"I believe so. They still do not know how many men we have, and they did not see any of our women or possessions. I think he was hoping they would be uninterested in us, but maybe also he did not want them to learn too much."

"Ugh," Hawɨlish said, dipping a paddle. "I do not like the sound of any of that."

"Me either," said Asku.

As they paddled, they kept a close eye on the heights, in case anyone was watching. Seeing no signs, they crossed at the calm spot just above where K̲'mɨł entered Nch'i-Wána, then beached the canoe on a small sandbar they knew well. When they had it well hidden, they made quick work of scaling the bluff. No one was in sight, so they began to follow the rim trail.

"Keep low and move one at a time," said Asku, "until we are in sight of their camp. We have to stay low until we spot the men." One by one, the boys took advantage of any cover they could find as they worked their way along. When they began to smell smoke, they slowed down, but there turned out to be no need for caution. The visitors had abandoned the campsite without fully dousing their fire.

"Around here, that's just stupid," said Hawilish.

"Maybe they don't care, man." said Kitchi in disgust. "But look around here. I think there were more than three of them. See? Places where six people slept." He started seeking their trail on his hands and knees. "Here is where they went. I think they left a short time ago, so we should expect to spot them someplace ahead."

"Then let's be very quiet," said Asku. "Six people make more noise than three, but they have twice as many ears and eyes."

Before the sun had gone much further, Hawilish peered out of a small draw and spotted their targets far ahead. "Six men," he said quietly. "They could turn around at any time."

"This is fine," said Asku. "All we need to do is see where they go without being seen, so let's stay at the edge of their sight. When they camp, we will close up on them somewhat and keep watch on them in turns."

The men made good time, but now and then they would stop to hunt, and then camped early so that some could climb down the bluffs to fish. They seemed unhurried. Asku and his friends had no trouble keeping up while staying hidden. With the sun past midday on the next day, they reached the place where Nch'i-Wána curved sharply around Toward the Great Mountains. Here the river flowed through a tight canyon, and on their side of Nch'i-Wána just beyond the canyon were the twin basalt towers known as the Two Sisters of legend. The six men still seemed unaware of the boys as they crossed the Walawála and followed it Toward the Rising Sun, leaving the great river behind.

Here the concealment became easier, thanks to the rolling topography of the broad valley. Even if the boys could not see their targets as often, they left obvious tracks in the trail's windblown, powdery silt. At a couple of places, the trail veered away from the meandering Walawála, only to find it again shortly. On the fourth day, with the Blue Mountains looming Toward the Rising Sun, the trail and the men bore left along a smaller river which Asku remembered as Tu-se.

"If they live up there," said Kitchi, pointing to the mountains, "why are they taking this trail? It looks like they are not getting any closer to home."

"Well, we are not sure where they live," said Asku. "That is what we are here to find out. But the Blue Mountains are very long and stretch far down Beyond Nch'i-Wána. The trail skirts around them. Soon it will turn Toward the Rising Sun."

"I see why the trail is on the side of Tu-se Toward the Setting Sun," Hawilish said, pointing. "It's all up and down hill on the other side. If a large party with elders and mothers were coming along, or with heavy loads, they would have no choice."

"There they are," said Kitchi. "Let's move."

The path continued in that fashion for another day, at which point Tu-se turned as Asku had advised them it would, and the trail on their side followed the river's floodplain. They increased their following distance to remain unseen, with the Blue Mountains coming closer with every step. On the night of the third day, the men camped at a fork in Tu-se, with the boys keeping watch from a safe distance. "How much further?" asked Hawilish.

"Tomorrow for sure," said Asku. "The trail goes away from the river, around the foothills of the Blue Mountains, and forks. We had better get up pretty early, so they don't get away from us."

"Everyone drink a lot of water before going to sleep, then," advised Hawilish.

"I'm glad," said Kitchi. "I am sick of jerky and acorn cakes. On the way back, we can get some fresh fish and do some hunting, maybe *xátxat*, and cook our dinner."

Asku took the first watch. He watched the moon and stars move through the sky, and well into the night before nudging Kitchi awake.

Hawilish woke Asku in the early dawn. "They are on the move," he whispered.

The friends packed up their gear in a hurry and worked their way closer than they had followed before, but something was different this morning. Two of the men packed and hustled away from the trail to the right, headed into the Blue Mountains, leaving the others sleeping.

"Now what?" asked Kitchi. "They split up. We can't follow those two without losing the others."

"Neither of those two is the leader," said Asku. "We can't do anything about them. We will wait and follow the others. The leader has a brighter wrap than the others, so we will follow whatever group he is with."

The rest of the group woke after dawn and seemed undisturbed by the first two men's absence. The remaining four ate, packed and continued on. Each hill rolled toward a larger one, until a hint of snow could be seen at the top of the tallest peak. The undulating terrain let the boys sneak up within a few bowshots of the four men by the time they reached an obvious fork in the well-worn trail.

Now we learn, thought Asku. His heart raced as they took cover in a clump of trees.

At the fork, the men turned right, a less traveled trail that went up into the base of the Blue Mountains. The boys watched until they were out of sight.

"So, what does all this mean?" asked Hawɨlish.

"It is not good news," said Asku. "They are Pyúsh P'ushtáayama, the Snake people, and most likely the same ones who attacked our village years ago."

"I was hoping they would just keep going Toward the Rising Sun and we could just forget about them," Hawɨlish sighed. "Like they were really just exploring."

"Me too, *pásiks*," Asku said. "Well, we know who they are now. I heard the Teacher say there are no other tribes anywhere near that area, so it has to be them."

"All right. *Áwna túxsha*…let's go home now," Kitchi said, standing tall and unslinging his spear from his sling. "But first, let's hunt."

"You can go," said Asku. "Meet us back along the trail; we will find a good spot to camp and get the fire going."

"Okay, you two girls do that. I'm gonna find us a x̱át̲x̲at...I need some duck."

"What do you think will happen?" Hawɨlish asked as they walked, the going so much easier without any need to stay hidden. "Will the Pyúsh return?"

"I don't know. I guess maybe the Chief will meet with the tribes nearest us, or maybe he will just make sure everyone is on the lookout."

"Yeah, that would be a good idea," Hawɨlish said, mostly to himself. They said little else until they reached the fork, where they began to set up camp. By later afternoon, the sun was at its hottest, and Asku's stomach was rumbling.

"How long has he been gone now?" Asku realized he was pacing. Hawɨlish just shrugged his shoulders, poking at the embers in the fire.

"Something's wrong, Hawɨlish." A sudden knot formed in his stomach. "He ought to be back here by now. Put out the fire and catch up with me."

While Asku headed down the trail, Hawɨlish threw dirt on the fire, then hurried to gather up their gear. Asku crouched low to the ground, looking for tracks and listening. With all the recent travel, it was difficult to figure out whose were whose, except that the boys' tracks were somewhat smaller. Then he came upon a spot where tracks went every which way.

"These are his tracks," he whispered. "They are fresh."

"But whose are these?" Hawɨlish bent over another set. "Do you think these are from those two guys we saw leave the other night?"

"How could that be? Those two headed off into the Blue Mountains and left the trail much earlier than this. How would they have come to this spot?"

"*Kúu mísh,*" Hawɨlish said, shaking his head. "You are right, this is not like Kitchi. Something is really wrong. Look, the tracks head off toward the forest and mountains. Three sets."

The boys followed the tracks into the thick forest. Asku thought he could smell a marsh nearby. The sign led into underbrush near a riverbed, where ferns grew to Asku's waist and blackberry bushes scratched his arms and stomach.

Then he heard a sound that stopped his heart: Kitchi's voice crying out in pain.

Both boys dropped to the ground. Asku pulled the long *chúksh* blade from his belt. Hawilish reached over his right shoulder, extracted a cedar arrow from his pack, and strung his bow. They waited and listened.

"Screw you, man," Kitchi hollered angrily. "I do not know who you are. I don't even know what you're saying."

A sickening crunch followed, punctuated by a yowl of agony. Asku made eye contact with Hawilish. He nodded, and they both crawled toward the sound of Kitchi's voice.

The blade between his teeth, Asku peered through the brush in front of him into a clearing. The two men were there along with a small camp and travelling gear. They were tall, lean, and dark-skinned, with long plaits that reached down to the middle of their backs. Red streaks and black dots decorated their scalps and around their eyes.

Kitchi was on his knees, his hands bound behind his back. His face was bruised. Blood ran from his nose and mouth.

The one standing over him held a long hunting knife to Kitchi's throat, speaking words that Asku could not understand. The angry man's voice got louder and angrier as the knife pressed deeper into Kitchi's skin. Beads of blood welled where the blade began to cut his flesh.

What should I do? Breathe, Asku, breathe, like you were taught. It is like hunting. He took two long, deep breaths through his nose.

The man backhanded Kitchi with the bone handle of his knife. Kitchi grunted but turned quickly and spat a mouthful of blood up into the man's face. The man bellowed in outrage and kicked Kitchi in the chest, knocking him flat on his back. He turned to shout something at the other man. His captors began to argue. Sensing the moment of disorder, Kitchi tried to stand up and run.

After that, everything happened so quickly that Asku would later remember it as just scenes flashing before his eyes.

The first man, seeing Kitchi's attempt to escape, pulled the tomahawk from his belt and swung it high above his head.

The other seemed to try and restrain him but didn't quite succeed.

Kitchi saw or sensed the weapon coming down toward his head and fell backward to dodge it. The stone axe struck him in the left leg with a crunching sound that turned Asku's stomach. He screamed in agony and fell to the ground.

While Asku moved in, Hawilish drew his bowstring.

The man raised his weapon again, pushing his companion away. Asku jumped to his feet, knife in hand, just as an arrow whizzed past his ear. It hit the tomahawk's wielder through the neck. The man dropped his weapon and stumbled backward, then fell to his knees making horrible noises.

The other man whirled around to where he thought the arrow had come from but got the direction just wrong enough. Asku leaped out and ran at him from behind, baring his knife and teeth in anger. The survivor caught the movement, but too late.

Asku grabbed him from behind and ripped his knife through the man's neck. He felt the blade pierce flesh, muscle, tendon—and life. His head fell grotesquely backward onto Asku's shoulder. Asku let him fall to the ground.

The other man was on his knees near Kitchi, trying to pull the arrow from his throat. He looked up at Asku in a gurgling, rasping plea for help.

A part of me wants to just let him die that way, slowly. He deserves that. But I am not his kind. Asku pulled the man's head back by the long plait of hair and sliced his throat. The man fell forward, dead almost instantly.

Asku stood in the shaking, hoarse-breathed, enraged, adrenaline-drugged state of the person who has just fought for life at close quarters and won. He looked down at his hands covered in blood, his knife dripping with death, and the two men whose lives he had just wiped out. He dropped the knife and tried to wipe the blood off on his trousers.

What helped him to pull himself together was Kitchi, moaning in pain, making the only noise other than the axe-wielder's final spasms. Hawilish was bending over Kitchi, whose leg was cut wide open. "Asku," he said, "he's bleeding bad. Very bad. Find something to stop it!"

Asku pulled his wrap from his sling, tore a strip with his teeth, folded it in half, and handed it to Hawilish. Kitchi's knee was already black and blue, with a deep gash a hand's length on the outside of his thigh. Hawilish began to bandage it. "Give me more!"

After three wrap-strips had been applied, the bleeding slowed to seepage. Kitchi finally passed out from the pain and loss of blood, giving Asku and Hawilish a few moments to wrap the hide strip tightly above the wound. "Not too tight," advised Hawilish. "If you do, he could lose the leg."

Now what do I do? He was not the only one with that question. He was simply the only one with the duty to answer it.

"*Pásiks*," Hawilish asked, "what now?"

Asku wracked his brain. *We are four nights from home. He will never survive that trip. Think, Asku!* "Can we carry him?" he asked.

Hawilish shook his head. "I doubt it. And he might get a lot worse over a long movement. It would cause more bleeding, and we could lose him. You could run home and get help, maybe?"

Asku worked that one out in his head. "No, it's too far. There has got to be something else."

Just then, he heard the Chief's voice in his head, and he knew what to do. Kitchi woke up and started rolling around again. Both boys knelt beside his head.

"Kitchi? Can you hear me?" asked Asku. "You are going to be okay."

"I hear ya, man," Kitchi forced out through clenched teeth.

Asku made a decision. "I will go for help. We will set up a camp here off the trail, well hidden, and you two wait until I return. I will find my way to the Wawyukyáma, my grandfather's people."

"They'll help us?" asked Hawilish.

"The Chief said they would. The Wawyukyáma chief is my grandfather. It can't be that far to Aputaput." Asku cleaned his knife on a nearby patch of grass and sheathed it at his belt. He left his sling and torn wrap behind.

"*Kitu, pásiks*," Hawilish urged. "Hurry."

Chapter 13

And Asku ran.

He had not mentioned that he had only been to his grandfather's village a couple of times and was unsure exactly how to find it. During the warm season, they lived on the Elk Plains, Toward the Great Mountains and the Rising Sun from the Patisapatisháma village. From here, though, it was Toward the Setting Sun and the Great Mountains. He stopped for breath and to think.

If I remember what my father taught me, there is a river that we would have come to had we gone past the trail fork, called Kimooenim by some people of the region. It flows in the direction of the Elk Plains but never reaches them; it joins Pikú-nen; eventually that river reaches Kw'sɨs and joins Nch'i-Wána. However, a river called Pa-lús joins Pikú-nen at Wíshpush Tɨnmá, the Beaver's Heart. The Elk Plains are up above Pa-lús, near the great waterfall of Aputaput. So, I will have to cross Pikú-nen, somewhere near the Beaver's Heart. I remember the story of Wíshpush Tɨnmá as my grandfather told it to me.

I also remember him telling me that they keep a canoe on the far side of Pikú-nen from Wíshpush Tɨnmá, just in case of an emergency.

Energized, Asku again took to the trail, but the sun was dropping quickly. With very little moonlight, he could not see well. He stuck to the trail as best he could.

Asku prayed to the Great Spirits as he ran—for Kitchi, for guidance, and for strength. He wasn't sure how far he had to go; he guessed that the Wawyukyáma village lay about a day away from where he had started. The only thing he could do was run and run he did. Once he came to the first small river, which he guessed to be Kimooenim, he followed its course at the best pace he could manage in the darkness.

The little river, which in fact was Kimooenim, ended in a great river which could only be Pikú-nen. Asku could not see far enough across it to know how far Toward the Setting Sun he should go. On he ran, hoping for some sign from the Spirits.

And then he found it—or received it. The riverside trail took him down to a small cove with a few scrubby trees. Behind them, and concealed with a mix of brush and driftwood, lay a two-person canoe with a paddle tucked underneath. Asku pushed the little canoe out into the river and jumped inside. The river was shallower than he remembered, but the rush of the water and current felt like home to him. He easily crossed, pulled the little canoe up high along the bank, tucked the cedar paddle underneath and looked around.

Wíshpush Tinmá was there, just where Pa-lús ended in Pikú-nen. The local legend was that Giant Beaver fought the five Wolf Brothers, falling to their spears after an epic battle. In his thrashing of agony at death, his claws and sharp teeth gouged out the areas jagged cliffs and waterfalls. The giant boulder at the end of Pa-lús was all that remained of Beaver, just his heart at the meeting of the two rivers. Asku dipped his hands into the slow ripple of Pa-lús, drinking his fill and splashing the water up his arms and down his neck and back. As he let the water cool him, he realized he had come this far without cleaning the blood from himself, and it was good to wash some of its violence away.

Just as the water trickled down his spine, he heard a low, deep grunt. He slowly lifted his eyes toward the sound and froze. The moon, just rising, cast an eerie light on Wíshpush Tinmá—and another creature.

The patch of white between his eyes gave him away.

"What are you doing here, *Pawaat-łá*?" he said, keeping his voice normal. *Just in case.*

The bear lifted his massive weight, standing on his hind legs. He sniffed the air to catch Asku's scent, then dropped to all fours and gave a grunt toward Asku, beckoning rather than aggressive. The bear nodded twice, then turned along the cliff edge and began to run following the streambed of Pa-lús.

"But my grandfather's village is above this stream on the Plains," Asku called out. "This valley will be hard to get out of."

The bear stopped momentarily and turned around, looked at him, then resumed his course. "I guess it can't be any clearer," muttered Asku, trotting after the bear.

He tried to keep the bear in sight, but no man on foot could keep up with a bear. After Asku lost him, he stopped for a drink from the river. *Am I going crazy? Is this the way, some sort of secret way? I sure hope so.*

Running, or walking where he must, Asku followed the Pa-lús riverbed. The rock wall to his left grew taller and taller like giant steps. Jagged slopes of loose rock littered the base. At times, Asku had to step out into the stream to go around landslide debris where the cliffside had collapsed into the river. At length, the river began to widen and Asku heard the roar of a waterfall nearby. *If I am right below my grandfather's village, I have no idea how I'm going to get up these cliffs, especially in the dark.* Aputaput, or Falling Water, was an amazing sight from above. He remembered standing back from the edge as a child. The river gushed over a jagged cliff and thundered to the bottom in a colorful pool of water before continuing its journey to Pikú-nen, to Nch'i-Wána, and to the Great Sea. He had the idle thought that if he had a raft or canoe, he could canoe all the way home.

Someday, perhaps.

Asku followed the little river as it turned Toward the Rising Sun, and there thundered Aputaput. The faintly moonlit beauty of the waterfall held nothing for him at this moment, walled in on all sides but the way back. He searched the top for the bear, hoping and praying, but nothing. He began to think he had lost too much valuable time and must turn back.

Then he saw a flash of something. He followed it and found his feet upon a hidden, narrow, and very steep trail. He began to climb, scrambling up the treacherous trail, placing hands and feet carefully with the moonlight unable to reach his side of the looming rocks. Halfway up the cliffside, the trail widened and became easier. In due course, with great care, he emerged atop the canyon not far from the falls.

When he had gone about as far onto the plateau as he could throw an acorn, a dark figure appeared in his path, and he heard another step out of the shadows behind him. That man quickly grabbed Asku's knife from his belt. There were others all around, some on horseback, although he had not heard horses approaching. He had heard no sound of them until now.

"State your business, young man," said the man before him, his voice deep and strong.

"Blessings, *síks*," Asku said, holding his hand at shoulder level to indicate peace. There was no response. "I am looking for the people of my grandfather. I need his help. Please."

"*Shínmash wá waních?*" the man spoke again. Asku could not read his expression.

"I am Askuwa'tu Haylaku," he said, remembering to introduce himself to possible strangers with confidence. "My mother is Chitsa Hihiwuti, and my father is Napayshni Hianayi, chief of the tribe of my people, the Patisapatisháma."

The man stepped into the light of the moon, a magnificent dark stallion near his left shoulder. He sounded less forbidding. "Asku, *píti*, the son of my sister? It is I, U'hitaykah."

I made it. Kitchi has a chance.

"But how have you entered our village from this side? Our people stay hidden on this side of the cliff. There is only one way up, and you found it in spite of the darkness. We watch it, but anyone climbing up makes noise that one may hear even over Aputaput."

"It is a long story, *káka*," Asku said. "Please, uncle, my *pásiks* is badly hurt, away past Wíshpush Tɨnmá and just before the Blue Mountains. I have come to seek your help."

"You came a good distance, and all by darkness. You did well to find us."

Asku decided not to mention the bear. "Some of the way I remembered from what I was taught and shown." *There, that is not a lie. Though it is definitely not all the truth.*

"You must have found our canoe. I am glad you remembered." U'hitaykah gave orders to a young man: *tomorrow, go find it and put it back. When you do, bring back some fish.*

U'hitaykah climbed onto the beautiful stallion's back and reached a hand down to Asku. The creature stood at Asku's shoulder, black as the night sky, his mane and tail blowing loose in the merciless Elk Plains wind. Leaving the young man to notify the chief of his grandson's appearance, four Wawyukyáma set out toward where Kitchi lay. U'hitaykah's people knew the best spot to ford Pikú-nen on horseback, which Asku found refreshing after his exhausting, sweaty, grimy journey through the darkness. The journey back seemed to take no time, but dawn was coming as they arrived.

Kitchi was sweating and shaking in shock, but his leg was no longer bleeding. Asku could see the long drag marks in the dirt where Hawɨlish must have dragged the bodies away. The tomahawk, now clean, rested next to Kitchi.

U'hitaykah looked over Kitchi's wound, then spoke: "Young man, you will be okay. We will take you to our village. You will have to be strong because the travel will be painful." Asku's uncle lifted Kitchi into his arms and set him on horseback in front of a young man not much older than Asku. They did not run at any speed, to avoid aggravating Kitchi's injury. As Asku looked back on one occasion, Kitchi was passed out, his head hanging against his chest. The young man sitting behind him seemed to be singing, or chanting, while holding Kitchi in place.

It was light out by the time they forded Pikú-nen, meeting a mounted lookout who joined up with them, and rode across the plateau to the village above the waterfall. Asku saw an elder coming toward them, his arms outstretched.

"Askuwa'tu Haylaku, grandson, my *tíla*!" Asku jumped down from the stallion's back and stepped forward into his grandfather's arms. The old man was tall and powerfully built, bigger even than Asku's father. He wore a large flowing bison hide over his shoulders, and a headdress of colorful feathers fell down his back. His gray hair and lined face bespoke wisdom, experience, and welcome.

"*Tíla*," Asku began, voice weak with exhaustion and relief, "grandfather…"

"How is it that your clothes are stained in blood, *myánash*?" he asked. Asku looked down at the blood on his trousers.

"I killed two men, *tíla*," Asku sighed. "But before I tell the story, I must make sure Kitchi is cared for."

The old eyes let slip a brief flash of satisfaction. "Our Healer is already gathering her medicines and preparing a place for him. You can do no more for him now. The women are preparing a morning meal. All there is now is to relate what has happened."

"*Kw'ałá, tíla.*" And then, seated next to Hawɨlish at the village's ceremonial firepit, Asku told the full tale to his grandfather, U'hitaykah, some *Nch'ínch'ima*, and several other men, some of whom had been along on the night ride. Asku told of the visitors at his village, of the Chief's assignment, and of the Pyúsh P'ushtáayama. The old man asked a question now and then. At its end, with all questions answered, all Asku wished for was food and sleep. As the food arrived, the chief hollered something that Asku did not understand.

The young man who had carried Kitchi on his horse came over. He was tall and slender, with long hair flowing freely down his bare back. His eyes seemed to dance with laughter. "Yes, *Wyánch'i?*"

"You must visit Napayshni, chief of the Patisapatisháma. Tell him of Askuwa'tu's arrival and Kitchi's injury. Tell him that we will look after them as long as needed. They are safe here."

The young man looked quickly at Asku with a slight nod and half a smile. "Yes, *Wyánch'i*," he said. They resumed eating, and Asku was not sure he had ever had such delicious breakfast in his life. As they were nearly finished, the messenger walked up on a beautiful horse. Asku had seen horses, of course, but few as magnificent as this one: tall and proud, his long mane blowing in the breeze; the brown color of river mud, with white painted up his legs, splashed along his shoulders and back and across most of his face and neck. The equine eyes were dark, confident, and intelligent. The messenger said his farewells, leapt onto the amazing creature in one swift motion, and was gone in the blink of an eye.

"You have done all you can, *tíla*," said Asku's grandfather.

Asku felt one tremendous wave of fatigue wash over him and nodded. But there was one more thing. "Would your Healer permit us to sleep near Kitchi, if we promise not to be in her way? We do not want to be away from him any longer if it can be helped."

That was not a problem.

▶──→

Asku woke up early in the afternoon. The Healer, an older woman whose kind face looked somehow familiar, rose from a seat next to Kitchi's sleeping form and came over. "Feeling better, *káła?*"

"Blessings, *lamyáy*, much better. Thank you for everything." The conversation stirred Hawɨlish, who rubbed his eyes, got up, and made his manners.

"I will sit with him, *káła*," she said. "Your grandfather would like to see you."

"Thank you, *lamyáy*," Asku stood and stretched his back and legs. He patted Kitchi's shoulder one last time before walking out.

The afternoon was cool and breezy, with the wind rushing across the Elk Plains. Asku went to the ceremonial fire, the logical place to seek out his grandfather, and indeed he was there. U'hitaykah stoked the fire with dried bison dung, which burned well, but smelled differently. A woman of middle age tended a maize dish and bison meat at the firepit while Asku's uncle and grandfather passed a *chalámat* around the fire. Soon four or five *Nch'ínch'ima* joined them. He guessed that customs were similar to those of the Patisapatisháma, and that a Council had been called. When the meal was ready, and the woman had served everyone, they all ate most of the meal in silence. As eager as Asku was to speak, he knew better.

"I think the two men you killed, Asku, came here not long before," the chief finally spoke.

Asku looked up from his bowl with interest.

"Yes," U'hitaykah said, waving his hand Toward the Setting Sun. "They tried to enter our village from the other side of the foothills. But they were impolite, and the Chief sensed their deception. We sent them away." He smiled slyly at his father, then spit into the fire.

"The Great Spirits are speaking to us," said the Chief. "We must listen." His eyes squinted at the fire, as if seeing a great distance. "My grandson's friend's wound has brought us a benefit, whether by accident or act of the Spirits. From Askuwa'tu's account, we now know that the evil band of Pyúsh P'ushtáayama are alive and plan to do us all harm again. We must Council, all of us: the Patisapatisháma and the Wanuukshiłáma, we must visit Wayám and spread the word. If we stand together, we may prevent a great sadness like we have not seen in a long time."

The men talked and debated well into the evening of war and strategy, peace and security. Asku kept silent, trying to take it all in. The other men finally stood and stretched their legs, said their blessings to the chief, and excused themselves into the darkness.

Asku spotted Hawilish asleep again behind a log near the fire, his wrap pulled tightly around his head. His grandfather smiled. "You must be exhausted. Let us turn in," he said, motioning for Asku to follow him. Asku opened his mouth, but his grandfather continued: "If Kitchi were not doing well, you would have been one of the first to know it, so the lack of news is more welcome than news. By now I am sure he is asleep, or your other friend would not have snuck up on us and gone to bed out here."

"Actually, *tíla,*" Asku pulled his torn wrap from the sling at his feet, "I will just sleep here, I think, with your permission." He found a place near Hawilish and curled up.

"As you wish," the old chief said. He removed the bison skin from his own back, laid it across his grandson and stoked the fire. "Sleep well, *myánash.*"

Chapter 14

Kitchi awoke the next morning with no sign of the fever, though he was in terrible pain. After drinking a special tea made by the Healer, though, he felt well enough to laugh and joke more like the Kitchi they knew.

Asku and Hawɨlish spent the daylight hours with his grandfather and U'hitaykah, walking with them on their rounds and meeting relatives. The days passed quickly, with gradual improvement for Kitchi beginning with the third. On the eve of the fourth day a celebration was planned: a celebration for Kitchi's life and healing, and in honor of Asku's arrival, their chief's grandson.

While they walked the village, the boys got an education about horses. Asku had not realized how essential the animal was to the Wawyukyáma. But, as his grandfather had explained, "When one hunts animals that run in great herds, on flat prairie land ranging for a moon's walk, one needs much assistance." The horses themselves had come not long ago from a tribe Beyond the Big River. They had changed life drastically on the Elk Plains.

"Was it the Pyúsh that brought the horses?" Hawɨlish asked.

"No. It was another tribe." The chief stopped and motioned for the boys to sit near an empty firepit. Asku recognized a lesson coming on.

"Before the horse," Asku's grandfather began, "we moved often from here to there, from the river to the mountain. Each season we packed all and carried all on our backs to where the food was. But when he came, we could now run with the mighty bison, he could carry a man, he could carry a man's supplies. He could even carry a bison's meat home on his back, one that had given his life to feed us."

The old man stopped walking and raised his hands to the Great Spirits. Asku listened with his heart, as the Teacher had conditioned him, to allow the images his grandfather's words could conjure.

Long ago, the sky was dark, Aanyáy had hidden her eyes from man, and ice covered the earth.

The horse was here. But she hid from man, from our ancestors, from our people. She was small, beaver size, with a long mane and tail, and thick fur to keep her warm. Aanyáy loved the horse. But when man had dishonored all of creation, she hid her face, and all became darkness.

"You must go from this place, átawit," she told the horse. "They are not worthy of you. Maybe someday you can return."

The horse nodded. A tear fell from her eyes, for she also had grown to love the man, although from afar. With great sadness the horse walked away. She walked a very long ways, never to see the man again, or so she feared.

As the horse walked, she passed many creatures, strange creatures that she had never seen before. They were walking toward the place where the man was. But she just put her head down in grief and kept walking, until the day Aanyáy told her this would be her new home. And there the horse thrived, grew tall and strong, very strong.

One day she saw the man as if in a dream; he was pale, like a ghost of men, and his eyes were blue with sadness. The horse could not help herself as she ran to him. But the man was strange, and the horse wondered how he got so far from home.

The horse and the Spirit Man grew close. She let him ride on her back and she helped him with many things. The horse learned the man's ways and began to realize the depth of his sadness, his guilt. He gained much, yet he never found peace. He always seemed to be looking for something, never finding it.

The horse decided she would lead the man home, and there, he would find himself again. There he would be happy once again, like he had been all that time ago before the ice and darkness. The horse devised her plan.

For many, many moons she travelled with the man; across land, across the Great Sea, walking and running. As the two approached the place where Aanyáy had turned her face away, she slowed down and she stopped.

The man jumped from her back, fell to his knees and cried out to Aanyáy.

"I am sorry," he wailed, his hands covered his face. "I am so sorry."

Aanyáy turned his direction. She saw the horse that she loved so dearly, and she smiled warmly down upon the man. "Myánash, it is because of her sacrifice to bring you home...for her love, you are forgiven."

Aanyáy glowed brightly, so brightly the horse closed her eyes to the warmth and the light. When she opened them again, the man was standing before her as she remembered him. His hair was dark, flowing down his bare back, his eyes piercing as midnight, and his skin tanned from Aanyáy's smile.

And to this day, they have never been parted—best friends, companions—man and horse.

There was silence for a bit. Asku heard horses' hooves not far away; someone going out or coming back. He opened his eyes.

I think that is very old, even before Saigwan. I wonder if he ever heard that story as a boy. Probably so. The horses my mind saw were not quite like the ones my grandfather's tribe has.

A horse and rider came up, dusty from head to toe, looking tired. It was the young messenger, returning from the River village, and he dismounted.

"Ah, yes. Blessings, Aanapay, welcome back," said the Chief. *"Túnmash wá táymun?"*

"The River Chief sends his gratitude. He and the tribe were becoming anxious for the boys. He will follow in a few days' time, *Wyánch'i.*"

"Did you see any sign of the Pyúsh P'ushtáayama?"

"None, *Wyánch'i*, other than the old tracks heading Toward the Rising Sun. The River Chief will send a scout ahead of him."

"Excellent. You have done well, *páya*. Go get some rest. When you have had some rest, I would like you and U'hitaykah to take my grandson and his friend to hunt the bison."

Hawilish and Asku traded glances, and both resisted the urge to jump up and yell for joy. After Aanapay headed off to care for his horse and get some rest, the Chief explained. Aanapay was the chief's nephew but had been raised as his son. A raid had ripped Aanapay's family apart when he was a small child, and he still grieved their loss. Asku tried to imagine himself in such a situation and could not. *Aanapay must be very strong*, he thought.

Aanapay had great skill with the horse, and within a short amount of time, he had Asku and Hawilish riding. Hawilish had been somewhat nervous at first but overcame it soon enough. Aanapay whispered to Asku that he had chosen Hawilish the most placid horse they had, one who would much rather stand around eating grass all day than run along the Elk Plains with the rest of them. They spent much of the day learning to ride, and then, the proper methods of care after riding. "You must always think of your horse's access to water and grass," said Aanapay, showing the boys the different prairie grasses horses liked. "If you take care of her, she will do the same for you. A horse is happy when she feels her rider's care and respect. She will ride herself to death if you ask her. She will eat herself to death if you let her. And when we hunt, she knows her work. Listen to her teachings."

Asku rode a trained Bison Horse, a painted mare: white with splashes of dark brown on either side, down her legs, between her eyes, even her tail and mane. When Asku leaned over her neck and entwined his fingers into her coarse mane, he felt like he could fly.

▶—→

The next day, with Aanapay rested up, the hunt began. Armed with his bow and sling of arrows, Asku rode alongside Hawilish and behind Aanapay, each keeping wide to the next man's flank to avoid eating a cloud of dust. Four other hunters' rode fanned out farther to the sides. U'hitaykah rode trail, far enough back not to suffer a similar fate, with two boys who led the load-haulers: two extra horses with travois slung aboard. They crossed the river above Aputaput, where it was easy to ford, and then rode out onto the Plains. The herd would be half a day's journey or more from the village, not far from a great lake. They rode for hours, battering

Asku's already-sore backside, but he would gladly have ridden that horse all day and all night and then some, soreness ignored. He ducked his head down close to her mane, felt the wind whip his hair behind him, felt the thick bands of muscles across her back move between his thighs with every hoofbeat, her breath heaving with his.

They stopped to water the animals well up Pa-lús, which in this area was merely a creek meandering among draws and gullies. The sun blazed down upon Asku's back. He tossed droplets of water across his neck and thought he heard them sizzle. *So hot. No shade, and a merciless wind.*

"Let me see that bow, *píti*," U'hitaykah said, interrupting his thoughts. "Where did you get this? I have never seen its equal." The men passed it around, admiring its craftsmanship.

"It was a gift from the Wanuukshiłáma chief," Asku said. "It is made from the rib bone of a whale. The carvings are of the sacred *sut'xwłá* hunt of their people."

"That is quite a gift," U'hitaykah said, with a look of tactful interest.

"It has been decided that the daughter of the Wanuukshiłáma chief will be my mate," Asku explained. "When she is ready, that is."

"I see," said U'hitaykah, raising an eyebrow and handing the bow back. "Let's go, brothers, the bison are waiting."

>——

The herd was not difficult to find, for the hunters could see a very long way on the prairie—and the herd was large. Asku could see hundreds, maybe even thousands, of the magnificent bison. Their tails flicked back and forth, and heads lowered to the ground as they munched away at a grassy area.

Not long before the bison heard the horses approaching, they began to move in a gigantic ball of dust. Asku had never seen such a thing before. Elk ran in herds, but they moved quietly and could run past a hunter before he even knew they were there. These animals sounded like a thunderstorm, their pounding hooves echoing off the distant foothills. Asku's mount leaped ahead of the rest, seeming to know what to do.

U'hitaykah had instructed Asku to choose an animal on the outside of the herd, not a mother with a young one, and the others would follow his lead.

Asku lifted his eyes to the sky, as best he could while clinging to a galloping horse. "Bless this hunt, Great Spirits, and bless the bison that will give his life for us."

Then Asku saw him, a large bull running along the outside of the herd. The horse sensed his choice and ran alongside the enormous animal. The herd turned quickly; yet again, the horse knew what to do and kept pace with the frightened group. Asku squinted to keep some of the dust out of his eyes, directing his attention toward the young bull. U'hitaykah had also taught him not to lose focus, because bison were unpredictable and dangerous even when not frightened and running.

He squeezed his thighs tightly to hold on and let go both hands, trusting the mare not to let him fall. Asku nocked an arrow, raised his bow, drew, aimed, and let go.

The arrow hit the massive animal at the shoulder and sank deep. The bull stumbled and continued running. But just as U'hitaykah had said he would, the animal broke away from the others. *Is he aware of his fate, and now thinks to lead the hunters away, giving his life for his herd?*

Long flint-tipped spears and feathered arrows whizzed past Asku from behind and beside his horse. The bison fell to the ground in a cloud of dust, many shafts rising from his hide. The others stampeded to safety. *Leaving the fallen brother behind, having sacrificed himself for his kind.*

Asku dismounted, approaching the dying animal. The bull tried desperately to rise but could only struggle and snort loudly. *How best to finish him? I must, and quickly.* U'hitaykah dismounted and came over, pointing to Asku's knife. The newest bison hunter nodded, drew his knife, and moved close enough to see the whites of the bison's eyes. They darted to and fro in fear, dust blowing up around his large nostrils as he labored out his last breaths.

Asku knelt, then plunged the knife into one side of the big bull's neck. A gush of blood signaled that he had found one of the great vessels at the neck. Much moved, Asku rested his hand upon the great beast's head and closed his eyes. "*Kw'ałá, síks,*" he said as the others approached with bowed heads. "May you be free, my friend."

The hunters worked quickly around Asku and Hawɨlish. "How will we get this thing back to the village?" Hawɨlish asked.

"I think it is safe to say they have that figured out," Asku said. "So, let's watch and learn, and do whatever we are told will help."

A quick, deep slice about the neck began to drain the animal's blood. One hunter held a small wooden cup under the steady stream until full, then set it aside. Others skinned the carcass, excised the heart, cut off the hooves and large hunks of flesh, the liver, and other internal organs. Another hunter reached into the beast's mouth and cut its tongue out, then wrapped it with care. Meanwhile, the boys had started unpacking the travois from the spare horses as soon as the hunt had stopped. Once the travois were rigged up, the boys led the horses over to the bison carcass to shorten the hunters' trips. So as not to feel useless, and after a few scowls from younger hunters, Asku and Hawɨlish found a role keeping control of the riderless hunting horses. The hunters seemed to have a very well-organized pattern for loading the travois, with no orders issued or needed.

Someone dug a shallow hole in the dirt and made a small fire. The hiss and crackle drew the others in. They began to chant.

U'hitaykah held the bison's warm heart in his hands momentarily, his eyes closed, before dropping it into the fire in a spray of sparks. Aanapay handed the steaming cup of lifeblood to Asku and intoned: "It is the custom of our people for the hunter to be one with his prey."

Asku nodded, took the cup and lifted it to his mouth. The blood was warm and thick in his throat. He drained it quickly and raised the cup into the air.

"*Kw'ałá, síks*," Asku said, formally. "We honor your sacrifice. May you be free in the next life, my brother."

Chapter 15

Asku spent the evening with the Healer, who happened to be his grandmother. In between caring for Kitchi, among others, she was making him a new wrap of soft animal hide. There had been some merriment when he had finally realized who she was.

"How is your mother, *kála*?" she asked, without looking up from her work. He held one side of the wrap tightly as she neatly stitched around the edges.

"She is well." He had not realized how much he missed her. "She is very well. Nayhali will mate this winter, with a very brave hunter of ours. And Susannawa climbs trees and jumps from them like a squirrel. We never know where he is. The little girls are beautiful. Mininaywah is growing like a weed. We have our hands full with her; she is two winters now. And Nis'hani is five, I think. At least it will be some time before I have to worry about who they will mate."

"And you, *myánash*?"

"Um, well, *kála*…the Chief has chosen a mate for me." Asku dropped his eyes to the wrap, picking at a sticky spot in the corner. "Her name is Kaliskah. She is the daughter of the Wanuukshiłáma chief. They will bring her to me when she is ready."

"Hmmm."

Asku continued to pick at the spot. "My father says she is sweet and kind, that she can cook and will take care of me. Oh, and that I will grow to love her. Or something like that."

"But?"

Do I want to talk about this? Perhaps I should whether I want to or not. "But *kála*, I love another, Hatayah, of my own tribe. She is who I want, I guess. If I were someone else, she is who I would have. But I do not get a choice, because I have responsibilities." He said the word as if it were 'lice.' "I forgot about those, but I have to obey them. It will be okay."

Asku's grandmother stopped and looked at him. "*Myánash,* much will be asked of you because of who you are. You will choose how much you give. Give some, and you will become Chief of the *great* Patisapatisháma. Give all, and you will become a *great* chief for your people, like your father and his father before him, and like your grandfather, of this tribe."

Asku could not help but smile. "I understand, *káła. Kw'ałá.*"

"Asku, I came from a tribe far away from here many winters ago. Chitsa left her people to join yours at the river; it was her sacrifice, and she gave all. Kaliskah will leave her people, and cling to you and yours. She also will give all."

"Yes, *káła.*"

>———→

That evening, Asku again sat with the chief and elders as they passed the *chalámat.* For the most part, he kept his mouth shut. After one elder spoke of a vision from his youth, there was a long silent stillness broken only by the sounds of passing the pipe and the flow of rings of smoke.

"*Tíla?*" Asku dared. His grandfather looked at him. "Do you know of Saigwan and the people of the cave?"

The old man stared at Asku for a long time, a deep questioning stare. "I do, Askuwa'tu. Do you?"

"Yes. He speaks to me, *tíla,* tells me stories of old. He teaches me." Asku picked up rocks at his feet and tossed them into the fire.

Another elder spoke without looking. "The Spirit of Saigwan speaks to you, you say?"

"He does."

"When?" pressed the second elder.

"Mostly when I awake early, before the sun, and go to our Totem. Sometimes when something happens to me, I live through an experience of the same sort, but as Saigwan. And then I am me again. It is confusing and makes me nervous."

The elder nodded in satisfaction. The chief spoke: "Saigwan is also ancestor to this tribe, although not directly." He blew smoke rings into the night sky. "You and your father are direct descendents of the Great Chief. We, however, are descendents of his sister-son.

"There are many stories of Saigwan and of the cave people. Times were much harder then. The mighty Aanyáy was hidden, and great coldness spread throughout this land. They struggled to survive. It is important that we do not forget these stories. It is good that your spirit calls to him, Askuwa'tu."

Asku chanced another question. "*Tíla*, do you know of the mammoth bear?"

The chief studied his grandson for some time. "It was said that as Saigwan aged, he had a *Pawaat-łá*, a bear much larger than those in our forests today. This bear came to Saigwan during his greatest need and led him through. But his people were afraid of the bear. Most would not speak of the animal, and some still do not. We believe a *Pawaat-łá* is an ancestor living within an animal, but the animal is still as such, an animal."

Asku's heart raced. "*Tíla*…I have a *Pawaat-łá*, a bear, black with a spot between his eyes. He showed me how to enter this village along the small mountain stream."

The old chief nodded, smiling around the pipe's mouthpiece. "Very interesting."

Saigwan woke, long before Aanyáy, in high excitement. Today would be his son's Páwanikt, his naming ceremony, a very special day for Saigwan and for the tribe. The Teacher would return this night, and then the celebration would begin.

But as he approached the night watch, he found the young man crouched over the cliff edge looking concerned. "Wyánch'i, something's amiss, though I do not quite know what."

Saigwan crouched next to him and watched out in the still darkness.

"There are strange calls coming from that way," he pointed
Toward the Rising Sun. *"At first I thought it was a creature. Now I am not
sure."*

"A man?"

"More than one, I fear."

"I have the watch. Go and wake Niyol," Saigwan commanded.

"Yes, Wyánch'i."

*Saigwan listened. All was quiet; too quiet. No animals roaming, no
crickets singing, nothing. Then Saigwan heard it: a man's call, and within
a few moments an answer from another direction, then a third voice.
Three men.*

Saigwan's mind raced as the watchman returned with Niyol. Is it
safe to just let them be, let them pass through? Are there any indications of
his people outside of the cave? Of course there are, they did not hide their
existence, why should they? If these men are hunters, then they will surely
see that there are people nearby.

But there are no other tribes for a moon's walk, at least. *Saigwan
knew of people toward the Great Sea, his mother's people, and he had
heard of people Toward the Rising Sun but had never met any in his
lifetime.*

No. We must know their purpose.

"We must investigate, yawtii," Saigwan whispered.

*Niyol nodded and went to summon three other hunters. When he
returned with them, he led them off the ledge and along the rocks to the
small draw leading onto the plateau. Saigwan said a prayer to the Great
Spirits before following. In hunters' silence, they crept out to a position
behind some heavy brush.*

*The first man wandered right past them. He was short and thick set
with dark skin, hair and beard. He wore torn buckskin trousers and
ragged foot coverings, with a shabby animal skin across his shoulders. An
old club hung on his belt, but no other weapons.*

*Saigwan jumped over the brush to land behind the man. Without a
sound, he had his long chert knife at the man's throat and his other hand
entangled in the man's matted hair. The stranger held his hands up in
silent surrender.*

"*Call to the others,*" *Saigwan hissed through his teeth into the stranger's ear. He did not seem to understand.*

Saigwan let go of the stranger's hair, motioned to his mouth, then to the scrubby nearby woods. "*Call to the others,*" *he repeated.*

The man put two fingers to his lips and whistled. The sound startled Saigwan, but he did not flinch. The whistle was returned once, then twice. The man whistled again; it was returned, this time closer, and again.

Soon enough, two others appeared from different directions, not far away. The first man held his arms up, waving a warning. Niyol and the other three men stepped out with nocked arrows, pulled the bows to half-draw and aimed them at the newcomers' feet. Saigwan gestured at them to lay their weapons on the ground. The two new arrivals looked at their helpless comrade, then at each other, and set down what weapons they had.

When a hunter had disarmed Saigwan's man, the young chief released him and gestured his fellows to stand with him. All three had the same unkempt look, and had carried thick, carved clubs. One, taller and leaner than the others, had also set down a short obsidian dagger.

"*Where do you come from?*" *Saigwan asked.*

The two looked at the leaner one, but the man only held his hands up and shook his head in confusion.

"*Where do you come from?*" *Saigwan asked again, directing his question to the tall lean fellow. He waved his hand around him toward the mountains and the sky.*

The leader nodded once. He looked up at the sky and pointed Toward the Rising Sun and Beyond Wy-east. Then he looked at Saigwan, held two fingers up, and pointed to the small sliver of the moon falling in the very early morning.

"*Two moons that direction?*" *Saigwan said to Niyol.*

"*Probably what he means, Wyánch'i.*"

"*What has brought you so far from home?*" *asked Saigwan.*

The leader did not seem to understand.

Saigwan touched his bare chest. "*Saigwan,*" *he said, then held his hand up in peace.*

The man nodded and responded, *"Manneha."* He touched his own chest and held his right hand up with the same sign of peace.

"My people," Saigwan touched his chest, then pointed to Niyol and the other hunters.

Manneha touched his own chest, said something, and pointed to the two men standing on either side of him.

Saigwan looked at Niyol. *"Well, what do you make of them? Are they dangerous rogues thrown out of a village for doing harm, or what?"*

Niyol kept his bow ready. *"Look at their eyes. They look tired, not greedy. They have had hard times. I suggest we show them hospitality, but carefully, and not give their weapons back yet until we know more."*

"That is good advice, pásiks. It is what we will do. Gather up their weapons to bring along but keep them in a wrap. We will go in and sit down by the fire at the cave entrance, all of us, and learn more."

As Niyol gathered up the dropped weapons, Saigwan led the newcomers to the mouth of the cave. While the other hunters re-stoked the fire, Saigwan remained standing. *"Niyol, see if you can communicate with these two, and get them some food and drink."* He turned to the tallest newcomer and beckoned. *"Manneha, please, walk with me."*

He led Manneha to his home, where Moema and the little ones were at the fire. The newest addition was asleep in his cradle, a wrap pulled tightly around his tiny chin. Saigwan kissed Moema on the cheek, ruffled his daughter's messy hair, and picked up his sleeping son.

"Mine," he smiled, touching his chest again and gesturing around his family.

Saigwan's daughter tugged on Manneha's trousers, waving her doll around for his attention. The young man reached a hand down and gently brushed her snarly hair from her eyes, then turned away.

That was not contempt for a child. That was grief. This one mourns a child. Perhaps a whole family. *Saigwan beckoned him to come along and led him to the ceremonial firepit.*

"Blessing today, Sapsikw'atá," Saigwan greeted the Teacher. *"I am happy for your safe return."*

"And also, to you." The Teacher began to prepare the chalámat. Manneha watched with interest and sat down where Saigwan gestured that he should.

"Watwáa naknúwim," the Teacher breathed deeply and chanted. *"Great Spirits, protect and take care of us."*

Manneha opened his eyes after exhaling long and hard. He looked at Saigwan and made a motion with one finger on his other palm.

"I am sorry, man," Saigwan replied in frustration.

After what was clearly a moment of thought, Manneha dropped off the bench to his knees and began to draw in the dirt using his fingers. He pointed to images already on the chamber wall, Yiska's artistic history of the tribe.

"Paint," Saigwan said. The Teacher nodded to Manneha, then got up to get supplies. *"You can tell us your story, Manneha. Sapsikw'atá, I am sure Yiska would both enjoy this, and help us understand it, especially as we will be borrowing his painting things."*

Yiska was happy to share his paints and brushes, and to see artistic effort. As Manneha began to paint on the cave wall behind the ceremonial fire, Saigwan and the Teacher passed the chalámat, watching the scene unfold.

At first, Manneha drew a family: a woman swelling with child and a very small boy holding her hand. Yiska nodded in appreciation; the newcomer was a talented artist who added many fine details. He drew three other families, each with small children, and a few older adults. Saigwan watched in fascination, feeling Manneha pour his very heart into each detail.

Finally, Manneha breathed deeply and turned toward them. He touched his heart, his hand lingering briefly, and then placed it in protective fashion over the woman with child and the small boy. Then he touched his chest and indicated the rest of the people.

"These are your people," Saigwan said, nodding.

The Teacher was studying Manneha's eyes. *"Wyánch'i, his heart is proud and sad. I begin to think he and his men are refugees of some kind."*

Manneha moved to the right to begin a new scene.

He drew three men hunting, one taller than the others. Saigwan could tell who they were by their weapons and clothing. The scene was just as detailed: a herd of elk, a mountain backdrop, the men working together to chase the herd against a steep mountainside. Then they were *clubbing a very large male, then Manneha drew a smaller scene of himself releasing the animal's spirit over a fire.*

Without turning around this time, Manneha began a third scene. It began with a bear twice the size of the people he had just drawn. The bear stood on its long hind legs, and had a short nose and broad forehead with tall pointed ears.

Manneha's motions became violent as he threw paint against the cave wall. He slapped it with his hands, his palms and knuckles scraping against the rocks, his own blood mixing with the red ochre.

Saigwan felt a rush of sorrow. He no longer wanted to know the end of this story.

Manneha drew his people again, some torn to pieces, blood everywhere. He drew his family—the beautiful pregnant woman and the little boy—dead in pools of blood.

Finally, the young man fell against the cave wall, one hand resting on the spot where he had drawn them.

Saigwan gave the young man a moment before approaching him.

"I am so sorry, yawtii," he said gently to Manneha, who had lost everything, who carried the same weight on his shoulders for his people, who must now feel anguish, anger, and regret all mixed together.

When Manneha finally looked up, he motioned with his hands back toward the cave-mouth, twice, pointed to the bear, and mimed the use of a club against it. Ahhhh. Manneha and his brothers are hunting the monster that killed their people, including Manneha's mate and son and unborn child. I would hunt him too.

Manneha drew the monstrous footprint of the bear, then laid his hand against it for comparison. The heel was twice the size of his hand. The claws were longer than Manneha's rather long fingers. He looked at Saigwan questioningly.

"No, man," Saigwan said with a shake of his head, "we have never seen a bear that size. I am sorry."

The night guard came into the main chamber and walked over to the ceremonial firepit. "Wyánch'i, sorry to interrupt you, but Niyol awaits your orders. He is somewhat impatient."

Saigwan nodded. "How are you all getting along with communicating?"

"We have made some progress. Niyol thinks they say they are on a great hunt for a bear. They do not look angry at us, and they were very grateful for the refreshments. They did not make any move toward their weapons, even though Niyol put them where they could at least make a try for them."

"That sounds good. Well done. None of it goes against what we have seen and heard here, so please tell Niyol these men are our brothers, and to bring them here, along with some more food and drink. I would like him to see something."

"Yes, Wyánch'i," and the night guard was gone.

"We will help you, Manneha," Saigwan said, placing a hand on Manneha's shoulder. "You are welcome here."

Manneha understood and rested his hand on Saigwan's shoulder in return.

Niyol arrived with everyone but the night guard. "Oh, no," he whispered, upon sight of the mural.

The two brothers slowly approached the scene. Each walked up and placed a hand over parts of the drawing. Their heads dropped as their chief came over, speaking quietly to them.

"I must attend to something, Niyol," Saigwan said. "Please make them comfortable as though they were relatives, with guest quarters and food, and water with which to clean up."

"I will take care of it, Wyánch'i."

Saigwan left them and went home to check on his family. His heart ached for what he had seen, and he wanted nothing more than to hold his own in his arms. Moema was working at the fire, her back to him. He reached his arms around her and pulled her body against his, burying his face in her hair. She patted his arms. "Are you all right, Saigwan?"

"I am now," he breathed into her ear crushing her body against his. "Where are the little ones, my átawit?"

"Sleeping. Shall we join them?"

"Let's do that."

He picked her up and carried her into the tent, and for a while, he lost track of time again.

)———→

"What do you want to do, yawtii?" Niyol asked as Saigwan paced near the back tunnel.

"I do not know, Niyol. How can we help them?"

"Well, they could stay here, right? We could welcome them into our tribe, couldn't we, Saigwan?"

"If you were them, would you stay, Niyol?"

"No way, man," Niyol admitted. "I would never stop until I had avenged my own."

"Or we could help them," Saigwan said, placing a hand on Niyol's shoulder. "We can outfit them. Spears, knives, food..."

Niyol nodded, but his smile looked a bit skeptical. "A bear the size of a mammoth? Are you kidding?"

That night, Saigwan dreamed of horrible things and awoke covered in sweat. He got up and paced for a long time, listening to the sleeping noises all around him and trying to calm down. Attempting sleep yet again, he dreamt of the giant bear and his family; its growl filled his head, its eyes red and angry. He could do nothing, could not even move, as the bear carried them away.

He gave up on sleep, dressed, and walked his rounds in the dead of night.

When he came to the ceremonial firepit, he found Manneha sitting in front of his drawing. Manneha opened his eyes briefly to nod at Saigwan, who sat down. He spoke to the Great Spirits for strength, for protection, for peace.

⊢—→

Day followed travel day. Night followed camping night. And the cold just kept getting colder; a chill that ran through his entire being, cracked at his emotions, wearied his very soul. After they left sight of Nch'i-Wána, Saigwan felt truly in a foreign place.

After many days of searching, the hunting party came upon the paw prints. Manneha gestured that they were a couple of days old, but most definitely the bear they hunted. The prints led up into the hills, where the hunting party followed the tracks higher and higher. Around midday, *the wind stopped howling, the snow stopped swirling, and the paw marks ended—at the mouth of a cave.*

Strategy decided, two hunters lit torches and stood outside the entrance. They began shouting and waving the light around, trying to entice the animal out. They would stop, listen, and resume. Stop, listen, resume.

Then Saigwan heard it. A soft growl, first from deep within the cave, then growing louder and louder. All backed away from the entrance as the enormous bear emerged.

The great beast stooped to exit the cave, stopped to blink its large black eyes, planted its feet and roared with enormous lungs; lips pulled back to reveal teeth the size of Saigwan's fingers. The great animal stood as tall as Saigwan's shoulder on all fours, mostly fur and massive bulkiness, but Saigwan could see the raw power that lurked beneath the matted hide. Its whole body shook with the sound of its anger.

The great animal caught the scent of hunters all around and began to sniff out his choice of prey. The men began to circle, and the dance began.

With a long scream of anger, mixed with great pain and suffering, Manneha broke the hunters' trance. He pulled his club from his belt and charged the great bear from the side, slugging it on top of the great head with all his might. The bear staggered and blinked its eyes. Others entered the dance, but Manneha had obtained the bear's undivided attention.

Manneha hit the animal again, this time in the face. The bear cried out in pain and anger and mauled out with a giant paw, catching Manneha in the side before he could start to dodge. It sent the young chief sprawling. Manneha tried to roll and get up, ignoring what looked like broken ribs, and swung his club in anguished rage.

The others came closer to distract the bear, but they could not stop the enormous creature from sinking its massive jaws into Manneha's shoulder. He screamed in pain, his club falling to the ground. The brothers jumped upon the bear's back and began to stab it with the spears Saigwan had given them. Yet the bear still knew nothing but it and the young chief.

As the bear shook Manneha—hard enough, Saigwan figured, that the first shake had probably snapped the young chief's neck—Saigwan lost all fear for himself. He stepped in, raised his spear, and stabbed with all his might into the animal's neck. He had just managed to wrest the weapon free when the bear dropped Manneha's limp form, stepped on it, and chose a new victim.

"Come on," Saigwan screamed, his hands waving in front of him, and stepped backward.

A sickening crunch echoed off the mountain tops and through the caverns when Niyol brought Manneha's club around, as if swinging a great axe at a tree with all his might, to strike the bear between the eyes. The club split, just as if Niyol had swung it at the cave wall, but the mammoth bear's skull buckled with the impact. The bear fell to the ground, unmoving but still breathing. Shaking his hands from the effect of the club's impact, Niyol slit the great beast's throat. Its lifeblood poured out upon the trampled snow at their feet.

Saigwan turned to a scene he would carry for the rest of his life: two brothers weeping in grief while holding their chief. One cradled his head, and the other fell over his chest. He knelt next to them; Manneha's neck was clearly broken, life gone.

He had known that there would be no way Manneha would survive.

Saigwan held one hand on Manneha's forehead, "Áwpam txána paláxs, yawtíi...now you have become one."

They buried Manneha at the mouth of the cave, beneath a cairn of rocks, along with the heart of the great bear. The two could never co-exist in life, but their spirits would forever be intertwined: the great mammoth bear and the boy who had to grow up too fast, yet never really got to live.

When the burial was done, and the two brothers completed a small ritual Saigwan did not understand, they turned to him. Both nodded at Saigwan with understanding, patted their hearts in a gesture of brotherhood, returned the weapons lent them, then walked away.

Saigwan sat near Manneha's tomb and watched as the men prepared the bear for skinning. "Are you well, Wyánch'i?" Niyol asked.

"Yes, Niyol, thank you." Saigwan cleared his throat. "Is this the way it had to happen? Do you think he had to die?"

Niyol sighed, ran his hands through his long hair and sat down. "I do."

"I guess I do too," Saigwan agreed, sadly.

>——→

Sometime after their return, Saigwan went to the ceremonial firepit.

"Saigwan," the old man began after a moment of greeting and welcomed return, "the Great Spirits refused to name your son. They told me that you will name him."

"What? I will name him?" Saigwan asked, flustered. "But how is this possible?"

"They said you will know."

The naming of the chief's first son was a special event for them all. The men passed the chalámat and the women danced. The little ones watched in admiration, their hands sticky with special sweetness saved for special occasions such as this.

When the dance was done, Niyol stood. With a great thundering voice, and to much oohing and ahhing from the people, he told the full tale of the great mammoth bear, of Manneha's bravery, and how the two spirits collided in a great and mighty death. Some of the smallest children trembled and held onto their mothers. Older ones cheered and hollered with excitement. Hunters' chins lifted in fierce approval as Niyol spoke of each man's deeds.

Finally, and with much drama, Niyol reached behind his back and pulled out one of the mammoth bear's enormous claws. He slashed the sharp object to and fro, causing a few of the women and children to scream, until finally the group erupted in applause.

Then the Teacher stood with hands raised for silence. "It is time, Saigwan," he beckoned.

Moema sat on the ground at Saigwan's feet, their young daughter just next to her. The baby boy lay asleep in her lap, wrapped loosely in a blanket of soft rabbit fur. He knelt in front of her, brushed her cheek with his hand, and lifted the infant. The wrap fell from the child, who now lay naked in his father's arms. A chill ran through the little body. Saigwan looked down momentarily upon the life he held in his arms.

"My son," he said in a voice full of pride, lifting the child high for all to see.

"His name will be Manneha."

Chapter 16

Asku awoke early, feeling homesick. He checked on Kitchi, stoked the fire next to Hawilish and went for a walk around the edge of the village.

As he walked, he thought of his mother and Nayhali. *They would be rising soon and preparing for the day. Maybe it's washing day. I miss the kids, Sus, Whirlwind...* Half a moon had passed since they left the village. He had never been away from home that long before. Then he thought of Hatayah, and pain washed over him again. He tried to exclude her from his thoughts.

Then he thought of his father, the chief of their people, a good man, and a good father. *Will I make him proud? Do I make him proud?*

The sun was creeping over the distant mountains, and its warmth filled his senses. He sat down, just where he was, and closed his eyes to feel Aanyáy's touch. Each morning, she ascended without a sound, yet she filled his heart with peace. He did not turn when quiet footsteps approached behind.

"May I join you, *píti?*" came a familiar deep voice.

"Blessings today, *káka,*" Asku said.

U'hitaykah smiled. "And to you, Askuwa'tu. How goes it today?"

"I am well. Can... can I ask you something?"

"Of course."

"Will you be ready to be chief? When the time comes, I mean?" Asku blurted.

"No," said U'hitaykah. "Will you?"

Asku rubbed a hand hard across his eyes and sighed.

"Right," his uncle continued. "But we will do what we must, what we are called to do. The Great Spirits have made their choice and that is our path. You and I will stand tall when they call us, though we may fear and doubt. We will still answer, 'I am ready,' even though we know that no one is ever ready."

"Never, *káka*?"

"Never," U'hitaykah replied, eyes boring deep into Asku's eyes and into his very spirit. "You just will do. You will take your place and your path will be before you."

Resignedly, Asku mumbled something that might have been a minor profanity.

U'hitaykah smiled. "But it doesn't mean you cannot try to prepare anyway." He stood and reached a hand down. "Come on, join me on my rounds this morning."

◆—→

Early in the morning of the next day, Asku was sitting next to his uncle and grandfather, whittling, when a messenger ran up.

"*Wyánch'i*," the young man began, "the Patisapatisháma chief is here."

Asku dropped the piece of wood and ran in the direction the man had pointed. Just outside the village, he stopped. *It will not do to run into his arms like I was still a child. I must say goodbye to those days and ways.* His father approached, flanked by Chaytan, Nayati, and a teenager named Maska.

As his father approached, Asku held his hand at shoulder height. "Blessings, *Wyánch'i*. How was your journey?"

His father smiled in satisfaction and pride. "Blessings, *tita*. You are well, thank the Great Spirits. We did not have a difficult trip."

"Askuwa'tu," Nayati asked, visibly controlling himself, "how is Kitchi?"

"He is improved and in good spirits. My grandfather's people have taken very good care of him. I am sure you would like to see him, so please come with me." He turned around and led them toward the firepit.

Did I just see my father trade glances with Chaytan, almost smiling?

Kitchi had just gone back into the tent to rest after sitting up for a while, and after pleasantries, Asku led Nayati there. When his father entered the tent, they all heard Kitchi's excited exclamation.

"Blessings, Napayshni," the old chief stood to embrace Asku's father.

"And to you, *Wyánch'i*. Kalataka, how can I ever repay you? You have done a great thing for me."

The old man waved his hand. "The Patisapatisháma are our friends. If one of our sons got injured further down Nch'i-Wána, I should hope they would go to you, and I know you would do no less. Askuwa'tu and his friends are welcome, as are you."

"How is my family?" Asku quietly asked Chaytan.

"They are all well, Asku," said Chaytan, lightly slapping his back. "They were beginning to worry about you, so when the horseman finally arrived with the news, we set out right away. They will be happy when you are home."

Asku heard his name and went to sit next to his father. His grandfather was talking.

"—has done us all a favor, Napayshni. We now know that this band of Pyúsh are alive and plan to do us harm. We must prepare."

"Yes," said Napayshni, "we must all come together. It is the time of the Patshatl, at the Great Sea during the next moon. Will you come?"

The old chief nodded thoughtfully. "I will, though we must consider how to protect our people in our absence. We must think long about this."

The two chiefs spoke most of the day and well into the night. Asku tried to listen as long as he could, but he soon fell asleep on the ground by the fire. He awoke the next morning with his grandfather's wrap over him.

>——→

The next morning, Nayati went to confer with the Grandmother about Kitchi's progress. He was still in some pain, but there was no sign of fever. "I believe it is safe for him to travel," said she, "but I must warn you that his leg may never be the way it once was. Kitchi, you must know this. You may always have difficulty and pain when you walk. I would advise giving it one more day, Nayati, if possible."

Kitchi looked unhappy but remembered his manners. "Thank you, *lamyáy*, for all your care."

"I was glad to give it, *myánash*. Do not try to do too much too soon, but when you can, exercise it. After a certain point, only using it will get it any better, and every day you do not will make it harder when you begin."

That evening, the Wawyukyáma held an elaborate celebration in honor of their visitors. Many gifts were given, but Kitchi's was one of the finest. A Wawyukyáma craftsman had made him an intricate cane, a single piece of beautiful, twisted wood sanded smooth, with a curved, knobby handle and detailed carvings of tomahawks, snakes and ducks. The artist had named the piece '*Xátxat* Killer.' There had been much good-natured laughter along with the general appreciation for the fine skill that had created such a cane, and even Kitchi had seen the humor. The Wawyukyáma gave other gifts to all the rest of the River visitors, and more for them to take home to their families and tribe.

I want to think this is all just generosity and family relations, thought Asku. *But it is not just that. The Wawyukyáma are family, but they also live closer to the Pyúsh P'ushtáayama. My grandfather is no fool. During times like these, everyone reaches out to make sure of alliances, partners and friends. Now they know they can count doubly upon us.*

And someday, I will have to make plans of that sort, and think that way, and if I fail, my people could pay a terrible price.

━━►

The group left on horseback at mid-morning the next day: Asku, Kitchi, Hawílish, Chaytan, Napayshni, Nayati, Maska (who had some challenges with his mount, and endured the expected kidding with fair humor). With them went U'hitaykah and Aanapay, leading a third horse loaded with supplies and gifts. U'hitaykah rode next to Napayshni, continuing their conversation of war and strategy. The Patisapatisháma had cached their canoes just above the Two Sisters, and U'hitaykah and Aanapay planned to see them speedily and safely to that point, then take the horses and turn for home.

But that night, Asku had trouble falling asleep again. He got up to watch the stars instead and found his father sitting alone in the dark. "Is sleep escaping you, my *tita*, as it is me?" Napayshni asked.

"Yes, I have not slept well since leaving home, *Wyánch'i*." Asku sat down next to him and pulled his new wrap tighter.

"Well, then sit with me for a while." The Chief pulled out his pipe. Asku watched him stuff the end with dried leaves. "What is on your mind, Asku?"

I dread this. But my father, I think, will understand.

"*Túta*," Asku began, clearing his throat, "those two men I killed...I just did it, I killed them. I do not know what came over me. I did not need to kill the second man. He would have died anyway with Hawilish's arrow stuck through his neck like it was. But I wanted to kill him, and I did, and I'm glad I did. And I am angry at them, still, for making me do it. And I am annoyed with myself, for continuing to think that they had families somewhere.

"That is not all of it, either. If I had been faster, or used more sense, perhaps Kitchi might have never been hurt. I feel somewhat at fault, that I let him down."

The Chief blew rings of smoke in front of him.

"Was I right, *Wyánch'i*? Did I do the right thing?"

"What does your heart tell you, *tita?*" his father asked.

Asku had not yet wrestled with that yet. *All I have done is relive the scene in my mind. What does my heart tell me?* "They were going to kill Kitchi," Asku answered, after some time. "I did what I had to do, *Wyánch'i*. But there still remains a fault of mine: I let him go off by himself in hostile country."

Napayshni blew some more smoke rings. "Askuwa'tu, there will be many times that you will just do what you have to do. You will do it because of who you are and the responsibility that you carry. You will doubt yourself often, but do not let that cloud your decisions. As for Kitchi, yes, he was your responsibility. I put you in charge. I am glad you do not forget that. But who knows him better than his *pásiks*? The way you described it to me before, he went off to hunt ducks for dinner. The men you were trailing had all gone away, or so a reasonable person could have decided.

"So, imagine yourself telling him, no, you can't go hunting by yourself. What would Kitchi have said?"

Asku managed to laugh a little. "'What am I, little *Wyánch'i*? A little girl pounding *wawachí*, waiting for her *Maɬáwitash*? Come on, man, do you think I cannot defeat a *x̱átx̱at* in deadly combat? Don't worry, *pásiks*.'"

"That's about right," said Napayshni with a chuckle. "So, you see, when you look back, you will always find things you wish you had done differently. But at the time, you decided with what you knew then, not what you learn later. But I know the feeling.

"I was a little younger than you are now when the Pyúsh P'ushtáayama band killed the chief and carried my sister away. Just a boy. They killed many of our people, abused our women. I watched some of this happen. The evil Pyúsh chief slit my father's throat in front of us. He spilled his blood there under the Totem. My eyes became those of a man, right there. After they left, we prepared. We followed them, me and four others. We came upon them in the night, as he lay on top of my sister."

Shudders of rage and disgust ran through Asku's body as he saw this in his mind, and the Chief continued.

"Rage overcame me, and I did not think. I did not feel. All I knew was he and I. The others were dead in an instant, and not by my hands. The Pyúsh chief sat alone as I moved my sister safely away. When I returned, his hands were bound, there was a fire…and I made him pay.

"Do I regret what I did? What I had to do?" The Chief looked toward Asku. "No."

There was a long pause.

"But do I still hear his cries of anguish and pleas for mercy?" the Chief continued. "Often."

Another long pause.

"There unfortunately will be others, my *tita*."

"Yes, I know. And perhaps soon."

After a while they talked about the stars, then of mundane things: Chitsa's cooking, Susannawa's moccasins, little Whirlwind's adventures. *The important things*.

By the second day, camped well down Walawála and nearly in sight of Nch'i-Wána, Asku could feel the excitement. He flitted about camp, helped Kitchi get ready, and boosted him onto his horse's back. He would see home before the sun set.

"Will you come all the way with us, *káka*?" Asku reached up to pat the flank of a horse that U'hitaykah was leading.

"No, not this time," he replied. "We will see you safely into your canoes, then return home."

Sadness seeped into Asku's voice. "It has been a good time in many ways. *Kw'alá,* for everything, *káka*."

U'hitaykah was a head taller than Asku, and much beefier. He smiled and gave his nephew a slap on the back, almost making him stumble. "You did well as a bison hunter. We will see you soon, *píti,* because we will head to the Great Sea together in not too long."

"Oh, yeah," Asku remembered. "The Patshatl."

"Yes, and we will finally get to check out this young maiden of yours. Won't we?"

Asku felt his face flushing with heat, made a futile effort at nonchalance. "Oh, yes. I suppose she will be there, won't she?"

U'hitaykah laughed, a deep honest salvo of chuckles. "Nervous, *píti*?"

"Just a little."

"Asku," said U'hitaykah in a quieter and more serious tone, "not ten days ago you killed two grown men to protect your friend. You travelled alone in the dark, a full day's journey, in less than a night, following a bear. This is small by comparison. I guarantee you will know what to do when the time comes."

"I guess," Asku said, trying to sound more confident than he felt.

"Yes, you will," his uncle added, "but I promise you that your first time will undoubtedly be as scary as a Pyúsh warrior with a tomahawk. Maybe scarier."

And he was laughing again.

>——→

They reached Nch'i-Wána by mid-morning where two canoes waited for them.

Aanapay and U'hitaykah stayed long enough to see Kitchi and all the gifts settled into the canoes. Then Asku laughed as the two horses, with the others tethered and following behind, took off in a great cloud of dust like thunder was chasing them.

They dropped Chaytan just before K'mił, as they had to stop on the far side to retrieve the canoe the boys had stashed upon setting forth. Chaytan would bring the tribe welcome news of the expedition's return and Kitchi's stable condition.

As the two canoes finally approached the bend, the Chief let out a loud call.

And from just ahead, the call was returned in many beautiful voices. Asku's heart leaped for joy to see so many of his people, at the river's edge and up on the bluff, present to welcome them all home.

Like everyone else, Asku received plenty of backslaps and welcomes. His mother in particular was delighted. "Askuwa'tu," she said, embracing him with that strength that always surprised him, "thank the Great Spirits. You have done very well, *myánash*, and I have missed you. You have made me very proud."

"That makes me even more glad to be home, *iła*. Nayhali, how goes it, *nána*?"

"I am well," she said, hugging him. "I am glad you are finally home, *nipa*. We got worried when you did not return on time."

Then his little siblings and Matahnu half tackled him, and there was a pleasant commotion for all. "I missed all you little chipmunks, too," said Asku, much moved. *This is what it is all about. This is why. This is the why of much that my father does, and that I do, and that I will have to do.*

In time, the throng migrated up the trail to the ridge. Kitchi still was unable to put any weight on his injured leg but had more help than anyone could want.

"Askuwa'tu Haylaku," the Teacher said, "blessings today." Asku had not even seen the old man.

"Blessings, *Sapsikw'ała*. I have a lot to tell you, and to ask your thoughts about."

"I am sure you do," the old man said with a nod. "I will look forward to that."

Asku looked around him. He briefly caught her eye and felt a twinge in his midsection. *Why does she have to be so pretty?* She dropped her eyes to the ground.

Asku looked away and tried to think of the time when he had been on horseback, and how much less complicated life had been.

As the group reached the village, the Teacher stopped, followed by everyone else. "*Kw'alá*, Great Spirits," he said, so all could hear. "Thank you, Great Mother, for returning our sons to us. *Inmíma átawitma tíinma*, my beloved people, we will celebrate tonight."

Asku and the Chief saw Kitchi settled with his family before heading home.

"He will be all right now," Asku reassured himself.

"Yes, thanks to you, my *tita*."

"Thanks also to Hawilish. But we have yet to see if he will walk again, *Wyánch'i*," Asku replied, ruefully. "Makes me think, if only I had reacted quicker—"

"Askuwa'tu," his father interrupted, "not another word like that, my *tita*. You saved his life. Stand tall."

"Yes, *Wyánch'i*."

Dinner was fresh-caught salmon, a favorite that Asku had missed very much on the Elk Plains, punctuated by the comfortable banter of motherly admonitions to children, Nayhali's occasional barb, and fatherly chuckles.

There was only one discordant note, and it was Susannawa, who seemed in Asku's absence to have become something of a little bully, lording it over his sisters. "I hope it is just a time he goes through," said Chitsa. "He was also unkind to Matahnu. I was tempted to put your headdress on him, Napayshni, and while he was trying to get out from under it, ask him if he truly felt like an important chief now. But that would have gotten it dirty." She threw Asku a look.

"It might have been worth it," said the Chief. "But maybe someone else who is back now has a better idea."

Asku looked from parent to parent. *Why me, and not Nayhali? I know the answer. Kúu mísh.* "Sus, come here."

The child took his sweet time coming over, bulling past Nisy, who objected in vocal terms. "What, Asku?"

"I understand you were very important in my absence, *nika*. Walking the rounds, that sort of thing."

"I was!"

"I also understand that you decided that, since the *Wyánch'i* was gone, you were pretty unbearable to everyone, and acted in ways you never saw me, nor our father behave. Why?"

Sus deflated, shocked. "I don't know."

Asku scowled. "Here is a suggestion. When I ask you why you did a thing, never again give me that answer. I will not take it. That is not an acceptable answer."

"I didn't think you were coming back," blurted Sus.

"What are you talking about?"

"You didn't come home, and then the *Wyánch'i* left…and it was just me. I tried to do what you do when the *Wyánch'i* is gone. I walked the rounds, I helped Mother, I carried my knife with me wherever I went."

"Well, Susannawa," said Asku, firmly, "I do not have any problem with that part. But I have a problem with the part you are not telling me."

"I told you everything!"

"Now you just told me a lie. Now you are in worse trouble, *nika*, for being dishonest to me. It offends me that you think I am dumb enough to believe—"

"I know, I know," Susannawa interrupted.

That was enough of that. "Susannawa. Be silent and listen. You don't interrupt me. All right?"

The child looked up at his older brother's eyes. "Yes, *yáya*," he said in a very small voice.

"Good," said Asku. "Why did you bully your sisters and Matahnu? Answer me right away."

The boy gulped. "I got angry. I was worried about you and our father."

"Let me tell you something about anger and fear. Where I was, with my *pásiks*, they were all I could depend on when I was angry and afraid. Matahnu is your *pásiks*. We saved Kitchi's life, and he trusted his *pásiks*. One day Mat may save your life. If you someday get hurt, do you want Mat to remember that you were mean to him?"

Susannawa shook his head.

"And your sisters. Suppose I was hurt like Kitchi. Nayhali would help take care of me. You need to realize that your sisters will be important to you for all your life. I never want to hear of you being bratty to them again. *Míshnam pamshtk'úksha'*, Susannawa?"

"Yes, Asku," he replied, meekly. "I understand. I am sorry."

"It would be a good start for you to tell them, not me. It was not me you bullied."

The boy looked as if he were about to cry but went over to Nis'hani and Mini. "I'm sorry, *litsáyin*. I won't be mean to you anymore. Someday you will be important to me!"

Two parents and two teenagers suppressed every impulse to laugh.

"Okay," Nis'hani said, planting a sloppy little girl kiss on his cheek. Sus looked as if he would push her away, but hearing Asku clear his throat, did not.

"That's a good start. Is there anything else you need to do?" Asku inquired.

"Yes, *yáya*," the little boy nodded.

They found Matahnu sitting all alone, poking a stick sadly into the fire.

"How goes it, Mat?" Asku asked.

"Oh, hi, Asku," Matahnu said. He smiled until he saw Susannawa. "Oh, it's you."

Susannawa stepped around Asku. "I am sorry, Mat. I was worried about my brother, and I forgot you are my *pásiks*, my best friend of anyone. You might save my life someday."

A smile crept across Matahnu's face. "Really, do you mean it?"

"I do."

"Okay, then you are my best friend too. Hey, I have got something to show you, come on." The little boy jumped to his feet, and Susannawa took off with him.

>——

Asku returned home, saw the salmon was still roasting on the hot rocks, and checked in on the Teacher. The Story House was empty. Feeling a little disappointed, Asku turned around the edge of the village for a walk instead.

Without really thinking, he turned the corner to Hatayah's home.

"Blessings today," he smiled. She was home alone.

Hatayah jumped in surprise. "Asku, uh, hi," she said, fumbling the moccasin she was assembling.

"*Míshnam wá,* Hatayah?"

She smiled, and his heart melted in it. "I am well, Asku, especially now that all of you are home. We were worried."

"Yea." He moved closer to her. "I really did not mean for us to worry anyone, though."

She laughed, a beautiful sound. "No, of course not."

He ran a nervous hand through his hair. "Stuff just happens to me, right? I don't get it sometimes," he said, taking another step closer.

Hatayah laughed again and looked up into his eyes. "That's not what I heard." She reached her hand out and touched his forearm. Asku fought the urge to touch her in turn, knew it was wrong, but his brain was losing the battle. "Everyone was talking about how you killed two men, saved Kitchi's life, and how you found your way to the Elk Plains People, all by yourself."

"Well, that makes it sound braver than it was," he said, embarrassed. Asku took a deep breath, and his mind lost the battle. He brushed her cheek with the back of his hand, ran his fingers down her neck and across her collarbone, then onto her shoulder. She closed her eyes and sighed.

But her face soon twisted in sadness.

His face and his hand fell. "What?"

"Asku—"

Some part of him feared what she would say and mounted a last-ditch effort to derail it. He took her around the waist, pulled her near and kissed her. Her lips were so soft and sweet, and she parted them slightly, falling into his arms. He held the length of her body pressed tightly against his. She reached her arms around his shoulders, and it all felt like paradise. If he had wondered about her inner feelings, he could wonder no longer.

And then she tried to step back. "No," she gasped. "Asku, stop."

He couldn't or didn't. He ran his lips down her neck, inhaling her.

"Asku, stop," she said, with more force. Her hands pushed hard against his chest. The spell broke. He took a step back.

"Hatayah, please," he begged.

She was firm. "No." He felt his heart breaking all over again.

"Please, *Atawishamash*…I love you. I need you."

"No," she responded, more gently. "Askuwa'tu Haylaku, you need to go. You must."

He tried to speak, but the words choked in his throat.

"Please. Go. Now." she said, without emotion. "And don't come back again. If you care about me, Asku, for me, walk away and do not look back."

Asku stood for a moment, looked into her eyes for weakness, and found none. There was nothing left but to do as she had said.

Chapter 17

In hope of avoiding everyone, Asku walked along the trail behind the village. *I am not sure if I want to run away, yell, punch something, or throw up. Maybe all of the above.*

"Hey, man," Hawilish said, startling him. "What's up?"

"Oh, hey," Asku replied, trying to pretend nothing was wrong. "Not much. You don't look very happy."

"I was just sitting with Kitchi. The Grandfather is poking around at his leg. Some of it opened up again on the way home." Hawilish had a queasy look on his face. He had a hard time with blood.

"Is everything okay?"

"I don't know."

"Come on. He might need us." *And maybe I might need to think about something that doesn't remind me of Hatayah in any way.*

They jogged down the trail and around the village to Kitchi's home. Nayati saw the boys at the door and invited them in.

Kitchi was lying in bed, biting down on a piece of rawhide, twitching every time the Grandfather put in a new stitch. Blood dripped down the sides of his knee. Asku knelt near Kitchi's stomach, grabbed his hand and patted his arm. "*Mishnam wá?*" he asked.

Kitchi nodded once, gritting it out. After a few delicate stitches, the Grandfather stopped. "We are done, my *tita*," he said, patting Kitchi's good leg.

"Thank you, Grandfather," Kitchi replied through clenched teeth.

"Will he walk again, Grandfather?" asked Nayati.

"It is too early to tell. When the wound heals, he must begin walking on it. He may need help at first." The old man turned to look at Kitchi. "If you do walk again, *tita*, I fear you may always limp, and your knee may always cause you pain. For that, I am sorry. We will pray to the

Great Spirits for healing of the muscles around your knee so that you will still be able to use it." The old man turned back to Nayati. "Be thankful for the Wawyukyáma Grandmother. Many would have just taken his leg and prayed he survived. Her work was very good."

Nayati nodded, expressionless.

Asku patted Kitchi on the shoulder "All right, man, you rest. I will come later and help you get to the Celebration."

"No. I am not going."

"Yes, you are. There are stories to tell."

"Yeah, and I'm not very good at it," added Hawɨlish.

Kitchi glared up at Asku, who returned the look. Kitchi finally succumbed. "*Kúu mish but* leave me alone for a while."

Stepping outside the tent, Asku and Hawɨlish found Kitchi's parents waiting for him. "He will be all right," Asku said, more hopeful than certain.

"*Kw'alá*, Askuwa'tu, Hawɨlish," said Kitchi's mother Ituha.

Hawɨlish found fascination in a tent peg. Asku answered, "Thank the Great Spirits, *lamyáy*. He would have done it for either of us."

"Yes, he would have. I am glad he has such friends." She nodded at him and went back inside their home.

"I'll see you later," Asku said to Hawɨlish. "I need to see the Teacher."

Asku took a detour back to the Teacher's home. He found the old man sitting in front of the Totem, the wrap around his shoulders. "Blessing, *Sapsikw'alá*," Asku said as he took a seat.

"And to you, Asku. How is Kitchi?"

"He will survive, though he may have a bad attitude for a very long time."

The Teacher nodded. "We will pray to the Great Spirits on his behalf. Kitchi has the makings of a very strong hunter."

Asku was quiet for a few moments, then: "*Sapsikw'alá*, Saigwan told me the story of Manneha and the great mammoth bear. Do you know this story?"

The old man nodded.

"My *Pawaat-lá*, my Spirit bear, led me to my grandfather's people. I was just running. I knew we could not get Kitchi home in time by ourselves. My bear led me into the canyon of Pa-lús, but I saw no way up. He showed me a secret way near Aputaput. He spoke to me, and I followed him."

The Teacher seemed to think for a while.

"*Sapsikw'alá*," Asku continued, "is he a real bear? I mean, is he a spirit or a bear?"

"He is both spirit and bear, my *tita*," the old man said with a smile. "So do not get too close."

"Yes, *Sapsikw'alá*," Asku laughed. "I have so much to tell you, but it is getting late. Can I come back tomorrow?"

The old man nodded. "Blessings, my *tita*."

"Blessings, *Sapsikw'alá*. I will see you in a little while."

Asku ran around the corner, his stomach reminding him of the salmon his mother and sister had been preparing. He found them all there, waiting for him.

"Well, there you are," the Chief said. "I was about to send Susannawa to go fetch you."

Asku apologized, washed up, and the meal began. Most of the conversation occurred between Napayshni and Chaytan, concerning a scout from whom they had not yet heard. It was impossible for him not to notice that Nayhali had eyes only for Chaytan.

"How is Kitchi, Askuwa'tu?" asked the Chief.

"Uh, the Grandfather had to re-stitch his knee a bit. The stitches came open on our journey. The Grandfather says we have to wait until the wound is healed to see how much he will recover."

The Chief nodded.

"He does not want to go tonight," Asku added. "But I am going over when we are done eating. I will carry him myself if I have to."

"Chaytan and I will join you, Asku. He should come, even if he thinks he does not want to."

▸——→

"*Míshnam wá?*" Asku said, entering Kitchi's family home. His friend was alone.

Kitchi snorted. "How do you think I'm doing?"

"Hopefully, well enough to join us tonight."

"*K'a'áay*. I am staying right here."

"Come on, Kitchi. This is important. You have to tell the story."

"You don't understand," he mumbled. "It's bad enough that I can't walk, and now I'm hanging out." Kitchi waved a hand down at the breechcloth, normally worn only when swimming or during periods of extreme heat or at celebrations like this one.

Trying not to laugh, Asku grabbed a deerhide cover from the bed. "I agree, you should not flash all that at the celebration. You were tough and brave enough already, and no one needs any more proof."

"Shut up, man," Kitchi groused, with a backhanded swipe at Asku's shoulder. Nevertheless, after a protracted session of complaining and swearing, Asku got Kitchi over to the chair they would carry him in.

Not much later, Nayati showed up with Chaytan and Napayshni. He and Napayshni took the front of the chair, while Chaytan and Asku took the back. All squatted down. "Ready? All together, lift!" ordered the Chief. All four men stood.

"Man, you are heavy," teased Asku. Kitchi hawked as if to spit in his direction.

"Knock it off, both of you," the Chief said. As they made their way toward the ceremonial fire, the Patisapatisháma began to gather.

>—→

"*Inmíma átawitma tíinma*," the Teacher beckoned, arms and hands outstretched in blessing, "my beloved people."

The old man passed the *chalámat* to the Chief. The others chatted quietly as more took their seats around the fire. Asku reflected on all the recent turmoil in his world: his grandmother's anger, his Spirit bear, the cave, Saigwan's stories, the Pyúsh, and his time on the Elk Plains. *I am fifteen winters. What have I accomplished? What have I done to make any of them proud? What have I done to be worthy?*

By his age, the Chief had seen his own father murdered in this very spot; had sought the men who did it, tortured and killed them; had become chief. Saigwan had borne his father's body a great distance in the snow, in spite of injuries; had become chief at a difficult time; had taken a beautiful young mate, only to bury her within a winter.

"I am fifteen," he whispered into the dancing flames.

The Teacher stood. Children rushed to find spots around the outskirts of the *Nch'inch'ima*.

"*Watwáa naknúwim*," he raised his hands into the dark night sky. "Thank you, Great Spirits, for the return of our young ones: Askuwa'tu Haylaku, Kitchi Malakaniha, and Hawilish Akaychayta. Thank you, Great Spirits, for the Wawyukyáma, our brothers and sisters. *Watwáa naknúwim,*" the old man finished, and waved for the celebration to begin.

Nayhali and other teen girls came forward, all dressed in matching buckskin dresses, wearing a wealth of fine jewelry and accessories. They danced with their hands held high in the air. From across the fire, Asku watched Kitchi sit a little taller in his chair.

As the girls danced to the deep thumping sound of the drums, the smoke and flames in the firepit seemed to join their movements. The Teacher chanted quietly, words Asku did not understand, and then all was quiet.

The old man told a story of the Pyúsh Pushtáayama arrival long ago. When he reached the part where the old Chief was murdered, and his young son set forth to avenge his death, Asku looked at his father. The *Wyánch'i*'s expression was impenetrable. The Teacher finished with the Pyúsh chief's more recent arrival, then turned toward Kitchi with an arm stretched in welcome.

Kitchi could not stand up, but he told a very vivid story nonetheless, one of bravery and strength, drawing many murmured reactions. At one point, he pulled the tomahawk out from behind him and swung it through the air, then finished with the dramatic scene of an arrow whizzing through the air to strike his tormentor in the neck, and then his best friend jumping out of the thicket with fire shining in his eyes.

"And then, I remember no more," he finished, with an arm outstretched in Asku's direction.

Asku began his part of the story with a bear, then of meeting his uncle above the waterfall and of the Wawyukyáma chief, Kalataka Wahchinksapa. The drums beat very softly as Asku spoke of the bison hunt and the way the one had given his life. Then he told the story of

Saigwan, Manneha, and the great mammoth bear hunt. As he finished the story, he gave his body over to the emotions of the experiences, lifting his eyes toward the stars.

"My son, Askuwa'tu Haylaku," he said in a voice that rang. The murmur received grew louder. Napayshni let it go on for a bit, then continued. "In one moon's time, we will travel to the Patshatl at the Great Sea. We will begin preparations."

Then he closed his eyes and lifted his arms toward the tribe with fingers outstretched. *"Inmíma átawitma tíinma*, blessings this night."

The villagers stood and stretched tingling legs, gathered up families and mats, and made their way home. Now the collective murmur combined excitement for the Patshatl with rather more immediate anticipation of rest. Kitchi got plenty of attention, from his wound to the tomahawk to his cane to its comical name.

They wanted to carry his chair home, and Asku saw no reason they should not.

It was not a night of bad dreams, but it did end for Asku before dawn.

Chapter 18

Saigwan awoke again to darkness, the image of the great bear's jaws crunching down upon Manneha's shoulder still fresh in his mind. It was always hard to get back to sleep after vividly bad dreams.

"Saigwan," Moema whispered, "are you all right?" Her hand groped for his under the thick elk skin, but he pulled away.

"Yes, I am fine. Go back to sleep, átawit."

He sat up, pulled the bison skin around his shoulders, and stepped out of his family's home into the nighttime chill. All seemed well again, discounting himself.

Saigwan walked toward the ceremonial fire to find the Teacher, wrap pulled tight, eyes closed. Saigwan sat down opposite the old man. He could not shake the scene. "Sapsikw'ałá," he began, "the great bear haunts my dreams. I see him in my mind, even now, he is there."

The Teacher said nothing.

"Am I eighteen winters, Sapsikw'ałá? I have seen many things, horrible things, great pain and death. Why does this bear now haunt me so?"

Some time passed in silence, other than the crackle of the fire, before the old man responded. "You must ask the animal's spirit, Saigwan. It may have some unfinished business with you." He paused, breathed deeply. "Yes, the animal is calling to you. And you must listen. He has something to teach you...or us, through you."

Another deep breath. "You must make a Spirit Journey."

"A Spirit Journey?" Saigwan whispered. A Spirit Journey was undertaken alone; a young person would leave the cave for a time of solitude, for his or her own reasons. "I have never taken a Spirit Journey, Sapsikw'ałá. Is it selfish to leave my people to do this?"

"I think you must, tita. But let us continue to ask the Spirits."

"Yes." Saigwan pulled his wrap tighter. It was cold.

>—→

Niyol found Saigwan in a small side chamber, repairing some of his travel gear. "What is going on? Are you going somewhere?" asked Niyol, sitting down with a pronounced grunt.

"I do not like it, man. Let me come with you."

Saigwan met his eyes. "Niyol, there is something I must do, alone. Please try to understand, yawtii."

"K̲'a'áay." Niyol stood and stormed away. This would not, of course, be the least or the last of the objections he could expect. They will take it as a bad omen. But I must speak to the spirit of the great bear.

"What is going on, yáya?" Kasa jumped to her feet and grabbed his arms later that day. "Why will you leave us?"

"Because I must. My mind will not be clear until I do. I am not leaving forever. It is as it must be."

Moema was fighting back tears and losing. "You must go, I know," she whispered through her hands, "but I dream as well, Wyánch'i."

He laid his hands on hers. "What are your dreams, Moema?"

Her eyes pierced his. "I dream of you, Wyánch'i, of great pain and suffering. I fear you will go and not come back. Please take Niyol with you."

He gathered both women into an embrace, but his voice stood its ground. "Ilksáas wínasha...I am going alone," he repeated. He turned and walked away.

>—→

Saigwan left well before the next dawn, when nearly everyone was asleep. Only Niyol and the Teacher were awake. With the old man's blessing and a frustrated glare from Niyol, he walked away from the cave.

He walked Toward the Rising Sun along the river, pulling his bison wrap tight to keep out the deepening chill. That night he found shelter against the base of a steep cliff, but the wind howled mercilessly. Saigwan tried and tried to get a fire started but gave up, huddling close to the rock wall beneath an overhang instead. He tucked the wrap up around his ears and chin and closed his eyes. He thought about his father, his grandfather, and then about his son. What life was Saigwan creating for him?

Saigwan did not eat or drink anything that night, and the next day when Aanyáy began her climb into the cloudy sky, he began walking again. I know where I am. I have no firm idea where I am going. That seems to be a summary of my whole life.

He walked along the heights above Nch'i-Wána until he came to a valley deeply carved by one of the many rivers that fed the Great River. The sound of the water pounding against the tall rock walls echoed in Saigwan's ears even from above. The cold wind followed as it rushed through the canyon above the foaming water.

Saigwan knew this particular river well, and that if he went away from Nch'i-Wána up its course for part of a day, he would come to a place where he might cross it without plunging into its lethal chill. He turned right, walking along the edge of the plateau.

And somewhere around midday, along that cliff edge, he saw her.

He saw her far below, a vision of a woman walking along the opposite bank, headed toward Nch'i-Wána. Saigwan turned and retraced his steps, seeking a way down. He soon found a narrow animal trail and slipped and jumped much of the way to the river's edge.

She was still there, walking downstream, dark hair long and flowing free behind her. A dress of white animal skin like he had never seen before dragged on the ground around her bare feet. Her arms moved as though she were singing to herself, dancing along to her own tune.

She was exactly as he remembered her.

"Una, átawit," he called to her from across the river. She did not turn or flinch, or even seem to know he was there at all. "Una, I am here!"

I am to follow her. Why else would she be here, right now, just as I am? Why would our paths be crossing here? *She continued walking, dancing Toward the Great Mountains along the riverbed, and Saigwan followed.*

When she reached a sandbar leading to brush and trees, the cliff no longer steep on her side of the river, she stopped and turned away from

Saigwan as if looking for something. Before long, Saigwan saw what she waited for. He was helpless to intervene.

He tried to cry out, but found his throat blocked as the great mammoth bear stepped out into the clearing, only steps away from her.

Saigwan ran forward into the icy water but stopped as he watched the great bear nuzzle the top of her head. The bear, then, must also be spirit rather than flesh. She reached her arms up and buried them in its thick, brown fur. Then she turned and continued walking Toward the Great Mountains, the great bear now following her.

The apparent crisis being past, it registered with Saigwan that he was standing in the nearest thing to liquid ice. He stepped backward onto dry ground, fell to his knees and screamed her name. Why could she not be at peace with the Great Spirits?

Moments passed until he felt his mind clearing. He got up and followed them. Saigwan continued to assail his own mind with the question to which a shadowed part of him already knew the answer.

The great bear walked slowly behind her, its enormous head moving along with the rhythm of her dance. It was a long, slow walk, and by the time the pair finally stopped, Saigwan felt the chill of evening, made worse thanks to his earlier wading. They both turned to face him.

"I am sorry," he called across the river, "can you not find peace?"

They stood there for moments, just looking at each other—the great bear, a mountain of brown fur, next to Saigwan's first love.

"How can I ease your pain?" he cried out.

They both turned around and walked away from him.

"Wait," he yelled. Neither turned, nor seemed to hear his call. They stepped into the trees and were gone from sight.

Saigwan looked once at the rushing river before him and made his choice.

"Come back," he yelled as he ran into the icy current of the river.

The water hit his flesh like a thousand mallets. His boots became waterlogged, and his bison wrap seemed much heavier. At mid-river, the current swept him off his footing and took him in its grip.

Saigwan swam as hard and as fast as he could, but the current was winning, moving him ever farther from where the two had disappeared.

He tried to keep fighting, but his strength waned as the chill pierced his vitals. He felt his limbs growing heavy and numb, wracked by violent shivers that came in waves.

Soon Saigwan realized it was all he could do just to keep his head above water. He untied the wrap from his neck and let it go, realizing the prized family heirloom could be the death of him. He could not get hold of anything on shore, nor find his footing in the swift river. At times he saw what he thought were fire lights, but he knew that was impossible.

Desperate to keep his head above water, he would gasp for a breath and then be pulled down again, banged against a rock, and sometimes both. He could see and feel the thundering waves rushing under him and over him.

Saigwan knew that he must find a way out of the water soon or it would take him. He felt a great drowsiness. Fighting, he focused on keeping his feet up where he could see them, and the river carried him farther and farther. His arms and legs felt like dead weight, and the act of breathing was painful labor now.

He felt the current fling him along the river's outer curve, and saw a large rock near the shore, protruding from the river just ahead. Saigwan tried to grab hold, but the water dragged him over it. A distant part of his mind registered that if he could feel pain right then, he would have just felt a great deal of it. Summoning all his remaining will, he pushed off the rock with both legs and landed halfway ashore on other sharp rocks.

He scrambled up out of the liquid, exhausted. He closed his eyes and he let go.

In his mind, the great bear spoke.

"Where will I go?" cried the bear, as great tears fell from his huge dark eyes. "Mine are no more…I am all alone. I am alone," it lamented.

"There is nothing left for me. No joy, no food, no place…and so, I will walk…and I will walk…" He drew a deep breath and turned away.

Saigwan awoke shaking, his eyes blurred and his body mostly numb. Something, or someone, held him close. A large fire blazed before him. Convulsive shivers rippled through his body from head to toe. Sharp stings made themselves felt across his body.

And then in his mind, she was there.

"I am glad for you, Wyánch'i," Una said, smiling sadly. "I will wait until the appointed time, and I will do all that was asked of me. There will be a time, and I will return.

"But until that day, know that I have loved you, Saigwan, Wyánch'i." She began to fade in his mind's eye. "And so, I will walk...and I will walk..."

And the great bear appeared again. This time Saigwan was there. He walked toward the animal with his arms open wide.

"Can I ease your pain, my brother?" Saigwan asked.

"Remember me," was all the great bear said.

"Wait," Saigwan yelled. He heard his own voice come out hoarse and painful. "Come back," he whispered.

"Saigwan," a familiar voice said from far away, "yawtii, wake up. Please."

He opened his eyes to the large, blazing fire, the heat of it beginning to warm his fingers and his toes. The shaking was easing. Niyol dabbed at the wounds on his shoulder and torso. Saigwan could see the dark red stains seeping through the cloth.

"Saigwan," Niyol pleaded again, "please?"

"Niyol," his eyes began to clear, his voice barely a whisper, "how...did you find me?"

"Oh, thank the Spirits," Niyol replied. "What has happened to you?"

"Niyol," he began, but could feel his consciousness fading again, "the bear was there...and so was she..."

He would later remember only bits and pieces of that time: Niyol struggling under his weight, people crying and voices speaking, other people rubbing his hands and arms and feet, bonfires and warmth.

Saigwan's next memory was the feel of the Grandmother's skilled hands presenting him a warm drink. Numbness had yielded to awareness of bruises, scrapes, and the beginnings of a cough.

He heard the people not far away; chanting, whispering, singing, talking, all over the crackle of fire. He knew he was in the home of the

Teacher. Saigwan wished to speak with him, with Niyol, Moema, his sister, but could not find his voice.

And then, he burned with the fever.

In his mind, Saigwan saw the great mammoth bear.

Aanyáy looked down upon the bear and she became sad, so sad…

"Where will you go, myánash?"

He just shook his mighty head, his fur glistening in her light. He had come so far and all alone.

"Where is your family?"

The bear dropped his muzzle toward the ground. Giant tears rolled off his cheeks and fell to the dirt making puddles that grew and grew.

"I am so sorry, myánash," Aanyáy replied. "What happened to them?"

He growled one long, deep and painful howl and she saw a picture in her mind's eye: of man, who had seen the great bear and coveted his fur for warmth, and his claws and teeth for tools. Man had watched for the bear to leave his home and had snuck in. Aanyáy could watch no more as man took the lives of the great bear's mate and offspring. She covered her eyes with her hands.

The puddles grew bigger and bigger, until soon a mighty river flowed from the feet of the bear as he continued walking. His great head rocked from side to side, low to the ground.

Aanyáy hid her face for a very long time. When she reappeared, she found man sitting by a fire, stringing beautiful teeth and claws on a necklace.

"Man," she asked, "what have you done?"

"I killed that monster," he boasted, "and I took my prize." He held up one fierce claw in his hand.

"Oh, myánash," Aanyáy replied with great sadness, "what you have done."

Saigwan awoke—or he thought he was awake—but he still could not open his eyes. He heard voices around him. His body shook with the fever as someone wiped a rag across his face. The cool water could not douse the fire.

"We must prepare the people," one voice said, male, elder.

"No. He will survive." Niyol stated. "He must survive."

"Niyol," the elder said again, "you must prepare."

"No!" Niyol shouted. "I will not!" Someone stormed loudly from the tent.

"My dear," the elder voice said, closer this time, "go rest, I will sit with him."

Someone sniffed and bent close to his face. Saigwan felt lips on his forehead. Long hair fell all around him.

"Átawishamash," said a young feminine voice, and she was gone.

Saigwan's body burned, then chilled, then burned again. At times his head ached as though he had hit it many times against a rock. When he coughed, the force seemed to tear at his lungs and throat. Yet through the darkness of pain and suffering, he heard the Teacher's voice.

"Saigwan, this is your journey. Listen to the Spirits, myánash. Listen...and return to us."

Asku looked up when the eagle cried overhead. His head hurt, but he breathed in the beautiful morning.

He took a step toward the Totem and rested a hand on the weathered wood. Black and red were the only colors still visible, but the shapes were definite, and eternal.

What an amazing tree this must have been once.

He took one more step toward home as the Chief came running toward him, much too fast for his morning rounds. It could mean nothing good.

"Wyánch'i?"

"Askuwa'tu," said Napayshni, eyes sad, "come with me, *tita*."

The two ran past the Teacher's home, down into the village, stopping at the door of Sunsaa, the man who had been his grandfather's best friend.

The Grandfather held Sunsaa's hand but did not look up when the Chief and Asku entered.

Napayshni knelt next to the dying old man. "How goes it, *mixa*?" he whispered.

Sunsaa opened his eyes. "Ah, Napayshni," he managed to say, "I will go now. Your father and all that I have loved…await me. Give me your blessing."

The Chief placed one hand on the old man's chest, the other on his forehead.

"*Kw'ałá, mixa*," he whispered. "Be at peace, my friend." As the old man took his last breath, Asku saw a tear roll down his father's cheek, and felt some of his own. *I am sorry, but also proud. Proud that I came to know him and be his friend, and that I gave him my time while he could receive it.*

That night the entire village celebrated Sunsaa's life with singing, dancing, music and feasting. There were many stories of him as a hunter, a fisherman, a lover, and a friend. The Chief sat quietly through most of the celebration, and when the time was right, he stood up. All eyes rested on him as Napayshni told his story from the heart: of a great man who rescued a young boy left alone and afraid by terrible evil, and of the boy becoming a man, and of the wisdom, guidance and support of his father's best friend, who had always been there to sustain him, teaching him without seeming to do so.

After this eulogy, such a eulogy, the tribe could only honor its eloquence and feeling with a time of silence as each person reflected. For a time, only the occasional cry of a baby could be heard over the sounds of fire.

Later, Asku sat alone with his father in front of their fire. The Chief smoked his pipe, taking short quick puffs and breathing out great rings of smoke that floated up into the starry sky.

"*Túta, míshnam wá?*"

The Chief smiled. "It is the great circle of life, *tita*."

"Yea," said Asku. "I guess."

"Askuwa'tu," said his father, staring at the Totem, "someday, I will leave this place." Asku began to protest, but the Chief waved his hand for silence. "Someday I will pass into the Spirit World, as those who have gone before me."

Asku nodded, staring blankly into the fire.

"When this happens, you must believe in yourself, Askuwa'tu Haylaku, and allow the Great Spirits to guide you." He took the short pipe from his mouth and pointed the end at Asku.

"And know that your father is proud."

Chapter 19

Sleep evaded Asku. All night long he tossed and turned thinking about Saigwan, the old man, and his father's words.

"Asku," Susannawa protested, "stop rolling over. You keep waking me up."

"Sorry, *nika*," Asku mumbled as he climbed out of bed. He grabbed his new wrap and made his familiar way in the darkness to the Totem.

The sky was mostly clear, the air free of the usual chilly nighttime breeze coming off the mountains. The stars flickered down upon Asku, lighting his path just a little.

The fire had died to embers. There was no one around at the Totem. Asku closed his eyes and listened to the nighttime noises—an owl hooting, a raccoon family chattering softly, a mouse scurrying nearby. He tucked the wrap around him to keep them all out, and just breathed.

Saigwan woke and found he could open his eyes, although it was dark. He found his toes and fingers and wiggled them. He took a deep breath, felt only minimal pain in his chest. He opened his mouth and tried to speak but felt his throat still painfully dry and cracked. He cleared it.

"Saigwan," said Niyol, rising from his sleeping furs in the corner. "Yawtii?"

"Water," Saigwan rasped.

Niyol held the small wooden bowl to Saigwan's lips. The water was like a cool mountain stream as it dripped down his throat. He felt life returning to his body. Another swallow and another, as the water seemed to wash away the last throes of fever.

"How goes it, Niyol?" he whispered.

Niyol sighed, an exhausted, painful sound. He grasped Saigwan's hand firmly, smiling through fatigue. He began to speak just as Kasa and Moema burst through the hide flap.

Saigwan raised a heavy hand to reassure them. "Do not worry," his voice cracked, "all is well."

Kasa spoke first. "Saigwan, we have been very worried. You have been lost in the fever for five nights, calling out and coughing. We could do nothing to help ease your suffering."

"Yes, lítsa, my dreams have been dark. But all is well now."

Both women kissed Saigwan before leaving to bring the little ones. Niyol remained by his side.

"Niyol, how did you find me?"

Niyol was quiet for a moment, contemplating something.

"The bear, Wyánch'i," he began. "The bear led me to the river. I saw your wrap first, washed up on the rocks." He pointed to the corner where the wrap hung. Saigwan smiled in thanks, a small weight off his heart.

"I ran in to grab it and then I saw you," he continued. "The bear stayed until I had you. Then he disappeared."

"Kw'ałá," he whispered, his voice beginning to clear. "Niyol, bring the Teacher. There is something I must talk with you both about."

Saigwan told them both of the bear, and of seeing Una again. He told them of the visions he had while in the river, and when the fever had him. He told them about his conversation with the great bear, and of the story he had seen.

The Teacher nodded in understanding. "This is a great gift to us, Saigwan," was all he said.

Saigwan knew it to be true.

Asku blinked his eyes as a hint of the sunrise appeared behind the Totem. The story of Saigwan's recovery left him with a peaceful afterglow.

Although sleep-deprived, he had important work ahead that day. His father had said they would leave in less than a moon, which did not leave him much time at all. He found Hawilish first thing in the morning, stoking up his family's firepit. "Today would be a good day to hunt, and I have to do some other stuff. Want to come?"

"Sure. Just let me stop by and see Kitchi and get my stuff."

"Will you see if he will lend us his *k'iplach*?"

"Okay."

They left after the morning meal. Asku led, heading for Łátax̱at Wána, where deer and elk were common. It was not a far journey over the hills, and they began to work their way upstream along the heights above the canyon.

"Are you sure we can carry a big bull elk's meat all the way home?" asked Hawilish as they eased down one of the many gullies etched into the hillside.

"Simple," Asku responded. "If we can't carry it all, we won't kill it."

"*Kúu mísh.*"

"How is Kitchi today?"

"Crabby, as usual."

"Give him time, he will come around."

"Yea, I guess. His mother said the Grandfather came by earlier today."

"Oh, yea, what did he say?"

"I guess he bent his knee a bit today," Hawilish rambled on. "So that's good, the Grandfather said so."

"That is good news," Asku replied. "Means his thigh muscle is still working, at least enough to move the rest of his leg."

"So, he will be able to walk, you think?" Hawilish asked, hopefully.

"Probably still too early to tell, but it sounds good to me."

"Hey, do you smell that?'

Asku sniffed the air. "Something dead. Not something small, either. Let's find it."

"What do we want with something dead and rotten?"

"That depends," said Asku. Then he looked down. "Hawɨlish. Stop and look."

Hawɨlish did. "*Kw'ayawi.* Cougar tracks, a couple of days old."

"Uh-oh," said Asku. "They go where we've been. See where they head up the hill?"

Hawɨlish's eyes followed the tracks. "Yeah. We'd better be careful. I doubt it's the *kw'ayawi* that died around here."

"Let's see what did," said Asku. "Look up."

A vulture glided high above. "That's pretty good. If the *kw'ayawi* were still at the kill, they'd stay away," observed Hawɨlish.

The boys followed the cougar's tracks up the slope and over into the next draw, the smell getting worse as they approached. There it was: the skeleton of a bull elk, a young one to go by the antlers, mostly picked clean. "That's perfect. That saves us a lot of work."

"Are you out of your mind?" asked Hawɨlish. "We cannot eat that, if there is even anything to eat. There will be flies and worms all over it, and I think I am going to throw up."

"I don't want it for food, *pásiks.* I want that rack. Come on."

"But you did not kill—" Hawɨlish stopped. "Wait a minute. You want the rack for what? I just want to know before I throw up helping you get it."

"I promise by the end of the day you will know," said Asku.

"Oh, all right, *kúu mish.* Then let's get this over with."

True to his prediction, within twenty paces of the fly-eaten carcass, Hawɨlish leaned over and threw up. But afterward, he edged closer, throwing up one more time. "Got the tomahawk?" inquired Asku.

"Yeah. Hurry up. I will keep watch for anything that comes, and if you don't mind too much, I think I can do it from upwind."

With the tomahawk, it took Asku a very short time to separate the antlers from the skull. He managed to do it without getting sick, headed up to where Hawɨlish sat on a rock outcrop, slung the antlers on his back and started to move out.

"That's all you need?" asked Hawɨlish, dubiously. "A pair of stinky elk antlers?"

"I will clean them up. But just one antler will do."

"Hmm."

At a fork in Łátaxat Wána, Asku turned up the tributary, away from Pahto and Toward the Rising Sun. "Now let's go to Yɨxa Xápaawish."

"That will be good. You can wash those things off. Although, Yɨxa Xápaawish may never be the same."

The river led up into higher country and onto a plateau. "I bet this is for the girl you are to be mated with from the Sea Chief's people, isn't it?" asked Hawɨlish.

"It might be. By the way, did you see Hatayah today?"

Hawɨlish lived very near Hatayah, and their mothers were friends. The question caught him off guard, and he tried to look away. "What?" he asked absentmindedly. "I mean, yeah, I saw her."

"What's up, *pásiks*?" Asku demanded.

"Nothing," Hawɨlish snapped back.

"Hawɨlish, what?"

"Nothing, man," Hawɨlish said, defensively. "We just, uh…we went for a walk this morning, that's all."

"What?" Asku snapped, instantly regretting it, then lost control again. "Really? Just the two of you?"

"Yea," Hawɨlish said. "She needs a friend, that's all."

Asku saw red momentarily, contained his anger, and increased his pace. Hawɨlish's long stride easily kept up. They continued on their way in silence for some time across the plateau.

It was a long hike to the waterfall, and the sun was well past its highest point before they arrived. Asku began to strip down. As Hawɨlish did the same, Asku pried up a rounded rock the size of a baby and set it by the pool.

"Okay, man, what is going on?" asked Hawɨlish, looking a bit nervous. "You said when we got here, I'd know. We are here."

"I will show you," said Asku, jumping into the water and swimming toward the falls.

Hawɨlish followed suit and swam over. Asku was against the side of the falls, pulling away a wedged branch and scooping handfuls of water onto something. As his friend arrived, Asku began to uncover the limestone rock.

"That is not the usual kind of stone around here," said Hawilish, taking a close look.

Asku washed off more mud and dirt, then pointed to the bluish-gray intrusion. "Neither is that."

Hawilish's eyes went wide. "Is that what I think it is?"

"Yea. The problem is getting some of it out of here."

"And how do you plan to do that?"

"It will not be easy, but I have an idea. We have no idea how far back this rock goes, but all we need is to break off a piece of it. If we can clear away enough dirt off the top of it, we might be able to hit it hard enough to break off a big chunk."

"We can't swim with that, man. Not even a *wishpush* could."

"We would not need to. It isn't far to the shallow part. If we have to, we can walk there on the bottom. When it is under water, it will not be as heavy, right? Just like when holding a person in the water?"

Hawilish nodded. "You're right. Let's get clearing some of this mud off and see what it takes." Using nearby sticks and their bare hands, the boys dug into the steep bank and underneath the rock. After about the time it would take to field-dress a couple of rabbits, they had cleared away enough dirt to expose a shelflike chunk of limestone, big enough for a small child to sit on.

"Now," said Asku, "the problem is how to get that rock over here and find a way to stand while we hit it. And hope we can hit it hard enough to break it off."

Hawilish shook his head. "If we can, you might ruin a lot of flint, man. You need a good-sized piece if you are planning what I think you are."

Asku looked over the limestone. "I think you are right. I think we are going to have to hammerstone it out. This will be a lot of work, even for two of us."

"In that case let's get started." Hawilish swam over to the shallows, where rounded rocks of all sizes were plentiful. Before long, both were chipping away at the limestone, and succeeded in exposing the flint intrusion. It was wider than a hand and went back into the rock portion still buried in the bank. Hawilish positioned his stone at a precise spot and held it while Asku delivered a heavy hammerstone blow, and a chunk came off that was about the size of two adult feet together. Asku gazed down in awe at the rare stone, looking for cracks. He found none.

"If you don't hide this, someone else may come along and find the rest," Hawilish said. They did their best to conceal the remaining stone portion beneath mud and the same branch they had used before. When they had washed all the mud and sweat from their bodies and made a start on cleaning the reek off the antlers, Asku loaded the stone into his sling, and they headed home.

The trip's final leg took longer than was good for Asku. The rock dug into his back, the antlers clanged, he was hungry, and the earlier subject kept after his mind like a buzzing fly. About halfway home from the waterfall, he finally boiled over. He grabbed Hawilish's arm, face flushed with anger. "Tell it to me straight, Hawilish. What is going on with you and Hatayah?"

Hawilish spun around to face him, jerking his arm away. "Back off, Asku," he snarled.

"What do you mean, she needs a friend?" Asku snapped again, "What are you up to?"

"Step *back*, Asku," Hawilish said, standing relaxed but ready for anything.

Asku dropped his hand to his side and looked out to their right, where he could see the cliffs Beyond Nch'i-Wána in the distance. He could think of nothing to say.

Hawilish broke the silence, looking away toward Wy-east. "You both need a friend. Maybe you even more than her. You are not the only person involved; she understands, but it hurts her too. Her heart looks like Kitchi's leg, man. The only way she can heal it up is if she can talk to someone, and that cannot be you, which you know if you think about it."

Processing that, Asku did not respond, and they kept walking. After a little while longer, Hawilish spoke again. "Look, if it makes you so mad, I will stop talking to her, if that's what you want."

Moments passed as Hawilish's words washed over him. "Well…you are a good friend," he replied.

"Am I?" Hawilish asked quietly, walking along.

"The best," Asku confirmed.

Hawilish finally turned around to look at him. "Thanks. So, you are okay with it? Can I hang out with her?"

"No," Asku replied, starting again for home. "But maybe I will feel different about it tomorrow."

"*Kúu mish*," Hawilish said.

It will be okay, once I adjust to it. Who better than my best friend?

➤

Asku got to work that night on the blade, banging away at the remaining limestone. "What is that Asku?" Nayhali asked as she pounded acorn meal at the little table.

"I believe it is a rock," he replied sarcastically, turning it over to work at the other side.

"I can see it is a rock, *nipa*." Her eyes narrowed in suspicion. "What are you doing with it?"

"Pounding it, *nána*," he bantered, in the same tone.

"You are *misht'ipni* sometimes, Asku."

"That is a fine way to talk to me. I just answered what you asked."

"Knock it off," Chitsa snapped. "Nayhali, please go round up the little ones and get them ready for sleep."

"Yes, *iła*." Nayhali aimed a kick at Asku's shin as she walked by.

"Where is the Chief?" asked Asku.

"He will be along soon," Chitsa replied. "He and Chaytan were scouting something."

Asku kept knocking bits of limestone loose. He barely even looked up when his father and Chaytan arrived. While Napayshni playfully did something to Chitsa that made her giggle, Chaytan sat down next to him.

"What are you making?"

"This? Oh, nothing much, just starting a new project," Asku replied.

"That's a beautiful piece of flint. Here—" Chaytan pointed at a spot—"if you turn it a bit, and hit right there, you should get a good chunk of the chalk rock loose."

Napayshni came over. "A new project?"

"It's nothing," said Asku. He did not look up to notice his father's smile.

While he worked, he listened as the two men discussed and debated over the scout's reports. As he listened, Asku began taking lighter strokes. He was running out of limestone and would soon be ready to start shaping the dagger. "He said it was the strangest thing he had ever seen," Chaytan stated. "Not sure what to make of it."

"Hmmm," the Chief said, rubbing his chin. "This could mean many things."

"But why would they move everything, even the women and children, sending them alone?" Chaytan asked.

Asku began to seek the soundest portion of the flint, suitable for a sturdy dagger. He ran his fingers across the bare flint surface, noting with satisfaction the absence of bubbles, cracks, and other fatal flaws. Then he remembered something. Asku set his leather and tools aside and took the piece over to his mother. "Can you help me with something, *iła*?"

Chitsa looked up from her work. "What is it, Asku?"

"Will you please lay your hand over this side of this flint?"

She did. Asku took a mental measurement. "Perfect. Thank you, *iła*." He did not see the glances and smiles his parents exchanged. Then something else occurred to him. "I am going to pay Kitchi a visit, see how he's doing," he said, rising and wrapping the stone and his tools in the leather that protected his thigh while working.

As he left, he noticed that Nayhali sat near enough Chaytan for their hips to touch, and although Chaytan paid attention only to the Chief, his left arm was hidden behind her.

Kitchi's family had just finished their evening meal. He was sitting in his chair, leg propped up, staring into the fire. Asku sat down next to him. "How goes it, *pásiks*?"

"What do you think, man?" he replied in a surly tone.

"Hey, you're up and out of the tent, so that's good. So, the Grandfather thinks you will walk again, huh?"

"Hmmpf."

"That's enough of this crap," said Asku, abruptly.

"What did you say?" growled Kitchi.

"I said 'that's enough of this crap,' Kitchi. Enough of you sitting around feeling sorry for yourself."

"That's easy for you to say, man." He looked at Asku with anger in his eyes. "You are still whole."

"Whatever," Asku continued. "You gonna sit around and feel sorry for yourself forever?"

"What do you know about it?" Kitchi snapped. His family did its studious best to pretend not to hear or see the exchange, though his mother exchanged glances with Nayati.

"I will tell you what I know. I know that you are my best friend, Kitchi. Best friends are not like wood carvings, man. I cannot trade for another *pásiks* at Wayám. So, I will not let you just sit around and mope. If I must, I will make moping more annoying than doing something about it."

Kitchi turned back to the fire again.

"Do you want to walk again?"

Kitchi nodded slightly, but his jaw tensed.

"Then walk again."

Hawilish happened by, and Kitchi's mood seemed to lift. Soon enough, the three of them were talking and laughing. After a bit, Ituha broke into their conversation without turning around. "Kitchi."

"Yes, *iła?*"

"I need that bowl of water over there by the door, please," she said.

Hawilish looked from Asku to Kitchi to Asku again. Kitchi watched his mother for a moment, then looked over at the bowl by the door. Hawilish started to rise.

"Kitchi can handle this," Ituha said, still without turning. Hawilish quickly sat back down.

Using his cane, Kitchi managed to lever himself to his feet. With hesitant and deliberate steps, he trundled over to the door, picked up the bowl, and started toward his mother. The water sloshed and spilled on the ground and down his trousers, but he kept walking. Finally, he set the cedar bowl down next to her.

"*Kw'ała, átawit,*" said his mother, without looking up from her acorn-pounding.

As Kitchi hobbled back over to his chair, Asku and Hawilish pretended nothing of note had happened. Then Asku remembered Kitchi's skill at stone working and pulled out his project. "Check this out, *pásiks*."

Kitchi ran a finger over the flint and let out a low whistle. "You can make something really nice out of that, if you take your time. What is it going to be?"

"It's for Kaliskah, the girl from the Wanuukshiłáma," said Asku. "I got some elk antlers for the handle, but I figured you would be able to help me make some decisions about how to work the blade." He paused for a moment. "It looks like special stuff, and in case Hawilish ever decides to make Hatayah something out of it, I want to know how best to help him work a piece of it."

Both Hawilish's and Kitchi's eyes went up, Hawilish's farthest. "Well," said Kitchi, "if you look at the end here, there are a few spots that are iffy..."

＞—→

Asku and the Chief sat together that night. While his father smoked his pipe, Asku shaved a piece of elk antler to smoothness.

"Will Kaliskah come back with us after the Patshatl?"

"It is hard to say," Napayshni replied.

"Okay," muttered Asku. "I was just wondering."

"She is very pretty and sweet, Askuwa'tu. Spunky, too." The Chief cleared his throat. "She is just a little older than you. Her mother died giving birth to her right around the time I became chief. She has grown up with my sister for her mother. It is the Sea People's custom that her brothers are responsible for her, but when she doesn't agree with them, she speaks her mind."

Asku let his father's words sink into his heart as he shaved away bumps and ridges on the antler. It seemed that every irregularity on the surface was a question, a worry, a fear...

Saigwan's strength slowly returned. Every day he felt a little better. After three days, he was able to rise and join the people in a celebration around the fire. He sat and watched from his chair while the mothers and young ones danced. Saigwan's own daughter joined in, to his great joy.

Saigwan raised his hands to speak.

"Inmíma átawitma tíinma, my beloved people," Saigwan began, speaking up despite the lingering pain in his throat, "the Great Spirits have spoken to me. They wish us to understand."

Saigwan spoke of the great mammoth bear's sorrow, of Aanyáy's heartbreaking misery, and of man's pride and boastfulness. Some nodded, and some bowed their heads in sadness. Others stared vacantly into the glowing embers. Yiska drew on the cave wall behind Saigwan, very near Manneha's drawing, making the gold and red blend with the brown and the charcoal. The wall looked as if it wept in sorrow.

Saigwan continued. "My people, we must never forget that all of this—" he waved his hands around him and above him— "is a gift to us. We are children of the land, and it is all for us, but we are its protectors."

A coughing fit wracked his body. While he regained his breath, the people waited.

"We must never forget this story."

>——

Niyol and Saigwan sat with the Teacher around the fire long after everyone had left.

"I want to travel to the place Manneha is buried," said Saigwan. That began another coughing fit, after which he cleared his throat and spat into the fire.

The cough had improved. At first he would cough so hard that his stomach would hurt terribly, and there would be blood in his mouth. But now, the coughing and pain had lessened, some.

"What will we do there, Wyánch'i?" Niyol asked.

"We will leave the story behind," Saigwan answered, tiredly. "We must tell the story for others to see. Our children, their children, and others."

The Teacher puffed on his pipe. "Yes. Yes, that would be wise."

"*Yawtii,*" *Saigwan asked, trying to stand, "will you help me home?"*

All was quiet and dark at Saigwan's tent as Niyol helped him under the flap and to the fur bed. Moema looked to be asleep. Saigwan got out of his clothing and laid down next to her.

"*Come,*" *Moema said, not asleep after all. "Let me hold you tonight."*

Saigwan fell into a peaceful sleep in the crook of her arm. He did not dream.

Chapter 20

Asku blinked his eyes, shook his head a bit. The peaceful visions were easier to wake up from than those that left him shaking or sweating or crying out. They all felt so real, as if he could reach out and touch the cave walls and the people there. He had heard the stories of old all his life. Now he felt the stories, he wept through the stories, he feared the stories. He lived the stories.

The village was already awake and had begun to buzz with general excitement. The Patshatl was a time for reunions, gifts, trades, and the display of crafts and finery. Every family was preparing in some way.

Asku found Hawilish on his way to the garden. "*Mishnam wá?*" Hawilish asked.

"It is a good day," Asku said, smiling. "What are you up to?"

"Garden. You?"

"Same," Asku smiled. "I hope I remember everything she wants."

Hawilish got them talking about ways to include Kitchi in this or that, and they became absorbed. They didn't see Hatayah coming their way until they heard her voice yelp in annoyance and embarrassment. She had tripped over something, sending her basket's contents everywhere. When the boys ran up, she looked mortified.

Asku took her hand, pulling her to her feet. "Hatayah, it happens. We will help you pick all this up."

Hatayah held her basket out while Asku and Hawilish gathered the fallen vegetables, the basket becoming heavier and heavier. Asku could see her arms beginning to strain under its weight, and he reached for it. It seemed like a great many vegetables for one family.

"*Mishnam wá*, Hatayah?" he asked.

"I am well," she answered, pleasantly. "And you?"

"Well, thanks," he replied, as Hawɨlish loaded the last of the vegetables. "Looks like quite a feast."

"Actually, I was trying to help out the mother next to us. She began her birth pains today and has no one to feed her little ones. I guess I overdid it."

"I am sure they will be thankful for that. But it does look pretty heavy for you. Not for Hawɨlish, though."

Hawɨlish and Hatayah both looked at Asku, who stepped back as if he had done the only natural thing. "Of course," Hawɨlish said, with a smile for Hatayah.

"*Kw'ałá,* Hawɨlish," Hatayah replied. "That would be wonderful."

Asku felt one more twinge, dismissed it. *Who better than him, anyway?*

And what all did Mother say for me to bring back? And where is Nayhali? Seven corn...I remember that much. Must be expecting Chaytan again tonight.

He twisted the corn carefully from the stalk, so as not to damage the plant, then took a moment to re-tie a portion of that corn stalk's attendant bean plant. The garden was empty except for one woman named Kimama, who was in the far corner picking berries with a little one on her back, humming a lullaby. He could see the drying shed across the trail, not far from the edge of the village. Plenty of traffic passed both garden and shed on the way to Nch'i-Wána, but hardly anyone went into the shed unless there on some errand.

As Asku glanced that way, the shed's door opened. Chaytan looked out, glanced both ways, and came out. Nayhali was right behind him. They both looked mussed, and Chaytan had done up his trousers strangely.

Asku stepped back out onto the trail and snorted, a bit too loudly. "*Míshnam wá,* Chaytan?"

Chaytan cleared his throat. "All is well, Asku. You?" Nayhali glared at her brother as she tucked her shirt back into her long skirt and tried to straighten up her hair.

"Um, just gathering some things for Mother." He tried, and failed, to cover another snort with a cough.

"Great. Well, I will be going now," Chaytan said, already halfway to the village trail.

Asku exploded with laughter, doubled over with tears streamed from his eyes and down his cheeks. His sister had not followed Chaytan and was looking daggers at him. "Are you happy?" she steamed.

"I am laughing my head off. Do I sound unhappy?"

"This is not funny!" she hissed. "Did you really have to do that?"

"Okay, sorry, Nayhali, but you could have picked a better place," Asku said, between viciously suppressed chuckles. He wiped away the current crop of tears.

"Well, we were just talking. I guess one thing just led to another, and we got carried away."

"Uh-huh." Asku snorted again. "What if Mother had come along instead of me?"

"Well, she did not, and Kimama is a friend of mine. I do not think she will remember having noticed anything, and I think if Mother came along, Kimama would find a way to let me know. Obviously, she did not realize that my brother is *misht'ipni*." Nayhali's voice shifted effortlessly to a wheedle. "Please do not tell Father, Asku? Please?"

"Why would I do that?"

"It's just…well, myself, I would not mind." she said. "But Chaytan worries so much about what Father thinks."

"Nayhali. I will not tell, all right?"

"*Kw'alá*," she sniffed.

"What were you two up to anyway?" he teased.

"Hmmm, that is none of your business," she said, royally.

"Yes, *Wyánch'i*."

"Shut up, Asku. What did Mother tell you to bring?" She headed around to the garden door and came in.

"Um, a medium-sized squash," he said, a snort leaking out. "Yech, I hate those things."

Nayhali chose a dark green squash, twisted it off with care, and placed in Asku's basket. "One squash. What else?"

"How come I have not heard anything about your mating ceremony, *nána*?"

"What else does she need?"

"Uhhh, beans. Grandchildren."

Nayhali rolled her eyes and sighed.

"Come on, *nána*."

Nayhali sighed and looked at the ground. "Father gave his approval, but he said we must wait until after your ceremony."

"What?" Asku stammered. "Why?"

"Yours is more important, I guess," she said with a sad little smile. "Oh, it's okay, *nipa,* don't look like that. It is more important to the people, you know."

"I am sorry, Nayhali," he mumbled.

"Knock it off. It's okay. Chaytan likes to hang out at our home anyway. That will change after the ceremony. We will have our own place, right?"

Asku walked toward the other half of the garden, where Kimama was still picking berries, apparently deaf to all recent events. "Blessings today, young *Wyánch'i*," she said, breaking into her lullaby. The baby was asleep.

"And to you," he said in a low voice, gathering a couple of handfuls from the *wisík* bushes in the corner. "Berries. Check."

"Great," Nayhali said. "If that's all, let's go."

Asku stopped at the Grandfather's herb garden. "No, there was one more thing."

"And you have forgotten it, of course."

"We are not all good at everything. Some of us are good at remembering garden errands, but not so great at 'talking' in private."

She swatted him on the shoulder and quietly called him a very unflattering name.

Asku closed his eyes, ignoring her. "Ummm. This is annoying me. Sage, chives...no. What was it?"

"Ugh, *nipa*," Nayhali snapped. "What is she making?"

"Well, Father took Sus fishing, so...I think she said trout and steamed vegetables."

"Satureja?" she asked, as if leading a slow child to the obvious conclusion.

"That is it! Thanks."

He looked over the rows of herbs and found the short round bush covered in little white savory flowers. He cut a handful off and handed them up to Nayhali.

"Do you love him?"

"With my heart," she replied with a deep sigh. "But…"

"But what?"

"But sometimes I wonder if he loves me because of Father."

I have somewhat wondered that too. Nayhali is not stupid. However, I have a feeling that if I tell her that I have had the same thought, it would be very bad.

"Well, I think you are wrong," he said. "Chaytan loves you too and he will take good care of you."

"I think he would. I just would not wish him to do that because he was afraid our father would disapprove. I would feel better if I believed he would want me even if I had no father, or an unimportant one. What about you, are you excited?"

"No, not in the slightest."

"Aw, come on, *nipa*," she teased as they walked through the gate and up the trail, "not at all?"

"Nope."

"There is my daughter," said Chitsa. "I was beginning to think we should send out a scouting party to track her down. *Mishpam mishana*? What have you been doing?"

Nayhali opened her mouth to answer, then shut it as Asku replied, "I met her along the way, *ila*. I asked her to help me. I had trouble remembering what all you wanted."

"*Kúu mish*," Chitsa said, taking the basket. "Askuwa'tu, will you watch the girls, please?"

"Sure. Where are they?"

She pointed to the tent as the two women collected their water baskets. As they headed down the trail, Nayhali turned once to smile at him.

Inside the tent, both little girls were sitting on the big bed playing with their shells from the Great Sea. They did not notice him, so he ducked back out before they did.

Asku got his project materials and sat down, laying the leather over his thigh and taking out the beautiful flint piece. After the talk with Kitchi, he was sure where to strike it. He began to make short, careful strikes, creating the overall dagger shape and examining the stone for revealed flaws. Where his work created premature edges, he roughed them off before continuing. He measured the future tang against the chosen portion of elk antler he had been smoothing; no point in hollowing that out until he knew exactly how wide the tang would be, for a close fit was desirable.

When he had the general shape near to what it would become, Asku decided to get some more smoothing done on the antler piece. *I still have to figure out what I'm going to carve on this handle. It will come to me.* After a while, he had the handle very near smooth, and probably enough to carve. It would be much easier to carve the design before fitting the handle to the tang. Something about the entire process made him feel light-hearted and grateful.

Kw'ałá, *spirit of the elk, for leaving part of you where I found you, and spirit of the cougar, for the way I benefited from your hunt.* Kw'ałá, *Yixa Xápaawish, for laying bare this rare stone that will enable me to give my future mate such a gift. You are all from my world. I know Kaliskah will honor you all as she uses it and respect your gifts to her.*

Asku next began to work the tang into the shape necessary to slot into the antler, stopping between each stroke to gauge the right point, angle and necessary force. It must not be too narrow, lest the dagger break easily during use; it must be suited for a tight and permanent fit. It made no sense to put the final edges on the blade until the very end. With careful pressure strokes from a deer antler, useful for finer work, he worked the tang into a shape that would fit well.

When Asku was ready for a break, he stuck his head in the tent. "I am going visiting Kitchi, unless no one here is interested in coming along."

Moments later, small warm hands grasped his own. The two little girls loved visiting. Boys generally roamed free, injuring themselves and testing unwise notions. In the busy drudgery of day-to-day life, girls did not often get far from their mothers.

Asku and his sisters arrived to find Kitchi sitting by the fire, talking with his father. Both were looking at something in a basket. Kitchi noticed them and beckoned. "Hey, man, come check this out."

Asku looked over Kitchi's shoulder. Crouched at the bottom of a tall, slender water basket were two of the largest scorpions Asku had ever seen. "Wow, where did you find those?"

"The rocks down by the river," said Nayati. "Have you ever seen ones like these before?"

"Not that big, at least not around here. On the plains and across the river a way, they may get that big. And it looks like it will be time for another chapter in Mat and Sus's lessons in which creatures do not make good toys."

Nayati held the basket up to let the little girls peek in. Nis'hani squealed and backed around Asku, burying her face in his trousers. Asku picked Mini up and parked her on his shoulder for safekeeping. "What's that?" she asked.

"That, little ones, is a scorpion," Asku pointed at it while gripping the squirmy little legs tightly with his other arm. "It has a stinger on its tail that can hurt you much worse than a yellowjacket or wasp. If you ever see one of those, you back away from it and get me or Father right away, or some other adult. *Mishnam pamshtk'úksha'*?"

There was no response. Asku grabbed Nisy by the shoulder and forced her to look into the basket. She did not like it but did not have much choice. "Make sure you remember what they look like, *litsa*."

Nis'hani opened her eyes, squealed, and turned away. "Can they jump up and bite me?" she asked.

"No, they cannot jump. And they do not bite, like you bite food. It is easy to step on them by mistake, so watch out."

"Well," said Nayati, picking up the basket, "I think the Grandfather will have a use for them."

Asku directed the girls to the wooden toys Ituha kept near the cooking area for her little ones.

"What are you up to today?" Kitchi shifted in his chair.

"Not much. Watching the girls. But the funniest thing happened today."

"What?" Kitchi asked, interest sparked.

"Well, I was at the garden today, trying to remember what I was supposed to bring home, and I happened to spot something interesting coming out of the drying shed." Asku started laughing all over again.

"What was it, man?" Kitchi prodded.

"Well, I kept watching, and out comes Chaytan with his trousers done wrong," Asku snorted with amusement. "Then out steps my sister, all mussed up."

"Good thing it was you and not the Chief. Could lead to a hunting accident, if you know what I mean. You gonna tell him?"

"No, why would I tell him?"

Now Kitchi looked serious. "Asku, he should not be doing that to your sister, man."

All of a sudden, the story was no longer funny. Asku's stomach tightened.

"You are right. Hey, what's up? You've never said anything like that before."

"Nothing," Kitchi said, looking embarrassed. After a pause: "Well, it's just that Nayhali's sweet, and I always wondered if Chaytan's good to her, you know? Plus, what if…you know? That would be bad, man."

"Yeah, you're right. I have to say something, I guess."

"Hey, before you do that, could you help me with something? I want to see if I can walk without my cane."

Asku tried not to sound as excited as he felt. "Do you think you might be able to?"

"That's why I want to try with no one around."

Asku smiled. "Let's do it."

"Okay." Kitchi took a deep breath and shifted his body in his chair, lifting his elevated foot and lowering it to the ground. His expression was pained.

"Does it hurt?"

Kitchi thought for a moment. "Naw, I guess I'm just afraid it will."

"*Awnam wá wishúwani,*" Asku said, standing at Kitchi's left. "Are you ready?"

Kitchi sighed, nodded, then slowly raised himself to his feet unassisted. He kept his left leg stiff and straight. He sucked in an involuntary hiss of pain.

"*Náy*…okay?" Asku asked.

"No. It does hurt, man," Kitchi hissed through gritted teeth.

"Want to sit back down? We can try another time, or I could get the cane."

"No. I am tired of sitting on my butt all day." Kitchi grabbed Asku's shoulder and stood tall, stretching his back and neck.

"Take a step," Asku encouraged.

"Gonna try." He leaned heavily on Asku for a moment, put a bit of weight on his left leg, and moved it forward a bit. As he did, he let out something like a viciously stifled scream, but held steady and shifted forward onto his right foot. He took another step, stifled another cry, and kept going for four or five steps. "*Kúu mish*. Now help me sit."

Asku pulled the chair around the firepit, and Kitchi sat down with a sigh, careful to keep his leg straight out in front of him. "Man, you did it! You walked!"

"Yeah, I did," Kitchi said, with a decompressing sigh.

Nisy clapped excitedly from the other side of the firepit. Kitchi took a small bow with his upper body.

"Have you tried to bend your knee?"

Without waiting for his answer, Asku took Kitchi's heel in his hands, lifted and slowly pushed it closer to the chair. Kitchi grabbed his thigh, his face scrunched up in pain, but this time he made no noise. The knee kept bending as Asku pushed it partway to its normal seated angle.

"Kitchi, look. Open your eyes."

Kitchi did. His leg was bent, about as far as it would normally bend while walking. "Wow," he said, half smiling. "Okay, let go now!" Asku put the leg back in its usual propped position.

"You did it," he said, patting Kitchi on the shoulder.

"Yeah, I guess I did." Nisy clapped again from her spot by the toys.

Kitchi and Asku talked for a while longer about the weather, hunting, and the Patshatl. When the girls became restless, he excused himself to take them home.

Nayati came up just as Asku and the girls were leaving. His eyes picked up on the shift in Kitchi's position, cane, and mood. "Blessings today," said Asku.

"And to you, Askuwa'tu, young *Wyánch'i*," replied Nayati.

They soon found the Chief and Susannawa cleaning two big trout. Chitsa was preparing the vegetables. "Blessings, Askuwa'tu," Chitsa said, looking up.

"And to you, *ita*. I have good news. Kitchi is beginning to make progress in walking."

That got Napayshni's attention. "How is he?"

"Better, *Wyánch'i*. There is no way to tell how well he will eventually walk, or if he will run again, but he now knows he can take a few steps without a cane and bend his injured knee."

His father smiled and returned his focus to his trout. "That is very good news, Asku."

"I thought so too." Asku turned to his sister. "Nayhali, may I speak with you for a moment?"

A nervous look crossed her face, but she put down her cooking preparations, and followed him out onto the trail anyway, then behind the dwelling. She wiped her wet hands on her skirt. "What?"

"I will have words with Chaytan."

"No, you will not," she said, hushed but indignant.

"I will."

Nayhali sighed, her shoulders falling. "Why, *nipa*?"

"Because" Asku began, "I want to know where he stands, what he plans to do."

"Please don't," she whispered.

"All right. Would you prefer that our father have the words?"

"Asku, you promised." She covered her face with her hands and started to cry.

"Nayhali," he said, not unkindly. "It has to be this way. We could talk with him together, if you prefer."

Nayhali paled. "*Kúu mísh*, but no, I don't want to go with you."

"Why do you cry?" he asked. "Do you think that I would block you from being happy?"

"I am sorry, Asku," she whispered through her tears. "I am afraid that he does not love me, and I thought...well, I thought that if I gave myself to him, that he would love me more than he loves the Chief."

Asku put a hand on her shoulder. "That is why I need to talk with him, Nayhali. It is my place."

She appeared about to protest, saw something in his eyes, and aborted the entreaty. When she had wiped away her tears, he led her back to the family's area. Chitsa and Napayshni both looked up, and neither missed their daughter's wet and puffy eyes.

"What's amiss, you two?"

"Nothing, *iła,*" Nayhali said, quietly resuming her work.

"I forgot something I have to do," said Asku.

The Chief stopped his filleting and looked at Asku for a moment. Nayhali looked away. After a moment, the Chief nodded his approval and resumed his work.

>——→

Asku went down to Nch'i-Wána, then worked his way upstream to a small but familiar indentation in the riverside. There he found Chaytan sitting on a rock, fishing. He looked up at Asku's approach, an odd look in his eyes. "Blessings, Asku. I expected you would come find me."

"And to you," said Asku, bottling his emotion as best he could. "How is the fishing?"

"I am not catching anything. Other than that, not bad."

Asku sat down, stared at Chaytan until he looked back. *Here we go.* "Chaytan, I need to know your plans with my sister."

Chaytan did not reply. Asku waited, then continued.

"Do you love my sister?"

Chaytan stared back at Asku for a long moment, then closed his eyes for a few seconds. "I do," he said, opening his eyes.

"Then you understand that she, and her future, are very important to me."

Chaytan cocked his head a bit, looked at Asku again. "And to me as well. Please know that I meant no disrespect to you, your father, or Nayhali."

Asku scowled. "You were not very discreet. I would rather we had spoken about this before learning about it while gathering in the garden."

"What would you have said?" asked Chaytan. "Have you never before had an interest in a girl?" He seemed to be on the verge of saying more, then held his tongue.

Asku felt a twinge and a sudden urge to punch Chaytan off the rock. He took a deep breath. "I do not know. But I cannot imagine that I would have been more concerned than I am now, finding something going on outside my knowledge."

Chaytan smiled. "But you do know what it feels like to care for a woman, and to want her, and to be unsure what you should do."

Inside his mind, Asku used most of the bad words he knew. *He's right. If it were me sitting on that rock, and an older brother of Hatayah's in front of me, what would I want from him?*

Some sense of understanding, maybe. Especially realizing that I might become part of his family. And I do not hate Chaytan. He is part of the family already, almost. I cannot imagine him mistreating Nayhali.

Okay.

"Chaytan, we need an understanding, you and me. You will watch yourself with my sister until after your ceremony. One day, I would be glad to call you my brother. But if you hurt my sister in any way, adopted uncle or not...*Mishnam pamshtk'úksha*'?"

"Yes." Chaytan ran his fingers through his long hair. "I understand you. It was wrong of me. I will control myself from now on."

Asku stood up and put a hand on Chaytan's shoulder. "Caring about my sister is not wrong. Just please, from now on, keep your belt tight."

Chaytan nodded. "Fair enough."

"You should haul in your line and come with me. She needs to see you. She is very angry with me, you realize."

"I see why she would be, but it was your place," said Chaytan. "You did what I would have done."

"My father has caught some trout. There should be a good dinner soon."

They took the long walk back up the trail. Neither spoke until they reached the edge of the village. Chaytan stopped.

"What will the Chief say, Asku?"

"Nothing, I expect, since he does not know. And since you have given me your promise, and I know you will honor it, and especially since that means Nayhali will not end up with child before she has a mate to provide for her, I see no reason why he would need to know."

"She will not be."

The two walked around the trail to Asku's home, where the family was gathered for dinner. Asku walked past them all and took a seat opposite the fire, where he had left his project and tools.

"Blessings today, *Wyánch'i*," Chaytan greeted Asku's father, his voice a bit shaky.

The Chief's eyes narrowed. "I have been looking for you."

"I am sorry, *Wyánch'i*. May I have a word with Nayhali first?"

"Of course. We can talk afterward."

"Yes, *Wyánch'i*." Chaytan reached for Nayhali's hand.

Once they had disappeared out onto the trail, Chitsa turned to her elder son. "Askuwa'tu Haylaku, what is going on?"

Napayshni spoke before Asku could. "Chitsa, it looks to me like Asku has things under control. Let's leave them all be."

Asku took out the elk antler piece and began to make some more of the slow progress of routing out the dagger's future haft. His mother came over to look at the piece. "I think that will be a very beautiful dagger. Do you have any plans to carve something on that?"

"I am still trying to decide, *ila*. I would like it to be special, with symbols that have meaning to the one who will use it. I believe I will know when I know."

"May I see the handle?" asked Chitsa. Asku handed it to her, and she took it in her hand as if a blade were installed in it. "Very good, Asku. It would be a little small for you, but for a woman's hand it would be just right," she said, handing it back. Asku did not see his parents' knowing smiles, but they happened all the same.

When Nayhali and Chaytan returned, they were holding hands and smiling. While Nayhali went to help her mother, Chaytan helped Napayshni and Susannawa clean up. Asku kept an ear tuned in that direction.

"He did not go all the way," Chaytan said, "just to the mountains again, where Asku went before."

"Well, someone must go the full distance to the village. We must know what they plan."

"I agree," Chaytan said. "I will go."

Nayhali looked up from her chopping, concern in her eyes. Then she noticed that Asku had caught her and dropped her gaze.

"I will go too," Asku added.

Chitsa spoke without looking up, quiet but firm. "I would rather you did not, Asku, if possible."

"Can you give me a reason, *átawit*?" asked the Chief.

"I can think of many, besides the help he gives Nayhali and I," said Chitsa, "but the greatest is that Kitchi's progress in healing is important to us all, and Asku's encouragement offers the best chance for that."

Napayshni remained quiet for some time. "You are right about that. However, Kitchi also has a family to encourage him, and seems well started on regaining use of his leg. Asku is known to the Wawyukyáma, your family, and his connection with them is important to our future. This is a chance for us to build those ties. And Chitsa, I believe that you would trust your son to your Elk Plains family above anyone but me. I will also send Hawilish, and we will send for U'hitaykah; he will want to be there too. Do not worry, *átawit*, he will be safe."

Chitsa looked dubious. Asku put an arm around his mother. "I will be fine, *iła*."

Chapter 21

The messenger was long gone to the Wawyukyáma, and the plans were set. Asku, Hawɨlish and Chaytan would leave before dawn. Kitchi, of course, could not go.

That night, Asku lay in bed next to Susannawa, listening to his family's quiet breathing in the silence of night. He could not stop thinking about Kaliskah. *What will she think of me? And what will her father, the chief at the Great Sea, make of me? What about her older brothers? I know how that can go from today.* After a restless night, he got up long before the sun and made his way toward the Totem.

Saigwan's story was just bits and pieces, scenes flashing behind Asku's eyes. Pain and fear, of not being strong enough, of hurting those he loved—it was Saigwan's pain, yet also his own.

"Blessings on this early morning, *myánash*," the Teacher said, in his habitually quiet voice.

"Blessings, *Sapsikw'ałá*," Asku replied sadly.

"What is in your heart, Asku?"

"*Sapsikw'ałá*, I feel a great weight upon my shoulders. And sometimes I feel I cannot bear it. Other times I feel I can." He paused. "I guess I just worry that I will fail, that I will let our people down."

The Teacher took a deep breath. "Your spirit is strong, and in your heart you understand what the Great Spirits have destined you for. You will make mistakes, that much is certain."

"That's what I am afraid of."

"Do not fear those mistakes, *myánash*. They make us who we are, and they make us stronger."

I do not understand, he thought, gazing up at the Totem. And then he gazed to the top, and upon the bear. *That's it! That bear is a symbol of my people.*

And I must carve it on Kaliskah's gift, so that it stands for myself and us. But it should not be all. Then what else? He gazed at the Totem for a moment. "*Sapsikw'atá*, I have a question."

"Ask anything in your heart."

"Thank you. I am making a special gift for Kaliskah. Until now, I had no idea how to decorate it in a suitable way. The Totem has inspired me to carve into it a great bear, like the one at the top. That will symbolize our people. But I do not know what to put on the other side, as a symbol of her people. I do not really know them."

The Teacher was silent for a few moments. "Her people know the Sea as we know Nch'i-Wána. I have been to the Great Sea. There is a fish, very distinctive, that swims in the sea but will not swim up Nch'i-Wána. I believe that it must have the salt that is in the Great Sea in order to live. At their village, I saw many decorations and images of fish, including the giant *sut'xwtá* that they hunt from canoes using great spears. It is more dangerous than a bison hunt in many ways, and men who hunt the giant fish are acclaimed mighty."

"Must I hunt such a fish in order to earn respect from Kaliskah?" Asku wondered aloud.

"I do not think so, though if you are offered the opportunity to join in such a hunt, you must surely not decline. Not, of course, that I believe you would even think of that. But there is a special fish found at the Great Sea. It is like a *sut'xwtá*, but not as big as others. It is black and white with a dorsal fin as tall as a man. It is the size of several dwellings. I hope you see one while you are there, but not too close. Many tribes along the Great Sea believe the Blackfish houses the spirits of warriors that have passed on, the Wanuukshitáma included. While the Sea Chief's people revere this fish, and do not kill him for food, neither do they crowd him when at sea, any more than you would crowd a great bear."

"Wow. So, he is to them much as this bear is to us?"

"Very much so."

"If I knew what this fish looked like, I could carve him on the other side of the handle of Kaliskah's dagger. Would that be respectful of their ways? I do not want to show up and offend their spirits."

The Teacher smiled. "There is something ancient and wise in you that emerges now and then, *myánash*. If you knew more about that, you would be more confident in your future. But to answer you directly, yes, it would be most respectful."

"Can you describe the Blackfish so that I can carve it, *Sapsikw'ałá*?"

"I cannot, not in a way that would enable you to represent it, because its markings are difficult to put into words. But I can help in another way. While you are out scouting, I will paint an image for you. I will show it to no one. By the time you return, you will have a picture to emulate."

Asku felt his heart leap. "*Kw'ałá, Sapsikw'ałá*. That is the final thing I needed in order to complete this gift." Asku saw the beginnings of the Rising Sun. "And now I must prepare for the travel."

"I will see you when you all come by for your blessings."

>——

"Are you prepared, *tita*?"

"I am," Asku replied. His knife was tucked into the sheath on his waist, the whalebone bow slung across his back. Chaytan and Hawilish flanked him.

"Stay hidden," the Chief instructed. "Go to the village, watch and listen as long as you need. We must know what they plan. U'hitaykah speaks the Pyúsh language. He will be able to understand them."

Asku nodded. "Yes, *túta*."

"Note how many able men they have, weapons, horses, anything else they may use against us," the Chief continued. "The scout said he saw women and children, all alone, heading Toward the Great Mountains."

"Yes, *Wyánch'i*, we will find out what they are up to."

"And Asku," the Chief said, taking his son by the shoulders, "be careful. This time, no one goes off alone."

"We will not. We will be alert."

And up the great river they paddled, leaving their canoe at the ford where the river bent Toward the Great Mountains, then walking at a quick pace. They did not hunt, but only scavenged berries and nuts along the way to supplement their trail rations. Other than the occasional trader's canoe on the first leg headed up Nch'i-Wána, they had no encounters. In the evenings, when possible, Asku worked away at routing the antler handle.

Four days later, the trail turned Toward the Great Mountain Range and brought them in sight of *Wíshpush Tínmá*, standing proud guard over the spot where Pa-lús joined Pikú-nen. "They are supposed to meet us here," said Asku. "But we should not make ourselves obvious."

"Then let's hide in the brush where they keep that canoe," suggested Hawilish.

"How are they supposed to find us, then?" asked Chaytan, slipping into the small hollow behind the brush.

"Like this," said Asku. He began to trill his tongue in a swift *aloo-aloo-aloo* like the crane, a bird that flew over the region in the thousands at the end of each year's cold season. The arrival brought the whole tribe out to celebrate the coming of a new season. He waited for a response, looked around and across the river, but nothing. "We must be early."

"Good. Then we can take a rest," said Hawilish, settling in for a nap. Chaytan whittled while Asku kept watch, gnawing on a piece of jerky in the shaded little grove. After about as long as it would normally take to paddle across Pikú-nen, Asku spotted three mounted men leading three riderless horses on the far bank. One rode the beautiful messenger horse, another the dark stallion, and the third rode a horse unfamiliar to Asku.

"That is them for sure," said Chaytan, quietly. "Hawilish. Wake up." As he shook their third member awake, Asku gave the crane-call once again. They did not seem to hear it yet. He watched them navigate to the ford, then ride their horses straight into the river at a swift pace. As they approached the bank, Asku saw U'hitaykah come into view and heard him give the crane-call. Asku answered with it, and soon the three Patisapatisháma were face to face with three Wawyukyáma warriors.

"Blessings on this fine day, *káka.*"

"And to you, young one," U'hitaykah said in his deep voice. "How is your injured friend? It is too bad he could not come."

"He is improving. You all have met Chaytan, I think, and Hawilish I know you have."

"Yes, we have. Blessings to you both as well. You remember Aanapay."

"It is good to see you, *káka*," said Asku, rubbing the dark stallion's neck. "And you, Aanapay. *Mishnam wá?*"

"I am well, Asku," Aanapay smiled, his joyful, contagious smile.

U'hitaykah introduced the third member of his party. "This is Mach'ni, another member of our tribe, who was away when you were last here. He is a fierce hunter. There are none braver, nor stronger."

Asku found it hard not to stare. The man was as big as a bear and had arms the size of Asku's thigh. His long hair was plaited down to the middle of his back. He wore a menacing knife, longer and sharper than any Asku had seen before, and had a colorful coup stick tied to his belt. He did not smile.

U'hitaykah's group secured their horses, then sat down near the river to discuss plans. Aanapay picked up a stick and began to draw in the dirt.

"On horseback, we will travel upstream along Kimooenim. It flows down from the mountains we will be going toward, and that will take us about two days. Well below their village, we will secure the horses and approach on foot. They have guards and dogs at certain spots around the edges of their camp, here and here," he said, drawing a circle and marking the two spots. "Our best time to approach is at twilight."

U'hitaykah nodded. "Twilight will be good."

"Will we split up?" Asku asked.

"Yes, we will go in pairs," said U'hitaykah as he reached for Aanapay's stick. "But we will not enter the village; that is too dangerous. Asku, you and I will find a spot to look into the village from this side," he said, pointing to a cluster of huts on the farthest side from where they would approach, "so we have to sneak around the village very cautiously. Chaytan and Mach'ni will make false tracks and a diversion here." U'hitaykah pointed to a spot across the main path and Toward the Rising Sun from the village. He then pointed out a cluster of trees on their way to the village. "Hawilish and Aanapay will wait for us here."

"The village has sparse river trees on either side, and the ground is sloped, so we should be able to approach in cover," Aanapay explained. "There is a fence surrounding the entire village, poles stuck in the ground. While it means we must get above it to see in, it means that not everyone inside can see out, either."

"They will be watching, though," U'hitaykah spoke again. "They attack often, as they are attacked often. It is their way. We must be very careful."

"Won't the dogs smell strange people approaching and alert them?" asked Chaytan.

Aanapay reached for a bag of dried sage. "Before we approach, we will smoke this, and then rub the ash all over ourselves. It should diminish our scent, and the dogs will not smell something interesting." He handed Asku a small bundle of the aromatic herb. Asku sniffed, then nodded.

"There are storage huts in a circle around here," Aanapay continued, drawing in the dirt just inside the fence at the spot where Asku and U'hitaykah would scout. He drew another, smaller circle in mid-camp. "These are family homes, and the ceremonial fire is here in the center. There are many smaller fires near each home, not unlike our own villages."

"The busiest place at twilight will be those fires," Chaytan said. "Especially up in the mountains. Even in the warm season, nights are cold there."

"Yes," Aanapay agreed. "Which means each should bring a wrap, so that if he is being motionless and observing, he will not freeze his balls off." There was laughter.

"Mach'ni, Chaytan," U'hitaykah began, "get close enough to look, but not too close. Note how many able-bodied men there are, what kind of weapons they carry. And get a good look at that chief and his heir, if you can tell who it is, before you create a diversion. Whatever you do, it has to be something that will keep dogs from tracking us to the horses. Once we get mounted up again, we will be fine." The two men nodded their understanding. To Asku, Mach'ni looked like more the type to rip out a pole from the palisade and rampage through the village swinging it like a club, but he seemed to accept the plan.

"Asku and I will scout from this side. If possible, we will get close enough to listen in on their plans, or at least take a good guess." U'hitaykah thought for a moment before turning toward Chaytan. "What did your scout say again?"

"He did not go to the village," Chaytan replied. "From the crossing he saw mothers and children walking, carrying many belongings."

"Which direction?" Aanapay asked.

"Toward the mountains that are in the direction of the Rising Sun," Chaytan replied.

"No escorts?" Mach'ni's rough voice sounded like something dragging over gravel.

"None. He said it was the strangest thing, just a line of mothers and children. All carrying things on their backs, about fifty of them, he said."

"Why would a tribe send their mothers and children away?" Mach'ni asked no one. "And to what place or people would they go?"

"It's hard to say," U'hitaykah stated. "That is why we must see for ourselves, brothers."

>——

Asku climbed onto the white painted mare's back and felt at home again. A pattern emerged: they would make good time for a while, and then Aanapay would stop the party to water the horses and inspect their feet and legs for trouble. After the stop, they would walk for a while to rest their mounts. As the sun fell low, Asku walked his horse next to his uncle's.

"How go things at the Great River, *píti*?" U'hitaykah asked.

"We are well. Busy preparing for the Patshatl, which is all very exciting…I guess."

"Yes, it is," U'hitaykah laughed, "for the women. For the rest of us, it is a lot of planning and worry." Asku laughed. "How is our young friend, Kitchi?"

"Kitchi is well, *káka*. He took a couple of steps recently without his cane, and even bent his knee a bit."

"That is very good news indeed."

The sun was dipping just below the horizon as they reached the trail junction Asku recalled from before. No one was in sight. Their path along pleasant little Kimooenim had made a gradual curve along with the river until it aimed them straight at the Blue Mountains. U'hitaykah pointed toward a grove of trees off the main trail. "We will sleep there. We cannot have a fire this night because it might give the Pyúsh P'ushtáayama a good reason to send out scouts."

"Tomorrow we must travel as if we could be observed any time," said Aanapay. "The less we are out in the open, the better. The only problem with riding horseback is that it makes us taller and much easier to spot. Our biggest danger is boys."

"Boys?" asked Hawilish, doubtfully.

"Well, older boys," explained Aanapay. "Who is most likely to decide to go downstream and look for something interesting to do, or to catch, or to climb? They would be alert for anything unfamiliar, such as us." Asku and Hawilish nodded understanding.

They snacked on pemmican and dried bison jerky in the darkness, and Asku broke out his antler and tools. He had left the blade home, where it could not be broken by accident. When everyone grew drowsy, like the rest, Asku pulled his wrap tight and lay down to sleep. The night was noisy along Kimooenim: bats, owls, mice, a pack of coyotes in the distance.

Exhausted from days of hard travel, Asku slept soon if not in peace. His dreams were filled with mothers and children walking with nowhere to go and no one to protect them, reaching forks in the road and not knowing which way to go.

━━➤

Aanapay rousted them awake well before dawn. "It is time for our method of foiling their dogs," he said, as his comrades rubbed sleep from their eyes. He already had a tiny fire going, which he fed only with tinder and fuel that produced minimal smoke.

"How does this work?" Asku inquired.

"First," said Aanapay, "we light these little bundles of sage. Fire can be seen for a long way at night, so it is important to hide it well. Try to get its smoke all over your body. We woke up in the dark because we have a better chance of hiding the small fires at night than hiding a column of smoke in the day. Rub the ash on yourself too, especially in your hair and under your arms."

"Won't the dogs still smell the horses?" asked Chaytan.

"On that, we hope for the best," said U'hitaykah. "We will at least rub some ash on them, though. If wind is blowing hard toward the village, we may have to tie the horses farther away. Dogs are always making noise. We just need to avoid them going crazier than usual when we get close."

Following Aanapay's guidance, they bathed in sage smoke and ash, then rubbed as much as they could on the horses. After breaking camp, the scouting party followed Kimooenim with care and at a distance, crossing draw after draw at a walk. "The Wind Spirits must not be very happy with the Pyúsh," commented U'hitaykah at a stop. "Right in our faces, just what we need."

"I can see why," said Asku. "The Pyúsh were probably rude to them also." Everyone muffled laughter.

In the afternoon, Aanapay and U'hitaykah conferred in a small grove of trees along Kimooenim, then stopped the party.

"Here we will tether the horses. The village is a short walk up the river, on the other side, and there is good cover all the way." U'hitaykah drew a small map on a sandbar. "One could walk there in the time it would take to clean some trout. We will approach on foot, on this side of the river. When we are just almost in sight of the village, Aanapay and Hawilish, you will hide well and be ready to cover our retreat if we have to leave in a hurry."

"He's a good shot," said Asku. "They learned that the first time." Mach'ni's face came within a shade of a smile.

"That is very good," said U'hitaykah. "So is Aanapay. The rest of us will cross the river closer to the village, then divide up. Asku, you and I will sneak up on the river side and try to find the best place to observe. Mach'ni, you and Chaytan will circle around the other side. If you can see anything useful, that will be great, but do not take chances. When their activity begins to die down for the night, start a brush fire and circle back to Aanapay and Hawilish. When they notice the fire, that will be Asku's and my signal to return as well."

"A fire will be suspicious, won't it? There is no storm," said Chaytan.

U'hitaykah nodded. "Definitely. But it will confuse them, and that is all we need. Also, they cannot avoid doing something about it, or their whole village could burn down. We will wade partway through Kimooenim on the way back, to confound tracking, then cross and untie the horses. If pursuit is too hot, cut the tethers; we brought spares. If all goes well, we will be past the trail crossing before they even figure out which direction to search."

When dusk fell, the six made their approach to the village. When the central fire was visible, Aanapay put a hand on Hawilish's shoulder and gestured him to find a good spot. As Chaytan and Mach'ni crossed the river and headed around the Rising Sun side of the village, U'hitaykah motioned Asku up the Setting Sun side. Staying low, they came in sight of the village under cover of the trees lining the river.

Asku's stomach was uneasy. *Where was it that my father caught up to the evil Snake chief all those winters ago? Am I near the spot where he saw the chief raping his sister? Where he heard her cries for help? Was it in this spot that the fifteen-year-old chief spilled the blood of another?*

There was plenty of noise from the village, with rays of firelight passing out through the palisade. This consisted of roughly barked tree trunks sharpened to points. Although side by side at the very base, the posts began leaning away from each other further up.

They stopped where the palisade began to curve away from the river. U'hitaykah looked around for a moment, then pointed to what looked like an enormous ancient willow set back a few steps behind the stream. Asku ducked under the long, droopy branches to find that it was not one old willow but a cluster of younger trees. He shinnied up one of the thicker trunks, inhaling the musty sharpness of its scent. Midway up, he found a branch sturdy enough that he could step out onto it while holding onto others. He moved carefully around until he found a good viewing perch. U'hitaykah lay below the tree and whistled once, like a hooting owl, to signal that there was no other trunk thick enough to hold his weight. It would fall to Asku to see what needed to be seen from this side of the village.

Asku closed his eyes first, listening, smelling, breathing. He smelled, he tasted: smoke, meat roasting, vegetables steaming, tobacco, the wet smell of old cedar and mud, bodily wastes. It smelled different than his village, somehow unhealthy. He would ever after associate that odor with the Pyúsh P'ushtáayama and with places where something was wrong.

He could see the outer row of storage huts, round pit houses partially underground with roofs of woven branches and grasses. Farther out, he could discern another row of similar but smaller buildings. These must be the family homes, although Asku could not see much sign of family activity.

Then Asku found a direct line of sight between two homes to the ceremonial firepit at the center of the village. Men sat around the blazing fire, sparks climbing in a thin line of smoke. Asku watched for a while, noting people, weapons, animals, all he could. *Thirty, maybe more. Eating, smoking, a couple of guards watching. Dressed as I remember with bare chests, trousers, not unlike my own people.* Some wore jewelry on wrists, necks, ears, or noses. All of their heads were bare but for the long strip of hair over the scalp, braided tight and long down their backs.

The chief was obvious, in his tall feather headdress that fell all the way down his back. He sat in silence, smoking a long pipe. Asku stayed up in the tree until he heard an owl's hoot. His uncle motioned him to come down, and Asku made his way to adjacent cover.

"How many men did you see?" U'hitaykah whispered.

"About thirty, *káka*. No women or children."

"Did you see the chief? Was it the same man?"

"Oh yea, it was him, the same man that came to our village," Asku said, a knot tightening in his stomach. U'hitaykah probed him for details about weapons, different tribal hairstyles and dress, everything one might ask about a village. Some details Asku had noted, and others he filed away as those he should have noted. He offered to go back up, but U'hitaykah declined, as they were close to the time when the diversion should begin. "If they need water, they will get it from the river. That means they will come our direction, so we must not delay getting out."

Asku thought for a moment. "*Káka*, those pit houses are permanent, right?"

U'hitaykah nodded.

"Don't the Pyúsh travel to Nch'i-Wána this time of year? There is often a group of them downriver, at Wayám. That village is a winter village. Why are they here now?"

"A good question." U'hitaykah looked toward the village once more. "Come on, Mach'ni." After about the time it would take to clean a large salmon, Asku heard a commotion. All the dogs in the village seemed to bark at once and run toward the back of the village, where the entrance was. Men raised their voices and followed. Asku watched as they ran toward the growing brush fire, within bowshot of their village. Some ran in opposite directions to gather baskets and water, others stopped to grab hides to smother the flames, and still others went for earth-moving tools.

"Píti," U'hitaykah whispered, "time to go." Once they began to get farther from the village, U'hitaykah walked in the river for about the length of a longhouse, then got out on the far side and made his way toward Aanapay's and Hawilish's position. Asku kept close behind, doing as his uncle did.

U'hitaykah stopped short and hooted, hearing the same in return. When they arrived, only Hawilish and Aanapay were present. No Mach'ni, no Chaytan. "They are not back yet?" asked U'hitaykah.

"They are," said Aanapay. "They took a captive and should already be with the horses by now. The Spirits were with us. We will tell you more when we are safely away, okay?" U'hitaykah nodded, and the four began to work their way toward the horses' position. Aanapay went last, watching for pursuit.

When they reached the horses, Mach'ni and Chaytan already had the mounts untied. Next to them, gagged and with hands tied behind his back, stood a slender young warrior with a long braid and scalp otherwise shaven. He radiated pride, anger and courage. "We will explain later," said Mach'ni. "For now, Hawilish, you ride with the prisoner." Hawilish nodded and helped Mach'ni to assist the captive onto his mount, then climbed on behind. Within moments, the scouting party was headed toward the trail crossing.

They rode carefully until they were near the trail, checked for campsites, then rode across it and headed farther up Kimooenim than they had previously camped. When Aanapay reined up at a good camping spot, they dismounted, hoisted the captive down, sat him down, and surrounded him.

"All right," said U'hitaykah. "What is all this about, Mach'ni?"

"The firemaking went well," growled Mach'ni. "We set it in several places so that by the time the Pyúsh noticed it, it would cause them a lot of worry. On our way back, Chaytan spotted this hunter, also watching the camp. We stopped, and I came around him and captured him. He did not resist or make noise, or try to alert the Pyúsh, which was wise on his part. So, we brought him back, and got him as far away from the village as possible right away. Now we can get some answers."

"Indeed, we can," said U'hitaykah. "You did right, Mach'ni. Now you can take his gag off."

Mach'ni did so, roughly. U'hitaykah spoke gently, yet sternly, in the Pyúsh tongue.

The young man spat at his feet.

Mach'ni backhanded the captive across the face, knocking him sideways. Blood streamed from his nose, and he spat it again in U'hitaykah's direction. This time, Mach'ni pulled out a knife and showed it to the captive, within a hand of his face.

The young man tried to rise to his knees and looked U'hitaykah in the eye. "Who are *you*?" he snarled.

Asku perked up. *That was the Elk Plains language, which is much like* Chiskin...*our way of speaking.*

"Ah," U'hitaykah said, smiling. "You speak our tongue. You are not Pyúsh P'ushtáayama?"

When the young man did not reply, Mach'ni squatted in front of him and pulled his head back by the long plait. "Now that we know you understand," Mach'ni growled, only a blade's width from the young man's face, "you will speak, or I will make sure you cannot speak ever again."

"No, I am not Pyúsh P'ushtáayama," the captive snarled. "Well, my father was. My mother was not. I am no longer one of them."

"No longer one of them?" U'hitaykah beckoned him to continue.

The captive did not answer. Mach'ni lifted his hand, but U'hitaykah gestured him to wait. Asku's uncle and knelt down in front of the young man. "You have nothing more to fear by us, *siks*," he said, gently. "If you speak."

"Who are you?" the young man asked again, one swelling eye fixed on Mach'ni.

U'hitaykah shook his head. "You are brave, young man, but for now, we are asking the questions. If you answer ours, you may get answers to yours. Now, your story. Begin with your name."

Mach'ni sat down near U'hitaykah. Both the young man and Asku breathed sighs of relief.

"I am called Keme. Many years ago, my mother was taken from a plains tribe during a raid and was brought here. My father took her as his mate. He took good care of her. I was born first, my brother next, and two sisters followed. My mother taught me your speech."

Aanapay stood quickly, causing everyone to turn in concern. "Your mother?" U'hitaykah silenced him with a warning eye and hand, gestured him to sit back down. Then he waved at Keme to continue.

"The chief was killed not long after, not far from here, actually." He nodded his head down the hill. "The stories say that a young river chief slew him."

U'hitaykah turned slightly toward Asku, whose heart was racing.

"The dead chief's son was made chief, although just a boy of ten or so, but his throat was slit in the night only a day later."

The young man lifted his head to the night sky momentarily. Then his eyes seemed to glaze over as he continued.

"The dead boy's uncle proclaimed himself chief immediately. Many believed he was the one who killed the boy. Now, even more believe this."

"Who is he?" U'hitaykah asked.

The young man spat at the ground, but not at U'hitaykah. "His real name is Matunaaga, but some call him Matchitehew—'Filled-With-Evil.'" Keme paused. "Matchitehew has many followers. They take what is not theirs, they quarrel often, and they hurt others. All fear them."

"Or hate them," snarled Mach'ni.

"Keep going," U'hitaykah ordered. "If we want you to stop, we will say so."

Keme nodded. "Some moons ago, Matchitehew came to my father. He desired my mother, but my father refused him. Later, when many men were away hunting, my father included, he took her. She fought back; there are scars on his flesh still to prove it."

Asku felt sick, imagining his own reaction to such an event. He no longer wanted to hear this story.

"Matchitehew dragged her by her hair to the ceremonial fire, where others held her as he had his way. He dishonored her in every way a man can dishonor a woman. Others did too. When they were finished, my mother tried to stand again, covered in blood and evil seed, and Matchitehew threw her into the fire. She burned there."

The young man continued, eyes like flint in the dim light. "When my father returned, with others loyal to him, they gathered the other women and children together in the night and sent them away to safety. I and my brother were to lead them." His eyes showed the pain of the memory. "I sent them on their way and promised to follow, but felt I had to return to check on my father. I crept to the village edge at nightfall.

"He had been caught. By the time I got there, my father hung there, at the fire, with three others. Their bodies were impaled on tall poles."

Keme was silent for a while, but U'hitaykah did not press him. Aanapay looked to U'hitaykah. U'hitaykah nodded, and Aanapay knelt in front of the young man. "Her name. What was your mother's name?" he asked, voice unsteady.

The young man met Aanapay's gaze. "Liseli, Warmest-of-Sunshine."

Aanapay's head fell in defeat. "But did you know of a woman named Aiyana? She was taken in a raid also, maybe about the time as your mother?"

Keme shook his head. "There was no one in this village by that name."

Aanapay stood up, crossed his arms, and walked away.

"Well, Keme," U'hitaykah said, "it seems we may share some history."

"Many years ago," Aanapay interrupted, his voice strained, "my mother was taken from us in a raid, possibly the same raid. Aiyana was her name, Eternal-Blooming-Flower."

U'hitaykah finished his sentence: "We have done all we can to find her. Others were taken also. We feared them all dead."

"I was a little boy when they took her away," Aanapay continued, steadying his voice by force of will. "My father and I had gone fishing when we saw smoke rising from the summer village. Horses were coming toward us. He pushed me into the bushes. I watched him try to fight them all off, try to save my mother and the others. I saw him die in the dust there. She was screaming for him. I ran after her, a very long way, before the Chief found me and carried me home."

Keme watched Aanapay for a moment, then looked to U'hitaykah. "You understand, then, that I must finish what my father started. I will be finished when I see Matchitehew's own agony."

"Yes, son," U'hitaykah nodded, "but you cannot achieve this alone."

"Where are your women and children?" Chaytan asked.

"They are five days Toward the Great Mountains and the Rising Sun," Keme said, pointing across Kimooenim. "At the village of one of the chief's mates. I have been there. They are safe, for now."

"Here, the Great Mountains must mean the ones that are also Toward the Rising Sun?" whispered Hawilish, to Asku. Asku nodded.

"But how long until Matchitehew follows?" Chaytan asked.

"He will not," Keme said. "Not yet anyway. Matchitehew will raid again, against the peoples Toward the Setting Sun from here. Then he will deal with the women and children who left. I expect he will show up where they have gone and demand their return."

Asku saw in his mind the great chief kneeling before the Totem, his blood spilt, its greatness crying out to the ground and to the ancestors, the evil angering the Great Spirits. And the mammoth bear watching from high above.

His young son, now chief, chasing in the darkness, adrenaline and hatred mingled with suspended sorrow pulsing through his veins. And the cries of a young girl—of pain and of fear.

U'hitaykah's voice brought Asku back to the present. "*Píti?*"

"Yes?"

"We must prepare." U'hitaykah turned back to Keme. "How long do we have?"

Keme looked from U'hitaykah to Asku and back again, realization dawning.

"He plans to attend the Patshatl with the Wanuukshiłáma during the next moon. He may scout the villages once more."

"How do we know this all is true?" Mach'ni spat. He stood up, pointing at Keme. "We are to believe him…one of them?"

Hands still bound, Keme jumped toward the bigger man, staring him down. His nose and lip still bled. "For two moons I have been hiding from what were my own people, sleeping during the day, sneaking into the camp by night, watching for my chance to kill him. This land holds nothing but pain for me. Its *buha*, its balance, is in ruin thanks to Matchitehew. But I will not leave until I avenge my mother and father, alone if I must. For them, my brother and sisters, and for my people."

Mach'ni sat down. Asku felt a chill of understanding.

U'hitaykah nodded. "You are no longer alone. Mach'ni, Keme is a gift from the Great Spirits. Please untie his hands. This is the answer we came in search of. We will spend the night and then we will head home to prepare."

Asku turned to look at Hawilish and Chaytan before nodding at his uncle. Mach'ni released Keme's bonds and returned his gear. "Come," Keme beckoned, looking up into the night sky, "I know a place we can rest the night."

They followed Keme a bit farther up the river, just past where it bent Toward the Setting Sun. Just up one of the rolling hills, Keme pointed in the darkness. "If we go past those riverbed trees, into that draw, there is a small cave."

"Mach'ni, you and Chaytan scout up with him while we see to the horses," said U'hitaykah. Before long, all seven were squeezed into a rather small cave nestled in the hillside. It had a small firepit in the center of the sandy floor. While Keme kindled a quick fire, the men arranged themselves as best they could fit into the small cave. Before long, exhaustion took everyone off to sleep.

Chapter 22

Come morning, Hawilish and Chaytan left to check on the horses and hunt for food. U'hitaykah had suggested that they make a late start of it, get some rest, and learn more about the intentions of the Pyúsh. He lit his *chalámat*.

"We must kill him," Mach'ni started again. He had been repeating it periodically since U'hitaykah's acceptance of Keme. "I will just sneak in and kill him. I will do it now!"

"It is futile," Keme said. "There are too many that will fight for him, and another will surely rise in his place."

"Why?" Mach'ni snapped. "Why do they follow him?"

Anger flashed across Keme's eyes. "He and his brother instilled fear in my people for two generations. Until you have lived in that way, you do not know how that is. Those that follow him see no other way and are afraid. My father said that Matchitehew would often tell them that other Pyúsh bands might come to attack them. And considering Matchitehew's actions, that was not impossible."

"How many men will remain loyal to him, Keme?" asked U'hitaykah. "Asku saw thirty or more."

Keme thought for a moment. "Right now, there are somewhere around thirty, but more are expected Toward the Rising Sun. Matchitehew has many likely allies. He has probably made them promises."

"Of what?" Mach'ni beckoned, breaking sticks and throwing them into the fire.

"Goods, horses, weapons, women," Keme stated, as if that were obvious.

"From our people, you mean?" Mach'ni snapped, looking from U'hitaykah to Asku and back again.

"And the Wanuukshiłáma," Keme added quietly. "Perhaps at Walawála and Tlakluit. I believe he would gladly raid his way down Nch'i-Wána and past Wayám, killing anyone who might get in his way. It would be his way to seek to kill other chiefs, in hopes of causing confusion and lack of leadership. He wants to control the river trade."

"I see his weakness," said U'hitaykah. "As one who rules by fear, he supposes others are like him. He does not imagine that some chiefs lead by respect, and that killing them would only make their tribes come together more strongly in anger."

The fire was blazing when the hunters returned, a young black-tailed deer across Chaytan's shoulders.

"Keme, our brother," U'hitaykah said, "tell us a story of the Pyúsh P'ushtáayama."

Keme took one long, deep breath off the *chalámat* before passing it to Asku.

"The Pyúsh…"

Long ago, our Mother was dark and void.

The Great Spirit moved across the vast nothingness and breathed life into her. He gave her night and also day. He placed the Sun in the sky and the stars each in their chosen place.

The ground and the waters He gathered in their place; mighty rivers flowed, infinite seas ebbed and tide, lesser streams trickled, immense lakes overflowed banks, shallow ponds rippled.

Then the Spirit breathed life to the land; mountains formed, ominous and grand; trees grew from the ground, roots reaching like tentacles toward water; plants of all kinds sprouted from the ground— fruits, vegetables, berries, nuts, flowers, herbs, and all the healing things.

The seas, the rivers, the streams, the lakes, the ponds filled with life. Fish and great animals of water jumped and swam for joy with their new being. The mountain, the tree, the sky, and all the land awoke and roamed freely to all corners of Mother Earth.

All creatures of the land, of the sky, of the water and all those in between cried out and danced and sang to their mighty Creator…

…and the Great Spirit was pleased.

But soon the Spirit realized something was missing. "My beautiful Sun, what is missing?"

She heard His great voice as it echoed off the veiled stars. "Oh, Great Spirit," she whispered, "what you have created is mighty, and glorious, and beyond compare..."

He spoke again, His voice like a soft breeze: "My lovely Sun, but what is missing?"

Sun closed her eyes, she thought long and hard, she rose and fell, and as she did, she watched the creatures as they came and went, as they woke and as they slept, and she wondered.

"Great Spirit," she whispered, "I would like to speak with one of them, to know what is in their hearts, to know what it is like to soar over the highest reaching mountain top on wings of brown and white...to blow cool, salty water from the top of one's enormous head as it climbs to the surface of the great dark deep...to feel the sand across one's belly as it slithers to and fro across the hot, glaring desert."

"Oh, Great Spirit, I smile down upon them every day and will do so until you choose the end of my existence. But what I desire more than anything else is to know what is in their hearts."

Just then, a whirlwind blew at the ground below her, and a form took shape from the very dust of the Earth. As the dust cleared, Sun could see the creature's form.

He stretched his limbs, wriggled toes and fingers and stood. Aanyáy giggled to herself. He had no wings, he had no scaly skin for moving across the ground, he had no blowhole or tail.

But then the Great Spirit spoke like a mighty wave, "My magnificent Sun, this is Man...and I am pleased."

Sun took a deep breath and warmed Man's nakedness with her rays of tenderness. He stood taller, stretched his back, and shielded his eyes as he tried to look up at her.

"Man," she affectionately whispered into the breeze, "tell me of all that is in your heart."

Man smiled, and Sun shined.

"Sun and man have always had an unstable relationship," Keme continued. "My mother told me similar stories from her people, stories of

Aanyáy. My father used to sit and listen with us. He loved listening to her."

Hawílish handed each man a skewer of meat ready for roasting, woven back and forth through a sharp stick. Asku held his over the flames and thought of Keme's mother and father. The sharp stick in his hand was an ugly reminder of man's capabilities.

Keme continued…

Sun loved Man. She loved watching him as he basked in her warmth or swam in the coolness of the lake or sat at the edge of the river fishing for the beautiful trout that lived within.

She began every day as the one before. "Man," she called, "what is in your heart?"

They had many talks of what the sand felt like between his toes, of her warmth upon his neck, of the juicy red berry upon his tongue, of the water trickling down his back. But soon Man seemed sad.

"What is wrong, Man?"

He said nothing but waved her away with his hand and turned his back to her. She followed him, shining brightly upon his path as he walked. Man walked for many days, turning into many moons.

"Man," Sun called out again, "tell me of your sadness."

He stopped and looked upon her, something different in his eyes. "Why am I here?" he shook his fist at her, raising his voice.

"Man," she whispered, upset at his anger, "why do you shout and shake your hand at me?"

"Sun," Man cried out again as tears dripped down his dark cheeks, "you rise and fall each day, you warm our Mother, you light the way, you cause the living things to grow and produce. But why am I here?"

A voice came from the sky like a whisper on the wind—and Man fell on his face.

"Man," the Great Spirit spoke, the wind wrapped around him like a gentle touch, "you are here because I put you here. You are here to care for your Mother, to watch over the beasts of the ground, of the sky and of the seas, to keep balance, Buha. You are here…and here you will remain."

Man sat on the ground in silence for a very long time. Sun waited.

Finally, Man stood, brushed himself off, looked once at her and turned his back again. Sun waited for the voice. She held her breath, knowing His wrath would be great, His voice like thunder shaking all the land, but nothing happened.

All was still and quiet, except for the soft footsteps of Man as he walked.

Time passed and Man did not come to Sun, not once. He built a shelter to hide from her presence, his head low when he came from it to fish or to bathe. She watched sadly as he needlessly killed many creatures and did not set their spirits free. Man cut down trees, not for firewood nor for shelter, but just to watch their mightiness fall. He purposely trampled beautiful things as he walked. Balance was lost. The Mother began to cry out in pain and great sadness.

Darkness fell as the Great Spirit moved, great rolling thunder in the distance and a deep growling breath of wind from the sky. Man felt the ground freeze below his feet, saw his breath as smoke from a fire, heard a soft cracking as the stream next to him froze in a great sheet of ice.

Man raised his eyes to Sun beckoningly. She could do nothing as she felt the sadness emanating from the Great Spirit, felt it in His breath as He veiled her in deep suffocating darkness—and she saw Man no more.

U'hitaykah handed Keme the *chalámat* as he awoke from the trancelike state of storytelling.

"Why do the Pyúsh P'ushtáayama call themselves Snake?" Chaytan asked as he handed Keme a sizzling skewer of meat.

"Many, many winters ago," Keme began, after taking a bite, "all of the Pyúsh lived along a narrow, winding river far from here, in the opposite direction you came to approach the village of Matchitehew and somewhat Toward the Rising Sun. The great mountains were on one side. And from the height of those mountains, I was told, the river looked like an unending snake. So, they took the name Pyúsh, after the river, or so I heard. Then later, as time went on, the great Pyúsh tribes split. Smaller bands travel here and there."

"But why do they bring destruction to others?" asked Hawilish.

"They have not always," Keme continued, "nor do all of them. My grandfather lives almost a moon's walk past Matchitehew's village. He is Pyúsh, and a good man. And my father was a good man too."

"My brothers, let us go as soon as our meal is done. We will journey home," said U'hitaykah. He looked at Keme. "Will you come with us?"

"I will," Keme nodded sadly, "but I cannot wait long. I must finish this. I must retrieve my family and start a new life somewhere. My brother and sisters need me."

⊶

Asku rode next to his uncle on the two-day trip back to the canoe cache. Conversation was sparse, mostly centered on ways to predict Matchitehew's troublemaking. Riding along Tu-se, he overheard bits and pieces of a conversation behind him.

"How many notches you got on that stick?" asked Keme from behind Aanapay on the painted messenger horse.

"More than you have seen in winters," Mach'ni growled.

"Really?"

"Do not get him started on that stick of his," Aanapay snorted. "He will take that as a challenge to add you to it." The group laughed.

Later in the day, as Nch'i-Wána came into sight, Asku's unease got the best of him. "*Káka*, what shall we plan then? About the Pyúsh P'ushtáayama, I mean?"

"We will come before the Patshatl," U'hitaykah answered. "We will work it all out then, *píti*."

And then it was time for them to part ways. Everyone exchanged blessings and goodbyes.

"Blessings, my new friend," Asku said, patting Keme on the shoulder. "You have shown me that not all is always as it might seem."

"And to you, until we meet again."

Asku found it very difficult to watch the horses recede into the distance.

The three Patisapatisháma began the next leg of their journey, traveling in silence much of the time. It was a good time to think. Asku had grown up to see the Pyúsh as enemies, and now he considered one a brother.

"Nch'i-Wána is rough today," Chaytan commented as they let the great river take them downstream. It took a certain skill to manage a canoe when the water foamed and swelled. At one point, they recognized the clothing and gear of some friendly Wayám fishermen they knew, and an older man raised a hand in blessing.

As Asku returned the greeting, Chaytan asked, "Why are they way up here?"

"*Kúu mísh*," Asku replied.

Soon home was so close that Asku could taste it on his tongue. His heart sped up in anticipation as they rounded the bend. Some of the tribe's fishermen stood over the *nixanásh* cages in the water, and one sighted him. A younger one rushed up the narrow path toward the village to spread the news.

Asku hopped out of the canoe as the fishermen helped to beach it, stretched his back and legs, and looked up to the bluff above. He saw his mother and father, his brother and sisters, Hawilish's family, and the Teacher. He recognized others as he led the climb.

"Blessings, *Wyánch'i*," Asku held his hand up.

"And to you, my *tita*," the Chief replied. "Welcome home. We are very interested in what you have learned, but it is easier if you are only asked to tell it once. You may want to rest for a while before then."

And Asku did, but not before checking in with someone.

❧——➤

Asku came upon the Teacher in his longhouse, mixing something up. "Blessings, *Sapsikw'alá*."

"Blessings, Askuwa'tu," said the Teacher. "I look forward to hearing your tale tonight."

"I do not look forward to telling it," said Asku with a smile.

"That is good. The less said about one's own brave deeds, the better. But in this case, you must. In the meantime, I promised you something." The elder rustled around and reached into a basket. "Come here and see."

Asku felt a thrill of anticipation as the Teacher unrolled the thin hide. Painted on it was a strange fish, which touched on dim memories of Asku's visit to the Great Sea early in his youth. Most of the fish was black, but it had white patches at the eye, just below the eye to the chin, and one more in mid-body. The fish was curved, as if caught in mid-leap to display prominent front fins, a tall dorsal fin, and a flat fluked tail.

For a moment he just stared. "And that is not the animal they fish for in Kaliskah's world?"

"No, they do not hunt the Blackfish. But they often see him. He is very large. The fish they hunt is even larger. There is no *wílaps* in Nch'i-Wána even nearly that size, not even the most ancient of elders, that is the length of three grown men. And as you know, and can see from the painting, the Blackfish is thicker than any sturgeon. So, imagine how enormous the fish is that the Sea Chief's people hunt."

"*Kw'ałá, Sapsikw'ałá*. This is beautiful. How do you recommend I color the dark parts so that they will not fade when she grips her dagger over time?"

The Teacher smiled. "Well, there is a trick I will teach you..."

The whole band made its way to the ceremonial fire. Asku sat cross-legged on a *tk'ú* mat next to the Chief. As the *Nch'ínch'ima* and others gathered, people stoked the fire and passed the *chalámat*.

There are things I must say. Am I strong enough? I must be.

There was dinner, of course, a celebratory affair. After the food cleared, the mothers and children headed home for the night, and the Chief stood up to begin the discussion.

"*Inmíma átawitma tíinma,*" he began, as always. "The Great Spirits have safely returned Askuwa'tu, Hawílish, and Chaytan, and for that, we are grateful." There were nods, and hands raised to the sky. "Please, Asku, tell us all of the Pyúsh P'ushtáayama and your journey."

It was silent but for the reassuring crackle and hiss of the fire as Asku spoke of their journey. He described every detail of the village, from the pointed fence posts to the winter pit lodgings. He told them of Keme and of the evil Pyúsh chief, Matunaaga or Matchitehew as the people called him. He stopped once to breathe deeply before he spoke of Liseli's death, her mate's choice, and the three brave men, their bodies hanging on sharp poles. Asku told Keme's story of the Great Spirit creating Mother Earth and of Sun's sadness.

Then he was silent for a time, as was the gathering.

"*Inmíma átawitma tíinma*," Asku went on. "Matchitehew plans to raid again. He awaits help from allies Toward the Rising Sun. Keme believes he will come to the Patshatl, and then, before the cold season, he will raid again somewhere Toward the Setting Sun from him." He sat down feeling drained, yet as if his task were incomplete.

"What is he after?" one elder asked from across the fire.

"Keme believes they seek horses, weapons and women. This man is evil, and possibly all the men left of this band also are. But not all the Pyúsh are. Of those who follow Matunaaga, many do it out of fear, or because they know no different. He wants to take from others and to preserve his own power. If we want to preserve our people, it is important to stop him."

Asku looked about the elders, warriors, and hunters. Many nodded; some even held his gaze without looking away. A young hunter stood abruptly, his long hair blowing about his face in the wind. "*Áwna wínasha…*let's go! Aieee!" he shouted, waving a menacing jawbone club. Others joined him.

The Chief let them calm down, then raised his hands. "Liwanu, we will discuss all ideas first. The time for that may come. For now, let us discuss."

The young hunter named Liwanu sat quietly, laying his club across his lap. Asku looked around, his heart beating hard, a yelling match in his head. He stood and the circle grew quiet again.

"I am sorry, *túta*, but Liwanu is right," he said.

Liwanu jumped to his feet again, waving his weapon. "Aieee," he screamed, turning in circles from his spot at the fire. Another young man, Sahkantiak, joined in the cry.

"It is the way of the young man to seek death…his own and others," an elder said, skeptically, from across the fire. His name was U'taktay, and he was still hale enough for combat. "Are you sure, young Askuwa'tu, that this Matchitehew is worth dying for?"

The circle grew quiet again. Liwanu sat down.

"You know nothing of tribal war. You are young." U'taktay looked from Asku to Liwanu to other young men, then back. "You will see your brother, your best friend, your neighbor cut down beside you, struggling to catch a final breath, the pain, the fear and the smells of death."

"I remember a young warrior not so different from these, U'taktay," the Teacher said. "A young one who would sooner fly off for a fight than enjoy a woman's company." Chuckles and snickers rolled around the firepit.

Asku turned toward his father. "*Túta*, we cannot sit here and wait for him to come."

"Are you sure he will come?" U'taktay asked.

"Keme believes—"

"Keme believes," U'taktay mocked. "Young *Wyánch'i*, are you willing to die for what Keme believes? Are you willing to see others die?"

Asku stared back. "I am willing to die for my people. As I believe you would have at my age, and still would if that came to be." Liwanu stood again, shouted a war-cry. Kitchi rose carefully to his feet, then Hawilish, then others.

Napayshni observed the division of opinion in silence, letting the discussion play out. Finally, he raised his hands, and all sat back down.

"First we will travel to the Patshatl," the Chief said, looking at Asku. "We must be patient and sure. While we attend the Patshatl, though, we will relocate those who are not attending; to Tlakluit, or to visit relatives at other villages if they wish. We are a peaceful tribe, though we have mighty hunters and fighters. I will not risk the lives of my son, or your sons—" he pointed around the circle— "nor will I spill innocent blood. Unless I must." The last words rang in the night air.

"But *túta*," Asku continued, anger brewing, "we could take him now, before the Patshatl."

"Or better yet," Liwanu added, "we send word down river, gather our strength at Wayám, and take him out before he even reaches the Patshatl!"

The group erupted once again and continued until the Chief stood. His voice boomed with authority. "I will meet with the *Nch'ínch'ima* now. Go home, rest. We all must be in our right minds for whatever may come our way."

»—→

This was the time when Asku celebrated the sixteenth winter of his birth, The Moon When Elk Cover Themselves in Mud. He wanted nothing more than an escape to Yixa X̲ápaawish to celebrate but getting Kitchi to come posed a problem. Asku and Hawɨlish put their heads together, thinking of ways to persuade him. "We could just offer to carry him in a chair," said Hawɨlish. "That would shame him into walking."

"Maybe we underestimate him," said Asku. "He just missed out on a big journey, and things happened while we were gone. Without us around, he was probably bored. Maybe he can't wait to get away for a while."

Sure enough, the moment his friends mentioned the trip, Kitchi stood up and began walking again. He did so slowly at first, with much pain and complaining. *But I notice that the more he walks, the less he complains. I hope that means he is suffering less.*

When they were just out of sight of the village, Asku looked back over his shoulder. "How goes it, man?"

"Shut up, and keep walking," Kitchi grumbled. "Not well enough. We are going to war, and I am as useless as a broken knife."

"That's not true, and you know it," said Hawɨlish from behind. "You can shoot a bow. Maybe you can't yet run nonstop to the Tlakluit, but it sounds like we will be attacked. If fighting comes close, it will be good to have your bow to pick off anyone who gets through."

"Yeah, real heroic, man," groused Kitchi, hobbling along.

It took them about twice as long as usual to reach the waterfall. They arrived just as the sun fell behind the mountains in a beautiful array of colors. While Kitchi found a spot to rest, Hawɨlish looked around for any recent signs of a large four-legged creature with a white spot on its forehead. None was in sight, so they made camp, caught some fish, and enjoyed a good dinner. "So, man," Kitchi began, "what do you think about the plan?"

"Makes me mad," Asku said. "I hate sitting around and waiting while he's getting together more allies. But I am not in charge."

"Yeah, I guess." Kitchi poked at the fire. "But if you get a clear shot at him at the Patshatl, you should take it. I mean, I get the whole 'meaning of the Patshatl,' but come on; he's there, you're there. He's gonna have to sleep sometime, right?"

"No, that would not be right," said Hawilish. "We can't just murder them in their sleep."

"Yeah," Asku said, "I guess the Chief is right. We have not been attacked—yet anyway. To kill Pyúsh P'ushtáayama at the Patshatl, while they are sleeping and defenseless, would be a dishonor. The Sea Chief, who is Kaliskah's father and with whom we must have good relations, would be furious. It would bring shame upon his hospitality. We would anger the Great Spirits, and it would tell every tribe around us not to trust us or be our friends. And what of the other Pyúsh bands?"

Hawilish took a bite of fish. "From what Keme said, some Pyúsh have nothing to do with Matchitehew and would not be his allies. But if they heard that people here were murdering Pyúsh without cause, then what?"

Kitchi pointed to his knee. "I have cause every time I take a step. I was doing nothing to harm them."

"And we killed two of them for that, as you recall," said Hawilish. "I know it does not heal up your leg that they died, but the ones responsible got what they deserved, didn't they?"

"I guess," Kitchi muttered into the fire. "I just do not like the idea of sitting around waiting, you know. I heard your story of what Keme said, and I thought, *what if he comes and we are not there, like what happened to Keme's mother*? That could be Nayhali. Or our mothers. Or Hatayah."

"*Kúu mish*," Asku replied in frustration. "I get it, all right?"

"I don't think you do, man," Kitchi said, coldly. "What about your little sisters? You know what they would do to them?"

"What do you want me to do?" Asku said, raising his voice.

"I want us to handle it like warriors! I want us to kill him and let the rest sort itself out!"

Hawilish spoke up, much louder than usual. "*Awkláw áw!* Stop now! This is not helping!"

After a moment of quiet, Kitchi said, "I just do not want anything to happen to any of them."

"Neither do I," said Asku. "I'm going for a walk."

>——→

After Asku returned, with tempers calmed, the boys talked for a long time about Hatayah and Kaliskah, Nayhali and Chaytan, and about Keme. Kitchi had his doubts about Keme. "If you could see him, Kitchi, you would not doubt," said Hawilish. "He has been closer to Matchitehew's brutal ways than any of us. We all at least grew up with Asku's father as *Wyánch'i*. He leads us with wisdom, not fear. No one in our tribe is scared of him." Kitchi grunted.

"You would like Keme," said Asku.

"And why is that?" asked Kitchi.

"Because he is like you, you hothead. And if you were in his place, you would do everything he is doing. Mach'ni clobbered him pretty good, and still he was not afraid. If anything, you would understand him better than anyone, *pásiks*."

Kitchi muttered a mild expletive. "*Kúu mísh*. Is anyone else getting tired?"

Asku fell asleep thinking about what it would be like to lose his mother and father, to send his family away and to be ultimately alone.

And somewhere in the darkness, his dreams became nightmares again…

Asku stood on a precipice somewhere above the Totem. Looking down, he saw Matchitehew and other Pyúsh, easily recognized by their long plaits and shaven heads. As he looked closer, Asku saw that Matchitehew held Chitsa in his arms. Asku tried to scream out, he looked for a way down, but it was as if he were floating on this precipice high above them.

As Asku watched, tormented by helplessness, Matchitehew used her and threw her aside. Asku screamed for her, but she did not move again. His anger burned toward Matchitehew. Then he saw his father kneeling before the Totem, his hands bound, his face bloody and bruised, his eyes on Chitsa's lifeless form. The evil chief raised his tomahawk and brought it down with all his might on the Chief's bowed head. Asku felt the crunch of bone. He saw his father's body fall, there at the Totem's feet…

"Asku, hey man," a voice called, from somewhere far away. "Wake up. Come on, wake up!"

Asku shook his head from side to side, trying to banish the picture from his mind.

"Are you all right?" asked Kitchi, his face coming into focus. Hawilish was behind him.

"Why?"

"You were yelling for help," Kitchi said. "Bad dream?"

"Just a dream," Asku mumbled.

"Okay. You all right then, little *Wyánch'i?*"

"Yeah." Asku sat up and threw another stick on the dying embers. "Go back to sleep. I'm fine."

Hawilish was soon snoring away. Kitchi tossed and turned, but his breathing finally slowed to the rhythmic sound of sleep. Asku watched the flames of the fire, feeling the heat's comfort on his face, mesmerized by the colors and the strange way they danced with the breeze. He closed his eyes as the Great Spirits called to him once again, and floated across time...

Chapter 23

All was ready for their journey into the mountains to the cave of the mammoth bear. Though the tribe had three moons supply of food, Saigwan felt uneasy about leaving. His sister and Moema were both blooming with child again, and the tribe lost at least one mother each winter on the child bed. He knew that he could not protect them from this fate if the Great Spirits deemed it theirs.

Five of them left at dawn; Saigwan, Niyol, two strong hunters, and Yiska, the gifted artist and storyteller of their tribe. Across his bent shoulders, one of which had been seriously injured in a fall years ago, Yiska carried a heavy sling filled to the brim with charcoal; twig brushes, the ends chewed until frayed; small wooden bowls for paint; sinew and fat for mixing.

Saigwan's cough had returned as soon as they ventured from the cave, sometimes violently, the stomach pains doubling him over at times. Niyol asked whether they should turn back, but Saigwan shook his head and waved him away, trying to hide the blood he spat.

Later that day, Saigwan warmed himself by the fire while Niyol and the others hunted. Yiska sat next to him, most of his face buried deep within his wrap for warmth. Saigwan watched the flames dance, enjoying the warmth on his face and hands. His chest hurt every time he took a breath, but the warmth helped.

"How do you feel, Wyánch'i?" asked Yiska.

Saigwan poked at the fire, "Some days I feel better. Some, worse."

"The others worry," Yiska said, pulling dried leaves from his sling to mix a hot tea for Saigwan.

"Yes, I know."

"It is the circle of life, my son. You will heal...or you will not." There was silence until the tea was ready, and Yiska handed the stone bowl to Saigwan.

"Kw'ałá," Saigwan nodded as the smell of the herbs soothed his aching chest.

That night Saigwan curled up in front of the fire and closed his eyes. The others sat around, passing the small *chalámat* and talking quietly, their voices and the crackle of the fire lulling him into a half-sleep. He felt himself lost somewhere between waking and dreaming, the fire warm on his face and his wrap tucked tightly around the rest of him.

In his mind, he heard the Teacher's voice clearly: *"Saigwan, be strong. Have courage. The Great Spirits will guide you. Listen to them..."*

Then he heard at a great distance: music, tapping, chanting, whispering. Saigwan knew it was them, his people, calling to him.

Saigwan awoke later to darkness, silent except for the whistle of the mountain wind and the quiet crackle of the remains of their fire. He sat up, stoked the fire and looked around. The old man and two hunters were asleep. Niyol stood at the edge of a ravine looking down.

"How goes it, yawtii?"

"Something is not right," Niyol said, nervously. *"It is too still, and there is a voice in the wind."*

Moments passed as they listened. The wind rose and fell, then seemed to roar down the side of the mountain and through the ravine. The wind spoke, although not in words he could understand.

"What is that?" Niyol asked.

"Kúu mísh," Saigwan replied, *"but it does not seem to mean us any harm. Go get some rest. I will sit up now."*

"No, I think I will stay right here."

"As you prefer. Wake me up if anything weird happens." Saigwan laid back down and pulled his wrap tight. It started to snow again. He watched the fire and he listened.

The wind picked up again and seemed to stop just above, and then roar over their heads. He could hear it yet could not feel it. It whooshed and moaned over his head. But it was just wind.

Then all became still, and he heard a voice.

"Saigwan," the voice said clearly, "Wyánch'i, my young Wyánch'i."

"Yes," Saigwan whispered, urging the voice, "I am here." He heard crying. "I am here, spirit," Saigwan said again. "Speak to me."

And in the fire, Saigwan saw a vision of what they sought: the great bear's cave and the two graves before it. He remembered it clearly from before.

"Yes, that is what we seek," he whispered.

Then the wind shifted from the other direction. It roared and cried, and it hit him hard. The wind swirled around their camp, churning up dust, snow, and debris around them. Saigwan stood in the midst of it all.

Confused and afraid, the others jumped to their feet and drew their knives. But the wind whirled around Saigwan only. His wrap fell to the ground. His long dark hair whipped around his face. Saigwan waved Niyol back.

The fire went completely out.

Saigwan closed his eyes. In his mind he saw the cave where Manneha and the great bear's bodies rested, though their spirits did not. Then he saw the other cave, the cave where the angry mammoth bear had massacred the mothers and young ones.

He opened his eyes, and the wind was still. His knees began to shake and give out. Niyol caught Saigwan just before he hit the ground.

"What was that?" Niyol asked. Had there been light, Saigwan would have seen him very pale.

Saigwan sat down. "I am not sure, yawtii. I felt a spirit pass through me, it spoke to me. I know where we are going."

Yiska smiled, and the hunters nodded. Niyol looked skeptical.

"Trust me, pásiks."

>——→

Saigwan stood at the mouth of the cave. It was the cave they sought, the one that haunted his dreams.

The graves stood as still and silent reminders. The head of the great bear was gone now. The stick remained, although slightly askew.

Animal tracks led around the graves and the open area in front of the cave, yet never seemed to enter.

Niyol approached the cave opening slowly, spear in hand. "None entered here. I cannot say why."

"Hmmm," Yiska whispered to Saigwan, "even the animals fear what has happened here."

One of the hunters knelt before a particularly large set of paw prints. "These tracks are fresh, Wyánch'i."

"Wolves?"

"Yes," the hunter nodded. "Five or six of them, I think."

"Okay. You two set a fire and keep watch. We will go in."

Saigwan stood before Manneha's grave and felt his throat tighten with emotion. He rested a hand on each mound and bowed his head.

When the fire was going, Niyol handed Saigwan a torch and entered the dark cave first. Saigwan and Yiska followed. They heard no animal sounds, no dripping, nothing indicating movement.

There was nothing in the cave. Saigwan approached a fur-scattered area marking the spot where the great mammoth bear must have slept for a very long time. Saigwan wondered how long the animal had stayed here, and what he had been waiting for.

"Let us build a fire here."

Soon the cave was alight and warm. As the smoke rose, Saigwan looked around. The side walls were rough and uneven in most places, but the back was relatively smooth. Yiska spread his wrap on the ground and began mixing his paints and preparing the wall.

Saigwan sat at the fire, facing the old man across the blaze, and closed his eyes. "Great Spirits," he whispered, "we are here, speak to us. May the great bear find peace from our visit, from his pain...from his story."

The flames roared up before them, crackling and snapping. Saigwan and Niyol quickly moved back as the flames danced in front of them: red, orange, yellow, blue. Saigwan blinked his eyes. He could make out faces in the flames.

The flames continued to grow. Oblivious to the fire behind him, Yiska began painting a scene: a bear, the great bear, his mate, and two younglings trailing behind as they walked along a steep cliff, their great feet leaving huge prints in the snow.

And Saigwan saw the scene in the fire: the mammoth bear walking, his family following him. The flames blue, the smoke swirling around them. The bear family seemed to walk closer and closer to where he sat. Saigwan held his hand up to them but felt only the heat of the fire. He blinked and they were gone.

Then a new scene erupted within the blue flames. Through them, Manneha waved. From somewhere behind, a little boy came running and jumped into Manneha's arms as he swung him around and around. A beautiful, dark-haired woman walked up from behind him, a child in her arms. Manneha put his arm around the woman and the little family turned. They followed the great bear family into the flames, until they were also gone.

And the old man began painting Aanyáy high in the sky, her rays beaming down upon the bear family, upon Manneha's small family, her smile vivid in the warmth of her rays.

The flames rose higher yet. Saigwan saw the two brothers, walking along a cliff edge in knee-deep snow, wraps pulled tightly around their faces as the flames swirled around them like a whipping wind. Then Saigwan saw the two in a dark cave, cold and still, lifeless, frozen in time.

The painting on the cave wall became the circle of life, though Yiska did not directly see the fire's story behind him. He drew the great and mighty deaths of Manneha and the bear, their lives and deaths intertwined.

Then a new scene appeared within the flames, and Saigwan's heart pounded: his sister lay upon the childbed. Her screams echoed out of the blue flames and off the cave walls. A child appeared, and then the two vanished.

The flames fell back into a small fire with regular cracks and pops. Saigwan closed his eyes...

And she was there again, behind his eyes. So beautiful, without a burden...without his burden.

She walked along the riverbed, her hands swirling in front of her, her hair whipping around her. She seemed to be singing, although Saigwan could not hear the words.

The great bear stepped out of the brush next to her and walked with her. His great head rolled from side to side, the same rhythm as her hands.

Saigwan stood on a precipice above them. He sat down cross-legged and watched.

Across the river, Manneha appeared: bare-chested, young and strong, unwounded. He matched her step for step. The two brothers stepped behind him, dropping the wraps from their shoulders, the knives and clubs from their hands, onto the ground. They walked, their steps matching Manneha's.

Saigwan breathed in and out, in and out, from where he sat on the cliff edge.

Above him, the clouds opened up as Aanyáy beamed down upon them, her rays of light and heat a smile upon her face. The spirits were swept up in one great whirlwind of sunshine and disappeared into the clouds above him.

He blinked once and the clouds had reformed, dark and ominous. Aanyáy was gone.

Saigwan opened his eyes. The story was all there, on the wall: the great mammoth bear's life and death, the mighty Manneha's pain and sorrow and agonizing revenge, and the brothers that followed him through it all.

A great whoosh of wind swirled through the cave, blowing out the fire. It carried voices: singing, weeping, and laughter swirled around them and rushed from the cave.

"Niyol...Yiska," Saigwan whispered.

"I am here," Niyol replied.

"Yes," said the old artist.

The two hunters came rushing in, torches dousing the darkness once more.

"Wyánch'i?" one asked, sounding badly rattled.

"Kúu mísh," he reassured the young man. "We are all okay."

"There were voices," the other man said, breathless. "It—or they, or whatever that was—came rushing out of the cave just moments ago."

"Yes," Saigwan said, standing up. "It is over."

He walked over to the wall and laid one hand upon the old painter's shoulder. "Kw'ałá, grandfather."

Saigwan felt Aanyáy upon his face as they emerged from the cave. Her warmth and light were a gentle touch. From that moment, Saigwan felt his strength return. He felt his lungs clear and his heart lift, and he could breathe without pain.

Asku opened his eyes just as light crested the horizon. It seemed as if the Spirits planned his waking from the visions always at that very moment, bringing him peace.

They spent the day hunting, swimming, and sunbathing, then spent the evenings eating, talking, and laughing around the fire. For a boy of sixteen winters, burdened by killing and danger and the past and future all at once, not much could be better.

At times like that, the wish to be someone else did not occur to him.

Chapter 24

As Asku's family prepared for breakfast, with Chitsa and Nayhali preparing *wák'amu* cakes and Napayshni bouncing a delighted little girl on each knee, a scout came running up to the Chief.

"The Wawyukyáma chief is coming, *Wyánch'i,*" the scout said, out of breath but smiling. "They will arrive very soon."

"Then breakfast can wait," said Chitsa, delighted. Within a moment, the entire family was headed down the trail toward the bluff, the women having left it to Asku and Napayshni to herd the little ones.

As the canoes came around the bend, the Chief cupped his hands around his mouth and called out at the top of his lungs. Chitsa nearly jumped up and down to hear the familiar deep voice answer. "See the canoes coming," she said, pointing downriver for the little ones. "That is your grandfather and your uncle. They are Elk Plains people, Wawyukyáma. When I was your age, I was growing up with them." Everyone went down to the shore to meet them, and Asku and Napayshni joined some other hunters and boys in helping pull the canoes ashore.

Asku smiled at the old man who sat in the lead canoe's bow. "Blessings today, *tíla.*"

"And to you, my *tíla,*" the old chief replied with a big smile.

"*Túta,*" Chitsa cried out in joy, embracing him.

"My *isha,*" the old chief sighed, holding her tightly, "my sweet little Chitsa."

"Blessings, *káka,*" Asku said as U'hitaykah exited the same canoe.

"How goes it, *píti?*" U'hitaykah socked him roughly in the ribs. "Napayshni," he said, nodding respectfully at Asku's father.

"U'hitaykah, my brother," the Chief grunted as they pulled the heavy canoe as far onto the beach as possible. "You are most welcome."

"*Litsa*," U'hitaykah turned and swung Chitsa up into his arms. Her skirt spun in giant circles around her, and she squealed like one of Asku's little sisters. Others who had come down greeted old friends and relatives. Asku scanned all the canoes and found whom he was looking for in the final one.

From it, Aanapay waved to him with a laugh, while Mach'ni offered a grunt as he jumped from the craft into the cold water, pulling the canoe ashore by himself. Keme leaped out to help, and the reunion was one of renewed friendship, with even an excuse for a smile from Mach'ni.

"How was the journey?"

"Dull," said Mach'ni. "Apparently, we need to take you along more often."

>——

That night, the Patisapatisháma threw a celebration in honor of the visitors. After it died down, the younger men sat around the ceremonial fire. The stars overhead cast an eerie glow upon the Totem, the mammoth bear's head illuminated at the top.

"It is cold here," Keme complained.

"Well, it is a good thing you are staying behind with Kitchi, then," Aanapay teased, poking a stick into the fire. "Everything is cold and wet there. But it is beautiful, so green and thick with moss and ferns. Like nothing you have ever seen before and certainly nothing like the Elk Plains. Right, Asku?"

Asku shook his head, "I dunno, I was little when I went with my father. Well, I do remember the sea. It has waves coming in and out, like Nch'i-Wána on its roughest day but much larger. The water that seemed to go on forever… that's it."

They talked well into the night, about the Patshatl and the Great Sea, and planned a fishing trip for early the next morning. Then they crashed around the warm fire.

>——

The sun was hot, but a morning breeze refreshed the young men as they set off down the trail. The river was a good place to be on a hot day.

Asku took his time along the way, explaining everything they saw. The delays enabled Kitchi to keep up. As they crested the bluff, Hatayah walked toward them with a water basket on her head and her little brother by the hand. She smiled, though part of her smile looked past him now. He felt a twinge in his stomach as Hawiłish took the basket from her head. "Blessings today, young *Wyánch'i*," she said to Asku.

"And to you," Asku replied, smiling. "You know where we'll be," he added to Hawiłish.

"Pretty girl," Keme commented as they continued down the slope.

"Yes, very." And it was all right.

They spent the morning fishing on the banks of the mighty Nch'i-Wána. The River boys taught the Plains boys how to fish the fast-moving water with weirs. The Wawyukyáma usually traded for dried salmon and salmon flour, but they knew how to fish with spears and dipnets. Keme watched, mesmerized, as fish swam mindlessly into the wickerwork cages.

By early afternoon the group had caught a basket full of salmon, each at least a forearm's length, along with a rather large *k'súyaas*. Kitchi carefully held the lamprey at arm's length, showing the sucker mouth and pointed teeth, before tossing it into a different basket that was shallow and filled halfway with water. Chitsa, who was heading the cooking, had instructed Asku how many fish, how big—and to hurry. Asku herded the group toward home. The fish would be slow roasted at the ceremonial fire.

After dinner, they would hold another council. Although each tribe had already made a decision in regard to the Pyúsh P'ushtáayama and the Patshatl, the question that remained was whether and to what degree the tribes would act in concert. *Nch'ínch'ima* from both tribes were gathering. They would share their decisions, then either make a plan together or decide to proceed independently. Afterward, the Patisapatisháma would send a messenger to the Wanuukshiłáma chief, while a Wawyukyáma messenger would speed away to inform those who had stayed behind on the plains. *I think I know what my father means to do*, thought Asku. *The Sea Chief must be busy preparing for the Patshatl, but he also has decisions to make. If we reach agreement with my grandfather's people,*

that means that if he joins in our plans, he has strong allies. I do not understand how my father sees things so far ahead.
    Maybe someday I will.

▸—→

After eating, the men argued well into the night. The *chalámat* made many circuits of the fire. Some believed the Pyúsh chief, Matchitehew, should be killed on his way to the Patshatl and his village raided before he was set to return. Others felt very strongly that the Patshatl was the first priority, then the Pyúsh chief. Still others, mostly younger men like Liwanu, felt that a hunting party should be sent now and the Patshatl used as cover. There was great interest in Keme, and he fielded many questions in a forthcoming way that won him general respect.

Liwanu and Sahkantiak quarreled, becoming so angry with each other that they were asked to leave until they could control themselves. Liwanu left around the back trail only to return a while later. Sahkantiak remained but stood just outside the ring of men with his arms crossed angrily over his chest.

Both chiefs sat quietly, just listening. Finally, Kalataka raised a hand, and the circle became quiet.

"Napayshni," he began, "let us hear from you, my son."

The Chief sat cross-legged next to Asku, his hands resting upon his knees. He raised his chin and began to speak in the deep, sure 'Chief voice.' "The Great Spirits have set a path before us. We know not what the result may be, but we must protect the people: the Wawyukyáma, the Wanuukshiłáma, the Patisapatisháma...and the Pyúsh P'ushtáayama."

That set off all manner of muttering and whispering. The Chief took a deep breath, raised his hand, and silence fell again.

"We do not risk destroying an entire village out of fear. We have good reason to believe that many Pyúsh are nothing like Matchitehew. We will be patient, and we will prepare with patience. When the Spirits lay the path before us, we will be ready." He paused. "What do you say, U'hitaykah, my brother?"

U'hitaykah nodded. "Too long have we worried about this band of Pyúsh P'ushtáayama. We have let evil reside near us and done nothing to stop it. Long ago, we allowed them to get away with destroying families"—he nodded at Aanapay— "and for this, I am sorry."

Aanapay looked at the ground.

U'hitaykah pounded a fist into the open palm of his hand. "We will destroy this evil chief," he said, with more than a hint of anger. Many in the group nodded and jeered, but U'hitaykah swiftly raised his hand for silence. "But we do not dishonor the Patshatl, we do not become like him. We must honor our traditions and the Great Spirits. We must celebrate the unity of our tribes. We must celebrate the union of Askuwa'tu Haylaku and the Wanuukshiłáma daughter. We cannot dishonor the Great Spirits. We are not Matchitehew. And we know now that not all Pyúsh are Matchitehew."

Silence.

"So, what, then?" a question came from somewhere around the fire.

"My brothers," U'hitaykah held his hand up as noise grew, "we have already made plans to protect the elders, the women and young ones while we are away. We have a place where they can go and be safe, and by now they are either there or getting close. After the Patshatl, we think it likely there will be a fight somewhere between our villages. We will prepare for that, so that we are not taken off our guard."

More shouting resumed, indicating some of both agreement and disagreement. The Teacher stood and pointed his stick at Asku.

"Inmíma átawitma tíinma. Let us hear from Askuwa'tu Haylaku, who has seen and learned the most about the Pyúsh."

Asku looked from his father to his grandfather before he took a deep breath and began.

"We will honor the Great Sprits. We will honor the Wanuukshiłáma. We will attend the Patshatl and honor the meaning of the ancient gathering. We will unite our tribes once again. We will do the right thing, my brothers and sisters, for the people." He looked directly at Keme. "Including yours."

Keme nodded, once. Only those who had come to know him could see the emotion behind the eyes. The circle was quiet but for the cracking and popping of the fire.

"Mach'ni and Aanapay will wait for the Pyúsh chief at the mountains," Asku's grandfather said, quietly. "They will watch his every move and follow him to the Patshatl."

"Yes," Asku's father said, nodding. "The Patisapatisháma *Nch'ínch'ima* will meet to decide how best to protect the village in our absence. If the Sea Chief invites the tribe, we may all go. If not, we must make other plans. Until then, we will redouble the watch around the village. We will have plenty of warning before he comes."

But Asku again felt the uneasy twinge in the pit of his stomach.

❧

He awoke late that night while the other young men slept around the smoldering fire. The Teacher, the Chief and his grandfather were still there, their voices in low whispers. He went back to sleep but awoke again not long after to a heated discussion. The Chief and Chaytan walked around the back side of the longhouse.

"Please, Napayshni," Chaytan said. "I need to go with you!"

"It will be as I have said it," answered the Chief, sternly.

"I cannot stand to be left behind again," Chaytan entreated. Asku had never heard him speak to Napayshni like this before.

After a moment, Asku heard his father say: "Get some rest, *nika*."

The next thing Asku saw was Chaytan moving out from behind the longhouse. He ran his fingers through his hair, disappeared behind the Totem and into the night.

❧

As the sun rose, Asku got up to sit in front of the Totem. The Great Spirits did speak, though differently than before. Their message came to Asku as a series of visions...

Saigwan and the others, their long trek home...
The people running to meet him...
Song and dance and celebration...
New life, a beautiful daughter and Niyol beside himself with joy...

Moema swelling with child, and so lovely in Saigwan's eyes...
The people's joy at Saigwan's healing...
And a new story painted on the cave wall...

When they had passed, Asku found himself moved to the soul.
"*Sapsikw'atá?*" Asku whispered. "The great bear...was it gone? I mean all gone forever, like the mammoth and the speartooth?"

"Yes," the old man said, nodding. "The Great Floods destroyed many things. And so did man."

"Oh," Asku said, sadly.

A few moments later, Asku heard familiar steps. "Blessings today," the Chief whispered, to the sleeping youths now beginning to stir, "to all of you. Asku, shall we?"

Asku got up to join his father on his rounds. "Chaytan did not come back last night, *Wyánch'i.*"

The Chief nodded as they walked.

"What was he so upset about?" he prodded.

"He wants to attend the Patshatl with us," the Chief sighed. "But I have asked him to stay behind and care for our people."

"Oh."

"Chaytan is my shadow, Askuwa'tu, my little brother." Napayshni smiled, deep in thought or memories. "He will go where I go. The thought of me going somewhere without him pains him greatly. It has always been so."

"Well, why does he have to stay behind, then?"

"Because I trust no one as much as I trust him," the Chief continued, as they walked out toward the garden. "He does not grasp this yet. But I am leaving all but one of my most valuable possessions behind, and I would trust no one else to care for them."

"I see."

"Well, maybe I should let him come. What do you think?"

Great Spirits! What do I think?

I think that what I heard in Chaytan's voice was a man whose loyalty could be pushed too far.

"*Túta*, Chaytan would lay down his life for you or our family without a second thought. I think that the hurt in his voice was deep. If anyone deserves consideration of you, for all he does, it is Chaytan."

Napayshni thought for a moment, nodded once. "*Kúu mísh*. Will you go find him and tell him? I must speak with the Teacher this morning."

"Of course. I know where he would go."

The Chief smiled. "This should be done immediately. Go now, please, and I will finish the rounds."

"Yes, *Wyánch'i*." Asku took off toward Nch'i-Wána at a run, passing mothers and grandmothers preparing for the day, sleepy-eyed children beginning their morning chores, and the tribe's fishermen already returning from the river, their baskets piled high with fish.

Asku found Chaytan up at the customary spot upstream of the fishing area, where the canyon tightened and the water churned through the deep walls of orange, red and brown rock. He sat with his feet dangling in the current, the white water splashing all around him.

Kicking off his moccasins, Asku sat down on a rock just an arm's length from where Chaytan sat. "Oh hey, man," Chaytan nodded.

"Hey."

"What's up?"

"The Chief sent me." Asku lifted his feet out of the chilly water, crossed them instead.

"What did he say?"

"He said to tell you that you will journey with us to the Patshatl."

Chaytan's head turned. "Really?"

"Yep," Asku looked up into the canyon. All seemed still except for the rushing water and the occasional blast of wind between the deep walls.

"That's good," Chaytan sighed. "I am glad."

After some time had passed, Asku picked up a small rock, threw it so that it would skip. It didn't. "My father is important to you."

"Your father is all I have."

Asku waited.

"All of my family died long ago. I was only a small boy," Chaytan began. "Some say it was an evil spirit in the village. Many died after being sick and suffering a long time; many old and the very young. I guess I was lucky."

Asku watched Chaytan as he spoke. "The old chief, your grandfather, took me in as his own. I guess I was the annoying little brother, always have been. That's probably how he still thinks," he added in a mumble.

"When Napayshni became chief during that great and terrible time, I stayed with him. Everyone was gone. His older brothers, his father, his sister was taken. His mother was no help. She blamed him for everything." Chaytan laughed mirthlessly. "He sat on that stool in the tent for a long time...a very long time. I can still see him in my mind."

Asku could also see his father, young—his own age—sitting on a stool with his head in his hands, a young Chaytan at his feet.

"I sat next to him, on the ground, just waiting." Chaytan glared across to the cliffs Beyond Nch'i-Wána. "I remember very clearly that moment. He sniffed and ran his hands through his hair, then he stood up and said, 'Chaytan, you must stay here, *nika*.' And then he was gone.

"He returned four nights later carrying his bruised and bleeding sister, and the old Pyúsh chief's ear strung through his belt." Chaytan cleared his throat and stood up.

"I will not be left behind again."

Chapter 25

The family sat together later that day, laughing about old times and telling stories as a delicious-smelling stew boiled over the fire. The Elk Plains chief had a little sister on each knee and a little boy at his feet. He spoke of Bison and Horse and a time when they were great friends on the plains. Then he began a funny story about Spilyáy. Coyote's antics had the little ones rolling with laughter, while Chitsa snickered from the little preparing table.

Asku enjoyed the scene as he began to carve the elk antler. He began with a bear, his bear, sketching it first with the tiny carving knife, then shaving out bit by bit to impose the bear's features on the sturdy piece.

"Why is Spilyáy always so grumpy, *tíla?*" Nisy asked.

"Because he is a sneaky, unhappy little thief, my beautiful one," the old man said, tucking a strand of hair behind her ear. "But he teaches us still. With every story, the grumpy little Spilyáy sends us a message."

Asku smiled as the bear's face took shape, a fine replica of the Totem he knew so well. Chitsa stood behind him for a moment, then said, "It is beautiful, *isha.*"

It is also a part of me. And now for a part of her. He turned the antler over, taking care to position the bear image perfectly face down.

"Who is it for, Asku?" Susannawa blurted.

"It is for the daughter of the chief at the Great Sea, *nika,*" Asku replied. "She will come here to live with us soon. Her name is Kaliskah."

The torchlight was dim in this part of the cave. It was hard to make out how much was in the back alcove, but it looked like not very much at all.

"*This is all there is?*" *Saigwan asked.*

"*Yes, Wyánch'i,*" *the older woman said, ruefully, "this is it."*

Her hands fumbled with the lid of the largest basket, one of three remaining. Three baskets, the last of the dried and ground berries and roots, after which starvation threatened.

"*It is okay, lamyáy. This is not your fault.*" *She would not meet his eyes.*

Why should she feel ashamed? The lack of food for my people is my fault alone.

The little ones were hungry, and the cold snap pierced even the cave. His people would not last the season with only three baskets left. And they were running low on wood. The men he sent out each day could find little due to the deep snow, and what they did bring back was often marginal.

Every day the women went out looking for nuts, roots and berries, but never found enough. The families had begun eating the soft inner bark from the wet wood. When roasted over a fire, it was not all that bad.

"*Will you please find Niyol, lamyáy, and go home to your family?*" *Saigwan patted her on the shoulder.*

"*Yes, Wyánch'i,*" *she said, sadly.*

Saigwan thought of his sister and the beautiful little girl they had buried not long after his arrival home. She had not wept for this child. Her milk had never flowed. He could still see her sitting at the fire, rocking the little one and singing softly. The little one had not even been named.

His own child would be born soon.

And Saigwan was angry. He was angry with himself.

The mothers could not suckle the little ones, because there was not enough sustenance for their own bodies. He heard the children's cries of hunger at night, not excepting his own. There had not been meat in three moons. Some went out every day, but the animals were no more eager to roam free in the snow and chill than were Saigwan's people. And meat was what the people must have or face the slow death of starvation.

It would begin with lethargy, swelling in places, and other maladies. If they did not find food soon, they would lose the capacity to try. If it continued, it would lead to desperate actions, good men and women turned mad and did things they otherwise would never think of.

And then there was the cold, always the cold, that seemed every day to seep further into their home.

Saigwan heard Niyol approach. "We must hunt," Saigwan said.
"Yes, Wyánch'i," he turned to go. "I will gather the men."

Asku and the older boys all sat around Kitchi's family firepit late in the day, talking and laughing, when Susannawa came running up. Matahnu trailed behind.

"The messenger is here," Susannawa exclaimed, out of breath and clutching his side.

"The Wanuukshiłáma messenger," Matahnu added, excited.

"The Chief wants you," Susannawa pointed a stubby little finger at Asku and smiled.

Keme was on his feet first. "Come on. *Áwna wínasha!*"

The boys had to thread their way through some crowding, for many people lingered in hopes of glimpsing the messenger from the Great Sea.

In due course, Asku made it through the crowd to where his father stood before the messenger. "Kohana," said Napayshni, "this is my son, Askuwa'tu Haylaku. Asku, this is Kohana, nephew and messenger of the Wanuukshiłáma chief."

The young man was short and stocky, with sparkling dark eyes and dark brown hair pulled back into two braids that hung across his shoulders. A long, sharp *áx̱sh'ax̱sh* shell protruded through the center of his nose. Tassels hung from his earlobes. He carried an intricately carved bow across his back and wore a white tusk-handled knife at his hip. He was barefoot.

"Askuwa'tu Haylaku," the young man began in Chiskin. Asku had been expecting Chinuk Wawa and had been brushing up. Upon hearing Kohana's practiced formality, all listening fell silent. "The great and mighty Sea Chief, Apenimon Kisecawchuck of the Great Sea, bids you welcome, young chief, and asks if you and your people would join him in a celebration of your union with his daughter, Kaliskah Sayen, at the Patshatl this time seven days hence?"

What am I supposed to say, exactly? Kohana stood awaiting Asku's response, the silence broken only by a baby's brief cry. Asku looked at the Teacher and then at the Chief, who smiled. His thoughts screamed inside his head, so loudly to him that it felt as if everyone else could hear. *Calm. Just stay calm. Breathe. Okay, hope this is right.*

Asku inhaled, drew himself up with dignity. "Thank you, my *síks*. I am most grateful to the mighty Wanuukshiłáma chief. I and my people are greatly anticipating the union of our tribes once again and welcome the opportunity to celebrate at the Patshatl this time seven days hence."

My mother is smiling, just a little. I can't have botched it up too badly.

The young man nodded, an act of state, then turned back toward Napayshni. "May I speak with the Wawyukyáma chief, please?"

Asku's grandfather stepped forward and nodded. "I am Kalataka Wahchinksapa, Chief of the Wawyukyáma."

Kohana began again: "The great and mighty Sea Chief, Apenimon Kisecawchuck of the Great Sea, bids you welcome, Kalataka Wahchinksapa, Chief of the Wawyukyáma, and asks if you and your people would join him in a celebration of the union of Askuwa'tu Haylaku with his daughter, Kaliskah Sayen, at the Patshatl this time seven days hence?"

The Elk Plains Chief met Kohana's gaze. "I speak for all the Wawyukyáma when I extend my thanks to the mighty chief, Apenimon Kisecawchuck of the Wanuukshiłáma, for the most gracious invitation to join his people for this Patshatl. The Sea Chief's hospitality is as famed as his strength and judgment. It will be our great honor to accept his invitation, and we look forward to seeing old friends and making new ones."

Kohana nodded, a bit more deliberately than before. There were a few scattered whispers. Napayshni spoke: "And now that all that is properly agreed, Kohana, please come up to the River village and sit with us, where we will share the *chalámat*." The entire procession worked its way up the trail, with Kohana asking intelligent questions about the lookouts they passed, the garden, and so on. The chiefs, their sons, and the elders all went to the ceremonial firepit and sat down.

"My chiefs," Kohana began, "my uncle feels as you all do. The Patshatl comes first, that we celebrate our union once again. Our tribes are the Mighty Three that control trade up and down Nch'i-Wána. My uncle is honored, Askuwa'tu, that you accept Kaliskah, and that the ties between Sea People, River People, and Elk Plains People will grow stronger and more cordial."

Now I am required to say something—but what? He took a deep breath. "We welcome those ties also, Kohana. I have heard many good things about Kaliskah, and I look forward to knowing her and welcoming her among our people as my mate."

"The Elk Plains people are the strongest tribe north of the Two Sisters along the waters that pour into Nch'i-Wána," said Napayshni. "Nothing may pass the river without our notice, and nothing may leave or enter it at the Great Sea without the consent of the Sea Chief. Nch'i-Wána is our fastest way to share news or goods, but it is also the fastest way for an invader to travel. When we help each other's strength and safety, we help our own tribes be safer."

And that is more like what I was supposed to have said!

Relax, Asku. You are not yet Wyánch'i, *nor will you be for many years.*

"But the Sea Chief also agrees that there is danger," responded Kohana. "For the safety of your loved ones, he invites you to bring them all with you. We have room enough for all of the Patisapatisháma and Wawyukyáma and would be pleased to welcome you all."

Napayshni nodded to Kohana. "Most considerate of the Sea Chief. But how is it you will have enough room for your people and ours? We have near two hundred within our village at any given time. The Wawyukyáma are as numerous."

Kohana nodded. "We have made room. The chief sent word to surrounding tribes. We have tents and food for plenty. However, as soon as we know how many will come, we should send word back to let them know."

Asku looked back at the Chief. "They will not all go, will they, *túta?*"

"No. Some will choose to travel to family at nearby tribes. Some may just remain with the Tlakluit or at Wayám. It is very busy and will be safe this time of year."

"Yes," Kohana nodded, "there were many visitors at the Falls when I came through, painted warriors from near Wy-east, well-armed and friendly."

"Yes," the Chief nodded, "they come from all over to trade. Kalataka, are the Wawyukyáma safe enough?"

The Elk Plains chief nodded. "Yes, they will be safe. I have sent them across the river Toward the Great Mountains, where they will stay with our sister tribes at the winter village. They will stay until I call them home. In any case, due to the distance, there would not be time to get many together to attend the Patshatl as an entire tribe, but certainly those of us who can accept the invitation will do so."

"Then all seems settled," said Napayshni. "Kohana, my mate Chitsa is the daughter of Kalataka, and she is a fine cook. We hope you will guest and dine with our family while you are here." The Chief smiled, gave Asku a light slap on the shoulder. "This one has been on many journeys lately, living on trail rations and making long travel days. He can eat like a bear." Everyone laughed, including Asku, and the meeting dissolved amid the spreading word that the entire tribe was welcome at the Patshatl. The gossip indicated that most planned to attend. The village came alive with excitement and planning.

Asku walked toward home. Kohana got up to follow him.

"May I have a word with you, Askuwa'tu?"

Asku led him along the trail toward Pahto, just far enough from the village for privacy. With a sly smile, Kohana pulled a small deerskin parcel from his sling.

"Kaliskah sends a message," Kohana said. "She says, 'Please be well, my young chief, accept this gift, wear it close to your heart until we meet, and know that I think of you often.'" He cleared his throat as he handed the soft pelt to Asku. "Kaliskah's brothers would have my tongue if they knew I carried a message to you. But Kaliskah can be very…well, you will soon find out, young chief. Let this be between us, okay?"

"*Kw'ałá, síks*," Asku said with a nod. The supple skin in his hands felt like it beat in time with his pounding heart.

"Well, if you will excuse me, I have a message I must deliver to your Teacher." Kohana smiled and turned to go, only to stop after a step or two. "One more thing. I was wondering if you would introduce me to this young Keme we have already heard so much about?"

Asku nodded, but really had no idea what Kohana had said to him. All he could think about was the package in his hands. Once the young man was out of sight, Asku untied the reed twine that sealed the fine wrapping of the secret gift, his heart jittery with anticipation.

The doeskin unwrapped to reveal a marvelous ornament: a simple, yet striking choker made from three hide strands strung with long, thin bone pieces and dark wooden beads. In the center hung three different lengths of twisted hide, also decorated with the white bone. The longest piece ended with a large, round, very smooth black stone. One could almost see the darkness of night within its depths.

In his mind, Asku could see Kaliskah's hands stringing each piece of bone and bead on the thin strip of animal skin. *If she sought to show me that she is skilled at crafts*, thought Asku, *she accomplished her goal.*

He tied the choker around his neck as he walked homeward. The clear black stone hung just below the hollow of his throat. It felt good around his neck, snug against his throat: just right.

The Chief's voice broke into his reverie. "You know, Asku, among some peoples, a choker is considered a symbol of leadership."

"Really?" Asku ran his fingers across the twisted hide, lingering on the black stone.

"It is quite a gift. Someone thinks a great deal of you."

>———

After much excitement, the group of canoes were loaded down with men, women and children, and gifts for the Wanuukshiłáma. They would travel a short distance downriver to Wayám, where they would portage around the falls on the far side. The crowded canoes would become lighter as those who elected to stay with friends or family disembarked there or crossed the river to others on the Tlakluit side. Once Napayshni was confident they would be safe, the boats would re-embark below the falls.

There were plenty of allies along this part of Nch'i-Wána, but the Chief had brought trade goods just in case. The Elk Plains people had also brought plenty of coveted bison hide, bone and hoof tools, and pemmican. Wayámpam, the loose term for the habitations on both sides of the river, had a small permanent population but a large transient one. While it could not mount large, organized campaigns as a unified tribe, it was unlikely Matchitehew could do it significant damage.

Even so, Asku found it reassuring to see a contingent of the painted warriors from around Wy-east at Wayám. Napayshni introduced himself and the senior leaders of both traveling tribes, communicating in the hand signs of the Wawa, which the painted warriors understood well enough to convey that they were friendly. About half of the Patisapatisháma contingent elected to stay behind, including Asku's mother and siblings, Kitchi's family, and Hatayah's family. When it was all sorted out, Napayshni took a moment to walk Asku through his assessment.

"Suppose the Snake People attacked here. I would guess that there are some five hundred people here all told. Of course, some could decide to leave, and others might arrive, so the number changes like the level of a river. There are always men of fighting age here as traders; they would fight to keep their goods from theft, and for families if they brought them. There are the men who live here and make it their home. The warriors from Wy-east add strength, and of course our own people remaining here would help. I would say that there are at least one hundred men fully capable of putting up a good fight, with another hundred boys and older men who might count for fifty in a crisis. Also, never discount the way women can fight if they feel their families are in danger. That would be another hundred who would count as fifty warriors, making up for lack of strength or skill with great ferocity. If you ever want to see how savagely a woman can fight, you have only to threaten her baby. My advice is not to do that unless you wish to join the Great Spirits."

Asku imagined Chitsa in such a case. He smiled. "So that is two hundred warriors, in effect, *túta?*"

"Yes, give or take who might come or go, but the number does not change too much in seven nights time. Based on what you learned from your scouting trip, I see no way Matchitehew could get anything here better than an arrow in his behind."

Asku nodded. "I see that. However, we also know he has allies. What if he brought two hundred including them?"

The Chief smiled. "That is a fair question, *tita*. Let us examine it. They would have to be fighting men who do not really respect the property and peace of others, would you agree?"

Asku thought for a moment. "Yes. That is why they associate with people like Matchitehew."

The Chief waited. *Which means...*

"Which means in the first place, a group that large might instead just decide to raid the Pyúsh P'ushtáayama village themselves."

His father nodded but said nothing.

"Which means also that Matchitehew could not really control them. If anything, they might control him. Instead of being the rider, the Pyúsh P'ushtáayama might find themselves the horse."

"And what might they do then?" prompted Napayshni.

Asku mulled it over. "There is no way to know. All we really know is that there is not much chance Matchitehew could show up with enough force to harm those here. But *túta*, the strength here is divided between the sides of the river. Could he not attack one and overwhelm it?"

"How long does it take you, Hawɨlish, and Kitchi to grab weapons and canoe across Nch'i-Wána?" asked the Chief.

"We could be there in the time it takes to eat dinner."

"And if you were doing so in order to protect women and elders and little children?"

"Quicker," said Asku, eyes hardening.

"So. Let us imagine Matchitehew tried that. He would have his hands full already, and then have to face twice as much strength, all of it very angry with him. That story would most likely end with Matchitehew meeting Apenimon."

Asku's head turned. "How would he somehow meet the Sea Chief?"

"He might not. It would depend on whether the *wílaps* were hungry or not. If they were hungry enough, his body would not reach the

Sea. More likely, though, the sturgeon would find his corpse too disgusting, and he would wash up on a sandbar."

They both laughed.

⯈⟶

The convoy continued downriver, with Asku steering a canoe carrying bison hides and his grandfather. They passed a number of fishing villages, with Asku's father and grandfather always raising a hand to shoulder level as a matter of prudence. Near the meeting of Łátaxat with Nch'i-Wána, they saw a herd of elk drinking along the water's edge, some with antlers as high and as wide as their own length. The scenery varied from dense forest to open flat plains, from towering cliffs to sandy beaches, from distant snow-capped mountains to valleys with small rivers.

About midday, where the canyon tightened past the shoals just Toward the Rising Sun of Łátaxat Wána, it began to rain and blow. The wind gusts proved much more difficult and dangerous to navigate, jostling the canoes and roiling up high swells on Nch'i-Wána. Near the Great Rapids, the Chief motioned the group to shore on the grassy flats along the bank Toward the Great Mountains.

A well-used firepit, crude benches and empty shelters marked the spot as a regular stop for river travelers. The people spread out, made camp, ate snacks, tried to fish, and stretched cramped legs. Some sheltered up the embankment under dense branches of evergreens so massive they seemed to reach the overcast sky. They would now be closer to Lawilat-łá, and Asku wished that she were visible.

Asku's grandfather cleared his throat and sat down against the trunk of a fir that was many times a great-grandmother of firs. Mothers hurried young ones to sit around his feet and hush, and once the chaos subsided, he began. "No one understands the strange wetness of the Setting Sun side of the Great Mountains more than Old Spilyáy."

"No one is more like Old Spilyáy than certain chiefs, *túta*," laughed U'hitaykah. The Elk Plains contingent chuckled. As Asku tried (and failed, abjectly) to imagine himself heckling his father before storytelling, his grandfather began to speak.

Spilyáy was hungry. He could not find anything to eat on the vast plains. He looked in all the usual places. The shallow dark tunnels of the ground squirrel, the grassy burrows of the jackrabbit, the tiny hole of the field mouse—but nothing.

Spilyáy was hungry.

He heard the birds talking of a place on the other side of Pahto. They spoke of wet greenness, mushiness and mud, water everywhere. Spilyáy knew that where there was water, there were bugs, and where there were bugs, there were yummy little things to eat.

Spilyáy's small muzzle dripped with saliva at the thought. He decided, then, to go.

He walked for days and nights with Aanyáy smiling down upon his dirty, silvery fur. His stomach growled louder with every soft-padded step he took, and his hide clung tighter to his ribcage.

Spilyáy found the pass over the mountains and looked up at Aanyáy for reassurance. "Are you sure it is this way...over that?"

She nodded, her rays shining love down upon the crotchety old coyote whom she loved so very much. "Yes, my dear, over that."

Spilyáy growled and complained as he ascended the mountains. The further he climbed, the colder it got. So, he moved faster. He willed his old limbs forward with each step.

But when the snow started falling, he stopped. "Are you sure, Aanyáy?"

"Yes, my dear old Spilyáy," she smiled again, annoying him more. "You must go down the other side."

After many days the hungry old coyote finally stepped foot on flat ground. His stomach growled again as he took in his surroundings. Ahead of him was a dense forest that seemed to reach to the sky, their branches gnarly and ominous, and covered in long, green prickles.

He sniffed the air. "Blech," he growled and spat, "what is that smell?"

Aanyáy laughed.

Spilyáy inched his way forward, step by step by step. He could see nothing except darkness in the forest. He stepped one paw between the trees. The ground was soft and squished under his paw. He pulled it back quickly.

"What is that?"

"Oh, go on, you grumpy old thing," Aanyáy teased.

Grumbling loudly, he stepped all four paws into the mushiness. The smell was stronger inside the forest. He sniffed the ground as he walked and decided it was definitely the green, smushy stuff that smelled so badly. "Blech," he complained again.

He heard something. Looking around, he saw movement— everywhere. There were squirrels chattering high above him, acorns in hand. There were ducks floating nearby in a small, swampy pond, unaware of his presence. There were enormous, fat salamanders resting on the trunks of tress. There was even a small deer drinking from the stream that entered the pond, not far from where he stood. The deer's little black tail flicked back and forth quickly.

The old coyote's tongue dripped with desire and his stomach rumbled loudly. He was certain they all heard it. And they did, their ears pricked, all of them, holding deathly still.

Then Spilyáy heard the rumble again, but it was not his stomach. The rumble grew louder this time, it seemed to come from the very ground he stood on. He cowered, crouched low to the mushiness, and inched his way toward a short fat tree with low branches. He hid under those branches, his heart pounding loudly.

He could not see Aanyáy anymore. He needed to see Aanyáy. She would tell him what that noise was.

He poked his little black nose out from under the tree branches to see if she was there. At that moment the sky cracked, a loud snap, and he cowered under the tree again.

Spilyáy no longer felt hungry, he just wanted to go home.

He waited a few moments and then poked his little nose out again, just the tiniest bit past the edge of the branches. The sky was dark grey. The clouds were thick and moving fast.

Just then, a giant ball of water fell from the sky and landed right in his eye. He yelped and stepped backwards, tripping over a rock. He rolled and smashed into the tree's scratchy trunk with a grunt. He pawed at his eye to clear it. His fur now covered in the thick, black mud and his eyes streaming from the sting of the water.

Then water dumped from the sky in buckets, and he found himself standing in a puddle under that little, fat tree.

Spilyáy did not like his feet to get wet. He loved the taste of cool water on his lips and on his tongue. But he did not like his paws to get wet at all.

He grumbled and complained as the puddle got deeper and deeper. The water was so deep now that it had begun to move. He saw the squirrel and the salamander scurry up the tree trunks. He saw the deer run on graceful, long legs for higher ground. He saw the duck family fly away.

And he knew he needed to get out of there.

He took off running as fast as his short, old legs would carry him. He ran to the edge of the forest and peeked out. A loud snap from the sky—he yelped and howled in fear. He took off running again, never stopping and never slowing down until he came down the other side of the mountains—back to the right side of Pahto.

Finally, when he felt the warmth of Aanyáy on his fur again, he skidded to a stop.

"My sweet, old friend," she smiled, with laughter silent upon her lips. "What has happened to you?"

He grumbled and complained about the other side of Pahto. How it had enticed him with its yummy things to eat; its scurrying squirrels and its black-tailed deer and its little duck family. But then, how the water had fallen from the angry sky.

"Too much green stuff," he growled, "and too wet."

She smiled at him with amusement. "My silly, old friend, you are all muddy. You need a bath."

He looked at his fur coated with black mud, moss, pinecones and needles. His fur clung to his body in a matted mess.

He grumbled something at her.

"What was that my sweet Spilyáy?" she asked.

"Never again," he mumbled, trotting off to his usual spots in search of food. His paws leaving muddy prints as he ran, and his little black nose sniffing left to right and back again on the dusty hard—but dry—ground.

And Aanyáy laughed to herself.

The old chief threw his head back and laughed, a great guffawing noise that made Asku and all the children giggle with amusement. "Sometimes I feel like that silly old Spilyáy," the Elk Plains chief chuckled, waving out into the rain and the dreary sky.

"About the rain or about needing a bath, old man?" Napayshni teased.

"Both," the old chief replied to more laughter.

"You haven't seen anything yet," Kohana whispered to Asku, "just wait for the Great Sea Wind to show his face."

"I do not doubt that" said Asku in a quiet voice. Others were now joking, laughing.

How swiftly the mood changed!

Chapter 26

The boats needed to beach at that spot anyway, because they had reached the top of the Whitewater of Wy-East, the great rapids of Nch'i-Wána. Only a very light canoe piloted by an expert boatman could pass those rapids safely. A lot of portage awaited this group. But Asku's father knew the portage trail well, and when the rain let up a little, the men hoisted the canoes over their shoulders. Napayshni led them to the sandbar below the last white water of the Great Rapids, where they reloaded and re-embarked out into the widening river.

The weather improved, although dark gray clouds loomed far off Toward the Setting Sun, running from the Great Mountains and Beyond Nch'i-Wána as far as Asku could see. They seemed to stop, as if run against a wall and waiting. Kohana said they were over the sea, and that they were usual. Nch'i-Wána bent Toward the Great Mountains, then back Toward the Setting Sun.

After midday they left Nch'i-Wána, turning into a wide bay and then up into the current of Skip-pi-náu-in, a much narrower and shallower body of water. By evening, Asku found his canoe facing a sandy beach with a number of Wanuukshiłáma tribesmen, plus some with darker skins wearing only breechcloths, who did not look like Wanuukshiłáma. As Kohana disembarked to greet his tribemates, the darker-skinned tribespeople began to unload the canoes. Some younger Patisapatisháma moved as if to help, but older members restrained them with gentle firmness. The breechclothed people began to carry the goods and supplies along a wide trail Toward the Setting Sun, singing softly. Although Asku did not understand the words, he found their sound chilling. Their hair was long, dark, and rather untidy.

"Shín pawá piiník?" he whispered to his father when he could do so without attracting attention. "Who are they?"

"*Ashwaníyama*...slaves," whispered the Chief.

"Oh."

The long line of Patisapatisháma, Wanuukshiłáma and *ashwaníyama* climbed a steep embankment and stopped at the top. Below lay the Great Sea in all its infinity. As the people began to reach the top behind him, Asku heard their exclamations of excitement. The vastness of the moving water, the place where the sky met the icy blueness so far in the distance, and the thundering of the crashing waves: a scene of majesty. And the wall of dark gray clouds still hovered just above the horizon, still far off in the distance.

He took a deep breath of the wet, salty air. Kohana raised his hands in blessing.

"*T'k-tók'te Tl'ka-ná-a Wé-ko-wa,*" he chanted, "Good Mother Sea, may you be pleased with this people."

They began the long, winding descent down the dunes and toward the beach. The sandy ground sprouted dune grasses and prickly, dry plants. A burr caught in Asku's trousers, and Kohana laughed as he watched Asku try to pry the thing loose without poking himself further. "Believe it or not," said Kohana, "that has a beautiful white flower on it much of the warm season. But right now, that thing wants to be your *shikhs*."

At the base of the embankment, the view was different but still awesome. The sea stretched forever out in front of them. Asku longed to throw his moccasins off, dig his toes into the sand, and run toward the moving water. Hawilish glanced at him with a smile, perhaps with the same thought. *There will be time,* Asku winked.

There was life everywhere: amusing white birds with skinny legs, webbed feet, and long, yellow, smiling beaks. There were masses of tiny gray birds that ran incredibly fast for something so small, moving airborne just above the sand like an enormous swarm of bees.

The large group followed Kohana Toward the Great Mountains, which Kohana explained was Toward Nch'i-Wána as well, along the edge of the beach until the embankment disappeared. Then they turned Toward the Rising Sun again, their backs to the sea, and entered a forest of strange, smooth, red trees. Asku could smell and hear a village close by. His heart raced with anticipation. *She is near!*

Just a short walk from the beach, yet buried within the red trees, was the Wanuukshiłáma village. And such a place it was.

Many large, beautifully decorated buildings encircled a considerable ceremonial fire. Around the outside circle, and tucked between the cedar homes, were dozens of temporary tents. The activity and energy of evening village life hit Asku immediately. As people stopped what they were doing to look at the visitors, Asku kept his eyes forward. When he was younger, the Chief had told him: "Askuwa'tu, when we go to other places, you will always be looked at. It is a greater burden than that of other children, because how you behave will affect the opinions of those you are visiting—not only of you, but of our people, and of me. Always remember that the feeling of the first time someone meets you will tend to stay with him. In your case, it is more important: what you do, or don't do, will affect our relations with them. At the beginning, there are always formalities, and that is the time to be as formal as others are. Later, though, when they have seen that you can be serious at need and are a respectful person, you can have fun."

So, I guess this is one of those times he meant. I can do this.

They followed Kohana past the ceremonial firepit and into the very center of the village. Three short Totems caught Asku's eye, all with beings carved on them: a raven, a whale, a bear unlike his own Totem's, people, and other images he could not figure out, all painted in intricate red and black and white. The center Totem stood taller than the others, and partway up it, he got a jolt: *that has to be the fish the Teacher taught me to carve and helped me to color. When we were finished, he told me that the sight must surely warm Kaliskah's heart. Soon we find out.*

The Wanuukshiłáma chief sat below the Totem, flanked by two young men. These two had painted faces and wore tall, pointed cedar hats covering their foreheads and a portion of their eyes, making them look like strange sentinel creatures. Both had long tassels in their ears, similar to Kohana's, connected to a thin, sharp *áxsh'axsh* protruding from the centers of their noses.

The Sea Chief smiled, and to Asku it seemed a kind, welcoming smile with eyes that seemed to dance. His face was lined with deep wrinkles and laugh lines, his skin tanned and leathery. His hair blew loose around his shoulders, gray with streaks of the whitest white.

"Aw, Napayshni…finally," said the Sea Chief, in Chinuk Wawa. The two chiefs embraced like old friends.

"Apenimon, blessings," answered Asku's father, also in Wawa.

The two young men on either side did not move. Asku felt their heavy stares and did not want to look away. He did so only when his father beckoned him forward, toward the Wanuukshiłáma chief.

"My son," the Chief said. "Askuwa'tu Haylaku."

The old man nodded, his eyes lingering momentarily on the choker at Asku's neck. "Come forward, son," Apenimon beckoned.

"Blessings, *ty-ee'*," Asku said in his best Chinuk Wawa.

"And to you," the old chief placed both hands on Asku's shoulders. "You are most welcome here, Askuwa'tu Haylaku. We have heard great and mighty stories of you already. We hope you will tell them while you are here."

"Of course, *ty-ee'*," Asku nodded, still feeling the malice emanating from either side of the jolly old chief. "Though many others played their great parts in those also, well worth telling."

Apenimon's eyes showed a flash of heightened interest. One hand on Asku's shoulder, he turned toward the young men. "Askuwa'tu, these are my sons. Pajackok Honiahaka, my eldest and heir."

The old chief waved toward the taller and leaner of the two boys, with a thick neck and broad shoulders. Pajackok had a narrow, grim face with high cheekbones and a long, ridged nose. His skin was paler than Asku's. The young man raised his hand in acknowledgement to the chief, his dark eyes still on Asku.

"Sunukkuhkau Ohanko," the Wanuukshiłáma chief said, turning to the shorter of the two at his other side. "My younger son."

The young man stepped forward with his hand raised. "Blessings, *ty-ee'*…uncle." Sunukkuhkau's voice was rough and deep. He stood a head shorter than Asku's father, perhaps two or three winters older than Asku, with an air of pride and power.

"And to you, my son," Asku's father smiled, patting him on the shoulder.

When the young man turned, he took two too many steps toward Asku. "Welcome, Askuwa'tu Haylaku."

Asku resisted the urge to step backward. Instead, he took a deep breath and stood tall, which helped because the young man's forehead was now at eye level.

"*Máh-sie, shikhs*," Asku replied, returning the stare.

For a moment, the tension electrified the gathering. Then the Wanuukshiłáma chief cracked it. "Kalataka, my old friend." Asku's grandfather stepped forward, arms outstretched.

"*Klahowya*," said the Elk Plains chief. "It has been too long."

The Chief guided Asku out of the way to allow introductions and pleasantries to continue. "*Tita*," the Chief whispered, "remind me to tell you the story of the first time I met your mother's brother. It is funny now, but at the time, was not."

"I am sure," Asku mumbled.

"I have a feeling, *tita*, that before you meet Kaliskah, you will need to win over two certain painted protectors."

"I can handle them."

At that moment, a hush overtook the village as a small group of men stepped between two cedar buildings. A golden orange glow from the dying day outlined the forms of three grown men following their escort. The latter walked toward the Wanuukshiłáma chief just as Kohana had done, hand raised in respect.

"Blessings, my *ty-ee'*." He stepped aside as he made the introduction, "The mighty chief of the Pyúsh P'ushtáayama, Matunaaga Sennulalatua."

Matchitehew looked much as he had on his visit to the Patisapatisháma village. His face was blank and emotionless. His eyes fidgeted, and looked droopy, as if deprived of sleep. He did not smile or speak. This time, however, he walked with an interesting cane with a ball on the end. Asku had never seen anything like it before.

He felt a chill from the evening breeze as his grandfather stepped back, allowing Matchitehew to approach. "Matunaaga," said Apenimon, as warmly as he had welcomed the others. "Welcome, my brother. I am glad that you have come."

Matchitehew nodded his head and looked over Pajackok and Sunukkuhkau, then held his hand up at shoulder height. "Apenimon," he said in Wawa, "thank you for inviting my brothers and I here for this celebration. We are honored to be included."

The Pyúsh chief then turned and walked toward the firepit, the two others following him. He stopped momentarily near Asku. The Chief nodded politely at him, and to Asku's surprise, the Snake chief nodded back.

Chaytan appeared out of nowhere near the Chief's left, both of his hands resting at his belt. The Snake chief eyed him momentarily before continuing to the very back of the fire and sitting down, eyes never still.

Matchitehew did not seem to notice that Mach'ni and Aanapay had materialized, somehow, between Kalataka and himself. Asku did but did not let on.

Then he realized, he had been holding his breath.

Chapter 27

After all the formalities, Asku helped Napayshni get their temporary tent settled. "Is it okay if I go look around now, *Wyánch'i?*"

"Yes, but there is someone I would like you to meet first," the Chief smiled. "My sister Huyana and her family."

"Kúu mísh," Asku said, begrudgingly.

"Askuwa'tu, listen carefully. You are not to go looking for Kaliskah. *Míshnam pamshtk'úksha"?*"

"Sure. Why not?"

"Customs are different here, *tita*, and we must respect that. Here you cannot have contact with a young woman unless her elder brother approves. And Pajackok is…well, you will find out soon enough. Let me just say that it will be a good action for you, for her, and for everyone, if you do not seek her out. Okay?"

Asku grunted something. "Askuwa'tu, I am serious about it."

"*Íi, Wyánch'i.*"

"Good. When you tell me that, I know you will do what is right."

Even if it drives me crazy, thought Asku.

As they approached a large, bustling family fire, a woman ran toward them trailing a long line of children. "Napay!" she cried out, flying into Asku's father's arms.

"*Míshnam wá, lítsa?*" said Napayshni, setting her down.

"We are well," she smiled, a very pretty smile. "We have been so excited for your visit. You didn't have much time at all the last time you came. You were in such a hurry." She was tall and slender, hair pulled neatly back and piled atop her head. Three or four little ones gathered around her long skirt.

The Chief put a hand on Asku's shoulder. "Huyana, you remember my oldest son, Askuwa'tu Haylaku."

"Blessings, *pámta*," she said, holding up a hand.

"And to you, *shisha*," Asku said. "I do not remember the last time; I was too small."

An older boy stepped from the house behind them, followed closely by Asku's grandmother.

"Blessings, *ila,*" the Chief said, holding up a polite hand.

"Napayshni," she said, nodding and sparing a glare for Asku.

All the uncertainty and self-doubt came back for a moment. Asku took a deep breath of the salt air, mastering his misgivings. "Blessings, *ála*," he said, in a calm but chilly voice.

The old woman snorted rudely, turned her nose up and walked away.

Napayshni, Asku, and Huyana all exchanged knowing looks of silent solidarity. Huyana then brought forward a smiling young man, perhaps a little older than Asku, with eyes that danced like those of the Sea Chief. He had the two long plaits in his hair, but nothing in his ears or lip. "Asku, this is my eldest son, Takoda."

"Blessings today," said Takoda.

"And to you, *yáya*." *For some reason, I like this Takoda right away. If we lived near each other, he would be with me and Hawilish and Kitchi.*

"Ah, Takoda, how goes it, young one?" the Chief said, slapping the boy on the back.

"I am well, uncle."

"Napay, where is Chaytan?" asked Huyana. "Please tell me you brought him?"

"Of course I brought him," answered Asku's father. "It was that or strap him to a tree."

"Well, go get him then! I want you both to meet my little one. Will you bless him, *yáya*, in our tongue?"

After the Chief raised the infant to the Great Spirits and said the words, Takoda offered to show Asku and Hawilish around the village and out to the sea. They walked a long, windy trail along the outskirts of the village.

"So, Askuwa'tu. You and Kaliskah, huh?"

Inside Asku, his guard went up. "Uh-huh. You can call me Asku."

"She's your sister, right?" Hawilish piped in.

"Half-sister. Her mother died not long after the child bed. Her mother, Paj and Sunu's, was my father's first mate. My mother is your chief's sister."

"Right," Hawilish said. "So, what is Kaliskah like?"

"Well, compared to other girls? I guess..." Takoda thought for a moment. "She's very sweet, you know, in a sister sort of way. But she always seems to be in trouble."

"What kind of trouble, man?" Asku asked, the ground becoming looser the further they walked out toward the Sea.

"Well, with Paj," the boy continued. "You see, she and Pajackok do not get along, never have. Which is not a good thing for her, if you know what I mean?"

"No, cousin," Asku said, stopping to look at him. "We definitely do not know what you mean."

Takoda looked at Asku carefully, then at Hawilish, and realized what was missing. "I see. Our customs are different from what you are used to. Our way is that a girl is her older brother's responsibility until she is mated before the Great Spirits. Until she is, therefore, Kaliskah belongs to Pajackok."

"She belongs to him. What exactly does that mean?" asked Asku, eyes narrowed.

Takoda looked surprised, then aghast for a moment. "Uh. I mean that she has to obey him. Just in how she lives her life."

"I am responsible for my sisters too," said Asku, "but they do not belong to me. In any way. My bow belongs to me. My moccasins belong to me. No people do."

"Well, our way is different, and in it, Kaliskah and Paj do not agree very often," the boy continued. "One time she defied him in front of many people and said a lot of insulting things about him. This happens often, because Kaliskah is the type to say what she is thinking. When she does, sometimes, he hits her."

"He hits her?" Hawilish repeated.

"Yep. My father does not like it much, but there isn't anything he can do. Our way allows it. My mother hates it a lot more. She is kind of careful, because this is her tribe now and he is the Chief's son, but I have seen her eyes. If I were Paj, I would not turn my back on her, ever."

"How often is this happening?" asked Asku.

"Oh, maybe once a moon, sometimes less. Last time he knocked her to the ground, but she came up and cracked him in the balls pretty good. I thought it was pretty funny." Hawilish snorted, looked up at Asku. "He threw up. Then he beat her."

Asku lost his breath momentarily, "He beat her?"

"Yeah, man. It happens sometimes, but apparently not where you guys are from. I am not saying he seriously injured her, or knocked out teeth, or broke bones, or disfigured her. I am sure he held back, because otherwise he could beat her to death. It is not like we're brutal or something."

"No, the Patisapatisháma do not usually have violence, unless the person has done something that is very much against our way of living."

Hawilish chimed in. "Asku, remember that time when your cousin—I forget his name—stole all that salmon and took it away to trade?"

"Yeah, I remember that. My father did hit him a couple of times. And they tied him to that post around back of the Story House for a while. But I do not think I could hit my sister Nayhali even if she hit me. I mean, I have even caught her at somewhat embarrassing moments, and looking back, no part of my heart wanted to hurt her. It is not our way."

"Well, things are different here, man," Takoda said with a shrug. "To be honest, I do not like it much. And most brothers do not hit their sisters. I have never seen the chief hit a woman or Sunu. But Paj is, well, a bit intense."

"I guess so," Hawilish added.

And I do not like it. Not one bit. That is my future mate he is hitting.

If he does it again, there is a good chance I will show him what a beating feels like.

"I think—well, let's be blunt, I know—that is why Kaliskah's so excited to get out of here," said Takoda with a smile. "In a way, this is good for you."

Asku looked at Takoda in surprise. "How can this be good for me in any way, man?"

Hawilish nodded. "Because Asku, she is not going to want to come back here. And you get to be the man who gets her away from Pajackok, so she is very glad you have come. She needs you to get her out of here."

They crested the top of the bluff. Behind them were red, barkless trees standing like sentinels. Ahead were rolling sand dunes with sparse patches of dune grass. Asku could hear the sea, but not see it.

Asku took off running, with Hawilish on his heels and Takoda trailing way behind. Making it over the last dune, he stopped to catch his breath. Running through dry sand was harder than he had expected.

They both looked up and down the beach, then at each other with a smile. No one else was around. Asku shed all his clothing and ran toward the water. The wind felt cool against his bare skin. As he reached the wet sand, a part of him registered that it was much colder than he had imagined. He could hear Hawilish's bare feet close behind him as they ran across the dark, soggy sand, sinking in only the width of a finger.

At the water's edge, Asku sped up, picking his legs up higher and higher to get further out into the waves. At thigh depth, when the first breaker hit him, he dove straight under it. He came up behind it in waist deep water, threw his hair back over his head and yelled. "Cold!"

Hawilish popped up very near him, cursing. They ran back toward the water's edge as the waves chased them from behind. Takoda laughed and laughed as they frantically pulled their shirts and trousers back on.

"You could have warned us, man!" Hawilish complained, shivering into his trousers. "What was that all about?"

"You didn't wait long enough," said Takoda between guffaws. "How was I to know that where you come from, all the water is warm?"

"It isn't," said Asku, pulling his shirt back on. "But it's not as cold as that, except in the winter. I am not sure my parts will ever recover from that shock. I wish you had said something."

"No way," Takoda snickered. "This was way more fun. But next time, I wouldn't go out that far either, at least not until I teach you some things. The rip tide can take you off your feet in a heartbeat."

"Do not worry," Hawilish grumbled.

"What's a rip tide?" asked Asku.

"The Sea has currents that are as strong as the wave that hit you, but which pull you out to deep water. If you get caught by one, and you panic, you could drown."

"I was ready to panic even without any of these rip tides," observed Asku. "So how do you escape it?"

"Swim sideways. You cannot swim against it, and you will just get exhausted. Then you are dead for sure. Look at the beach and swim along it, to get out of the rip tide, which is not very wide. Then swim to the shallows."

They walked along the beach as the sun reached to touch the horizon. The boys passed mothers digging for clams with long pointed sticks. Another group stood knee-deep in the water scraping black mussels from the sides of rocks with sharp, flat-edged stones.

"What is that?" Hawilish pointed down the beach. "Are those the bones of the great fish your tribe hunts?"

Down the beach stood large pieces of wood, as tall as trees, sticking straight out of the sand at awkward angles. It resembled a large wooden skeleton.

"That's a Floating House," Takoda stated, as if everyone knew.

Asku stared at it. "A what? Houses do not float."

"Haven't you heard the stories," Takoda asked, "of the Ghost Men...the ones who came here long ago?"

"No," Hawilish and Asku replied.

"Oh, you've missed a good one, then," Takoda said. "A long time ago, a Floating House appeared out there, a big canoe of sorts. My ancestors were afraid. They feared the Great Spirits were angry, that they had done something wrong. They watched and they waited until small canoes were lowered from it and came toward the shore. The chief sent the mothers and children away, while he and the men waited there at the beach for whatever their punishment was."

Asku looked out toward the horizon, trying to imagine such a strange thing.

"As the canoes came closer, the chief saw that men sat in them...ghost men, with pale white skin. The men were afraid. Some threw rocks and others yelled, trying to make the spirits go back. A loud sound came from one of the canoes and a man fell to the ground, blood pouring from his chest. The others picked him up and ran for the safety of the trees. The Ghost Men came to shore. When they came within sight of the trees, my ancestors killed them all."

"Really," Hawilish asked, "Ghost Men?"

"Yep, and eventually the Floating House tipped over in a storm and washed up here," Takoda said, pointing toward the frame.

They reached the tall logs and walked through it, touching the sides and gaping at its size. "Did the man die?" asked Hawilish.

"Yes, and it did not take long."

"Did you ever figure out how the Ghost Men killed him?" Asku wondered out loud.

"A Biting Spear," Takoda said.

"Ah. It was like a spear but with poison or something?" Asku asked.

"We do not know," said Takoda. "The men captured some off the bodies of the dead Ghost Men but did not understand how they worked. We found a ball of heavy metal in one of the Biting Spears, and most of the Ghost Men had bags of these metal balls. That is what I was told, anyway. Our elders talked about what we should do. Some thought we should try to figure out the Biting Spears, and that we should use the wood of the Floating House since it was already cut. But the majority said that if we kept the items in our village, it would attract evil spirits. So, we still do not use the wood, and we threw the Biting Spears into where the Great River pours into the Sea."

"Have you ever seen anything like this, still floating?" Hawilish asked.

Takoda pointed out to sea. "Some say they have seen Floating Houses again, but none have come close. We have heard stories from Beyond the Great Mountains though, similar stories."

"Really?" Asku wondered, inspecting the wood.

"Yes." Takoda rested his hand on a piece of the eerie skeleton and looked up. "We have family far beyond the Great River, near the Land that Floats in the Sea. They say the Ghost Men have returned."

"This is oak, I think," said Asku, running his hand along a portion of the frame, "although I do not know the cut at all. What did the Floating House look like? Do the stories say?"

"Yea, it had many white cloth pieces hanging from it, tied with rope. The stories say that from a distance, they looked like hides, maybe from something bigger than a bison, but some pieces of them eventually washed ashore, and they turned out to be woven cloth. The largest had two intersecting red lines. The elders speak of that sign often, so that all generations will remember how to know when Ghost Men are near."

"Why?" Hawilish asked.

"In case they ever come back again," Takoda said, walking out of the structure.

Asku followed him. "You have never seen those Biting Spears, the ones that killed the man?" Asku inquired as they walked along the dark, wet sand.

"No, although my father saw one near the Land that Floats in the Sea, but the man kept it very close, and he never saw how it worked."

"Then in that Land, they are not worried about attracting evil spirits," Hawilish observed.

"I guess not," said Takoda. "But that does not mean they have not attracted any. I notice my father did not trade for it and bring it back."

>—→

Later that evening, they sat around the firepit as darkness set in. Asku looked around at the women and older girls, some of whom were being either subtle or obvious about trying to get his attention.

"She is not here," Takoda whispered, leaning close to Asku.

"Where is she?"

Takoda pointed to a nearby tent. "There. She won't come out until tomorrow's ceremony, and believe me, she is not happy about it. And I would not be surprised if she found a way to communicate."

Asku resisted an impulse to touch his choker. *Ha. No, Takoda, that would not surprise me either.*

Aanapay and Mach'ni soon arrived, and Asku introduced his Elk Plains comrades. He soon found that they had convened an impromptu "Funny Stories About Asku" session, in which everyone present could participate. The older two rolled with laughter as Takoda painted the scene of two boys screaming and running, the cold waves chasing their naked behinds. After the first three or four, including Hawilish's tale of a childhood mishap where Asku sat down on the wrong rock near a firepit, Asku had the impulse to say that he'd heard enough. And from rather deeper inside him, something said: *no, I should appreciate this. Even Mach'ni is laughing. The only reason this is happening is because they are all my friends, though they come from three different peoples, and I am what they have in common.*

Aanapay shared a moment in which Asku had been standing next to his horse's head, and the animal had sneezed a horsey quantity of snot onto his ear. He gestured to indicate enough to fill a man's hand. Takoda was almost in tears.

And remembering the moment, Asku was too.

Soon the Wanuukshiłáma chief appeared, raised his hands and shouted, "It is time!"

Everyone hurried to clean up and put on his best clothing. Asku donned the small headdress that denoted a Chief's son and was glad for its lightness in comparison to what his father wore. The mighty River Chief's headdress displayed two rows of eagle feathers that climbed high above his head and fell to the ground behind him. The bead and bone decorations clinked together when he walked. Asku had picked up the ancient *tamáawish* once, and marveled that his father could wear it without falling over.

Asku and his father stepped out of the tent to much applause from the ceremonial fire area. Women carried children, large baskets of food, or both, all the while herding other children in little coveys. *It is a lot of work for them*, thought Asku, *but they are showing off too: their cooking, their children, their crafts.*

The Wanuukshiłáma chief waved Asku and his father over, seating them on his right side, the Wawyukyáma chief and U'hitaykah on his left. Then the gifts were brought forth.

Many things were given away: beautifully carved ivory knives, jewelry, blankets with intricate designs woven into them, some more of that oolichan oil which Chitsa so loved in spite of its awful smell, and much more.

Then Apenimon pointed to two young women huddled together on the outskirts of the fire and motioned them as a gift to the Patisapatisháma.

The taller woman sighed as she led the other by the hand toward Asku and his father, where they knelt all the way to the ground, still holding hands. Asku's father nodded in thanks and waved for them to rise and go about celebration business.

The Wanuukshiłáma were excited about the bison and elk meat, horns, and hooves that the Elk Plains people had sent. The women became equally excited from the outskirts as Chaytan presented the stack of mountain goat skins from the Patisapatisháma, obtained on long trips toward Pahto. They passed each item around for all to touch.

After the gift-giving, the women presented food beginning with the chiefs. Takoda explained each dish to Asku. In addition to the standard fare of venison, salmon and sturgeon, there were all kinds of sea creatures to taste: whale meat, otter, clams, mussels. Asku gagged on the mussels but forced them down in case anyone was watching. The sea urchin was worse, with a spiky shell that seemed as if it were still moving. Asku looked around, while Takoda nodded with a smirk. The orange innards tasted bitter and salty and terrible. As Asku made a face and passed on the rest, Takoda burst out laughing.

Except for shellfish that tasted like fishy bison tendons, and sea urchins that tasted like something one might eat in order to throw up poisonous berries, the feast was perhaps the finest of Asku's life. When it wound down, and the women and older girls began cleaning up, an old man lit and passed the *chalámat* to the Wanuukshiłáma chief. When it was Asku's turn, he took a careful breath of the pungent, nose-burning mix. The smoke mingled with that from the fire in front of him, swirling up to the dark cloudless sky. The fire kept the night chill at bay.

After the post-dinner smoke, the Sea Chief stood and raised his hands in front of him, a striking white fur draped over his shoulders. "Welcome, my friends," he shouted. "Welcome all."

Great cheering erupted around him.

"My brothers," he continued, "tonight we feast, tonight we celebrate our reunion." He turned toward Pajackok with an outstretched hand. "Tomorrow, we celebrate the union of this tribe with the great tribe of the people at the River once again."

There was another barrage of cheering and yelling. Pajackok stood, then raised his hand to speak and turned toward Asku. "Soon, we will hunt the whale that will give its life to us. Will you join my brothers and me, young chief of the Patisapatisháma?"

Asku's heart pounded with excitement. "I will," he replied, head held high. He did not look around to see the faces of the Patisapatisháma present, but he felt their pride in the air and in his spirit.

After another round of cheering and whooping, the Sea Chief raised his hand again. "Long have this people been proud," he began, now in a forceful tone. "Long have this people been mighty, long have this people been filled with courage!" He raised his fists up over his head, shaking them as the crowd yelled.

"Was it not so, long ago, that we came here, across the sea of never-ending ice and coldness, the sky dark and void, the mighty Sun hidden from her people? Was it not so, long ago, when the Ghosts of Men arrived?"

This is a master of speaking to many people, thought Asku. *He has something of Spirit. He has the attention of everyone. I think even babies inside their mothers are hearing him.* Like all others, Asku's eyes were fixed on the mighty Wanuukshiláma chief with the voice of thunder and shaking fists. "They came on their Floating Houses, with their Biting Spears, and we—" he pounded his chest, hard—"we, this people, …sent…them…back!"

More cheers and shouting.

All became quiet as the chief spoke softer, his eyes closed. He gestured toward Kalataka. "Long have this people been proud, long have this people been strong!" Then Apenimon gestured likewise toward Napayshni: "Long have this people been united, long…have we been brothers!"

After another round of cheers, two men entered the circle dressed in grass skirts and short cedar wraps. A makeshift bark canoe hung from their shoulders on long strips of hide. They danced around the fire, dramatizing the story the Wanuukshiláma chief told:

Two brothers: weary and hungry and homesick…travelled.
The Sun was hidden and the waters, ice. They could not find land.
The ice crept out to sea, pushing them further and further from home.
Father Wind howled around them, blowing them without care.

The younger spoke into the wind. "Take us where you may, my old friend, for we are now lost. We are far from home."

The older spoke too. "But let this place where you lead us be warm," he spat in anger, "for I hate this never-ending cold!"

"Do not say such things," the younger one snapped, "you will anger the Spirits!"

Father Wind blew angrily, and the canoe moved faster and faster, out of control, then spinning in circles. The brothers fell to the floor of the canoe, covering their heads with their white bear cloaks as Father Wind screamed around them. They reached for each other, holding tightly.

The younger whispered. "Oh, Great Spirit, protect us from this evil...oh, Great Spirit, protect us from this evil...oh, Great Spirit, protect us from this evil..."

"Father Wind, forgive my brother. He knows not what he says."
Then all was still.

The younger brother lifted his head slightly. Great drops of water flew into his eyes; not snow, not ice...just water.

"Brother, look," he exclaimed pointing into the night sky, "Mother Moon!"

The other brother refused to lift his head. He mumbled incoherently from the bottom of the canoe.

The younger brother noticed something moving next to the canoe. The creature lifted its head above the water and looked at him. Its sleek body shined in the moonlight; its eyes, bright and beautiful; its nose, hooked, and its tail, flapped; black and red spots on its scaly flesh.

Asku laughed out loud as someone held a long stick out very near the men and the canoe, waving it around. On the end of the stick was the head of a salmon painted red, black and green. Even Matchitehew laughed.

"Hello, my friend," the brother whispered. "Can you tell me where we are?"

The creature winked and began to swim toward the shore.

The boy saw a trail through the ice. He put his hands into the water on either side of the canoe and paddled. He wished for nothing more than to follow the beautiful creature he had just seen.

He paddled hard and fast while his brother, still huddled in fear, spoke words he could not understand.

The boy kept his eye ever on the mystical creature in front of his canoe. Every now and then she stopped and looked back at him. The shore appeared as she led him through the ice.

"What is this place?" he called up to her.

She turned her head and seemed to smile, then disappeared under the surface.

The boy screamed for her, deathly afraid of losing her. "Come back, please come back! Do not leave me!"

Then, a woman stepped from the depths. He could see her clearly.

Her head broke through the icy waters first; long, sleek hair as black as the night sky fell over her shoulders. She walked from the depths; he could see her back, her arms and her legs. As her midnight hair fell down her back, it covered her nakedness from him once again.

Asku laughed aloud again, as another man appeared wearing nothing but a breechcloth and black grass on his head that hung down almost to the ground. He danced around, pulling the grass around his front to cover his pretend nakedness, and shaking his backside in others' faces.

The boy put his hands back into the water and paddled ferociously, following the beautiful creature.

As her bare toes reached the edge of the water, she ran across the small beach and disappeared into the thickness of a dark forest.

"Wait," the boy called, "please wait!"

He jumped from the canoe into the icy waters and swam with all his might the rest of the distance. Reaching the water's edge, his body numb with the cold, he turned back. The canoe and his brother were gone. He called to him, screamed with all his breath, but nothing.

He looked at the forest, the trees stood like mountains before him, their arms reaching toward the night sky.

She appeared there, her skin and hair radiating like the night sky he had not seen in a very long time. The boy ran toward her, and she held her hands out to him. He took them both and the two disappeared into the forest.

The old chief laughed. "I love that story! But that, my brothers, is why we honor the salmon. Do not forget to always send your first salmon back into the water with the blessing song, for otherwise, you may miss your chance at seeing the beautiful black-haired woman-fish…nakedness and all." That got another round of chuckles, which Apenimon joined as he added, "Some of us have been begging Mother Moon for this one to come true our whole lives!"

Chapter 28

Asku could not get comfortable that night. Whatever was in that *chalámat*, or perhaps those disgusting mussels, had given him a stomachache. His head felt fuzzy, and his ears were still ringing from the crowd noise. He rubbed his temples in small circles as a sliver of firelight appeared at the tent door.

Asku lifted his head, just catching Aanapay's cheeky grin as he pointed toward Asku's cot. Darkness fell once again when the tent flap closed behind.

A dark, shrouded figure seemed to float toward him. Asku had not felt truly safe here since the moment the Pyúsh P'ushtáayama had arrived, but this was obviously not them. The figure knelt next to his head. Like a soft breeze on a warm day came a gentle scent of woman, a tender touch, a line drawn along his chin, his neck, down the twisted hide, a coolness that rested over his heart, the smooth, black stone beneath.

"Kaliskah?" he whispered into the night. His heart pounded under the black stone and her cool touch, and he slid back her hood. Her eyes sparkled in the darkness. He touched her face, felt the soft curve down her jaw to her chin. She closed her eyes to his touch.

Kaliskah took both of his hands and pulled him to his feet. He thought momentarily about what his father had said, but that fleeting thought faded as he followed his heart. He grabbed his wrap from the cot. She led him to the back of the tent and lifted a loose part of the hide. He followed her under and outside.

She covered her head, looked left to right, then darted across the open fire area while pulling Asku along behind her. He did not know or care where she was leading him. He longed to see her, to hear her voice, to hold her in his arms at last. Her hand was small and soft and cool inside of his, but she gripped his hand as if she would never let him go again.

They walked through the thick underbrush of the red, barkless forest until a narrow trail began to slope upward, with jagged rocky areas. He watched her carefully, bracing to catch her if she stumbled, but she went up it like a mountain goat. Soon they emerged on a flat, rocky cliff edge, from which Asku could hear the crashing waves of water on the beach below, exactly where he had been earlier that day. The moonlight accented the wrecked wooden skeleton.

He gripped her hand tightly as they looked over the long dropoff. The sea was as infinite as the night sky on the horizon. The countless stars twinkled from their created places and the sliver of moon smiled at him as he breathed the salty air.

But the sea held nothing for him, not with her finally so close.

He turned to face her. Kaliskah dropped the hood from her head, and her hair swam around her face in the wind. Her smile reached her eyes as they danced like Apenimon's, although she had the drawn features of her older painted protector. Her lips were full and red, like a sunset back home. He longed to touch her, to feel her skin and her heartbeat under his fingers.

Her head cocked to one side as she looked at him. He stepped closer, moving both of them away from the treacherous cliff edge.

"Kaliskah," he stammered, "I—"

She closed the distance between them and held a finger to his lips. Her body was so close now that he could smell her, a mixture of honey and salt.

She slid both hands around to the back of his neck, sending tingles down his spine. Then, roughly and with surprising strength for her size, she pulled his head down, and his lips met hers.

He slipped his hands inside her wrap, found her waist, and pulled her to him. Her satisfied sigh told him everything. He enjoyed the taste of her tongue as it roamed along his lips and teeth.

Moments passed, maybe longer, until she stepped back. Asku gasped for air.

"I am sorry, Askuwa'tu Haylaku." Her voice was a beautiful song in his ears. "It is just that I have been waiting a long time, and I wanted our first meeting to be special."

Asku laughed out loud. "Asku, please, and you succeeded. You are beautiful, Kaliskah." He knelt in front of her, reached into his wrap and pulled out the sheathed dagger he had made, then presented to her in its sheath, hilt first. The moonlight revealed the patterns colored into the leather, the carved and colored antler handle, and the top of the exquisite bluish-gray blade. Her eyes grew wide.

"I made this for you," he whispered. "It is my promise to you that, with every last breath in my chest, and every beat of my heart, that I will protect you, I will honor you, and I will love you."

She accepted the dagger, turned it over, held it in the moonlight to examine the artwork. Her eyes lit up as she examined the orca and the bear. Kaliskah looked down at him as if she were about to cry, and then one small, silent tear fell. He reached up to brush it away and she grabbed both of his hands.

"Asku, this is so beautiful," she said, looking deep into his soul. "*Máh-sie*…thank you."

He spread his wrap on the ground there at the top of the cliff. The night air was cold, but they sat there hand in hand, and after a while, she leaned into his shoulder. He shivered often, but not from a chill.

"Are you afraid, Kaliskah?" he asked after a while.

"Of what?"

"Of leaving all of this." He waved his hand out toward the sea. "Of coming up Nch'i-Wána to live with me?"

She searched him again with her piercing eyes, then leaned back against his shoulder. "Not anymore," she whispered. "Tell me about the river, Asku. Tell me about your mother."

Asku felt like he went on and on, but he loved talking about home and about his family and wanted her to be excited. The two talked about everything and nothing at all, until light began to appear behind them.

Asku stood quickly, waking from his wonderful dream to their precarious reality. "Kaliskah, I must get you home before everyone awakens."

As the sunlight grew Toward the Rising Sun, he could see the color of her skin, her hair and her eyes. She took his breath away. She stood and touched his bare chest, hands soft and warm now against his cool skin. She moved them down his rib cage, encircled his waist and laid her head against his neck. She seemed to fit perfectly under his chin as he wrapped his arms around her. He dropped his face into her hair, breathed her smell deeply, willing himself never to forget it.

"I am glad you are finally here, my young chief."

As they approached the ceremonial firepit, she squeezed his hand, looked up into his eyes one last time, and disappeared through a back door entrance into one of the large cedar homes. He continued between two of the buildings, feeling as if he could fly.

Chaytan and Napayshni were having a quiet talk while Aanapay stoked the glowing embers. Asku pretended to adjust his trousers as if he had just relieved himself, then walked up.

"Sleep well, young chief?" Aanapay teased with a quiet chuckle. "I am certain yours was sweeter than mine."

The Chief looked from Aanapay to Asku and back again, some sort of recognition dawning. "Come, *tita*," he beckoned.

They sat at the fire talking about the day and the upcoming whale hunt. Scuffling and shouting from the other side of the fire soon cut their conversation short.

Pajackok came around the corner, hauling Kaliskah by the hair. Sunukkuhkau was not far behind, arguing with his brother. Kaliskah fought back, but in vain; Pajackok was a giant next to her. Just then, the Sea Chief exited the tent farthest from them.

Asku hurried toward the scene, his eyes flashing anger.

"Asku, no," he heard his father insist.

"Pajackok," Apenimon demanded, rising to his full height, "what is the meaning of this?"

Pajackok hurled Kaliskah at the Chief's feet. She fell to her hands and knees in the dust just as Asku skidded to a stop behind them. Others gathered around.

"She has dishonored you, *tl-ka-má-ma*," he spat, "and she has dishonored me." He grabbed her by the wrist, raising it high in the air. Kaliskah gasped in pain at his grip, then again as he threw her back down.

"Not now, Pajackok," the old chief said, bending to help his daughter to her feet.

Pajackok turned on his heels to face Asku, face full of fury. He raised a long finger and pointed it at Asku. "She never came to bed last night. She has dishonored us with him!"

Asku's stomach knotted. *What have I done?*

"*Nakst*...no, I did not!" Kaliskah hissed.

"Paj, that is enough," Sunu said, but Pajackok shoved him away.

Asku stepped forward with a hand raised in respect. "No, she has not, *shikhs*."

His father grabbed his arm from behind again. "Asku, *no*."

"I will not have a false thing said of me or her, *túta*." Asku turned to Pajackok. "We went for a walk. That is all."

"She disobeyed me. She must be punished. You know our custom." Pajackok shouted. A crowd was gathering.

Kaliskah brushed her skirt off and rubbed her sore wrist. "Pajackok, leave me alone, and you leave him out of it! You cannot tell me what to do forever! *Tl-ka-má-ma*," Kaliskah added, turning toward Apenimon, "I took Asku to the cliff. We talked all night. He did not touch me, father, I promise."

Asku tried not to wince at the partial lie.

"Well...I kissed him," she added quietly, as the villagers gasped. "It was my fault, though. I did it, father. I kissed him. I am sorry."

Pajackok stepped in front of her and backhanded her down to his feet. Something snapped in Asku: *I made a promise last night. It is time to keep it.* He moved between them and stood over her, fists clenched. "*Kopet'*...stop!" he hissed. "You will not touch her again."

Pajackok jumped back in surprise but recovered and glared back. "Move away, Askuwa'tu. She is my responsibility, not my father's and not yet yours. Mine!"

The two stared at each other for a long time until the Sea Chief spoke.

"Askuwa'tu," he said quietly, "I am afraid that Pajackok is right. Kaliskah Sayen is his responsibility. It is our custom, my son."

Asku looked from Pajackok to the Sea Chief and back again. He looked down at Kaliskah, her angry tears making muddy streaks down her beautiful face, a large bruise already forming on her right cheek. He had promised.

And he knew what he had to do.

He took a deep breath. "Then I will take her punishment," he said to Pajackok with a glare that dared him to refuse.

Pajackok looked from Asku, to his father, to Sunu and back again, unsure how to proceed. "What's the matter, Pajackok? I respect your custom; there is punishment for violating a rule. I will take it. Here I am."

"*Nakst*...no!" Kaliskah tried to move past Asku, but he blocked her path. He could not block her voice. "No, Pajackok! We did nothing wrong. Leave him out of this."

Asku looked at the Sea Chief. "*Ty-ee'*, I would appreciate if you would ask your daughter to step back. I choose to take her punishment."

The old man betrayed no emotion as he glanced toward Asku's father. There was something like a nod of understanding or agreement. The Wanuukshiɫáma chief turned back toward Asku and nodded.

"No!" Kaliskah tried to push past Asku. Pajackok seemed unsure what to do.

"Kaliskah, you must go, my dear," the Sea Chief said, in a voice accustomed to obedience.

"I will not!"

"Kaliskah, you will go now," the chief said, angrily this time. "That is final. Sunukkuhkau, take her home and see that she does not leave."

As Sunu stepped toward her, Kaliskah raised a hand to stop him momentarily. She turned to face Asku but did not touch him. She pitched her voice loud enough for all to hear. "Askuwa'tu, you are the only one who has ever stood up for me. *Máh-sie*...thank you."

And with that, she let Sunu drag her away with only modest resistance.

Pajackok stood still, snorting like a caged animal. Some villagers called out in disgust and shook their fists in the air, including what sounded like anger at Pajackok.

Asku dropped to his knees and laced his fingers behind his back, looking up in defiance. "Well?" he asked.

"No!" Hawɨlish shouted. He sprinted past Asku and struck Pajackok hard in the face. Pajackok stumbled backward but regained his balance quickly. He wiped the back of his hand across his bleeding and already swelling lower lip. His eyes narrowed as he spat blood at Hawilish's feet.

"Hawilish," the Chief sternly called to him.

Hawilish did not seem to hear his Chief's command. He stood at the ready. "Hawilish," whispered Asku, "I must do this."

Hawilish looked at Asku, searched his face, looked up at Pajackok with a look that said, *go too far and it may be the last thing you ever do*, then ran a frustrated hand through his hair and fell back to the others.

"Let us be done with this," Asku said angrily. "We have a whale to hunt."

Pajackok stood over Asku. "Did you touch my sister?" he spat.

"Yes, I did," said Asku. "But I did no more than kiss her and sit with her."

Pajackok growled, then belted Asku across the face. Asku felt his teeth slice the inside of his cheek and a sting as his lower lip split. He spat out blood. "When this is over," Asku snarled, glaring back, "if you ever lay a hand on her again, I will hunt you down and kill you very slowly."

"Did you defile my sister?" Pajackok demanded through his teeth, ignoring Asku's comment.

"No. I did not."

Asku braced himself this time. Pajackok's hand came down hard, higher on his face. He felt the impact against his cheekbone and eye, then the warm trickle of blood down his cheek and chin.

He looked up with one eye. "You are nothing but a coward," Asku said, disdainfully. "Beating up your little sister and a man who refuses to fight back, and for what? Honor? This is not honor. You have a problem, man."

Pajackok snorted and raised his hand, striking Asku again across the right cheek. His cheek and the inside of his mouth were numb, but he could feel the blood dripping from his nose and into his mouth. He spat again to clear it.

"Is that all you have?" Asku taunted.

The young man raised his hand again. "*Ko-pet'*," Apenimon ordered. "Enough!"

Pajackok looked as if he would defy his father, then looked to the Sea Chief and back to Asku again, then turned on his heel and stalked away.

Asku unlaced his fingers and forced himself to stand up unassisted. "Asku," his father asked, "are you all right, *tita?*"

"Yes." He spat more blood from his mouth. "I am fine."

Well, my heart is not fine. My heart wants to go after Pajackok and kick his cowardly backside all the way to the Two Sisters, and then get rough with him. But that would give him satisfaction. Asku breathed in and out to steady himself, tried to open the injured eye, and with great pain, managed it.

"You are very brave, my son," the Sea Chief said. He smiled and held out a clean cloth.

"Apenimon...your Grandfather, please?" Napayshni asked.

"Of course. I will show you the way."

Asku heard many whispers as he followed the old chief around the firepit toward the home of the village's healer. He held his head high.

"Wow, *píti,*" U'hitaykah chuckled, from somewhere nearby.

"I told you, man," Takoda chimed in.

"Do you need help, Napayshni?" asked Kalataka.

"No, he will be fine," said Asku's father.

"We will come by in a bit, then."

Asku, Hawilish, and Napayshni entered the Wanuukshiłáma Grandfather's tent. It smelled of sweet incense. Hawilish leaned in for a look. "Oh man, Asku, your eye is a mess."

"Go outside. I will be fine."

"*Kúu mísh.* I will be right outside."

Asku heard him leave. His head was pounding. "Where does it hurt, my son?" asked a kind voice from somewhere nearby.

"My head. Though the rest of my face is not doing so well either," he said, clenching his teeth against the various pains that all blended into a head full of discomfort.

An old man came into the vision range of Asku's good eye, handing him a cup. "Drink this. It will help."

Whatever it was, it was bitter. It stung his cut lip and burned his throat when he swallowed, but he soon felt the burning liquid fall into his stomach. His fingers and toes started to tingle.

"Is that better, *tita*?" his father asked.

"Uh-huh," he mumbled. He felt warm hands feeling his head, probing for sore spots. He felt fingers probing in his mouth for broken teeth and at the cuts on his cheek. He felt something in his nose, and a gentle pull.

"His nose is not broken, Napayshni, nor has he any broken teeth," the old man said. "That is good."

"Young Askuwa'tu," the Grandfather said, from the side with the battered eye, "can you hear me?"

"Uh-hunh."

"I believe you will heal, *ten'-as*. You did not suffer serious damage, though I am sure it feels serious enough. I could try to stitch the spot below your lip, but not your eye. Either way, you will always carry a scar. Napayshni?"

"I think he will be fine," laughed the Chief. "We have our share of scars. Don't we, Asku?"

"Sure," Asku mumbled. "What's another scar or two?"

"All right," said the Grandfather. "I will make a poultice for the cuts. You will need to lie still for awhile."

"That sounds good," mumbled Asku, reclining on the furs. The Grandfather sat down next to them and began mixing up some grandfatherly healing concoction.

"So, Asku...the whale hunt," the Chief began. "I was worried about you being out there on the open sea with Paj and Sunu and knowing the two of them fairly well."

Asku was silent. The Grandfather chuckled as he mixed something else into his work.

"But I am thinking they will have a new appreciation for you, my *tita*, after this whole affair. I am proud of you, Askuwa'tu."

The Grandfather chuckled again, kindly, as he put the mixture on the cut under Asku's mouth. The poultice smelled pungent and earthen but felt cool and only stung a little after the initial twinge of touch. Then the old man wetted a small, supple hide and laid it across Asku's forehead.

"I never should've gone with her last night," Asku said. "I am sorry."

"What is done is done. I must go talk with Apenimon now. We will put the hunt off until tomorrow when you are feeling better. Will you be all right?"

Asku nodded.

As he turned to leave, Napayshni stopped. Asku could just see a sly smile. "By the way, what did you think of her?"

Asku smiled, in spite of the immediate pain it caused. "She is special."

"Good. I will send in Hawilish. You rest."

Just as Hawilish came in, Asku heard a new confrontation begin outside. "Not now, *ila!*" growled his father from somewhere nearby. Asku could not make out his grandmother's answer, but it sounded angry. "It is none of your concern!" continued Napayshni. "You will leave this place at once, and you may not come near my son under any circumstances. If you try, I will see to it you are stopped."

The voices became muffled and eventually disappeared. Asku peered out at Hawilish, who whispered, "Mach'ni is outside. I am here." With that, Asku fell asleep.

)——→

When Asku opened his eyes again, his headache was fading but his face felt like freshly pounded *wawachi*. He heard voices outside the tent, two deep male tones and a woman's voice. He looked around.

Hawilish moved his stool closer to Asku's head. He nodded toward the door. "It's either Pajackok or his brother, or your grandmother. They have all been snooping around here all day. I am not sure if they are keeping an eye on you or making sure Kaliskah doesn't get to you. But don't worry. Mach'ni and Chaytan are also right outside. Last time I looked, Mach'ni was cleaning his fingernails with that big knife of his."

Asku laughed a little, which hurt.

"Is she worth it?" Hawilish asked, after a moment or two, quietly.

Asku kept his head in his hands.

"Because, man, all I am saying is…well, you have known her, what, one day? And look at you."

"Okay, I get your point," Asku muttered. "And yes, she is worth it. Now, will you please help me get out of here?"

Hawɨlish stood to help Asku stand up. "*Náy…*okay?" he asked.

"Yep, just a moment. Still a little dizzy."

"Maybe you should sit back down, then."

Asku looked his best friend in the eye, steadied himself on his feet. "*Kw'ałá, pásiks.*"

"Sure," Hawɨlish replied, "just take it easy. *Náy?*"

"For what you did, I mean."

"Humph," Hawɨlish grunted, "a lot of good it did you."

Asku rubbed his temples. "It was what I wanted to do but could not. And it was a nice punch. Did you see his lip?"

"If it were Hatayah, and I was her future mate, and someone roughed her up and was about to hit me to punish her—"

"I would not stop with one hit. But it was good that you did, here and now."

Hawɨlish smiled, beginning from somewhere deep within.

▶—

She did not come to him that night. As much as he longed to see her, Asku was thankful. His headache was gone, but his throbbing face inhibited his sleep. He was beginning to regret having refused another dose of the Grandfather's drink. Even though Mach'ni sat awake outside the tent door, peeking in now and then to check, Asku could not rest easily.

The whale hunt preparations would begin at the new dawn. He would either prove himself to the Wanuukshiłáma people or make things worse again. Asku would help to paddle one of the long hunting canoes, hand weapons to the hunters, and be available as needed. It was a sacred hunt to the Wanuukshiłáma, and an honor to participate even on a paddle. *And it is also very dangerous. My father explained it to me: it takes a great deal of skill, and they can only afford to have one green crewman along, and then only to do as told without hesitation. Pajackok started behind a paddle, and I am sure the Sea Chief did also. Why are they allowing me to participate?*

Is it out of respect for my father and grandfather? Or is it a test by Kaliskah's brothers?

If I were them, that is probably what it would be. Either way, much is at stake. No matter the reason, I cannot embarrass myself, or I will embarrass my people.

Asku gave up on sleep long before the sunrise. The old Wanuukshiłáma chief sat in front of the three Totems, his wrap pulled tightly around his shoulders.

"May I join you, *ty-ee*?" Asku said, quietly.

The Sea Chief gave a slight nod. Asku down sat cross-legged next to the old man and pulled his wrap tightly around his own shoulders. He closed his eyes, listening, feeling, breathing in the coming day, and trying to release the events up to now.

"You are a good choice for my Kaliskah," he said, kindly. "There is strength about you, my son. You will do great things for your people." Apenimon sighed. "And you will care for my Kaliskah."

"I will."

"Hmm. By the way, just outside your tent is a breechcloth. You should go put it on."

Chapter 29

Sunukkuhkau approached Asku as dawn dispelled the early dusk. Other young men had begun to gather around the morning fire. Asku nodded.

"I am sorry about what happened," said Sunu, very softly. "However, I am not sorry for our custom. It is who we are."

Asku said nothing.

Sunu sighed. "Paj, he just, well…he feels a lot of pressure."

Asku turned his still-swollen face toward the Sea Chief's son. "That, I understand. But he will not touch Kaliskah again. I have agreed to this union, to take her as my mate, uniting our tribes once again. I say how she will be treated. He will not lay a hand on her again."

"I do not think Pajackok feels that way. She is still his to worry about and to take care of, for now."

"Then we will have a problem."

Sunu stared at Asku for what felt like a long time. "You think you are better than us," he stated.

"Not at all, Sunukkuhkau. This has nothing to do with customs. It has to do with people. I have agreed to this union with Kaliskah, and I have a problem with a man twice her size treating her roughly, brother or not. And if Pajackok thinks about it, he should not want me to feel any other way. If he wants the best for Kaliskah, he will respect my position."

"How is it that you care so much about my sister when you have spent one night together?" There was more than a hint of challenge in the tone.

Asku turned to look Sunu in the eyes. "I cannot explain exactly why. I think maybe only elders understand how all that works. Even before I met her, I had a sense of good feeling toward her. But in that night, we talked a lot about her home and mine. She wanted to know about my mother, and she told me what she knew about hers, yours."

"And that is mostly what you did?" Sunu's eyes bored into Asku's.

Asku met them. "It is the truth. Did we touch? Yes, but not as parents do."

"Did you kiss?"

"Yes. But in truth, we spent almost all the time getting to know each other's lives and minds. If you must know, I would probably not have known to do anything else, and even if I tried, I might have made a great fool out of myself. She did not encourage anything else, anyway, and I am glad. That is my word."

"What if she had?"

"I have not thought about that, because all our talk that night made me think of her mind, and what she hopes for in her future. So, I do not know."

Sunu looked at him for a few moments. "I believe you, Askuwa'tu. As you can guess, Paj is not so easily convinced."

Asku smiled a bit. "*Máh-sie*. Look, man, I understand your need to test me, to see if I am worthy enough for your sister, but—"

"Are you?" Sunu interrupted.

"I will take care of her."

One corner of Sunu's mouth turned up, and he nodded. "We will make sure of that, River boy."

"Okay then," Asku half smiled back. "Pass the message along to your brother, will you?"

Sunu nodded and walked away. Asku realized he had been clenching his jaw tightly, making his face hurt again.

Hawilish sat down next to him, without preamble. "Where did you come from?" Asku asked.

"I was here the whole time."

Asku's jaw lifted in a smile, but the beginning of a drum prompted him to be silent. Soon the Sea People's Teacher joined in the drum's rhythm with a chanted song, probably the blessing song Asku's father had explained was part of the preparation.

It was a chilly morning, especially in nothing but a breechcloth. The chiefs, their sons, and the whale hunting party—all in breechcloths, and Asku was certain his backside stuck out—followed the Teacher toward the sweat lodge. A cold mist fell.

Pajackok, Sunukkuhkau, and Asku stood before the Teacher before entering the *xwayátsh*, the sweat lodge. The elder lit a smudge stick, chanted words in the Wanuukshiłáma language, and blessed each of them in turn. He raised the stick to Asku's head, down his body, out each arm, then across his back. Asku followed the other two into a cramped building with a pit in the middle, where dozens of hot rocks glowed red. A stoic man, who matched his father's description of the Keeper of the Fire, brought in another red-glowing rock with a set of long tongs.

When all were present, the Sea Chief lit and passed the *chalámat* to Asku's grandfather, who passed it to Napayshni, who continued to send it around the circle. The Keeper came and went in silence, adding more hot rocks. When the last man was seated, the Keeper handed the Teacher a small pitcher, then left and closed the door flap.

The Teacher began to chant, softly, pouring water onto the hot rocks. Before long, the lodge was hotter and more humid than anything Asku could remember, and the breechcloth seemed like a good idea. The steam filled his lungs and his senses. The saltiness dripped down his forehead and face, stinging the cuts.

Asku closed his eyes and listened to the drumbeat coming from somewhere within. The teacher shook a rattle in his hands, hitting it rhythmically against his knee. No one spoke. Each man's experience was his own alone.

Asku spoke to the Great Spirits, thanked them, and beseeched them to make him strong enough.

Saigwan spoke to him, there in the *xwayátsh* at the Wanuukshiłáma village…

Moema lay on the bed of furs, the new life in her arms. The little boy suckled noisily as Saigwan knelt at her side. He no longer stopped his tears.

Three nights into the child's life, she had not stopped bleeding. The Grandmother had cut the child from between her legs, explaining that the alternative was certain death for mother and child. But the flow of blood did not slow, even with the Grandmother's chanting and chasing away of the evil spirits.

He tried to make her comfortable, but the sight of her losing the struggle for life ripped the heart from his body. Her breath was ragged now, and her beautiful skin had turned a ghostly gray.

He could smell death there, in their home. And he could do nothing.

"Saigwan," she whispered, through dry, cracked lips.

He looked deep into her eyes, willing himself to smile.

"I have been happy." The words were testament to her own will.

"Rest, átawit," he said. "Do not speak. Save your strength."

"No, Saigwan, you must hear what I say." She touched his face. "I did what I needed to do. I have loved you. You will go on, and they will go on." She motioned to the little one at her breast. You must go on, for our people. I will pass on, but you must go on. Do you hear me? For me?"

He shook his head.

"Take care of them," she breathed. "Átawishamash."

But it did not matter how strong he was, nor how much love he could give her. Neither could save her.

As Asku felt his awareness returning to the *xwayátsh*, he shook his head. The lodge was quiet but for the soft hiss as water hit the hot rocks.

He looked around at his grandfather, his father, his uncle; proud men, strong, from the prime of life to elderhood. Then Asku's eyes rested on Matchitehew. The dark, roaming eyes meant everything that his grandfather and father were not. Hawilish happened to be seated next to the Pyúsh chief, and for a moment Asku longed to jump over the hot rocks and introduce Matchitehew's face to them.

Then Asku thought back to Saigwan. His tribe was the same tribe, although his life was so different. His people had plenty, and no longer had to hide from the biting cold. Yet the people existed because of the great chief, Saigwan, and many before him, and many after.

But am I strong enough? Am I strong enough to face what most certainly lies ahead?

Saigwan could find peace only in solitude, and only outside of the cave. There were too many memories within the ancient, cold walls...three in particular. The youngest suckled with another mother who had excess milk. The older two went to live with Kasa.

Each day, Saigwan went to visit them, and each day his flood of grief returned. As he would walk away, Manneha always ran after him, cried out for him, but Saigwan could not bring himself to turn around.

He knew he needed to get away, but he was afraid to leave his people. He sensed something, something coming, and winter was approaching. The days were getting shorter. Snow had already fallen on the hills all around them.

The Teacher watched him late one evening. "Is it time to hunt again, Saigwan?"

"Yes. Winter is almost here."

"I fear this winter will be different. A change is coming, for good or for worse."

Saigwan stared into the fire. "Yes, Sapsikw'atá. We must be prepared for whatever comes."

"Will you hunt the mammoth?"

"We will try, but we have not found the herd in a long time. They no longer walk the plains Toward the Great Mountains, nor is there any sign of them Toward the Rising Sun. I am not hopeful."

"I have had a tk'i."

Saigwan looked up from the fire, waited.

"You must head Toward the Great Mountains and the Setting Sun, across Nch'i-Wána, toward the sea."

"Pit'xanuk Lawilat-tá, the People below the Trees of the Mountain...my mother's people?"

"Íi."

"We will not find the herd there."

"Maybe not, but something awaits you there."

They walked across Nch'i-Wána's thick ice just after leaving home. The sound of moving water beneath was a reassurance, but he wondered how long it would keep flowing, and what would happen if or when it stopped. Ancient stories told of a time when the people had relied upon the salmon. The Teacher once spoke of a salmon-type creature, longer than the height of a man, with fangs protruding from the tip of its nose. The salmon had not come up the river from the sea, not since before Saigwan's father died. He remembered the season they had not come when they were expected. The people had been afraid and wanted to move on, but the elders felt they must be patient and wait for the salmon to return.

Saigwan hoped he would live to see the day the salmon swam Nch'i-Wána again.

The hills rolled into high, rocky cliffs overlooking the icy river below. They kept Nch'i-Wána on their left for a time, then turned partly Toward the Great Mountains and the Setting Sun. He could not see them, but Saigwan knew the Great Mountains loomed ahead.

Saigwan lost count of the days they had been walking. The snowstorm had begun the day they left the cave. The wind whipped the snow around them as they walked, erasing their footprints behind them. The days were dark, the nights even darker. They walked slowly, cautious of what lay ahead or underfoot that could not be seen.

And as they walked, they saw no sign of the herds, of any herd.

But despite the relentless wind and swirling snow, Saigwan knew the way. He had been to his grandfather's home a number of times when he was young. There had been a time when the tribes had gathered together to celebrate a plentiful year. That had not happened in a while.

Lawilat-łá, Fire Mountain, stood somewhere ahead of them. At some distance Saigwan recognized the cluster of rocky hills at her base, and at times they seemed to pick up and move further away with each tired step. As the hunters finally dragged themselves up to the base of the rocky incline, a warning call echoed from above.

Saigwan raised his hand to the unseen weapons certainly facing him. "Blessings this day, my brothers, I seek the Pɨt'xanuk Lawilat-łá, the people of my grandfather," he called into the wind and snow.

The lookouts recognized him, lowered the weapons, and called Saigwan's party to advance. Inside, at warmth and in firelight, he recognized his grandfather easily enough. Deep wrinkles filled his round face. His eyes sparkled with wisdom and understanding. He looked like Saigwan's mother.

"Tíla," Saigwan dropped his eyes.

"Míshnam wá, my tíla? How are you?" The old chief stepped back, keeping his hands upon Saigwan's shoulders. "You look so like her."

"Funny," Saigwan chuckled, "that is what I thought when I saw you."

"You have come a great distance, my tíla. We have not heard from the Nch'i-Wána Tánawit in a long time, and we have feared for you. Come, you will find rest here for a time."

Their hosts ushered Saigwan's men in for warmth and a scant but welcome meal. The Teacher chanted a soft, sad song as Saigwan spoke of everything in his heart, everything that had happened in the many intervening winters. He laughed, he wept, he shouted in anger. He no longer felt so alone.

Here was a place where he was not Chief, just Saigwan.

His grandfather just listened, puffing rhythmically on a small clay chalámat.

"How do I go on, tíla?" Saigwan knew it was a childish question but could not help himself.

The old man breathed deeply on the pipe before speaking. "You will go on because you must. For a chief, in fact for any man, looking back is nothing you can spare time for. A people need their chief to be ever looking forward, despite his own pain. Your pain means nothing. The pain of your people means everything, and there is nothing that you would not do to protect them from it."

They stayed for three nights. Saigwan sat with his grandfather the entire time, sleeping only when he could no longer keep his eyes open. Niyol stayed by his side. As they finally prepared to leave, a young girl stood before him.

"What can I do for you, myánash?" he asked.

The pretty girl looked at the ground. "My name is Ayashe. Will you take me with you, Wyánch'i?" she entreated.

Saigwan looked at the young girl and back at his grandfather. "I am sorry, young one. I cannot—"

His grandfather's tone brooked no debate. "Saigwan, this is Ayashe, the daughter of our greatest hunter. He was a fierce warrior and a good man. You will take her with you, and you will care for her."

This not why I came here. I do not want to take this child. *"Tíla, I cannot. I cannot love again. Someone is always hurt because of who I am. I cannot."*

The old man took him by the shoulder. "Saigwan, you will love again. And you will lose again. Death is just a pathway to the next life; you cannot stop it, and you cannot control it. Worry about controlling the things that you can. It is time you became the man the Great Spirits designed you to become." He stepped back and put his hands on Saigwan's face, "Now, you will take Ayashe with you and you will go home, and you will not leave your people again. I fear change is coming. The herds are gone, and the land is colder than ever. Míshnam pamshtk'úksha', my tíla?"

He nodded, finally, and looked back at the young girl with the pleading eyes. What could pain a young one so much? But he of all people knew the answer.

The old chief laid an arm over her shoulders. "Ayashe is all alone. I took her in my home out of great respect to her father, but there is no peace for her here. And I made a promise. Ayashe, lead them to the wák'amu meadow, so they know how to find it next warm season, if it returns. You know the time. We will meet you there."

She nodded.

Saigwan met her eyes. "How old are you?" he asked, kindly.

"I am fourteen winters."

"We traveled a very great distance. We live above Nch'i-Wána. We will hunt on the way home…if there is anything to hunt. We have had great hardship. If you come, you will share in great hardship."

She nodded. "Please take me with you."

He looked at Niyol, who shrugged acceptance.

They left the next morning, carrying gifts from his grandfather's tribe. There were things for his sister, which had belonged to their grandmother. There were things for the Teacher, who still had living relatives there. Ayashe carried a precious basket of wák'amu flour on her back, all that could be spared, and two other hunters carried woven baskets filled to the brim with pit-roasted wák'amu bulbs.

Ayashe led them Toward the Rising Sun, below Pahto, to a meadow surrounded by ancient trees. She explained: once the snow melted, the meadow would be a field of blue flowers. Just before winter's approach, the women and children would pull the now-wilted plant from the soil, including the precious bulb. Once the bulbs were pit-roasted, women pounded them into flour that would keep all year if well preserved and secured. The Pɨt'xanuk Lawilat-ɬá still hunted the herds when they could, but the wák'amu flour sustained them when the winters were long.

Saigwan began to feel hope. They had not found the mammoth herd again, but they had found something else that might sustain. Its name, wák'amu, had a sense of hope for him. We will meet the Pɨt'xanuk Lawilat-ɬá at the meadow when the snow melts and learn the way of the wák'amu. We must prepare gifts to celebrate this new knowledge. We must thank the Pɨt'xanuk Lawilat-ɬá, and we must thank the Great Spirits. If we are ungrateful, perhaps the Spirits will decide we do not appreciate what they give, and perhaps then these wák'amu bulbs will no longer grow beneath the ground.

Saigwan enjoyed Ayashe's company from the first moment of their journey home. Her smile lightened his heart. At first he found her childish, but he soon realized he was seeing joy. He did not yet know what had broken her heart or what she had fled, but her joy was contagious. She said funny things, she laughed a great deal, and often she tripped over nothing. Amid the bitter snowstorms and merciless wind, Ayashe made everyone smile and laugh. And as everyone knew, the best winter wrap was laughter and a good attitude in the face of hardship.

When he called up to the lookout, the answering call was a beautiful sound. Soon Manneha was bounding into his arms.

"My tita," he said, burying his face in Manneha's little boy smell, *"I have missed you so. I am home now."*

Much to Asku's relief, the door flap opened. Cool, crisp coastal morning air wafted through the open door, reaching even his spot in the very back of the sweat lodge. The Keeper of the Fire hooked the door flap open. Slowly, the men began to evacuate the steamy, and now very stinky *xwayátsh*.

They cleaned the sweat from their bodies with coarse sea sponges, dipping them into buckets of cold water, squeezing it over their shoulders and heads. The water seemed to sizzle on Asku's hot skin, and he noticed that he stood right next to Matchitehew. The older man was bent over, dunking his sponge again in the bucket of water.

With a jolt to his stomach, Asku saw the long white scars across the back of his neck and shoulders.

Matchitehew seemed to feel the heat of Asku's stare. He turned around, eyes narrowing. Asku refused to look away. Now he also saw the scars down the side of Matchitehew's face, long white lines in the telltale fingernail pattern, the same one seen on his back: the emblems of the abuse of women.

Of one woman in particular.

I feel relief. Anger, yes, great anger, and I admit a bit of fear, but mostly relief. I will have revenge. We will have revenge. I do not know how, but it will happen.

But will I be strong enough?

The Pyúsh chief finally looked away.

Chapter 30

The whale hunters brought no food or water, which was fine with Asku. His mouth still hurt, and his stomach was unsettled.

The teacher chanted words of blessing and protection as they sat around the blazing fire in silence. Huyana braided Asku's hair into a tight plait, twining it around a thin piece of bark at the crown of his head. Then he moved to Hawilish, who was not going to sea, but would help when the hunting party returned to shore. Hawilish was not nearly as quiet about having his hair combed and plaited. The others snickered as he squirmed and complained. *"Cheechako,"* Pajackok snorted.

The entire village followed them down the coast, away from the mouth of Nch'i-Wána and toward a bonfire someone had started on the heights. On the way down, Pajackok gave Asku some lessons in a businesslike tone, as if there were nothing else between them.

"You will paddle with the other men," he began. "Since you do not speak our language, do as they do and stay in rhythm. I am told you have hunted bison, but this is much harder. You can be trampled by bison, but if you fall off your horse while doing it, you will not drown. If I need anything specific from you, I will tell you, so you understand. I expect you to obey without question, as all our lives may depend on it. This is also not like taking a canoe up Nch'i-Wána. On the Sea, with the *eh'-ko-lie* in sight, I must make decisions very rapidly and there is no time to do anything but follow them."

"May I ask questions?"

"Yes, but only now. Not at sea."

"Why is our hair tied up?"

"So, it will not be caught in anything, such as a rope. When the harpoon strikes the *eh'-ko-lie*, if it is a good throw, he will run hard. The rope will pay out as fast as an arrow can fly. The canoe could turn in any direction the sea sends it. If that rope were to catch on your hair, or your hand, it would drag you away to drown. There would probably be no way to save you. Men die each year doing this, even experienced hunters."

"Where will I sit in the canoe?"

"You must sit where you can see the others paddling, so that if I order them to back paddle right, or hold paddles steady on the left, you can do as they do. Sunu will be near you. If he needs you to do something, he will tell you in Wawa."

"Okay. I understand. I will not hesitate to do as told." *It is interesting that he is not attempting to dominate me, but I like him better this way. This Pajackok reminds me of his father, and mine.*

"That is most important," said Pajackok. "It happens very fast. I could tell you to jump out of the canoe and do something, and you must trust me to have a good reason."

Asku nodded. "I will."

"Do you get sick on the water?"

"I never have before, but I have seen it happen to others."

"People who would not usually in a boat on Nch'i-Wána might do so on the Great Sea. Let's hope you do not, but if you do, you must keep to your duties even if you are miserable. You are a River man, so I assume you are a good swimmer?"

"Yes, I am," said Asku. "Is there anything else I should know?"

"Yes. No hunt you will ever experience in your whole life will compare to this. It is a sacred gift of the Great Spirits. Your mind is prepared and calm, or I would not have you along. Proceed with respect for the spirits, the Great Sea, the *eh'-ko-lie*, and the customs of the hunt, and we may find that conditions favor us." There was even a hint of a proud smile, around the still-swollen lip Hawilish had punched.

"*Máh-sie.* I am grateful to join you."

Pajackok grunted and nodded. The hunting party filed down to the water, where two long canoes sat near the surf. The incoming waves just touched their bows.

Asku skimmed his hand along the smooth curve at the stern of one. It reached to his chest. Carven into it were tiny scenes of animals and men, of wind and storm, water and land.

The Wanuukshiłáma chief laid a hand on Pajackok's shoulder, raising the other in blessing to the hunters. *"T'k-tók-te Tl'ka-ná-a Wé-ko-wa,"* he shouted above the beach sounds. "Good Mother Sea, protect our young hunters. May their arms not fail in the throw, may their eyes be alert on the watch, may the sea and waves protect them, and may the Mighty One give itself to them and come ashore."

Sunu positioned Asku just in front of him and on the opposite side, gesturing where he should sit when the canoe was launched. Pajackok did a final and exacting equipment check of lines, harpoons, paddles, baling bucket, everything needed for the hunt. Then Pajackok, his brothers, other tribesmen, and Asku pushed a canoe out into the oncoming waves, each hunter jumping in as he was thigh deep.

The full complement consisted of Sunu at the stern, Pajackok at the bow, Asku in front of Sunu facing forward as the other paddlers did, and the rest between Asku and Pajackok. Each man took a paddle and paddled in rhythm to Pajackok's chant. Over the shoulder of Takoda, who was in front of him, Asku watched as the beach grew smaller and smaller as they paddled backward out to sea. He could still see his father and grandfather, each with an arm raised in silent blessing.

The canoe rose and fell, up and over waves, again and again, as the men paddled madly between each wall of water. Asku was used to the movement of water, but the swells here were heavier than Nch'i-Wána on its stormiest day. His stomach turned a bit until they reached the calmer open sea. At an order from Pajackok, the pace of paddling slowed.

"It is easier on the way in," Takoda whispered to Asku, who was out of breath. The other canoe appeared alongside theirs, Kohana at the bow.

"Now what?" Asku whispered over his shoulder to Sunu.

"Now we wait. Our watchers will signal us; that is why they are on the bluffs where they can see farthest. One carries the *Wé-ko-wa* shell. When blown in, the sound can be heard at a great distance. *Eh'-ko-lie* groups have already been seen along our coast. They travel Away from the Midday Sun during the warm season, then return past the mouth of the Big River as the cold blows in." Sunu pointed toward a bluff farther from Nch'i-Wána than where they'd left the people. "But the Blackfish controls the sea. The legends say that he has a lair under the water, where all come to pay homage to him."

Takoda snorted. Sunu's scowl came out in his voice. "What, do you not believe, *ow*?"

"Uh, well," Takoda stuttered under what was for sure his older brother's angry glare, "the Blackfish is really important, but a lair under the sea? Really, *káhp-ho*?"

"Keep it down," said Pajackok. The brothers were still arguing, albeit quietly, when everyone heard a distinct noise from the bluff: a short blow and two longer blows on what must have been the *Wé-ko-wa* shell.

"Toward the Big River, *shikhs*," Pajackok called as the paddlers quickly turned the canoes in that direction. When the canoe had come about, Pajackok bellowed, "Full ahead!"

Asku's heart raced with anticipation, nerves, the unfamiliar environment, and the adrenaline of imminent action. *I am just glad that, so far, I do not seem to have committed some error. If I do nothing of note, it will mean I did my full part. I see why this is the test they put me through, because it is the test they know.*

The harpoons rested in small props mounted inside the canoe below the gunwales. Each was almost twice as long as Asku, and as wide as his balled fist, the kind of giant spear he could imagine Mach'ni throwing. The sharp black shell tip had elk horn barbs on either side. His father had explained that the harpoon was meant to fall apart when it hit. About midway on the harpoon was a loop hook with a long line of rope and a handful of sealskin floats.

Pajackok called out and pointed, and Asku saw his first whales.

The pod was not far from the canoes, four or five of the great beasts. They seemed to pay the hunters no attention. A gray and white back appeared, then slid back under the surface; a spout of water, another a small distance off; a dark tail quietly slapped the water, then disappeared again.

Asku's heart pounded as he continued paddling in time with the others. Pajackok reached carefully over them toward the stern. Sunu snapped an order and all paddles on the starboard side lifted, enabling Pajackok to lift a harpoon clear. Asku could not see what the brothers were doing but could see the tip of the harpoon out to starboard, about shoulder high. Pajackok waved the other canoe to fall behind.

Right then a large whale surfaced to starboard, near enough to roll a heavy wave under them. For a moment Asku felt the insane impulse to run regardless of anything else, to swim, to get farther from something so enormous. Courage won. Sunu hissed an order, and all the paddlers shipped their paddles. Asku watched out to his left, the canoe's starboard. The whale did not seem to end.

I have never known such anticipation in my life.

Asku risked a glance at Pajackok who stood perfectly still, watching and waiting for the target spot. Sunu and one other stood behind him, ready to add muscle to the cast, checking the coiled line for any sign it might catch or snag.

"*Al-tákh!*" Pajackok yelled, as the three men pierced the whale between the shoulders. He shouted another order, and the paddlers sent the canoe into reverse. Just as the canoe began to gain way backward with some speed, the whale's powerful tail came out of the water and swatted all over the place, a reflex reaction to sudden unexplained impact. Rope and floats whistled over the side as the animal thrashed at the invasion.

If we had been near that tail, this canoe would have looked like a bunch of firewood on which someone had butchered several elk, and not in a tidy way.

"*Al-tákh...Al'-ta!*" Pajackok shouted again.

Asku looked around for the other canoe and saw Kohana's crew had come along the whale's other side, where two men were throwing shorter spears. The foremost paddler in Pajackok's canoe had cunningly aligned the craft so that the harpoon rope paid out directly over the bow.

"Keep up," Paj shouted again, "he will slow soon enough!"

Asku felt his arms burning as the men bent to their work, battling the whale's pull once it hit the end of the line. Finally, and not soon enough, Asku felt the movement slowing. At the same time, he heard animal sounds—loud, angry, commanding sounds. He saw the rest of the pod turn once, then abandon their stricken comrade and speed out to sea. Pajackok called out an order; the canoes reversed direction again, toward the whale.

Soon their canoes were close enough now that Asku could see the wound as the whale rocked slowly from side to side. Blood welled along the beautiful gray skin and spread throughout the cold, dark waters. "How long?" he asked.

"It depends," Pajackok said, sounding compassionate. "The spear is meant to go deep and kill quickly, right through the heart. If we were close enough, and aimed well, it should not take long."

Asku closed his eyes and prayed to the Great Spirits to end the animal's suffering, to free the spirit of the whale. The only sound was the soft splash of the paddles as the hunters tried to maintain a safe distance. Asku felt his own mortality at that very moment: the vastness of the sea, the large animal whose fate rested in their hands, and the risks of conflict he knew would come.

Pajackok nodded to Sunu and to Kohana's first mate. Both threw harpoons into the animal's side. Then a young man in the other canoe stood and dove into the water beside the whale.

"What is he doing?" Asku whispered to Takoda aghast.

"He is lacing the Mighty One's mouth shut." Takoda took one look at his older brother over his shoulder with a brotherly sneer. "So, he will not leave us and pay homage to the Blackfish in his lair…or take us with him."

The young swimmer returned within a few moments, and with no orders, they drifted on the waves. After a while, and to the hunters' excitement, the animal turned toward shore. Sunu explained to Asku: "Sometimes, a wounded whale will head for the beach. That is the best result. I do not think this one will make it, though, so we may have a lot of work ahead."

Sunu was right. Shortly, the whale ceased its shoreward progress, and now the whalers had to tow it in. That was slow going, for even without resistance, the whale still weighed a great deal. As they approached shore, Pajackok and Sunu made course corrections to ensure a straight-in arrival.

"What happens if we come in wrong?" Asku asked of Sunu.

"We all go for a swim in the surf with a big wooden canoe, our paddles, spare harpoons, and our shipmates landing on top of us."

As they began to move the canoes up the beach, the whale gave one last surge of strength in the shallow surf. The waves rolled the enormous animal ashore on its side, and there it lay still. The *Eh'-ko-lie's* last great breath had been to throw itself at the feet of the people.

Asku felt a great sudden sorrow and humility, more than he had ever felt taking game. He ran his hand across the whale's side; it was cool and smooth, like the black stone resting on his chest. The whale's back was covered in long lines of barnacles and old scars. The people gathered around, Patisapatisháma and Wanuukshiláma alike. Following the lead of the Sea People, the attending River People bowed heads and held their hands out in front of them, palms facing toward the sky as they chanted an ancient, sad song.

"It is dead," Paj whispered. "It did not suffer long, a shot through the heart. Let me show you." He and Asku yanked the harpoon free of the animal's skin; blood, water and blubber spilled at their feet.

Asku turned around. Apenimon was nearby. "*Ty-ee'*, it is our custom, the custom of the Patisapatisháma, to honor the spirit of the animal by removing the heart and sending it away in fire. Would this be acceptable here?"

The old chief smiled and held a hand up in respect. "It would. However, you would not be able to reach it for some time, as there is a great deal of cutting ahead. And when you did, you would find that it is more than you can carry. But your custom is in the same spirit as our ways and should not be delayed. Will it honor your custom if you take blood from the wound to the heart, and put that upon a fire?"

Asku looked to his father. "*Wyánch'i?*"

"Yes, since the Wanuukshiláma *Ty-ee'* permits it. This is the home of the Sea People, and their customs have precedence."

A Wanuukshiláma elder handed Asku a large oyster shell half. Asku briefly rested his hand on the side of the animal, saying, "*Kw'alá, yáya.*" Then he set the shell against the side at a spot where blood would fill it up. When it was done, he turned toward the tide line. The people followed him, palms still facing the sky and heads bowed.

Hawilish and Aanapay had kindled up a smaller fire from dry driftwood, and Asku headed that direction. He walked past a shrouded figure, the hood covering her beautiful, laughing eyes. Napayshni, Apenimon, Kalataka, Pajackok, and U'hitaykah walked with him.

Asku raised the shell high above his head. *"Kw'ałá, síks,"* he said. "Thank you, friend. Thank you, Great Spirits, for our brother, the Mighty One." He knelt and poured the heart's blood into the fire, releasing the animal's spirit into the beyond. A murmur of approval rippled through the assembled hundreds.

Asku stood there with a humble heart, watching the dancing flames.

"For the young hunter as well," the Wanuukshiłáma chief said, offering a steaming cup of something warm. "I am told it is like the Wawyukyáma custom."

Remembering the bison's blood, Asku tried not to gag at the thought. *This I had not expected. But it is their way, and everyone is watching. I can do this.* He lifted the cup high. The liquid was thick and hot in his throat, but he swallowed quickly, willing himself not to throw up, and wiped his mouth with the back of his hand. The people cheered.

A wave of excitement passed through him. *I did it. I must have done as I was expected, or there would not be approval. Tonight, she will be presented to me, and I will accept her. Then she will be brought to my village, and we will finally be together.*

A voice jarred Asku out of his thoughts. "You did well," Pajackok said. Then, more quietly, "And I was not sorry to see it, Askuwa'tu." The people were dispersing. Although a number stayed behind to prepare the animal's carcass, most began to walk down the beach, and Pajackok trailed them.

I cannot say I now like him, but I seem to have earned his respect, and I must admit he now has some of mine. But I hope my beat-up face makes me look tough and brave.

"I only do what I feel is right," added Pajackok, looking out to sea.

"I understand," replied Asku. "But are there not other ways, more honorable, to gain obedience?"

"Yes, maybe," Pajackok sighed. "But Kaliskah is, well...she is difficult. She is hot-headed and she listens to no one."

"I did not notice that roughing her up improved her hearing. Did you?"

"Hmmm." Pajackok rubbed his hand across his eyes. "You do not understand."

"Maybe I do not." Asku took a deep breath. "I do not claim to understand everything. Here is what I do understand. After tonight, when the arrangement is done, Kaliskah will be my mate. Then she will be my responsibility. And from then on, no one will lay a hand on her again." He stared deeply into Pajackok's dark eyes. "Do you understand me?"

After some time Pajackok nodded, then something else crossed his face. "I do not know if she told you, but her time has come upon her, it began just before your arrival, young *ty-ee'.*"

"No, she did not tell me. We spoke of other matters, mostly about my family and people since she is very curious about where she will live."

Pajackok smiled. "Tonight, you will formally accept the offer of a union with my people. In just a few days, we will bring her to your village. If, of course, you still wish it, and give your permission."

Then it all hit him. It was time, now, already. Suddenly he felt like he would much rather be on the sea hunting the great *sut'xwłá—eh'-ko-lie* in the Wawa—for the rest of his life. Pajackok quietly chuckled at Asku's stunned silence.

Asku swore inwardly, puffed his chest out the best he could, and tried to recover. "Then we will make plans before we head home," he nodded. A pause, then: "Thank you for the honor of inviting me to join in the sacred *eh'-ko-lie* hunt, Pajackok. It was like no other experience."

"Most people call me Paj," he said, walking back toward the whale carcass.

Chapter 31

Kaliskah stood before him.

The bonfire's flames danced in her eyes and her skin glowed in the firelight. He could not take his eyes off her. When she smiled at him, his heart fluttered.

Her father jolted him from that reverie by taking them both by the wrists, raising their arms high. "My daughter Kaliskah Sayen of the Wé-ko-wa Til'lig-hum," he shouted for all to hear, especially Asku whose ear happened to be within a hand's length, "and Askuwa'tu Haylaku, son of Napayshni Hianayi of the Patisapatisháma, and grandson of Kalataka Wahchinksapa of the Wawyukyáma! The union of our people shall once again take place at the Patisapatisháma village within the moon!"

To great cheers, he placed their hands together, still holding them high in the air. But not for long, as a horde of excited young women soon whisked Kaliskah away in a sea of giggles.

Apenimon handed Asku a heavy cedar mask. "*Eh'-ko-lie*," said the Sea Chief, pounding his chest. "*Sut'xwłá* in the language of our friends." He held his hand out to Asku's grandfather. "Tell us of Sut'xwłayáy and X̱ux̱ux̱yáy."

The Wanuukshiłáma chief sat cross-legged in front of the glowing fire. Asku's grandfather stood and clasped his hands behind his back. The whale mask had two great jaws that opened and closed, snapping together loudly. Asku put it on and tested them. Asku wondered momentarily how his grandfather knew a story of Whale and Raven. *I will have to ask.* But his thoughts were interrupted as a drumbeat began, a soft one nearby, and the old Elk Plains chief spoke.

Sut'xwłayáy danced and splashed in the sunlight near the mouth of the great river. He knew this spot well. When he was young, he and his family came often to eat of the tasty things floating in and out with the rush of water. So many creatures travelled upstream, and he loved to watch for them and catch them as they began their long journeys home, especially this season—when day is longer than night—when salmon swim in schools and Aanyáy shines most bright. For the mouth was not often known to Aanyáy; her face was usually hidden amongst ominous sea storms. When she did shine, all creatures basked in her beauty at the mouth of the Nch'i-Wána.

Asku danced about, snapping the jaws and stomping, doing rolls forward like a whale diving and surfacing. The group cheered and laughed.

Xuxuxyáy always met Whale there. Whale and Raven loved to play in Aanyáy's warmth together. Raven would fly high above and tell him when the salmon were swimming. Whale would catch them and toss a couple up to Raven. Sometimes Raven would land on Whale's sleek back and would talk and talk and talk. That one loved to talk.

Asku kept dancing and snapping the jaws at Pajackok, as Xuxuxyáy, who ran around flapping a pair of black feather wings strapped to his back. Pajackok almost knocked Asku on the ground trying to climb onto his back, to great hilarity all around.

The story ended with Raven flying into the mouth of a larger whale, and Whale still being able to hear his friend talking while inside the belly of the large gray whale. Asku lifted the heavy whale's mask over his head, still laughing along with the crowd.

Then came other stories, some from experiences, some legendary. Hawilish spoke of the lonely gray wolf. U'hitaykah told a sad story of Bison and Horse, and Asku's grandfather told the story of Spilyáy and the other side of the mountains. The whole intoxicating celebration lasted late into the night.

>——→

Sometime in the night, a hand on Asku awakened him. It was Chaytan. "Asku, get up. Sunu is here to see you."

"What does he want at this hour? Doesn't he sleep?"

"I have no idea. But you had better get up."

Asku's eyes began to clear as he got dressed and went outside. "Sunu. What is up, *shikhs*?"

Sunukkuhkau backed from the tent and motioned for Asku to follow. Chaytan did not follow, though his eyes looked as if he considered that against his better judgment.

Asku followed Sunu, now noticing the dark shadow of Pajackok over his other shoulder. The trail began to feel familiar.

They continued out onto the beach where a bonfire blazed high into the dark sky. Others were there already. Hawilish even appeared, although slightly out of breath. Without speaking, each young man took his place around the hissing fire, backs resting against large pieces of driftwood. The waves crashed far off in the distance.

Pajackok held a long tassel connected to a very sharp bone hook. Asku could see it glistening in the light of the fire. Pieces of whale bone and teeth decorated the tassel, strung on thin sinew thread—and he understood. Paj held the bone hook tassel in the air, chanting words Asku could not understand.

Then he knelt before Asku and winked.

Asku braced himself, willing himself not to cry out or move.

With an expert poke and a quick tug, the tassel hung from Asku's right earlobe. *Okay, that did hurt, but less than him punching me in the face.*

Paj offered a hand and pulled him to his feet. Sunu handed him a small whale mask, similar to but lighter than the one he had worn at the feast. They danced around the fire, then the young men told other stories. With no Pyúsh P'ushtáayama present, Hawilish told the story of Kitchi's bravery, and how he received the Xátxat Killer cane.

By the time the sun's light began to lift the veil of night, the whalers stood up and made their way back to the village. They would not get much sleep before their morning meal, after which the goodbyes would begin.

Asku's new trophy bounced against his neck, reminding him of all his experiences at the Sea. *I do not want to leave Kaliskah.*

And when she comes to me, and I bring her to my home as my mate, I will not have to leave her again.

>———

"They are gone," Kohana whispered to the Chief during breakfast. He looked as if he had not slept much.

"When did they take off?" asked Napayshni.

"Well before the sun."

"How far did you follow his trail?" U'hitaykah asked.

"As far as we could. They crossed Skip-pi-náu-in and then Nak-i-kláu-a-nak. They are on foot, but we lost them after that."

Asku looked from the Chief to his grandfather, to U'hitaykah and back at Kohana. "What does this mean?"

The Chief laid a hand on Asku's shoulder. "Maybe nothing, my *tita*. Hopefully nothing."

"But in case it is not nothing, we should go after them. All our people are at Wayám or visiting other villages!"

"They are moving fast," Kohana continued. "They can easily get canoes and cross at will. There are tribes always looking to barter along this section of the Nch'i-Wána, and they left with plenty to barter with. And since a lot of goods will land on the trading flow of Nch'i-Wána, but have not yet done so, they will get better bargains by leaving now."

"We should go back to Wayám and regroup," said U'hitaykah.

Asku nodded, but all he could think about was his family. The little ones, Kitchi with his leg propped up, Hatayah, Matahnu...he knew they would be safe at Wayám, but he worried, nonetheless. "Yes, we should go," he said, jumping up from his spot at the fire. He looked directly at Napayshni. "*Áwna túxsha.* Let's go home now."

"Askuwa'tu, we will go shortly, but for now please finish your morning meal. Remember the way we considered the situation? They are safe at the Wayám village. Many warriors and hunters call the Falls home for moons at a time. But we should not linger any longer."

Asku and the Chief spent some time with the Wanuukshiłáma elders after the morning meal, coordinating the process that would bring

Kaliskah along and scheduling a new celebration. Three days thence, the Wanuukshiłáma would depart for the Patisapatisháma village.

While Asku prepared to take his place in the canoe, the Sea Chief took him by the shoulders. *"Máh-sie,"* he said.

Even as they exited Skip-pi-náu-in and began the long push up Nch'i-Wána, Asku had no idea why Apenimon had thanked him.

)——→

The trip upstream was much more difficult, and not just because of the current. They had gained more in return than they had given away at the Patshatl, including the two young slave girls, who sat in the bow of Aanapay's canoe with the sea furs. Asku remembered seeing the girls looking very nervous at the trip's start, but by the end of that first day, Aanapay had the eldest sister paddling the canoe and the younger laughing at his impish antics. They traveled three nights and most of that day, including both portages, but the stop at Wayám was all they had anticipated.

Asku and the Chief walked through the busy village, telling of the Patshatl and spreading word for the Patisapatisháma to prepare to head home. Finally, out of nowhere, Susannawa flew into Asku's arms. "How goes it, *nika?*" he whispered into his ear, holding the little boy tightly and thanking the Great Spirits for their safety.

"Good, Asku! I helped mother with the fire, and helped keep track of the sisters, and went for water! I even walked around checking on our people each morning like you and the Chief do, and the *Sapsikw'ałá* went with me!"

Asku put the boy back on his feet, looking him up and down. *"Kw'ałá*...thank you, little one."

As he looked up at Asku, Susannawa's left eyebrow arched just like Napayshni's. "What happened to you, Asku? Did you get in a fight? And what is that thing hanging off your ear?"

"It is okay, *nika.* I will tell you about it later."

He turned to find Chitsa in Napayshni's arms. They were having a quiet conversation. When his mother came over to greet him, thankfully, there were no questions about his face or the tassel.

They found Kitchi sitting on lookout duty Toward the Rising Sun, his leg propped up beside him, whittling away on a thick piece of wood. "Whoa, man!" he hollered. "Who did you get in a fight with?"

"Ha-ha," Asku teased, "you know me."

"Looks like you won, anyway, and got an award for it, little *Wyánch'i,*" Kitchi jibed, flicking the tassel in Asku's ear.

"You might say that." said Asku. Hawilish snorted.

"Well, let's hear it, then," Kitchi insisted, putting his knife and piece of wood dramatically down next to him.

"It is a long story, *pásiks.* I will tell you on the ride home," Asku smacked him on the shoulder. "*Túnmash wá táymun?*"

"Fine, quiet. Nothing to tell. Let's hear your news now, man. I am not waiting until the ride home. Is she ugly?"

"Oh, *kúu mish.* I guess we have time while everyone is packing up. And no, she isn't."

Asku began with the Pajackok incident. He was barely a breath into the story when Kitchi rounded on Hawilish. "Where were you during all this? You should have beat this guy up!"

"Whoa," said Hawilish. "Will you be quiet and hear what happened before you yell at me?"

Kitchi snorted. Hawilish ran his hand through his hair.

"That's better. Hawilish came out of nowhere, I did not even see him coming. He slugged old stiff Pajackok right in the mouth, and it was still swollen when we left two days later. He was like a guard dog. He would not back off until the Chief started hollering."

Kitchi narrowed his eyes and nodded at Hawilish.

"Lot of good it did," Hawilish mumbled.

"Yeah, well, you had to back off. It wasn't your fault."

"What does that mean?" Kitchi looked back and forth between the two of them. "You guys are talking in code, knock it off. Why would any of us back off when one of us is on the ground at some wannabe chief's feet?"

Hawilish lost his patience. "Cuz the Chief told me to, you loudmouth!" he yelled.

"How am I supposed to tell about this if you two cannot calm down? Now hush." Asku waited, then continued. "Hawilish had to back off because the Chief told him to, because I told him to, and because we would have had a war between our tribe and theirs right there in the middle of the Patshatl."

"Hmmm," Kitchi growled.

"Liwanu had already drawn that jawbone club of his," Hawilish added quietly.

"He did? No wonder my father settled it down so quickly."

Kitchi shook his head. "Well, I do not like the sound of any of that. I don't know what I would have done."

"Probably would have caused a lot of trouble," said Hawilish. "Look, Kitchi. Different peoples have different ways. We were in their village as guests."

"Guests who get beat up by their hosts. I do not like these people's customs."

"I do not like all of them either," said Asku. "And I was the one who got to take the brunt of them. But Kitchi, fact is, you would be protective of a sister too. Pajackok didn't know much about me or us. And he did not spend the rest of the time giving me trouble. In fact, he was the captain of my whaling canoe, and he treated me just fine. He was like some other people we know, who lose their tempers and then think later."

Kitchi scowled but remained silent.

"Then came the whale hunt, which was a very big deal." Asku went on about the sweat lodge, the training, and all their experiences. Kitchi was especially interested in the whale hunt, and he laughed as the boys tried to describe how cold the water was.

"So, she's not ugly then, obviously."

"No, she is amazing," Asku replied. "And she is coming to our village in three days for the ceremony."

"What?!" they both exclaimed.

"Why didn't you tell me, Asku?" Hawilish protested. "So, will the ceremony be then or not for a while? How does it all work?"

"Never mind the ceremony," said Kitchi. "The important thing is that in three days you will be the first one to stick your—" Hawilish pushed him backward off the log, where he landed hard on his backside with a grunt.

"Are you all right?" Asku laughed, reaching down to give him a hand up.

"What was that for?" demanded Kitchi.

"Screw you, Kitchi," said Hawilish. "Have you seen Asku's face?"

"No. I have been very busy and have not taken any time to notice it. Of course, I've seen his face! I may be lame, but I'm not blind, man!"

"Do you use your head at all?" Hawilish said, hotly. "Don't you realize what he has done for her? Have you been listening at all?"

Kitchi got up awkwardly, brushing his backside off. He mumbled something that sounded like an apology and sat back down on the log, although a little farther away from Hawilish. "You will be the first, that's all. I guess you probably won't tell us what it's like either, will ya?" he turned to Asku, a gleam in his eye.

"No, probably not," Asku laughed. He stood up to leave. "*Áwna túxsha*…let's go home now."

>———→

The trip home was a sort of loosely organized ongoing reunion, with some catching their evening meals along the way. The village was in good shape, except for some elk and badger depredations here and there. Chitsa and Nayhali cooked a beautiful meal later that evening. After serving all the men around her fire, including their Elk Plains relatives, Chitsa turned her attention to the rest of the family, and then to the poor young girls that sat quietly near the door of their home, looking scared.

The girls had learned some Chinuk Wawa, but not quite enough to tell their story. The Chief sent Susannawa to bring the Teacher, whom he thought might know something similar to their tribe's language.

The Teacher did and was able to translate the story of their young lives. "We think all our people are dead, except for the few who are slaves at the Wanuukshiłáma. We believe that an evil spirit came to our village not long after the Ghost Men arrived from the sea in a Floating House. He brought cooking pots that did not burn, Biting Spears that some of our men went crazy over, and the stupid water that we had only heard about before. But after the Floating House left, the people became very sick. The old and very young suffered and died first." The younger sister began to sob as her sibling continued.

"Not long after, a tribe from Toward the Rising Sun raided and killed the men who remained and took the rest as slaves. Not long after, they traded us to the Wanuukshiłáma chief. He treated us kindly, for the most part."

"We can help you to get home, to find what may be left of your people," said Napayshni. The Teacher translated.

The girls looked at each other. The older girl spoke again. The Teacher relayed: "Thank you, great Chief and his son, for offering this. However, we do not think our people exist anymore. We would return only to an empty place, bones and evil spirits. The best we could hope for is to find a new home, and mates, and regain some status and our freedom."

"That is not difficult. I can arrange everything but the mates; those you must attract and choose for yourselves." Their faces lit up as the Teacher relayed the meaning. "You are free now, *pt'ilíma*. You may stay here with the Patisapatisháma if you wish. Or—" the Chief glanced at Aanapay, then winked—"perhaps the Wawyukyáma would welcome you. They are our allies, and we are confident they would treat you just as well, if the Wawyukyáma Chief agrees?"

Kalataka looked at Aanapay, then nodded. Aanapay stood, cleared his throat and laced his hands behind his back to speak formally. "With your permission, *Wyánch'i* of the Patisapatisháma, I will care for them both at our village."

"If that is what they wish, I give permission," Asku's father said, formally but with a smile.

After translation and discussion, the eldest sister held the younger tightly, whispering something in her ear. Then she smiled and nodded. "Well," the Chief laughed, "that is happily settled, then."

The village was in a tizzy at the impending arrival of their young chief's mate and the ceremony that would follow. It meant everyone paying Asku far more attention than he found comfortable, and he went toward the Totem in hopes of some time alone. It was an unwise choice. A group of women sat around the mating tent, talking and decorating the sides with designs of beautiful colors. To his great embarrassment, they stopped work and conversation to give him formal greetings. *And I do not know exactly what those looks in their eyes are saying, but I know they are laughing at me. This is ridiculous. But I must be polite.* Avoiding their eyes, Asku praised and thanked them for their hard work.

Another woman walked up the trail, little one strapped tightly to her back and two others in tow. She carried a neatly folded goatskin, its long white fur bright in the sunlight, and set it on a growing pile. Asku realized their purpose, paled, and barged into the Teacher's home without even the common courtesy of knocking, leaving behind him muffled giggles.

The Teacher was waving a lit smudge stick in some pattern. "Blessings, Asku. What is your hurry?"

Realizing what he'd done, Asku gulped. "Blessings, *Sapsikw'ałá*, and I apologize for being so rude. I... well, I just needed a quick escape."

"If it is an emergency, you did nothing wrong. What is wrong?"

Asku stopped, then plunged ahead. "I went to the Totem to try and straighten out my thoughts. All I found there were women smirking at me, like everyone but me knew a secret, and I wanted to get away. I know it sounds stupid."

The Teacher smiled. "I take no offense, Asku. Take sanctuary here as often as you need."

"*Kw'ałá, Sapsikw'ałá.*" He took a deep breath and sat down. "She will arrive in the morning, and there will be a great ceremony. Can you tell me what that will involve?"

The Teacher wove the smudge stick high into the air, down to the ground, left, then right, then wafting the smoke to his own face. He breathed deeply before responding. "Well, we will celebrate with a feast and the telling of stories. There will be music and dancing, of course," added the old man, walking around the room waving the stick.

"Then I will say the blessing," he continued, now holding the stick over Asku's head. He moved it down toward Asku's feet, left to right, and then blew the smoke in his face. Asku closed his eyes, breathing in the sweet incense...*lavender, sage, lemon grass...and something else.*

The old man set the stick back on the little altar. "Then, you will enter the tent and consummate your union."

Asku felt the blood drain from his face. "Will everyone be there, *Sapsikw'alá*? Listening, I mean?"

Only the Teacher's eyes smiled. "No, *myánash*. The people will disperse. They will give you your privacy."

"*Kúu mísh*," Asku sighed. "That's good."

Chapter 32

From where he stood atop the bluff, Asku could see two canoes. In one, Kaliskah sat between Pajackok and Sunukkuhkau. He did not recognize the rest of the Sea People at that distance, but the delegation was far smaller than expected. Something seemed wrong.

"I have a bad feeling," said Napayshni. "Chaytan, go bring the Grandfather, right away. Everyone else, let's go." Chaytan turned on his heel and took off for the village, while Asku and the others ran down the trail to the water.

It took an agonizing time for the canoes to come into nearer view. When it did, Asku could see that Sunu looked abnormally pale, with blood leaking from a makeshift bandage below his arm, and some from his mouth. He sat leaning against Kaliskah, who looked grieved.

When the canoes came near, Asku and the Chief joined the men who waded in to pull them ashore. Kaliskah looked unhurt, sad, angry, and quite ready to use the bow and arrows in her lap. Pajackok seemed unharmed.

Kaliskah leaped out of the canoe and prepared to help Sunu disembark. Asku moved to help Pajackok. "What is up, *shikhs*?" he asked urgently.

"They are coming," Pajackok growled. "My father is dead."

A murmur of anger and alarm passed through the gathered Patisapatisháma. Napayshni raised a hand for a moment, expression much moved, and nodded very deliberately to Pajackok. It was enough to say: *he was a great chief, a great ally, a great man, and I respected him as my peer.*

Chitsa came forward to Kaliskah, reached out. "*Isha*, Asku is my son. I wish the welcome were in a better situation, but I welcome you anyway." Kaliskah set down her bow and quiver and went to Chitsa's arms while Asku put out an arm to steady Sunu. The combined strength of several men was plenty to hoist the wounded Wanuukshiłáma whale hunter out of the canoe and onto the beach. Asku looked uphill to see the Grandfather working his way down the trail, Chaytan standing near in case the elder should lose footing. The Chief lifted the bandage at Sunu's shoulder to reveal a wide, deep wound just at the young man's armpit, bleeding badly. Napayshni glanced over at Pajackok.

"It was a spear. He pulled it out himself."

Nodding, the Chief put firm pressure on the wound. "What happened?"

"They attacked us early this morning," Paj rumbled. "We were not far from here, on the outskirts of Wayám, which as you know is very crowded. We considered it safe there. In hindsight, it was not. It was a small party of intruders, not an assault, and they came on us by surprise. We tried to fight them off. I have no idea how many there are, more than the three for sure. They killed my father during the fight, and I believe that was their main aim since they fled after that. Kohana is injured but not badly. I sent him home with a couple of slaves and my father's body, to inform our people. Your healer has a reputation greater than any at Wayám, and this was the destination we had planned in any case, thus safest for us."

"I see the wisdom of your decision, Pajackok. Be assured we will do our best for Sunukkuhkau and will keep you all as safe as our own people." He pointed up the trail. The Grandfather and Chaytan were coming, and behind them were four young men with poles and blankets.

Pajackok nodded. "*Máh-sie*, River *Ty-ee'*."

"As my mate said, I wish the circumstances were as happy as we meant them to be, but despite that, we welcome our Wanuukshiłáma friends. When there is time, of course, there are formalities, but right now I would appreciate all you can tell me: who the attackers are, where they might go, and what they intend. We will also have to guard against raids."

"So far as we could determine, they were on foot, and Beyond Nch'i-Wána," Pajackok explained. "I do not know how long it will take them to get here, or where they will cross, or even if they will come here for sure. We packed and left immediately, so as not to waste time explaining everything to everyone at Wayám. The place will be awash in rumors, though, and they could surely see we had been attacked, so I hope they will be on guard. Make no mistake, *Ty-ee'*, danger is about."

"I do not doubt that," said Napayshni. Pajackok bent over Sunu's head, patted the shoulder on his good side, and whispered something in his ear. Sunu nodded, whispered something back. Then Pajackok turned to Kaliskah, sheltered under Chitsa's arm. "I must go, *ats*."

"I wish you did not have to," said Kaliskah.

"I wish that also, sister, but you know that our people's need comes before our own. I must take up my duties and be sure they are prepared. You must stay with Sunukkuhkau. I will come back when I am sure the people are safe."

At that moment, the Grandfather reached them and began to examine Sunu's wound. Pajackok and Kaliskah knelt down next to their brother, who appeared to have a difficult time remaining stoic through the pain. After a few moments of gentle exploration, the elder looked up at Pajackok. "This is a dangerous wound, deep and made with a very sharp spear tip. You judged rightly that he cannot be taken back yet. He must rest. The reason he is spitting out blood is that it is leaking into his breathing. That is very dangerous. If he receives rest, and we can keep the wound clean, he may recover. I will take care of him."

"*Máh-sie*, Healer." Pajackok stood. He looked from the Chief to Asku, his eyes still dark and hard. "I am sorry to leave. If there is to be a fight, I would prefer not to miss it, as this is the work of Matchitehew in some form. But I must go."

"Of course," said Napayshni. "I would do the same in your position. Know that we will care for Sunukkuhkau and Kaliskah as our own." As Pajackok prepared to re-embark, the Grandfather directed the young men to prepare a stretcher from a blanket and poles, then supervised their lifting of Sunu onto the platform. Weakly, Sunu waved his good arm. Pajackok looked back once, nodded, and gave the order for both canoes to shove off.

In their wake, Asku held up a hand in blessing, silently asking the Great Spirits for protection—for Pajackok, for the Sea People, and for his own people. The entire party began to climb the trail.

Halfway up, the Chief cut into Asku's thoughts. "Askuwa'tu, take Keme and Hawilish and go to the crossing. Do not be seen or heard. Find them, and which direction they come, and how many. *Míshnam pamshtk'úksha'*? They will not cross here, because we can see very far. They certainly will not cross Toward the Setting Sun from here. At this point, they will not go near Wayám. Word will be out, and not only will they be unwelcome, but there are those at Wayám who would be glad to bring their heads to the Sea People for a reward. Surely they will head Toward the Rising Sun. While you do that, your grandfather and I will prepare to defend our people. We will not be taken unaware."

"Yes, *Wyánch'i*," Asku nodded.

"*Kitu*...hurry."

Asku took off at a run with Hawɨlish behind him. By the time they had rounded up Keme and gathered up their gear and weapons, the alarm was raised in full. He saw women hurrying about, young ones in tow toward the Teacher's longhouse, while the men—and some women— gathered weapons and prepared to fight.

The scouting party came first to the ridgeline overlooking K̲'mɨł Canyon, immediately Toward the Rising Sun from the village, and stopped to scan across the canyon. No one was in sight, and they began the descent down to K̲'mɨł. At this time of year, it was just a creek, but during some winters it was a torrent. They ascended the far side with care, keeping Nch'i-Wána on their right, working their way to a bluff well known to the River People, from which one could see a great distance. Asku stopped and crawled toward the crest of the bluff, motioning his comrades to do the same.

"I don't see anyone," said Hawɨlish.

"Neither do I," said Keme. "Do we go down and cross?"

"Not here. They could see us from very far away." Asku closed his eyes, and in his mind he saw Saigwan, he saw his father, he saw the mighty Wanuukshiłáma chief with his kind eyes, and he saw his grandfather. *Help me*, he called out to all of them.

Asku opened his eyes and scanned Beyond Nch'i-Wána once more—and saw movement in the left field of his vision, on their side of the river. The bear's fur shone in the sunlight as he stood up on his hind legs, nose high, as if tasting the air for Asku's scent.

Asku raised his hand. "It is me, *anahúy*."

The bear dropped to his feet and nodded, then turned and ran along the ridgeline ahead of them. "*Kɨtu!*" he said, keeping his voice low.

They followed the bear along the bluff, down and up canyons as they came. When they came to a good viewpoint, Asku would gesture for a halt. They saw no signs of the Pyúsh chief or the others, but the bear was still there.

Midday heat beat down upon Asku's bare back as they kept following the bear, running when it was safe, slowing when necessary. As they worked their way through rolling hills near the bluff, the bear vanished. Asku crawled up to the nearest overlook.

Across the river at the water's edge were men, with a dozen or more canoes. Some of the men seemed to pace, while others sat around a small firepit. Asku scanned the cliffside behind them and saw another group of men inching their way down a steep, rocky trail that switched back and forth. There were five or so of them, definitely the Pyúsh P'ushtáayama he had seen at their village and the sea, and at least twenty more at the water's edge. A line of horses waited along the rim.

"That is him," Hawɨlish whispered, pointing to the men on the switchbacks. "Do you see him there?"

"Oh, it's him all right, and a few other Pyúsh," Keme replied, "but those are Sxíxtama...from the Sts'áat Mountains Toward the Rising Sun."

"Who?" Hawɨlish asked.

"No one you want to know, man," Keme sighed.

Hawɨlish shielded his eyes from the sun with a hand. "Do you think they will cross here?"

"I don't think that would make sense," said Keme.

"No," said Asku, "because the bluff on this side is too steep. I expect they will ride the river until they can climb up, probably someplace before K̲'mɨł Canyon. We should watch carefully Toward the Rising Sun. Let's get back and report."

⊶

The sun was dropping low in the sky when they arrived back in the village. Asku's thighs and calves burned, and his feet ached. They had only stopped once for water, at K̲'mɨł, when they were very near home.

The Chief was out inspecting the watch perimeter over a draw of K'mił that represented one of the few likely ways attackers might sneak in. "What did you learn?" he asked.

"The Pyúsh are with allies. Keme identified them as Sxíxtama. I counted thirteen canoes, and they have horses on the heights. A total of twenty-five warriors, including Matchitehew, but that many canoes mean there are others somewhere."

"Sxíxtama," repeated Napayshni, thoughtful. "They will only be reliable for him as long as they see opportunity to gain. If he gets into trouble, they will vanish like wind. Where are they?"

"They are Beyond Nch'i-Wána, *Wyánch'i*, at the white water where the cliffs are very high."

"That is not far away at all. Were you seen?"

"I am sure we were not, *Wyánch'i*. We kept well hidden and were on the other side of the river to begin with."

"Also," said Keme, "I watched them for signs of reaction. If we had been seen, someone would have pointed us out to Matchitehew. That did not happen."

"Well done, all of you," said the Chief. "Even if they have enough others to fill all those canoes, they are outnumbered, so they must hope to pull some trickery on us and attempt to overwhelm us in one spot. That is their only advantage: we must defend all of a large area, whereas they need defend nothing."

Asku nodded. "Then the way to defend ourselves is for our watchers to be very sharp-eyed."

"That, and to be able to identify their main attack, and move enough warriors into place to drive them back. We will be ready. Asku, you probably want to check on Kaliskah and Sunu. After that, come help me to set up our defenses."

They found Chaytan first, testing a ladder positioned against the Story House. Women and children still bustled about, but some were headed into the Story House with food and water and weapons. Everyone was armed in some way. Asku told Chaytan of all they had seen. "Where are Kaliskah and Sunu?" he asked.

"The Grandfather's. The Chief will return shortly, and he will decide what to do with them."

Asku entered the Grandfather's home quietly. Sunu seemed to be sleeping, although not peacefully. His skin was the color of clouds on a gloomy day and his limbs twitched. The wound on his shoulder was covered with a small cloth. Asku thought he could hear a quiet sucking sound coming from under it as his chest rose and fell. Kaliskah sat at Sunu's side.

"We will not be able to move him far, Askuwa'tu, if at all," the Grandfather whispered. Kaliskah looked up. "He will not survive it."

Asku nodded in understanding. He walked over to Kaliskah and put a hand on her shoulder. "I am sorry, Kaliskah."

She put an arm around his waist and held on but did not cry.

>——→

When the Chief arrived with Chaytan, it was time to settle the matter. Napayshni called the men outside.

"We must move him into the longhouse," Chaytan insisted. "This tent is too vulnerable. We need everyone who cannot fight in one spot, and the Story House is the strongest refuge."

"He will die if we do," the Grandfather said. "I will stay with him. The wound must be sealed, and soon. If we move him and the wound is not sealed, that will kill him." The old man turned to Asku's father. "Napayshni, this is my job, my gift from the Great Spirits, no matter the outcome. I will care for this young man. I have all I need here to seal the wound, and I have the small drying pit in my house. We will remain down there. Please leave us here."

The Chief studied the old man for a long time. Finally, he nodded. "You will not be far away from the others, but you must try to keep him quiet." He rested a hand on the old man's shoulder, "*Kw'ałá, x̱ı̱tway.*"

The Grandfather nodded and entered his home to prepare. "Napayshni," Chaytan began again, "it will be hard enough to watch the longhouse, now we must watch the–"

"We must do it as best we can." The Chief held his hand up and turned toward Asku. "My *títa*, gather the men. Set the watch at the river. Chaytan, take Liwanu and his men. Make a line along K̲'mił Canyon, from the Watch Tree all the way to the first warrior on the bluff above the river."

Asku looked from his father to Chaytan and back again, "Yes, *Wyánch'i.*"

"Do not put everyone out on watch, but keep strong groups back from the lookouts, to move where the fighting goes. I will set a line Toward the Great Mountains and the Setting Sun. They all will need to be ready to move in any direction at any time. I will watch for signals from atop the Story House, where I can see very far, with a group of warriors who can move to the thickest fighting. And remember, this village itself is not important. We can get more things. We cannot get people back once lost. Thus, we must protect our people at all costs, including Sunukkuhkau and the Grandfather. *Míshnam pamshtk'úksha'?*"

"Yes, *túta.* But what of Kaliskah?" asked Asku.

The Chief looked at him. "Send her into the longhouse, *tita,* it is safer."

"She will not like it at all, *Wyánch'i.* She will not want to leave Sunu, for one thing. For another, she will want to fight, and you have seen that she is fierce. And she is not the only young woman who will want to take a stand."

"No one likes any of this!" exclaimed the Chief, irritated. Then he softened. "Everyone has wants, Askuwa'tu. However, I must think for all our people. And I must have my leaders, like you and Chaytan, and they cannot be even more distracted and worried. I am sure she can handle herself. But I need you to focus on what I have asked you to do, and for that, you must know that she is safe."

"Yes, *Wyánch'i.*"

"Also, there is another reason. You remember how we sized up the defense strength of Wayám?" Asku nodded. "Suppose things were to go very badly. If so, those young women, plus some older men and even children, will provide some defense of last resort. And you remember what I told you about a mother and her baby."

"I see, *túta.*"

"Good. Now your work is to explain that to Kaliskah and get her to the Story House, then do what I sent you to do. And quickly."

The men went inside the Grandfather's house and moved Sunu into the drying pit, four or five rammed-earth steps leading into a sort of cellar. As the men covered the pit entrance with planks of cedar, *tk'ú* mats and furs for added protection, Kaliskah moved to go with Sunu, but Asku put a hand on her shoulder. She turned in surprise. "Please come outside," he said. "We must talk."

She complied, at least that far. "What is it, Asku?"

"Kaliskah, I need you to go into the Story House with the others."

"No. I will not leave *káhp-ho*…or you. I can help, let me help. Do not ask me to do this."

"I would prefer to ask you than to tell you, but you must do it."

She put a hand on her hip, where the beautiful dagger rested. "Oh? Why must I?"

I begin to see how my father feels. Asku quelled his annoyance with an effort. "Here is why, and there is not much time, so you must go immediately. There is almost no chance they will notice Sunu down there, and we cannot move him farther. The Story House is where all the women will be."

Kaliskah's eyes narrowed. "You think I cannot fight, Patisapatisháma *Ty-ee*?"

"That is not what I think. Many women can and will fight, and that is why you are needed there. They may need inspiration. Some may need calming, and my mother needs you to help her. As for the rest, you will be their Chief's mate one day, and they need to know you at your best, to show the girls how to be strong women. I want you to watch the back window and protect my brother and sisters. I hope you will all be safe, but if war reaches you, fight well."

For a moment she looked as if she would resist. It passed. "All right, Asku. But I will worry." She put on a brave smile and patted her bow. "And yes, we will guard all of the windows just in case and barricade the door." She squeezed his hand one last time before disappearing behind another family into the Story House.

Chapter 33

The Patisapatisháma village sat on a plateau. The living area was perhaps an extreme arcing bowshot in width, leaving it surrounded with a much larger open area. It was roughly circular, with the garden and drying shed slightly below and outside the living area nearest Nch'i-Wána, the longhouses and ceremonial firepit at the farthest side from the river.

In the direction of Pahto, and Toward the Setting Sun, was a long gradual draw that poured occasional rainstorms and snowmelt into Nch'i-Wána just downstream of the tribe's washing and canoe storage area. There, Asku and Hawɨlish had slain the starving old wolf not long before. On the side opposite Nch'i-Wána was mainly open plateau, with small hills and slopes as the only obstacles, and now and then a boulder or rock outcrop. Continuing Toward the Rising Sun, not long before the canyon of K̲'mɨł, was the solitary, somewhat forlorn tree that the Patisapatisháma had never cut down for fuel or timber: the Watch Tree, left alone for its obvious value in the only area where outsiders could approach the village without obstacles. Then came K̲'mɨł, a steep canyon which poured or trickled into Nch'i-Wána upstream of the washing and fishing area. A hearty man could walk across this area in the time it took to eat a big dinner and could walk a circuit of its entire perimeter in about four times that.

The Chief's defensive plan involved a perimeter of lookouts, sparser in the less threatened zones and denser in the more dangerous regions. The lower part of K̲'mɨł and the cliffs above Nch'i-Wána would be time-consuming and perilous for attackers and needed only sentinels to make sure Matchitehew did not succeed simply by doing something so dumb that no one would guard against it. The runoff draw toward Pahto might be easier to cross but afforded a good view of any crossing from the village side and had a medium density of lookouts. The most worrisome area extended from the end of the runoff draw Toward the Rising Sun past the Watch Tree to upper K'mił, which was still a difficult crossing and climb for attackers, but more feasible until the point where K'mił snaked back Toward the Setting Sun before its final canyon emptying directly into Nch'i-Wána.

The job of watchers was to see and signal, and if need be, to withdraw. Most were teenage boys and young men with keen eyes, especially in darkness. About a hundred paces beyond the watch perimeter waited three groups of warriors, about twelve each, who would react as the situation required. One, led by Chaytan and including the Elk Plains contingent, positioned itself between the runoff draw and the Watch Tree. Liwanu's group, eager for action, backed up the line between and including the Watch Tree extending to K'mił. Asku's group, including Hawiłish and Kitchi, overwatched K'mił from Liwanu's area to the steep lower part of its canyon. A steep draw that emptied into K'mił from near the village itself split his perimeter at one point, but the watchers could see each other well. While Kitchi could not keep up with rapid movement, he would catch up as need be.

Asku sat with Hawiłish and Kitchi behind the midpoint of his area, watching and listening. While Kitchi inspected his arrows, and Hawiłish scanned for movement, Asku closed his eyes and spoke to the Great Spirits.

Help me to be strong enough. Give me strength, give me wisdom, for whatever comes. And keep them safe...all of them.

Young boys, employed as messengers and gofers, brought jerky and water out to the watchers. The sun fell below the horizon, splashing the sky with another of the pink, orange, and deep crimson skyscapes that marked this country. As the sky Toward the Rising Sun grew dark, Asku could hear the scurrying of twilight creatures. He tried to remain calm and attentive.

He found no calm, at least not for long.

Toward the Great Mountains, he heard distant shouts, some of pain. Liwanu, who waited just at the limit of where signals could be seen, gestured: *we will investigate.* "The Watch Tree," said Hawiłish.

Asku waved his agreement to Liwanu. "Hawiłish," Asku whispered, "warn down the line toward Nch'i-Wána, then run to tell the

Chief there is action at the Watch Tree." He looked to Wahkan, a seasoned warrior of middle age but still hale. "I am going to find out what happened. I will be back. Wahkan, lead this group until I return."

Wahkan nodded, as did Hawilish, who signaled the next watch point along K'mił and took off running. Asku ran after Liwanu's warriors and caught up with them in brushy cover about a rock's long throw from the Watch Tree.

A young man staggered toward them from the direction of the Watch Tree, dragging someone through the scrubby grass. Only when they were very close did Asku recognize Haysutu, one winter younger than himself, dragging his little brother Maska. Someone else was crawling over from the side of the Watch Tree Toward the Great Mountains to investigate as well, probably Ashkii, the oldest brother of Haysutu and Maska. Asku nodded to Liwanu, who crouched forward with another warrior to help Haysutu and Maska back into cover.

In the dusk, Asku had to get very close to see what was wrong with Maska and Haysutu. The younger was in bad shape, with a broken arrow shaft in his chest and blood all over his face. Haysutu was bleeding from the upper arm, where an arrow had passed clear through the flesh. "What happened, *siks*?" Asku whispered.

"Maska was in the Tree," began Haysutu, bitterly. "I was at the base, as we usually do. There was a noise, maybe a rock thrown, and I turned around to see what it was. We were concerned they might somehow sneak around us in the dark. At that point, I heard arrows fly, and one hit me in the arm. That is nothing. But Maska yelled in pain and then I heard him fall. I think he is dead."

Liwanu put a hand just near Maska's mouth and nose as Ashkii arrived. "He is not breathing. It looks like the fall drove the arrow in deeper, but where it hit him would have been dangerous in any case. Look at that arrow's fletching, though."

Asku gently finished breaking the nock end from the arrow, held it close enough to his eyes to see, then handed it to Liwanu. "That is not a Pyúsh arrow. That is Sxíxtama fletching. Keme taught me how to recognize them while we were traveling."

"We will kill them for this," snarled Liwanu.

"Any we can, or can catch," agreed Asku. "Ashkii, Haysutu, I am very sorry. If there were a chance to save Maska, I would say take him back to the Story House, but it looks bad."

Haysutu spat. "We have lost him."

"We will stay," hissed Ashkii. "I will go up the tree; we must a watcher there, and I am the thinnest of us and can hide best in the branches. Maybe they will shoot at me, but I will stay well hidden. Cover us, okay? Come on, *nika*." The rest nocked arrows and watched as the brothers low-crawled toward the Watch Tree. Haysutu took cover at its base, while Ashkii climbed up the covered side.

There was movement—in two places, at medium bowshot, from behind large clumps of brush. Four bows twanged toward the movement as an arrow flew toward the Watch Tree, sticking into it with a *thud*. There was a yell of pain, a deep adult male voice, but no more movement.

Liwanu stood and yelled, dancing from side to side. "How do you like that lesson? Try again and we will teach you some more!" An arrow flew past. "How do you even get food if you are such lousy shots! Aiieeeeee!" Liwanu turned around, slapped his backside, and got back into cover.

Liwanu's warriors were chuckling. "They probably did not understand a word you said, but they understood that you have no respect for them," said Asku. *And I wish you hadn't done that, but I could hardly stop you.* "What is your plan now?"

"*Wyánch'i*, I will leave two men here to help watch, and to help protect the brothers," said Liwanu. "We need to keep in touch with our watchers."

Asku nodded. "*Kúu mísh.* I think they are trying to get us to react more than we should. I will go back to the group I left with Wahkan. Make sure no one gets through here without a fight." Asku took off, first at a crouched trot, then at a run.

A few minutes after Asku returned to his group, Hawilish appeared behind him out of breath. "We are under attack from two sides so far, although we have yet to see most of our attackers. A group of archers are hidden somewhere Toward the Great Mountains, across the runoff draw. They have not tried to cross it. The Chief said to stay on watch, be careful of sneak attacks, and to send me back with word when anything changes."

Asku nodded. "There has been an attack at the Watch Tree, and Maska is dead, but they are just probing. Liwanu has the situation under control. Send word to the watchers down K̲'mił what has happened, then come back. It is getting dark fast, and it will be harder to see movement, so we will need to be closer to the watch line."

Asku looked at the terrain in front of him. Toward the Rising Sun was gently rolling land beyond the K̲'mił Canyon, the cliffsides of which were steeper and more dangerous than the runoff draw. *I hope they are fools enough to come across the canyon, or sneak through it, he thought. They do not know it as we do. If they try, they will be sorry.*

He thought about Maska, a happy-go-lucky boy fond of jokes and fishing. *As for me, I am already sorry.* He shook his head to clear it.

A whistle came from Liwanu's direction. Asku turned and watched. The young warrior held two hands out, fingers outstretched, one time and pointed Toward the Great Mountains. Then he did the same and pointed Toward the Rising Sun and upper K̲'mił Canyon. Asku nodded, waved his group of defenders to gather, and ran toward Hawilish.

"What's happening?" Kitchi whispered as Asku whistled and gestured with his hands toward the next watcher.

"Ten approach along K̲'mił, and a group of similar size is headed for Chaytan. Tell those on watch to be ready. We will shift forward to be nearer the watch perimeter. *Wyanúukim íchin.*" Asku led the way.

"*Watwáa naknúwim,*" Hawilish whispered. "Protect and take care of us."

Asku's men advanced nearer Liwanu's group. *If I do not let him play a warrior's part, I will demean my friend. Plus, he is too brave to waste what he can do.* "Kitchi," he said, "sneak out where you can see into upper K̲'mił and see if you can spot them. Kitchi nodded and crouched forward until he was at a perimeter point looking into the canyon, then signaled back: *they have crossed far up K̲'mił in a side draw.* That meant it would depend on where they exited the draw toward the perimeter.

"*Wyánch'i,*" rumbled Wahkan, "they can see no better than we can in the dusk, and maybe not as well, since we know this ground like we know our mates' eyes. If they advance here, they will expect us to be far back, where we are now. If we advanced past the watchers, we would be where they do not expect us, and give them a bad surprise."

"They deserve one. I agree. Stay here while I explain the plan to Liwanu, then I will signal you forward."

Asku worked his way toward Liwanu's position, using all available cover, and told him what Wahkan had suggested. "That sounds good, *Wyánch'i*. And if your people have to retreat, you can retreat past us, and we will attack from their side." Asku waved Wahkan forward and crept ahead to catch up with his group.

"Should we send word to the *Wyánch'i*?" whispered Hawilish, as they edged ahead.

"We should, but I cannot spare anyone."

"The only question is when they will come out of that side canyon," said Wahkan. "At some point, they must. They probably decided it would be too dangerous to come further down K'mił, and too hard to climb up."

"*Kúu mish,* maybe," Asku replied.

"Probably thought they could get out to the River this way. *Misht'ipni*," Wahkan spat. "They were smart not to try carrying that through."

"Do the Pyúsh fight in the dark?"

Wahkan shook his head. "Many tribes don't, but I do not think we should count on it. But look, *Wyánch'i*." Wahkan was pointing back across lower K'mił. Asku's eyes followed and saw fires. Several fires, almost certainly Toward the Rising Sun of K'mił.

"Hmmm," he thought aloud. "It will spread fast."

"*Íi,*" Wahkan nodded. "But it will not cross K'mił, nor will it give them cover if they try to do so. It is a cheap distraction, I think. It will only help them if our men keep staring at it, as it is bad for their sight in the dark, and in any case, is not where they ought to look."

"Yes. Do not look at the fires. Eyes straight ahead and look for movement." After a moment, he added: "The Chief is expecting a report from me by now. Wahkan, I will be back soon." The elder warrior nodded. Asku nodded to him and to Hawilish before heading back toward the village.

He found his father in the center of the village, on top of the Story House. "Askuwa'tu," the Chief called out. "*Túnmash wá táymun?*"

"*Wyánch'i*, as you have seen, they have lit fires across K'miⱡ. You know that they tested us near the Watch Tree; they paid for that."

"How are our men positioned now?"

"The lookouts are in their normal positions in our area," said Asku. "We have seen ten warriors cross the upper part of K'miⱡ and move Toward the Setting Sun along our line. Wahkan suggested my group move forward, so if they moved toward us, we could ambush them. Liwanu's group is still in position. How is the other side? We heard there was another group of ten, headed toward Chaytan."

"Chaytan has not sent word, so I do not know." The Chief ran a hand along his forehead and through his hair. "But remember that their line is closer to here than yours is. If no one has attacked your group or Liwanu's by the time you get back, you should pull back inside our watchers, in case we need you back here on short notice."

"*Íi*," Asku nodded.

"Find Chaytan," the Chief ordered. "Tell him about the situation on your front and find out how his is doing. Send a messenger from his group to tell me, too, then get back and if all is well, pull your group back to reinforce this side."

"Yes, *Wyánch'i.*"

Asku looked once at the silent Story House, full of almost everyone he loved, before running up the trail Toward the Great Mountains. At the top of the runoff draw, he found the first watcher waiting behind a thick patch of sage grass, an arrow nocked and ready.

"*Náy?*" Asku asked.

"*Íi*," the young man said. He pointed Toward the Rising Sun. "Chaytan is that direction."

Asku followed the line of men, staying low to the ground and watching carefully for movement ahead. At the point of the line nearest the village, he found Chaytan crouched behind a boulder the size of his family's tent. On the other side crouched Sahkantiak, looking eager to engage. Chaytan's group was fanned out in cover on both sides of the boulder, about fifty paces inside the sentinel line. Asku stopped behind the rock. "*Túnmash wá táymun?*"

"Ten or fifteen warriors moving fast. They are not Pyúsh, but Sxíxtama." Chaytan drew a *chcháya* arrow from his quiver, licked his fingers, then ran them across the eagle feathers on the end. "Our watchers will fire one shot, then evade. As the Sxíxtama advance, we will pick them off. If they angle past us, we will hit them from behind."

"Chaytan, so you know, we have the other group ahead of us near upper K̲'mił. We think they will at least come forward to take shots at us. Also, the fires you see are across lower K̲'mił. The Chief and I think that both are just meant to confuse us and tie us down, so that leaves only one place for the main attack, assuming there is to be one."

Chaytan nodded, keeping his eyes toward the horizon. Asku saw signaling ahead in the dusk. "They have stopped," Chaytan whispered. "Just out of reach. Asku, I think you're right. You had better get back to your group soon, before you are cut off from them."

"I will. The *Wyánch'i* says for you to send a report back to him."

"I do not like to spare a man, but he does need to know. I will do it. Now I suggest you get moving."

He did not, quite yet. There were bow-twangs in the dusk, and Chaytan's watchers soon fell back from the perimeter. Asku could see movements beyond them. "Stay well covered," whispered Chaytan to his men. "If you get a good target, shoot." Chaytan swung outside the boulder half a second longer than it would take to shoot and drew an arrow cracking against the boulder's edge to glance away. Asku saw two of Chaytan's men answer and heard a half-stifled grunt of pain from out in the dusk. Chaytan crawled over to a young warrior of fourteen, briefed him, and sent him to report to the Chief as fast as he could safely get there.

Staying low, Asku made his way back toward Wahkan's positions, stopping to confer with Liwanu. Carefully, of course, because Liwanu's men were engaged as Chaytan's had been. The Patisapatisháma archers were holding ground, exchanging arrows and taunts. Liwanu crouched with U'taktay, the battle-experienced elder who had grilled Asku before about the need for warfare.

Darkness was setting in, and it would be a while until the moon proved useful, but his eyes slowly adjusted as he ran the line. The Patisapatisháma archers were holding ground. Arrows were flying, with plenty of taunting. Both sets of warriors had cover and could hold out for a while. Asku ducked behind a rock with Liwanu and U'taktay.

"Túnmash wá táymun?" U'taktay asked.

"There are fires across K̲'mił, and Pyúsh or Sxíxtama warriors probing all along the perimeter," Asku whispered. U'taktay nodded, swung out of cover, saw no shot, and returned to concealment. "Do you foresee them getting through here?"

"Not in my lifetime," said Liwanu. "Is Chaytan holding?"

"Yes, they just came under attack, much like here."

"Young *Wyánch'i,*" U'taktay said, "They will not cross this open area, not in the dark. We have the advantage. For fifty-two winters I have walked these hills, I could find them in the dark."

"*Kúu mish,*" Asku nodded. "But be careful."

Asku ducked low and began making his way toward Wahkan's positions. He did not get far before, well to his rear in the direction of Chaytan's positions, a war call echoed across the plateau. It sent sharp spikes of adrenaline through his veins. He swung the whalebone bow from his back, nocked a cedar arrow and ran back along the watch line where he had come.

Between Liwanu and Chaytan's positions, Asku looked about for a watcher and found none. He gave a bird whistle, heard nothing, and scouted around. No one, and no enemies. He ran back to the last watcher's post. "I think they have broken through. Signal that down to Liwanu and Wahkan, and signal Liwanu to send another watcher." By the time he began, Asku was moving toward the village with an arrow ready to nock.

On the way, he saw two shadowy figures, also headed for the village. One whistled, and Asku responded in kind. "Chaytan sent us to find out about the yelling," said the older. Both carried obsidian-tipped spears as well as bows.

"The watcher behind me is not at his post," said Asku. "I am concerned, but there is not time to hunt about for him. If they have gotten into the village, we are needed there, and if not, we need to warn them. Come on."

At a run, they neared the village in about the time it would take a small child's attention to wander. With its firepits, especially the ceremonial fire, it was not hard to see figures moving about the dwellings at a distance. Asku had asked his father about leaving the fires lit, and Napayshni had explained that since they already knew the location of the village, light favored the defenders because they would be able to tell friend from foe at a greater distance and would thus not accidentally shoot at each other in panic. Now he could hear shouts in both Chiskin and some other language. Asku led his men toward the Totem, the nearest part of the village to his approach. "Go right and see if there are enemies looting or searching about that side of the village. There is no need to take live prisoners. I will check on my father."

The men hesitated a moment, then said, "*Kúu mísh, Wyánch'i.*" They readied their bows and approached the village at the part nearest Pahto.

Someone was crouched at the Totem, with someone else on the ground sitting against it. Asku nocked an arrow. As he got closer, the crouching figure's slight build grew familiar.

Nayhali.

Great Spirits, if ever we needed your protection, it would be now.

It all seemed to happen so slowly, though it took so little actual time.

She had a knife in her hand, shielding the sitting figure. Then Asku saw three men, Sxíxtama by their look, emerge from between the dwellings into the ceremonial fire area. Two, both short and stocky, carried thick bone tomahawks. The tallest carried a dagger, and each had a coupstick on his hip. One of the shorter Sxíxtama, with more elaborate ornamentation, seemed in charge.

All three began to walk toward Nayhali, leering. One made a gesture of unmistakable obscenity. "*Łík,*" Nayhali spat, brandishing a knife.

My sister is as brave as the eagle. I am proud of her.

At that moment Asku saw movement at the Story House door, heard a twang. The stocky man in charge yelled out in pain as the arrow hit him in the midsection. While he staggered back, struggling to pull the arrow out in a panic, the other two rushed ahead. One headed toward Nayhali, and the other toward the Story House.

Asku had just time to recognize Kaliskah hurrying to nock another arrow at the Story House doorway. He rushed forward into the light, yelled out a terrible insult, and waited until Kaliskah's presumptive attacker turned to look. Then Asku let go the arrow.

He had meant to shoot for the chest, but for whatever reason, the arrow went high. That was not a bad thing. The obsidian point struck the tallest man just under the chin. He keeled over backward, pawing madly at the arrow and giving out a sort of gurgled scream.

The remaining man snarled and rushed Nayhali, who kept herself between the Sxíxtama and the figure slumped against the Totem. Asku drew his knife and charged but failed to arrive in time. Nayhali held her dagger at the ready—*and I see she remembered the fighting methods I taught her*—and prepared to slash away.

Twunnnng.

Kaliskah, after all, had not had just the one arrow.

This one hit the Sxíxtama in the backside. Had it arrived an instant sooner, it would have gone into his hip and brought him down. He let forth a scream of pain and bellowed something in his own language, probably a cry for help.

As he did, Nayhali did the thing her attacker least expected. She rushed him and slashed at his arm, managing a deep cut into the underside of his forearm, then kept moving past him. It was fortunate for her that she did, for his tomahawk narrowly missed her back.

My chance.

Asku slashed his dagger into Nayhali's attacker's leg from behind, just above the knee. The leg collapsed, and Asku looked into the eyes of a stricken man who knew his dying day had come.

Drawn by the action, the other two scouts arrived. Both rushed ahead with spears and finished off the wounded. "We found some dead, *Wyánch'i*, and saw a few fleeing," said the older scout. "We will keep looking."

"Asku!" called Nayhali. Now he got a good look at the figure slumped against the Totem.

Nayhali was on her knees in front of the Chief. As he raised his bowed head, Asku caught a glimpse of the arrow shaft sticking out of his chest. Blood dripped slowly down Napayshni's chin, ribs, and stomach as he struggled to breathe.

"Take a message back to the watchers," Asku ordered. "Tell them what happened here, that the Chief is wounded, and to watch for those fleeing."

The men looked from Asku to the Chief and back again. The older warrior nodded. "We will," he hissed through his teeth.

Kaliskah rushed up, bringing Chitsa. She did not make a sound until she reached his side. "Napayshni," she whispered, "can you hear me?"

"Asku," the Chief said, forcing out the word.

"I am here, *túta*."

"Get them back inside the longhouse, close up the gap," the Chief gasped.

"Yes, *Wyánch'i*," Asku took his mother by the shoulders. She did not protest, except to whisper something into the Chief's ear before taking Nayhali and Kaliskah by the hand and hurrying back toward the door. Had Asku looked, he would have seen Kaliskah take up a guard position at the door, but at that point two of Wahkan's warriors ran up.

"Help me," Asku waved to them. The three of them hoisted Napayshni up, as gently as they could. The Chief did not make a sound as they carried him through the door of the Grandfather's healing tent. "Grandfather?" Asku called down, lifting a cedar plank from the underground storage room. "We need you."

"Asku, *winak*," the Chief ordered.

Asku looked once at his father, then nodded and slipped back through the doorway. A deep breath did nothing for the anger and fear growing inside him.

Within an hour, messengers reported that the attackers had fled into the night. Six Patisapatisháma were dead, with ten more wounded, two seriously including the Chief. A full count of dead enemies would have to wait for daylight. Asku went out to the perimeter, moving along the watch line covering K̲'mił. Wahkan's group had skirmished and taken the least harm. Asku found Liwanu near the place he had left him, although now he stood out of cover, eyes angry, arms folded. "It is over, then?" Liwanu asked.

"Seems to be," Asku answered, watching the fires in the distance across K̲'mił. The only movement in sight was that of the tall grass in the wind. "I have yet to check on Chaytan, but the word is that his group caught and killed some of those who got through. The rest have run away. We will track them. They will not get far."

"Ours ran as well," Liwanu spat.

"What about Matchitehew? Did you see him?"

"No. He and the other Pyúsh did not even come close enough for a shot." He spat on the ground in disgust. "But I will go after him, right now. Just say the word."

"I am going after him," Asku stated. "*Ilksáas wínasha.*"

"No, you are not going alone," Liwanu said, lifting his chin. "And it looks like I am not the only one who sees it that way." Keme and Hawilish were just running up, loaded up and armed for travel. Keme tossed another bag at Asku before walking past him and taking the trail toward the Watch Tree.

"I have just one question, young *Wyánch'i*," interjected U'taktay. Asku turned and nodded for him to ask. "How do you plan to see their trail, or follow it, in the dark?"

"There is some moonlight. It cannot be that hard," said Liwanu.

U'taktay nodded. "At dawn, it will not be. But let us remember what we know. They came in more than one group, because we faced more men than the scouting expedition reported. They left tracks both coming and going. There will be a lot to sort out, and a lot depends on what one can notice. They crossed K'mił in both directions, or at least some of them did, and they probably left few traces, so they could have moved along the canyon bed and come out at a different place. You will have to locate that in order to pick up their trail. You may find many trails. Maybe they split up."

Liwanu muttered something, but quietly enough to avoid open insolence. "They will get a long head start if we wait," Asku countered. "In fact, they already have one."

"Do you believe you can do this by a little moonlight, when you are already tired from a long and tense watch and fighting, young *Wyánch'i*?"

I have no answer to that; at least, none that I want to hear myself. "What do you advise?"

U'taktay smiled a little. "Well, it is obvious that we will need to keep a watch over the night. We do not know if they might regroup and return. I do not think we wiped out their whole force. Maybe some of it stayed around. After a group band together for a bad purpose, if that purpose mainly fails, it tends to fall apart. It is possible that the Sxíxtama and Pyúsh P'ushtáayama went separate ways." In the darkness, Asku just saw U'taktay raise an eyebrow, then shift his eyes toward Liwanu.

I see. "Liwanu. I would like it if you would hunt down and kill any Sxíxtama that fled toward Pahto and upper Iksíks Wána. Take five other men only," added Asku, "and start at first light tracking from the group that engaged Chaytan. Make sure that none get home to say: 'It is easy and fun to attack the weak Patisapatisháma.' But you must wait for dawn."

Liwanu smiled, a smile of fury and malice. "We will do it, young *Wyánch'i*."

"Good hunting."

"Those of you who are going tracking, then," said U'taktay, "should get some sleep while you can, because you will want to be moving as soon as it is light enough to see anything useful. In the meantime, those of us who are not going to track them can maintain the watch, with some relieving others so no one falls asleep. The women and children and elders can relax a little."

"We are giving them a very long head start," grumbled Liwanu.

"There are only a few of you," said the elder. "Fewer always move faster. You are younger, for the most part. You also have an advantage: you know you are pursuing them. They do not know if you are or not, or how many men you have. Every time they stop, for any reason, is a time you will not. They also can become tired and may rest soon; they had a long trip to get here and will have to travel well into the night in order to camp in what they think is safety. And unless they left all their wounded to die, they may have some who slow them down. Some may straggle and be easy prey for you, and perhaps provide information."

"It is hard to just go to bed," grumbled Asku. Liwanu muttered agreement.

"Without a doubt," said Hawilish. "But he is right, if you think about it. If we run after them now, we may even mess up the trail without seeing it. We might never find them. I am not sure if I can sleep at all, but if we want to find and punish Matchitehew, we should do as U'taktay recommends."

Asku nodded. "Yes, that is what we will do. Keme, Hawilish, be ready for a very early start. Liwanu, select your men and do the same.

U'taktay, can you make sure we are all awakened at the earliest sensible time?"

"Of course, young *Wyánch'i*. I just wish I were fast enough to keep up with you, for I would go myself. But you have good companions, including one who knows Matchitehew's habits and ways," he said, nodding toward Keme. "And he will help you remember that our conflict is not with all Pyúsh." Keme said nothing, but nodded gratitude. "There is just one other thing to consider: our Wawyukyáma allies. You, young *Wyánch'i*, will probably find that Matchitehew headed for his home country. The Elk Plains People are the experts in that country, and more importantly, what will they think if you do not ask them to join you?"

"I did not even think of that. There is much on my mind, U'taktay."

"That is what elders are for, to think of the other things," said U'taktay. "Let us now go to the Wawyukyáma *Wyánch'i*, talk with him, decide what they want to do, and then get you some sleep."

In the end, it was a simple discussion. Kalataka would remain at the River for the time being. U'hitaykah, Aanapay and Mach'ni would go with Asku, and if possible, check on their vacant village.

As for Matchitehew, he would pay.

Chapter 34

Asku spent that night in restless sleep near his father. He did not even check on Kaliskah, Chitsa, Nayhali, or anyone else. Sure enough, U'taktay came in the pre-dawn to wake him up. Asku dressed in haste, gathered his travel weapons and equipment, and went to the ceremonial firepit. *Right now*, he thought, *I do not feel spirits so much. Maybe this is what it is to be blind with rage and grief. I wish never to feel this way again.*

U'taktay came by with a basket of fresh-made *wawachi* scones. Asku took one with thanks. "Thank my mate, who got up early to make them for you. But quickly, there is one more thing."

Asku waited.

"You understand that you of all people really should not be running off right now, and that it would be best to let Keme and Hawílish and Liwanu and U'hitaykah and their comrades handle this. They are not destined to be *Wyánch'i* here, and you are. Everyone here needs you right now."

Asku felt anger rise in him and bottled it with an effort. "Perhaps so. But this is something I must do."

"So it was for your father, Askuwa'tu, many winters ago. I am not saying you must not. You will, so it is pointless to argue. But the day will come when you may no longer indulge a strong feeling that means abandoning your people."

Too quickly, Asku snarled, "I am not abandoning them. I am hunting down their enemies. This is not fair, U'taktay."

"You have plenty of capable men. Your father is too injured to lead in an active way as *Wyánch'i*. Be truthful to yourself, young *Wyánch'i*. This act by you comes at the expense of your people, a people already in pain. Only you will know when you speak truth to your own soul. I can not know that."

Bereft of anything to say, Asku stood silent, glaring.

"I am simply advising you that someday you will need to think of this, even when you are enraged. Even at those times, we will still need you."

So, it was for Saigwan. A chief cannot just do what he wants. He must care for his people.

Well, I am not chief. But... "Náy, U'taktay. I understand your meaning."

"May the Spirits protect us from any such need in the future," said the elder, giving Asku a light slap on the back. "And in the meantime, good hunting."

Liwanu and his men showed up, received blessings and well-wishes, and headed out to track. Keme, Hawilish and the Elk Plains contingent arrived just after, were blessed, and began to move out.

"My advice is that we walk just past the perimeter from Ꝁ'mił Toward the Setting Sun," said Keme. "We may find a dying enemy that will tell us where they were. Failing that, we may find other sign, such as something dropped in the dark, or Matchitehew's own tracks."

"How will we know those?" U'hitaykah asked.

Keme smiled, studying the ground. "He has a cane with a big ball on the end. He sometimes uses it as a walking stick, always in his right hand. So, if you see a man's prints with a sort of round mark to their right, they are his. He would not use it while running, though."

"I remember seeing that at the Sea," Asku mumbled.

In the end, it was easier. In a small depression past the enemy skirmish line, they found an attacker who had crawled away with an arrow deep in his midsection. He was still alive. Keme mouthed to Asku, *Let me.* Asku nodded.

Keme knelt over the man, who could barely speak. There was a conversational exchange. Asku heard the word 'Matunaaga.' Then Keme cut his throat, and the man died almost immediately.

"Well?" Asku inquired.

Keme smirked. "A simple bargain. I knew him to be Pyúsh and asked if he knew he was dying. He did. I asked him where Matchitehew had been, and where he might flee. If he told me all, I promised to end his suffering immediately, and if not, I told him I would blind him and leave him to die. He made the wiser choice."

"Very good," said Aanapay. "So where do we go?"

Keme explained that Matchitehew had been just beyond this position and would probably not try to get to his canoes, expecting an ambush. Instead, he would head overland toward Iksíks Wána, which emptied into Nch'i-Wána not far from where Pikú-nen did the same. "He said one more thing," added Keme. "He says Matunaaga has an evil spirit in him, and he hopes that we skin him alive. I think our enemy made promises to his men that he could not or did not keep."

"Does not surprise me," Mach'ni rumbled.

For Asku, the tracking was a distraction from the mass of feelings within him: rage, grief, guilt, worry. The dying Pyúsh seemed to have told the truth, as a trail led back to a small rise with many footprints and other signs of recent, hasty passing. Amid the residue, Hawilish came across something else. "Keme, are these the prints you described?"

Asku took a look, and Keme confirmed it. "Yes, those are his. See the walking stick. Prints leading away from here by multiple men will include his, though he will not be using the cane until their tracks say they are not running."

Once they identified those, tracking became easy. The trail crossed upper K'mił and a dry tributary streambed, headed mostly Toward the Rising Sun. Most of this land was dusty plateaus broken up by draws that would only bear water for short periods in heavy rains, all toward Nch'i-Wána. There looked to be seven men's tracks, and soon they found obvious signs of a hasty campsite hastily departed: bedroll marks, unburied bodily wastes, a few flint chips. One set of prints led away toward Nch'i-Wána upstream of K'mił, and the rest continued toward Iksís Wána. "I think there was a fight here, or a scuffle," said Mach'ni. He pointed to a confused mess of tracks, and a single darkened drop of blood.

"What do you make of it, Keme?" asked U'hitaykah.

"They are probably arguing. Maybe one of them thought they were going in a bad direction, and they told him to do as he wished. Someone got nicked or cut, maybe a bloody nose. In any case, the main group will still be with Matchitehew. We are on the right path."

Doing his best to think of tracking and pursuit, Asku tried to shut reality out with a curtain of focused rage. Even so, some leaked through. *My father may already be dead. The women will not have me to help them. What must Kaliskah think? Chaytan may be overwhelmed, even with my grandfather there. Who will walk the rounds and check on the wounded?*

U'taktay talked to me like a young fool...because I am one.

Then the sooner we skin Matchitehew alive, the sooner we get back.

The Patisapatisháma knew well the land between Nch'i-Wána and Iksíks Wána, for it was a good hunting ground. One part was a favorite nesting area for beautiful blue birds, whose discarded feathers traded well. It would not be strange to encounter other tribes here, but so far they had seen no sign. While everyone else tracked, Aanapay kept his eyes far ahead in hope of spotting their quarry. Now and then he traded roles with Mach'ni or U'hitaykah. At times, the fleeing Pyúsh P'ushtáayama's tracks showed that they were running.

Asku, late in the day, turned to Keme: "Do you think Matchitehew senses that we are after him?"

"I think he runs like a frightened rabbit who was chased out of a garden. I think he feels it. He will move as fast as he can, though his people may slow him down. They know that they can scatter any time, and that we will hunt him above all, so maybe they do not care so much."

"It is only what he deserves," said Hawilish.

"And will get," Mach'ni said, patting his knife.

"Even so," said Keme, "We are nearly out of daylight by which to track. Soon we must camp. My guess is that we will catch him sometime tomorrow."

>——>

Asku slept no better that night than the one before. With a good early start, though, the trackers made their way to Iksíks Wána by midday. The tracks led along the riverside, which sometimes was a low floodplain, other times framed by tight cliffs. "Matchitehew is stupid," U'hitaykah remarked. "Or lazy. If he had waded along these shallows for about as long as it would take to walk across a village, he would have wet feet, but we would be completely lost. The trail would end, and we would have to swim across the river, where we would find no trail there."

"That is true," said Aanapay. "Then we would wonder if we had missed something, or where he had got out of the river, or if he had somehow gotten a canoe. In the meantime, he would still be walking along the river, far ahead, laughing at us."

"If he were not stupid, he would not lead with fear," said Keme. "Leaders like the River Chief and the Elk Plains Chief do not want or need fear, and neither do decent Pyúsh. I have seen it. Your chiefs are followed for their wisdom and because they sacrifice for their people."

Except when they get very angry, thought Asku. He forced reason aside once again, reminded himself that they might soon confront Matchitehew, and thought of what he would do to the Pyúsh P'ushtáayama chief.

Late in the day, as they moved along the river, U'hitaykah signaled a halt and called them together. "Very near up ahead, Iksíks Wána bends sharply to our left. There is an excellent camping spot at the bend on both sides, which I believe the Patisapatisháma know well." Hawilish and Asku nodded. "There is always driftwood there to build a fire, trees that fell into the river farther upstream and get lodged at the bend, so it is very convenient. We should approach it cautiously, because by now they might consider themselves safe and expect to get a good rest."

Soon the group made their way to a slope-sheltered riverside meadow dotted with scrub oak, cottonwood, and cedar trees. Staying in cover, the tracking party worked its way forward. Hawilish signaled a halt, put a hand to his ear.

Asku heard the noises of camp being set up just ahead. Adrenaline pulsed painfully through his veins.

The hunters crouched in a small gully mostly obscured by brush and trees. Asku counted six Pyúsh, no Sxíxtama. One sat on an old log along the river, looking bored, glancing about in their direction and across the water. The rest were building a fire and setting up camp. At the sight and sound of Matchitehew, giving orders and looking nervously about, Asku felt rage begin to blind him to all but the desire for blood. Hawilish laid one hand on his back, rather firmly. Mach'ni motioned that they should withdraw a bit for ease of planning.

"This is the side from which they expect trouble," Mach'ni whispered, one gully back. "If we all attack from here, some may get away."

"In that case," said U'hitaykah, "it would be good for some of us to circle around. They attacked us in dusk. We can do the same. They cannot escape up the hill, which will hide movement for those of us that circle around to the far side. Any that survive will have to surrender or leap into the river and take their chances, and we can probably hit them with arrows. Asku, what do you think?"

"I think I want to cut Matchitehew into small pieces," snarled Asku.

Mach'ni and U'hitaykah traded glances. "You will get your chance," said U'hitaykah. "For now, our work is to give it to you. Aanapay, Keme, Hawilish, when it is safe, you move back up to where we were or closer. The rest of us will work our way around them and get as close as we can. By that time, they may be attentive. Mach'ni is our best at sneak attacks, so he will attack first. Asku and I will follow immediately, making a lot of noise. Aanapay, that will be your signal to attack. The distraction should let you get very close. Hawilish, I am told you are a very good shot. Is it true?"

Hawilish nodded. "Not our best, but I do well."

"Good," said U'hitaykah. "When your group attacks, you stay back and take safe bow shots that will not hit any of us, but always be ready to shoot anyone who jumps into the river."

"I will."

"Good. Any questions?"

U'hitaykah's party moved out. First they backtracked to a place where they could climb the steep slope onto the plateau that overlooked the Pyúsh encampment. "They ought to have camped up here," commented Mach'ni. "They could have seen us a long way off."

"Glad they didn't," said U'hitaykah. "I wonder where the other Pyúsh P'ushtáayama warriors are. We will have to go out to their village to be sure. I fear something has happened."

As the Setting Sun touched the horizon, they worked their way down one of the steep gullies and toward the enemy camp. A dry canyon provided them complete cover until they crouched within medium bow shot of the campfire. The smell of cooked fish was a reminder that they had not had fresh food since their departure. There was still a lookout, eating his fish and watching toward Aanapay's position. Asku could hear Matchitehew arguing with two of the men, who seemed to question his leadership. *They are even less attentive*, he thought. *Well, soon enough we will give them a good reason to pay attention.* He banished all other thoughts.

The actual fight, as a later observer would say of a very different conflict, did not last long enough to light a pipe.

Asku and U'hitaykah lay concealed behind Mach'ni and to his right. Lining himself up with a small tree near where Matchitehew and four of his warriors sat around the fire eating trout, he leaped forward with his enormous club. The man sitting before him, facing away, did not have a chance. The crunch of the man's skull shattering under Mach'ni's mighty blow was a signal impossible to ignore.

U'hitaykah leaped to his feet and charged with a war-cry. That would have been inadequate to describe what came from Asku. Every emotion of his last few days, all that he had held back, now exploded from his soul in a cry one might have expected from a cougar. Even Mach'ni seemed to notice. Paying no attention that direction, with Matchitehew and the lookout in front of him, Asku did not see Mach'ni's mirthless smile.

The lookout faced about to see U'hitaykah, while Matchitehew picked up a long spear. A man to Mach'ni's front and left turned and tried to stand, but his shoulder turned directly into the swing of Mach'ni's club. Something cracked, and the man stumbled, trying to draw a dagger with his remaining good arm.

The firelight enabled Asku to see Aanapay and Keme sprinting in from the far side. The racket of combat drowned out the sound of Hawilish's shot, but not its impact. Asku saw an arrow sink deep into the lookout's torso. *I should not have looked* flashed through Asku's brain as Matchitehew seized the moment to jab at Asku with the spear.

Only a sudden reflexive shift made the spear-thrust miss, mostly, the flint blade raising a shallow cut on Asku's side. If he felt the pain, it was to embrace it. As Matchitehew drew back the spear again, U'hitaykah flung a big handful of dirt into his eyes, nose, and mouth. The Pyúsh chief bellowed with rage.

Across the fire, the last two unhurt men drew knives to face Mach'ni, who took that moment to bash in the ribcage of the man he had just wounded. Mach'ni saw Keme and Aanapay rushing forward but gave no sign. As the one on Mach'ni's left started to sidestep in an effort to flank him, Aanapay stabbed a long dagger deep into his neck. The man fell limp. To Aanapay's left, Keme disposed of the other easily.

Matchitehew was trying to get his vision back while jabbing and slashing with his spear. *Take him alive*, said something inside Asku. Dodging the blind thrusts, Asku slipped inside the weapon's reach. Before, his pain and grief and rage had gone into sound. Now it all flowed through his knife arm. He slashed up, once, at Matchitehew's fingers on the spear, and the spear fell. As it did, Asku stabbed into the side of Matchitehew's knee and twisted. The Pyúsh cut loose with a scream of agony that would have affected all but the coldest heart.

As it was, he had done enough to chill any heart, and no one cared. U'hitaykah lunged and finished the former lookout. Asku grabbed the spear and threw it behind him, then yanked away the dagger Matchitehew was trying to draw.

With five dead or mortally wounded, Matchitehew lay still, trying to glare defiant rage through eyes still trying to blink the dust and sand out. U'hitaykah looked at Asku. "It is up to you, *píti*. He has done your people the most harm. Because of him, your *pásiks* was tortured, your people killed, your father wounded. Now you choose what is done with him."

It is still not over with in my heart, thought Asku. *But there are others to consider. I must remember others.* "Mach'ni, *káka*, for now, tie him up. I think he is likely to become difficult." U'hitaykah and Mach'ni began to truss up Matchitehew with leather thonging scavenged from the dead. When they had him bound hand and foot, Mach'ni and Aanapay hoisted the captive into a painful kneeling position.

Asku looked down at his enemy. The firelit dusk was enough for him to see the long white fingernail marks on either side of his face, and Asku's stomach tightened in anger once more.

"Where are the others?" he hissed in Chinuk Wawa. "Where did you send them?"

Matchitehew's top lip curled back as he spat at Asku's feet. Asku nodded to Mach'ni, who brought his hand across Matchitehew's mouth. The sound echoed off the trees. Blood ran from the bound man's nose and mouth.

U'hitaykah squatted just to Asku's right and spoke in the Pyúsh P'ushtáayama language. Matchitehew still did not respond. His eyes remained locked on Asku.

Asku nodded again to Mach'ni, who yanked the man's head back by his long plait and held it there. Matchitehew gasped for breath, his airway distorted. Mach'ni drew his long hunting knife slowly across the man's cheek.

U'hitaykah repeated the question, louder, but still no response. U'hitaykah nodded at Mach'ni, not waiting for Asku. "Sometimes I myself do not feel much like conversation," sneered Mach'ni. "Maybe this will help you find your voice." Mach'ni grabbed the long bone piece that hung from one ear and tore it clear by the tassel. Matchitehew cried out momentarily, then began yelling incomprehensible things, spitting as he spoke.

"You see how that motivates you to speak up?" Mach'ni jibed. "You are finding your voice." He yanked the tassel from Matchitehew's other ear. The man did not cry out this time, but sagged limp in the grasp of Mach'ni and Aanapay.

"Did you kill the Sea Chief?" Asku demanded again, his head spinning in anger. "Did you wound the River Chief?" U'hitaykah repeated it in Pyúsh, enunciating with care. The Pyúsh chief glared at U'hitaykah and then back at Asku, shaking his head.

"*Ty-ee',*" he smiled, with blood in his teeth. "*Mem'-a-loost.*"

Asku's throat constricted at the words, but Mach'ni kicked Matchitehew in the wounded knee. The bound man screamed in anguish—a sound that would remain forever in Asku's mind, a sound that he would hear in the middle of the night like a haunting ghost.

Aanapay let go of him and the man fell forward again. Mach'ni stepped a big, sure foot into the middle of his back, forcing him all the way to the ground. The big man turned to Asku and held out Asku's own obsidian knife, the notched antler handle first. Asku had not realized he had dropped it.

The handle felt heavy and burning hot in his hand. His heart raced. Visions passed before his eyes. He saw...

Saigwan's sacrifices and trials...

His father, a young boy, killing the first evil Pyúsh P'ushtáayama chief...

His father again, now gravely wounded...

His people, hidden in the longhouse, and what this man intended for them...

The Great Sea Chief and his jovial son, both good men who had embraced him, one dead, one seriously wounded...

The bravery of the Patisapatisháma, who had risked and in some cases given lives for their tribe...

His sister, outmatched, valiant, defiant...

Kaliskah, just as brave...

Kitchi, tormented then crippled...

This is for them all. But others also have cause for anger.

"Keme. Hawɨlish. This man has done harm to people you care for and cared for. What do you say we should do?"

Keme's dark eyes looked dangerous. "He should die slowly, the way he caused others to suffer. I would be glad to see him rolled into the fire."

"I admit part of me hates it, *pásiks*," said Hawɨlish. "But if Matchitehew cannot deserve such a death, no one can. He gave others worse. For Kitchi, Keme's family and my *Wyánch'i*, there must be great punishment. No one would have bothered him had he just stayed home. He brought this on himself."

At the mention of his father, Asku felt a deep twinge. *I have the terrible feeling he will not live when I return.*

And neither will the man responsible for it all.

Asku motioned Mach'ni and Aanapay to put the prisoner's face in the dirt. Then he knelt on Matchitehew's back and yanked his head back by the long plait. Matchitehew cried out in fear and expected pain. As Asku held the braid back, he drew the long knife across the Pyúsh chief's scalp.

The man writhed and screamed into the earth, but the land was as deaf to his pain as were his captors. They lifted his limp form to its knees once again. Keme stood an arm's length away.

Matchitehew's face was wet with blood and covered in dirt. He appeared semi-conscious. "Keme. Do you have any advice for this worthless excuse for a chief?"

Keme leaned over and hissed something into Matchitehew's ear. The captive's eyes focused with sudden realization. "I think that may help him understand," said Keme, a terrible look in his eyes.

Is that how I now look? Great Spirits.

This must end.

Asku took Matchitehew by one armpit. "Keme?"

Keme nodded. Matchitehew struggled, a bit, against the thongs that immobilized him. Aanapay prodded the fire a little, baring the pile of red coals in the center. With a strong heave, Asku and Keme lifted up Matchitehew so that he faced the fire.

Visions flashed before Asku's eyes again—Saigwan, his grandfather, his father, Chaytan, Kaliskah, his mother.

Asku and Keme half dragged, half tossed Matchitehew face first into his own campfire.

The screams did not last very long. The smell of burning flesh filled the air, and Asku inhaled it in fury. Matchitehew continued moving until his screams became soft moans of great pain. As they wound down, Asku felt U'hitaykah's hand on his shoulder. "When he stops moving or making sounds, *píti*, for the good of your spirit, you must leave this behind and let it be done. Carry it along, and it will poison your heart."

"But we are not done."

"The work may not be. The revenge is. How do you think the Matunaagas of the land come to be?"

Matchitehew's final moans and movements stopped.

Asku looked at the plait in his hands. He looked around the fire, at U'hitaykah. He looked up into the night sky, then closed his eyes.

When he opened them again, he threw the plait into the fire.

Chapter 35

Asku sat down next to U'hitaykah and watched the fire for a long time. Nobody wanted anything belonging to Matchitehew's men, not even Keme. The others dragged both bodies and possessions, including that walking stick, onto the fire, building it up to a great blaze. It was now obsidian-dark, with only the faintest remnant of daylight purpling the far horizon.

"We need to finish this," said Asku.

"We need to get you home," U'hitaykah replied.

"*Káka,* we need to go to the village. *I* need to go to the village."

"Your people need you, Askuwa'tu."

"Please, I need to see this through."

"*Píti*, no. Hear me out."

The rest imperceptibly gave them space.

"We do not know your father's condition," U'hitaykah began. "I fear the worst. I know you do too. Your people will now look to you for stability and leadership, and they deserve it of you. Every day you are absent will harm your people. You must return to them."

Asku tossed a twig into the blaze. "Without being able to tell them it is done?"

"The force behind it is done. As *Wyánch'i* someday, you must learn how to trust others to carry out your wishes, as your father trusted you to scout. He did not go himself. He sent trusted people. Mach'ni, Aanapay and I are going that direction anyway, to check in on our village. We will detour toward his camp, see what state it is in, and if it is safe, go and bring our people home. That is our own duty. Our own *wyánch'i* trusts us to do it. He stayed behind, in part to help fill the empty space of guidance *you* left behind. We trust him to your people. You can trust this to us."

Asku felt the weight of his life fall onto his back. All of a sudden, he was just Askuwa'tu—just a boy facing worry, fear and pain.

"If my father is gone, I am by no means ready to be Chief of the Patisapatisháma."

"Neither was he when his time came," said U'hitaykah, gently. "I believe that when you are as old as your grandfather, you will tell your grandson that no one ever is."

They sat in silence for some time.

Asku decided.

"Keme is the best one to assess what happened with the Pyúsh P'ushtáayama. He should go with you. I would consider it a help, *káka*, if Aanapay could come back with Hawilish and I. There may yet be small groups of Sxíxtama about the prairies, and I would value his counsel back home."

U'hitaykah met his nephew's eyes, nodded. "If you get moving now, with no need to track, you can be home late tomorrow."

"*Íi. Kw'ałá, káka.*"

▸——→

The return trip was quick and uneventful. Late the next afternoon, Hawilish sighted the Watch Tree in the distance. There was movement in it, and a young man leaped out of the lowest branch and headed for them at a run. Banishing fatigue, Asku took off to meet him. It was Haysutu.

As soon as Asku saw the youth's expression, he knew.

"*Wyánch'i*, it is very sad. *Áw icháawi.* He is with the Spirits now."

Aanapay put a hand on his back. "I am very sorry, *píti*," he whispered.

Asku felt anger wash over him. A part of him had not allowed himself to believe what he knew to be quite likely. His mind was unable to sort out any feelings but numbness and grief. Thoughts pierced the mental fog in disconnected bursts:

I want to run. To turn, to run, and never look back again.

Right now, I would trade places with Kitchi, including a lame knee.

Someone like U'taktay is much more able to do this.

Everyone will want to say things, and I do not want to see anyone.

They will judge me for running off.
I was not with my father during his last moments.
The world has no fairness.
I am going to take my time walking the rest of the way.

A figure approached from the distance, walking well but with a cane. In due time, they met. Kitchi looked somber and angry. "Did you get him?"

"We did," Asku answered. "He paid."

Kitchi's eyes flashed fierce satisfaction. "He could never pay enough, but he is not going to bother anyone else again. That's as best you could do."

Asku gave him an unreadable look. "Yes and no. But it is what happened, and if nothing else, Haysutu can run to tell the people that Matchitehew and those nearest him are definitely dead."

Haysutu took off like a rabbit. "How is the village?" Asku forced out.

"Like you would expect," said Kitchi.

"Sunu?"

"The Grandfather says he is fragile but improving and should pull through."

"Good. How are Sus and the little sisters? For that matter, how are Nayhali and Kaliskah, and my mother?"

Kitchi cleared his throat. "She spends most of her time by the ceremonial firepit. It is not a good situation. They need you, *pásiks*." His voice had a new tone: wise tact, without sarcasm, and his simple words burned off the fog, echoed across the void in Asku's heart. *I think I just heard what Kitchi will sound like one day as an elder. He is right. They need me. I am full of my own pain. I am not the only one in pain. I cannot be selfish. If I am, here and now, then I should not be chief of anything.*

As they neared the village, Kalataka came out to meet his grandson. The Teacher was not far behind. Asku raised a hand. "Blessings, *tíla*."

His grandfather drew him into an embrace. "Thank the Great Spirits you are safe, *tíla*."

"U'hitaykah, Mach'ni and Keme are unhurt. They went to check on the Elk Plains village and what was once Matchitehew's village. They will return and let us know what they find." He looked deep into his grandfather's eyes, then the Teacher's. "It is finished."

Both nodded. The Teacher raised his hands in blessing upon each of the men returned, spoke the ritual words of thanks. The only words that jolted him were "...Askuwa'tu Haylaku, our young *wyánch'i.*"

They need me. But am I strong enough?

I will have to be.

As Asku neared the Totem, he saw what he expected to see: a bier near the Totem, roughly the height of a tall man, with seven hide-and-mat-wrapped forms lain on top. Flowers, baskets, tools, and weapons lined the sides and top of the bier: gifts for the Spirit Journeys of the fallen.

"The *Nch'inch'ima* felt it best none of them make the journey alone, *Wyánch'i,* and the families agreed," said the Teacher, very gently. "So, we gathered them all together, and we waited for you."

"It was right, *Sapsikw'alá.* Others lost fathers, brothers, sons. There is enough grief for everyone," said Asku, finishing bitterly. His family was at the bier's edge: Chitsa was weaving, Nayhali was wiping dirt off Susannawa's face, and Kaliskah leaned against the Story House with an armload of Mini and Nis'hani, who clutched her new bear.

You are right, Kitchi. They need me.

Asku turned toward the Totem and took a deep breath. Tears burned their way down his cheeks and nose. *Great Spirits give me strength. Let me be strong enough for them. Let me not run from my pain and my responsibility. Saigwan, hear me.*

Father, hear me. I need you.

He willed his feet to move forward, one quiet step at a time. As his family finally looked up, Asku knelt next to Chitsa and reached to embrace her. She set her weaving aside, and for the first time in his life, his mother felt not like a power figure, but a woman seeking solace in the elder male strength of her family.

"I am very sorry, *ila,*" he whispered.

"Is it over, *isha?*" she asked, dully.

"Yes, I killed him." Asku stifled back a kaleidoscope of emotions. "Your brother and Keme and Mach'ni are investigating their village and will probably burn it. It is done."

She nodded once, let go of him, and returned to her weaving.

Asku greeted the rest his surviving family, each in turn from youngest to oldest, collecting tears and child snot with each embrace. Nayhali was even more listless and unresponsive than his mother. "*Nána, where is Chaytan?*" She shook her head and refused to answer.

Then he went to Kaliskah. Silent tears ran down her cheeks. Neither said anything, but she reached her hand up to his face and brushed his cheek.

And now, for me.

Asku went to the bier and laid a hand on his father's wrapped head, easily distinguished by symbols on the wrapping that described his life. He would not cry again.

"*Kw'alá, túta...Wyánch'i*. Thank you for sacrificing yourself—for me, and for our people. Thank you for giving all."

)⟶

After that, Asku lost track of time for a while. He would later recall that he spent most of the day just sitting with his family until his legs were asleep and his back ached. He began to regain awareness of the world when he realized the sun was falling in the sky. Nisy and Mini were asleep in his arms, and Susannawa still sniffed quietly. Kalataka sat next to Chitsa. Hawilish and Kitchi sat on the ground near the Totem, where the Teacher leaned on his teaching stick.

As his head began to clear, Asku knew what he needed to do.

With Kaliskah's help, he tucked the little ones into his bed, all together. They fell asleep rather easily, a tiny clutch of future and hope. Then he took Kaliskah by the hand and led her to his family's firepit. It was out, and he began to rekindle it. *I have never seen this fire out cold, and I never want to see it that way again. And there is no water. How long has it been since any of them have eaten?*

He took a deep breath and turned his attention to Kaliskah. Her face was in her hands. Asku sat down next to her but did not touch her.

"Kaliskah." She did not look up. "Kaliskah, I mourn him with you."

She took a deep breath and wiped her eyes. At last, she looked up, fixed him for a moment with a penetrating stare that reminded him of their first meeting, then dropped her gaze to the ground again. "My heart is broken for my people, Asku," she whispered. "And for yours.

"When I saw them coming for your father..." Her voice trailed off. "*Ul-há-i-pa,*" she spat at the ground in disgust. "Demon Men." Kaliskah spoke in a combination of the Wawa and of the Wanuukshiláma, with now and then a word of Chiskin. He could make out enough to understand. "They took us by surprise."

Asku waited, and she went on. "He was shot through the chest. It happened so quickly. We saw it. When the warrior moved forward to take scalp, that was enough for us. Your mother killed that man before Nayhali, or I were even out the door. She shot him through the window. I killed another coming toward the Story House after your mother. Then you showed up, and you saw the rest."

I did. They were brave. I was not as much use.

Kaliskah's voice dropped. "Asku, I am very sorry that we did not save your father. We were not ready. I should have been ready."

He met her eyes. "Kaliskah, they were determined to kill him, and it was night. You fought bravely for my family. I am as sorry at your loss as you are at mine, and it is not our fault. It is Matchitehew's, and he has paid all he could afford. Now we have more to do. I am proud of you, and I need you." He took her hands and held them.

"Asku, what are we going to do? *Ti-tum-má-ma, mi-sái-ka klim-sá-ma-ma...*my father, your father...?"

Asku stifled a sudden urge to punch something. He wrestled and pinned it until it passed. In her eyes, he saw them all: Apenimon, Pajackok, and Sunukkuhkau. Then he saw in them his father and his own family, including Kaliskah.

The fire was now a warming blaze. He put an arm around her. "Kaliskah, I cannot do this without you. I need you." He waved a hand toward the tent, toward the little ones sleeping. "Will you stay with them for me? I have something I must do."

She nodded. He put his arms around her again, drew her close and buried his face in her unkempt hair. He wished for what had been meant for them, that this had all been a very bad dream, and that he would wake up to find himself still at the sea, with her tucked in the crook of his shoulder at the spot high above the crashing waves, his spirit leaping with young love.

But when he lifted his head, they were still at his family firepit. His nightmare was real. He stood to go. "I will send someone for water and salmon. Can you feed them when they wake?"

Kaliskah reached into a pocket in her long skirt and pulled out a piece of white cord. She tied her hair back and nodded as he turned to go.

>——→

The Teacher sat in silence by the bier, eyes closed. Asku approached and sat next to him, with Hawɨlish and Kitchi close behind.

"What happens now, *Sapsikw'atá*?"

"We must honor them, but first you must be named chief."

"Then let us prepare for that."

"We will. But you also must prepare. This is a good time for you to consider how you feel about everything in life that makes you uncomfortable."

"Why is that?"

"Because the *Nch'inch'ima* surely have."

I have a feeling I am not going to like this at all. Asku nodded. "Where is Chaytan?" No one spoke for a moment. Asku turned to Kitchi, then to Hawɨlish, but no one answered him. "Well, where is he?"

The Teacher laid a hand on Asku's shoulder. "You know the place." The elder got up and walked away.

>——→

Asku found him out on the rocks down near K̲'mɨł, his usual place. Chaytan did not look up. He was dirty, still wearing the same clothes Asku recognized from the Pyúsh battle and looked as if he had neither eaten nor slept.

"Hey, man," Asku sat down on a rock.

Chaytan did not respond.

"Have you been out here the whole time we were gone?"

Chaytan nodded slightly. The wind whipped his long hair around him.

"I know what you are thinking, but it is not your fault. There is nothing you could have done."

Chaytan shook his head and grimaced. "None of that matters now. He is gone. He's gone."

Asku fought back the pain and numbness. "Yes, the Chief is gone."

"There is nothing for me here now. He was the last of my brothers and my best friend. It is over."

"That is not so, Chaytan. I am here. Nayhali is. We need you. Even if only for me, and for my father's sake, please be for me what you were for my father."

Chaytan shook his head again but smiled a little. "That job is already taken."

I want to argue...but I can't. Chaytan cannot replace Hawɨlish and Kitchi, and he knows it. "Where will you go?"

"*Kúu mish.*" Chaytan looked at Asku. "But I cannot stay here."

I understand. It will be like another death of someone we need, whom I have always known, but I do understand. "Send word back, *náy*?"

Chaytan nodded, but his eyes did not. "Tell Nayhali..." His voice caught in his throat, and he could not finish the sentence.

"I will, my brother."

>——→

That evening, Asku passed the *chalámat* with the *Nch'inch'ima* for a long time. They asked him first to describe the story of the entire Pyúsh campaign in his own words, including the end of Matchitehew. Then they requested he tell them the entire content of his Saigwan visions. The elders then began to question him.

"How do you know that you are strong enough to care for this tribe?"

"Why did you go yourself after Matunaaga, rather than stay and help your people?"

"At heart, does a part of you just want to turn and run from all this?"

"Tell me. In your view, how many hours of a woman's life does it take to bring her mate a single *wawachí*-flour cake?"

"In your observations, how could we best improve the site of our village?"

"Did your father ever make a mistake in your opinion? How should he have handled it?"

"If you make a decision, and half the people dissent from it and do not want to follow your direction, how would you handle that?"

"Do you understand why your grandmother mistreated you? What do you think of her attitude now?"

"You will never have a *Małáwitash*, much less waddle around with a baby inside you. What makes you feel that you understand the burdens borne by a woman of this tribe?"

"We have just suffered seven deaths and several more wounds. That is a disaster. How would you lead us toward a safer future in spite of this serious loss of strength?"

"The next time you decide to put your own anger and desire for revenge above the welfare of your people, how do you wish us to react?"

"If we decide you are not suitable to be *Wyánch'i*, what will you do then?"

"Will you see this people to success or to shame?"

By the time it was over, Asku had half a mind to ask them to pick someone else. He was not sure they liked half his answers, and he was sure he disliked at least that many. But in the end, he stood before them all with as much courage as he could muster. "I will do what is laid before me with all of my strength and with all of my heart, as did my father and my father's father. If you will let me."

In the end, the elders had agreed. Despite the fact that he came from a long line of beloved chiefs, Asku was still unsure that he was worthy. But when they excused him to prepare for the ceremony, he looked once at the Teacher. The old man's nod of encouragement gave him strength.

He turned and walked down the path. Behind him shuffled two sets of feet, one with a limp.

Late that night, the Teacher handed him the old *tamáawish*. The firelight glowed eerily on the long white and black feathers. The tassels, beads and bone knocked together softly, but the sound rang loudly in his ears.

How many great men have worn this? How many have given all?

He set it on his head. The soft leather strap around his forehead fit snugly, but it felt heavier on his head than it had in his hands. *And that probably is a lesson right there. It feels even heavier on my heart, come to think of it. My father was younger than I am now when this moment came for him.*

The Teacher beckoned him to take the traditional place of the *Wyánch'i*. The people were quiet, even the little ones around the outside of the ceremonial fire, waiting for him.

Kitchi's words rang in his ears, along with the soft clacks of the tassels. *They need you, man.*

Asku was thankful for the hand the Teacher extended. When he stood, the weight of the ancient *tamáawish* felt like it might tip him over. The strength of that hand steadied him.

He stepped forward, one careful foot in front of the other.

Raising his hands into the night sky, he chanted, "*Watwáa naknúwim*," over and over, gaining strength from the words.

A drum beat softly from somewhere behind him. The people chanted the ancient words, softly, very softly.

"*Watwáa naknúwim…*"

He pulled the long *chúksh* blade from his belt. The smoke in the fire rose in time to the drum and to the words coming softly from all around him. The eagle feathers seemed to move in rhythm. He could feel the hum of the words in the pressure of the band around his forehead. *I feel like the ancestors are chanting as well. I feel Saigwan.*

Asku raised the blade high above his head. The black rock sparkled in the glow of the orange firelight as he chanted louder. "*Watwáa naknúwim…*"

The people echoed his words as he drew the knife across the palm of his hand, stoic against the sting. Blood welled up and dripped from the cut. Asku balled his fist, holding it over the fire. Blood dripped into the flames below. The fire hissed its welcome.

The people fell silent again.

"My blood will protect this people. My blood will lead this people. My blood will spill for this people: the blood of my father, the blood of my grandfather, the blood of the great chief, Saigwan…my blood for this people."

All around the fire the people chanted again, "*Watwáa naknúwim…*"

They sat at the fire all night. As the sun rose, light just beginning to touch the village, the people walked toward the bluff in kinship groups. Those who were bereaved carried their fallen. Four strong elders carried Napayshni toward his final rest, eyes stolid. Others brought flowers, food and gifts for the spirits of the fallen, whether friends or family, for the long journey that lay ahead.

At the top of the bluff facing Toward the Rising Sun were seven deep holes, the bottoms lined with grasses and thick *tk'ú* mats. Each grave sloped gradually on one short side, to facilitate entry. One by one, with the people chanting the funerary chant, those bearing the bodies laid them carefully into the holes. Those bringing gifts and supplies for the next life laid them within the graves.

Asku watched the ceremony and let the memories fill his heart and his mind. He saw visions of his father: walking the trail each morning, caring for them all. Asku saw Napayshni's strong arms lifting Chitsa off her feet. He saw Susannawa fly out of a tree, landing on his father's shoulders. He saw the pain in his eyes as he told Asku of what must be with Kaliskah.

Most of all, he saw time. His father had given him the best gift a father could give a son: time. Despite his burdens, he had always given Asku time. *And I will cherish it all. When Kaliskah has my children, I will always have time to give them.*

Asku stepped down into his father's grave. "*Kw'ałá, túta,*" he whispered, letting the hand he had sliced open linger on the covered body. "My *Wyánch'i.*"

Chitsa stepped down into the grave, weeping quietly. As Asku took her by the shoulders, he noticed a small rattlesnake satchel tucked carefully and lovingly under the Chief's right arm. He turned quickly to see the backside of the small boy with his hand nestled in that of the Wawyukyáma chief.

The Teacher picked up a handful of dust, chanted words that Asku could not understand, and threw the dust on top of the first body. He did the same for the other six. The people stood in silence at the bluff as men shoveled dirt into the graves and lined the tops with rocks. Women, elders and children laid flowers among the rocks. The people would gather there at sunset, for a moon's time, to say a blessing again in honor of their fallen.

The wind picked up, and Nch'i-Wána flowed, as if reminding Asku that it always had.

Chapter 36

Two days later, Liwanu's hunting party returned to the River village. They had brought company, though the company had not wanted to come.

"How was your search?" Asku began. "I see you took one alive."

"Yes, *Wyánch'i*. He does not speak Chiskin or Wawa. We felt that he might be able to give useful information, and we had no one who understood any of his language."

"That was wise, Liwanu, well done." Asku filled Liwanu and his men in on the events that they had missed. Eyes fell at the recitation of casualties. "So, what else happened?"

"He was with three others. We killed them in an ambush. Hoping to find more, we took a different way back, but saw no others. I think the rest fled far away."

"They had better stay far away. They have caused too much trouble." He turned to Aanapay. "Is he Pyúsh P'ushtáayama?"

"No," said Aanapay, "he is Sxíxtama, and a young and rather unseasoned one to go by his decorations." He was also bound and hobbled; Liwanu's men had taken no chances.

"*Kúu mísh.* Please translate for me." Through Aanapay, Asku began the questioning by holding a *chúksh* blade to the man's throat while Liwanu pulled the long plait back. "Of what people are you?"

"Sxíxtama," the man answered, scanning the group.

"Did you participate in the attack on the Patisapatisháma?" Asku demanded, feeling the rage begin to rise inside. He breathed to calm it.

"Yes. Matunaaga promised us horses and goods, but he killed the Wanuukshiláma chief and wounded his son. We did not like this. The Sxíxtama do not want trouble with the Wanuukshiláma."

"Well, I would say you have it anyway."

"We followed Matunaaga across Nch'i-Wána. There were warriors all around the village. It was better defended than he said it would be. The Sxíxtama know the River People have no horses, but we went with him anyway. Matunaaga is evil, but we greatly fear the Pyúsh bands Beyond Nch'i-Wána. Matunaaga told us to create a diversion, to keep the Patisapatisháma warriors busy."

Asku's heart raced. *I do not want to hear this story.* "Keep telling," he ordered, feeling a great gaping hole growing in his heart.

"Matunaaga sent four or five of us into the center of the village, where he said the River Chief would be. I was not among them. He promised horses, women, and weapons to the man that killed the mighty Patisapatisháma Chief and brought back his scalp. He said whoever did it would have glory up and down Nch'i-Wána, could control the river trade and receive all the power that the Great Chief had." The Sxíxtama seemed more and more agitated. "We did not want this. The Great Spirits will be angry with us."

"They are not the only ones angry," snarled Asku. His knuckles grew white on the knife handle. "This is your fault," he hissed. Blood began to well where the knife pierced the man's painted, dark skin.

"No, it is not!"

"Asku," Aanapay said, "I believe he is telling the truth."

"Then who killed Apenimon, and my father? Answer quickly, Sxíxtama!"

"My brothers and I did not kill either chief. We wanted to leave as soon as it began, but could not, or Matunaaga and other Pyúsh might take it out on our people."

"You could have stopped this," Asku hissed. His muscles tensed to push the knife forward. The man struggled and protested.

"Askuwa'tu," said his grandfather in a command tone, "*awkłáw áw!*"

Asku turned, and just swallowed what he was about to blurt: *I am Chief here, not you. You do not give me orders here.* With a great effort, he mastered most of his rage and took a step back. *It is different now. Now, if I say what I am thinking in the moment, I will damage our people's relations. He is my grandfather, but he is an allied chief as well, and he will look out for his people first, as I must watch over mine. If he must ever choose between his own people and me, he must and will choose them, not me or us.*

My father would never have been idiot enough to put him in that position. I had better not be.

Asku looked at the Wawyukyáma chief, then back at the young Sxíxtama warrior.

I know what you are about to do, said his grandfather's eyes. *I cannot stop you, nor will I try. But I do not approve.*

The rage rose again. This time it nearly won. Asku looked around, daring the others to tell him to stop.

No one did, but he could see it in their eyes.

A voice whispered, very low and close. "You have every right," said U'taktay. "The question is whether our loss is best avenged by an execution in cold blood, or by using this man to help our people live better."

I wonder what my father would do.

He would hunt down Matchitehew, the source of the danger. I know this because he went out and did just like that.

U'taktay cannot, here and now, make a suggestion to me in the open. It would diminish my authority. He is showing me respect. But I can ask him.

"U'taktay. *Tíla.* Can either of you think of a way we can use this man to help keep all our tribes safer? I would ask Pajackok if he were here, or Sunukkuhkau but he is in no condition."

Asku felt a bit of the surrounding tension dissipate. "*Wyánch'i,*" U'taktay began, "the Wawyukyáma *Wyánch'i* would know better than I. The Elk Plains people live closer to both the Pyúsh P'ushtáayama and Sxíxtama than we do. Aanapay might have insight as well, as he knows more about them still." A warm glance of understanding passed, ever so briefly, between U'taktay and Kalataka.

"Well," began the Elk Plains chief, "if he is released alive, he can carry a message back to his people. If he makes it back. That is his problem, no one else's."

"Aanapay," said Asku, "if we were to release him, would that tell the Sxíxtama that we are weak and that we should be trifled with?"

Aanapay shook his head. "I do not think so. They are already very nervous, according to this prisoner. The Sxíxtama have taken heavy losses, and they know that siding with Matchitehew was foolish. I think they want to make peace with everyone they can. Sending this one back to tell his story will say to them: 'We are willing to have peace, but never come back and make war on us again.'"

A low murmur of approval rippled through those present. Even Liwanu nodded. *Well, that says all that needs saying.* "Kúu mísh, Sxíxtama. Do you have a name?"

"I am Yahto."

"Go back to your people, Yahto. Your people have wronged the Patisapatisháma, and for no reason other than fear and greed. You would have done better to make friends of the Wawyukyáma. They are our friends and are led by much wiser people than Matchitehew. Together you might have felt safer against the Pyúsh. You have also wronged the Wanuukshiłáma, offended the peace of Wayám and the spirits of the Patshatl, and created enmity and fear as far as waters run that join Nch'i-Wána. You killed the father of my mate-to-be, who never did you wrong, in addition to my own father. What have you to say for yourself, Yahto?"

At that point, it registered with the captive that he was going to live. "Patisapatisháma chief, thank you for my life. I swear that I will return home and tell my people what happened. I will encourage them to reach out to the Peoples of Nch'i-Wána for peace."

"Good enough. Liwanu, untie him, then give him enough of his weapons and gear to get started home. Yahto, if I were you I would keep clear of the Elk Plains. You may meet Wawyukyáma on the way. If you do, surrender and hope that they let you explain. Our anger, and that of our friends, is so great that we could easily band together for a punitive expedition, so your people could see what it feels like."

Yahto nodded. In no longer than it took to clean some salmon, he was gone.

>———

The next few days were mercifully uneventful. Asku walked his rounds, tried to do as his father had done, visited the homes of those who had lost, accepted condolences, and spent time with his family. It seemed to help Chitsa, who began by degrees to resume her normal activities, if not her former good cheer. Kalataka's presence seemed to lift her spirits a bit, especially his ability to distract and entertain the younger children.

Not long after, a lookout from the Watch Tree reported to Asku. "*Wyánch'i*, the Wawyukyáma who went to investigate the Pyúsh are returning. They have a man with them, and he is not a captive. They look unhurt."

Kalataka lifted Nis'hani off his knee, where he had been bouncing her, to her vocal delight. "Shall we go out to meet them?"

"Yes, let's do so," said Asku. "I am just glad they are home safe, and their news may help us put all this trouble further in the past. At least, I hope."

U'hitaykah, Mach'ni, and Keme looked tired, as did the fourth member of their party. By now Asku knew Pyúsh fashions better than he had ever wished, but anyone his uncle would bring freely to the River village could not be an enemy. U'hitaykah greeted them. "Blessings, *píti, túta.*"

The Elk Plains chief smiled but was silent; Asku recognized deference when he saw it. Being Chief would take getting used to. "Blessings and welcome back, *káka*, Mach'ni, Keme. It seems you have brought a visitor."

Keme spoke and gestured. "This is Mahkah, a Pyúsh P'ushtáayama we met at Matchitehew's former village. He is of the Mountain Pyúsh tribes, a chief's grandson, in fact." Keme then translated that into what was presumably Pyúsh.

The young leader was tall, with a long braid nearly to his waist. He wore a beaded hide headband that sat at the very top of his forehead with five tall owl feathers and porcupine quills sticking straight up out of the back of it, and the recognizable *k'iplach* at his belt. He stepped forward, standing to full height and examining Asku. "*Tu-cubin-noonie,*" he said.

"He greets you. In our language it means 'I am your friend,'" said Keme.

"Please make the polite answer."

"*Noonie-tu-cubin,*" said Keme.

Mahkah seemed to relax a bit. "*Iiooie,*" he said.

"He says he is well. It implies that he hopes you are too. If you say the same thing back, that is the standard answer."

Asku nodded. *"Iiooie*, Mahkah. Be welcome into our village." The men all followed him. As they walked, Asku told the returning scouts what had happened, including the death and funeral of Napayshni. Keme asked in a whisper if he should translate it all. "If I do, it will be the politest action, since it means we are not talking so he cannot understand us," said Keme, and Asku nodded assent.

"This is sad for our people as well," said U'hitaykah. "He was my sister's mate. When we gather our people once again at our village, we will remember our friend. I am so very sorry, *Wyánch'i*."

How strange it feels for my uncle to call me that, thought Asku. *But I think I understand. He is making the point of speaking to me with respect, here in my village. He is giving me support.* "*Kw'ałá*, U'hitaykah...*káka*. I hope I can be as much a friend to the Wawyukyáma as my father was."

"I am sure you will, *píti*." Later, when he recalled the exchange, Asku would realize why the subtle tension had dissipated during that walk. For the moment, he just felt everyone relax a bit more, and was glad to have one less thing on his mind.

The sight of U'hitaykah stirred Chitsa to begin food preparation, and Nayhali brought water, giving the women something to do. When everyone was seated around the ceremonial fire, and a few elders and other interested persons had shown up—whether to view the visitor or to hear the conversation—Asku began. "Keme, he does not speak much Wawa, right?" Keme nodded. "Then we will try to slow down enough so you can translate." Keme translated that to Mahkah, who nodded gratitude.

"Our village itself was not damaged," U'hitaykah began. "We made our way to Matchitehew's village. When we got there, it was completely still. No fire, no movement, no voices; nothing. There were many dead bodies, and it smelled horrible. Scavengers had been at some of them.

"Keme recognized some of the men, whom he said were good. One had been a friend to Keme's father. Keme believes that this man stood up to Matchitehew and was killed for it. It was a sad time for him.

"At that point, we met five Pyúsh warriors, who also came in the entrance. Keme recognized them as Pyúsh but not Matchitehew's men, and they greeted him as a friend. Mahkah is their leader. He told us that they had come to get Matunaaga. They were looking for his body. We told him what had happened to the man, and they seemed satisfied."

"May I explain?" asked Mahkah.

"Please do," replied Asku.

"As Keme explained, I am the grandson of the chief of the largest band of Pyúsh Beyond Wy-East. We are the Mountain Tribes.

"My grandfather sent me to bring back Matunaaga because the great chiefs of all Pyúsh tribes are angry with him. They fear he will disrupt the *Buha* of our people. That is our word for the natural balance of power. If we had found him, we meant to dishonor him, kill him, and absorb the remnants of his people into other Pyúsh bands. As it was, we burned Matunaaga's village. Keme, Mach'ni and U'hitaykah helped us. I sent the rest of my men home to give my people the news.

"I am very sorry for what has happened. When they learn, my people will be very angry and very sad at heart. It is humiliating to know what the evil Matunaaga has done to those who meant him no harm. I understand he was even disrespectful to his hosts at the Patshatl, which is unthinkable and not our way at all. That is one reason I came alone, to express my shame and regret in person to you face to face.

"In particular, I am very sorry for the murder of your father, the other men of your tribe, and the Sea Chief as well. Had we known what Matunaaga intended, and especially that he was using Sxíxtama to do it, we would have stopped him by force much sooner.

"If I may say so, you did wisely to release the Sxíxtama captive. Better to have him able to talk about the whole disaster than to have them out running around your country trying to find out. But we owe you a debt because we did not prevent this great evil from befalling our friends.

"If they do threaten you, we will make them regret it. Before, the worries that man described to you were mostly without much good reason, but their actions have made the worries real for their people."

Mahkah paused, then his manner became a bit more formal. "*Mamook kloshe tumtum, Ty-ee'?*" he asked, in broken Wawa.

Asku looked at Keme, then toward Hawilish and Kitchi, who had sat with him in silence, then to his grandfather and U'hitaykah. No one seemed to advise against it.

"*Mamook kloshe tumtum,*" Asku nodded. "Yes, we will have peace. I cannot speak for the new Sea Chief, but I think our decisions will influence his. He is the brother of the woman who will soon be my mate."

Mahkah nodded, then turned to Kalataka. "*Mamook kloshe tumtum, Ty-ee'*?"

The Wawyukyáma chief gazed at Mahkah for a moment. "*Mamook kloshe tumtum.* We will leave with good feelings for the Pyúsh bands Beyond Wy-East."

Mahkah nodded at Asku. The Teacher, listening quietly, pulled out the *chalámat* and filled the end from a smaller satchel with dried *yúxpass*. The men sat cross-legged on the ground for some time, passing the pipe, speaking of weather, terrain, trading, and anything else except for what had happened.

>——

Asku invited Mahkah to stay the night in the village. The next day, the Elk Plains chief announced that it was time for him to go. "While I would like to remain for your ceremony, the danger is over, and it is our duty to go bring our people back to begin winter preparations. Mahkah, will you come with us to our village on your return trip?"

"I will," he said. "If we understand each other better, there is less chance of trouble." The tall Pyúsh turned to Asku. "*Máh-sie,* Patisapatisháma *Ty-ee'*. I hope that my grandfather will encourage a trading party to go to Wayám, and that if they stop first to trade with the Patisapatisháma, they will be welcomed."

"Of course," Asku nodded. "*Tu-cubin-noonie.*"

Mahkah smiled. "*Noonie-tu-cubin,*" he said.

"*Iiooie,*" replied Asku, and received the same answer. "Keme, was that a correct way to say goodbye?"

"Not quite," answered Keme, "but he understands what you meant, and that is what matters. And I also thank you. You did not treat me as an enemy."

"You never behaved like one. You are welcome here any time."

His grandfather and U'hitaykah raised their hands in blessing one last time. Asku replied, then watched them begin their journey. Kitchi rested a hand on his shoulder. "We are with you, *pásiks*," he said.

"*Táaminwa*," said Hawilish, "always."

As he watched them depart, Asku remembered his grandfather's words from the night before. They had sat around the ceremonial fire well into the night.

"We are not far away, tíla," the old chief puffed on the short *chalámat* at *his lips.*

"Yes," Asku nodded, staring into the fire.

"You send for us," U'hitaykah's deep voice said, "and we will be here."

Asku looked up, at both of them.

"Askuwa'tu," the old chief closed his eyes and sighed, "You are strong enough. Míshnam pamshtk'úksha'?"

Asku nodded without looking up from the fire.

"You can and you will do this," the old man stated.

The words rang in his ears, but never penetrated his soul.

Asku turned to his two best friends. "Will you check on my family, please?"

They nodded and went in that direction. Asku continued alone, the long, slow walk that took him around the village. At every home someone would respectfully raise a hand, saying, "Blessing today, *Wyánch'i*."

And every time he heard those words, he wanted nothing more than to look over his shoulder and find that the words meant his father was behind him. And every time, the words twisted a knife in his heart.

>—→

Two days later, Pajackok arrived with his mother and a few others. As Huyana stepped from the canoe, she fell into Chitsa's arms and wept. Asku greeted Pajackok, who was his usual somber self, and reported that Sunu was improving by degrees. He touched on the high points of events, and Pajackok accepted that he would learn the details later. Then Asku's aunt looked at him, still holding Chitsa's hand. "Blessings today, *Wyánch'i*."

Asku embraced her. "Blessings. I am deeply sorry, *shísha*."

She stepped back, keeping a hand on his face. "You look so like him," she whispered. "*Kw'ałá*. Thank you for taking care of Sunukkuhkau and Kaliskah. Now, Apenimon's children are all I have left of him."

They went to see Sunukkuhkau first. He was able to sit up and move around a little now, although still with great pain, but very excited to see his family. Huyana and Chitsa soon found gladness—or distraction—in the mating ceremony preparations.

Asku passed the *chalámat* with the Wanuukshiłáma brothers later that night. Sunu sat propped up in Kitchi's chair, furs tucked around and behind him. When he coughed, his pain was obvious, but he tried to discourage them from waiting on him. "I am fine, *káhp-ho*…really," he said. "I feel better every day."

Pajackok sat on the tightly woven *tk'ú* mat, looking like a bow pulled tight. His eyes narrowed to thin slits as he stared into the fire, deep in thought, pain, or painful thought. Asku told them all of the Pyúsh battle, of the Sxíxtama, and of catching up to Matunaaga. He spoke of the Mountain Pyúsh grandson, Mahkah, and his promise of peace.

"I know Mahkah," Pajackok interjected. "My father and his grandfather were friends once. His father died in another battle long ago."

The young men sat in silence for some time.

"We will set my father's spirit free, on the *wé-ko-wa ok-ó-la*, the waves of the great sea, after your ceremony," Pajackok said quietly. "Will you come, *ow*?"

Asku breathed the *chalámat* for a moment as he looked at his future in-laws. "I would be honored. He was a great man, and I also need to say goodbye to him."

He suddenly felt less alone.

Chapter 37

The days that followed did not give Asku much reason to feel like an important chief. More than anything, they gave him reason to feel like an incapable child. All the women in his life were hard at work pouring their hearts into the preparations, and he did not even know what to do to help.

And I am mostly in the way, he thought, awakening before dawn one morning, and unable to return to sleep. He grabbed his wrap and went out to the Totem.

In his mind, he saw Saigwan and Niyol returning to the cave, and he saw the young and beautiful Ayashe. The vision swept him away…

Unable to sleep, Saigwan sat at the mouth of the cave keeping watch. He stoked the small fire, pulled the bison wrap tighter, and looked up into the cloudy midnight sky.

As Saigwan watched, a break appeared in the cloud cover. He saw stars, thousands of them, filling his heart with great joy and hope.

"Kw'alá, Great Spirits," he murmured into the night. "Be pleased in this people. Be pleased in me."

As the Spirits continued to shine down upon him, he thought of Moema and her sacrifice. He thought about his children, especially Manneha, who would be chief of this tribe one day in his turn. He thought about all the mistakes he had made in his life. He willed himself not to make the same ones again.

He would love his children, and he would be a father to them.

His sister would care for Ayashe until her Maławitash, and then she would become his mate, his companion, and his friend.

And he would care for his people.

He would love and lose again. He breathed in and out, seeing it all there in the beauty of the night, a gift from the Great Spirits.

He thought about the ceremony that had celebrated his return, the dancing and singing, and the offerings that were given to bring Aanyáy back. It felt as though they had danced and sang for days and nights. Yiska had recorded the story in color on the wall behind the fire. The people prayed for the ice to recede, for the herds to return and for the fish to swim in the river again.

And now the stars appeared.

Saigwan took them as a sign of reassurance. He could handle whatever was laid at his feet. He would be strong enough for his people.

He had to be.

The preparations were almost complete: baskets and baskets of food for the feasting, the painted mating tent with its pile of soft furs, everyone's best finery and jewelry. Asku watched the women and older girls as they ran around putting all in order. His mother and aunt stood at a preparing table near the Teacher's home, laughing and talking as they pounded and kneaded what would become something delicious, he was sure of it. But he gave them a wide berth, lest they either ask him a question he did not want to answer or give him looks that said *stay out of the way.*

It was almost a relief that the cut on his hand needed doctoring, providing in turn an excuse to check on Sunukkuhkau. Asku went into the Grandfather's tent. The old man waved him toward the tall table covered in furs in the very center of the room.

Sunukkuhkau was propped up in what had been Kitchi's chair. "How are you feeling, *shikhs*?" Asku asked.

"Better every day, *Ty-ee'*, thanks to your Grandfather."

"I am sure your people are missing you," Asku said, as the Grandfather approached with a basket-woven tray of tools.

"Yes, I am anxious to see how they fare, and anxious to release my father's spirit."

"I understand."

The Grandfather hummed as he coated the broken skin on Asku's hand in one of his green, gritty herbal mixtures.

"*Máh-sie*, Asku," Sunu said. "For all that you did."

As the Grandfather wrapped his hand, Asku replied, "I think it is no more than you and Paj would have done for me."

Despite all the hubbub that consumed the rest of the day, Asku was again restless that night.

Saigwan entered the tent. Though it was the third time in his life, it felt like the nervous anticipation of the first. He was somewhere near twenty winters. In them, he had already fathered four children and released the spirits of two beautiful women, both he had loved dearly.

Saigwan had no more tears for his losses. He found time to retreat to the inner ritual chamber, where the voices were heard. They called to him from the walls, and he let their words and their memories overcome him. He heard Una and Moema, and even his mother, speaking or singing to him. Their voices reminded Saigwan that all life was connected, past, present, and future—and that when a loved one passed on, she did not truly leave.

Ayashe had grown into a beautiful young woman. The people had celebrated her sacred time with much joy, for this would help him to be again the father and leader that that they needed him to be. Her laughter and joy filled the cave in ways he could not even have imagined, like rays of warming sunlight slipping past the clouds.

Now she lay before him, covered in the same furs he had seen twice before. Until now, he had wondered if he would ever see her as more than a girl. Almost the day that her time had come upon her, it was as if blinders were lifted from his eyes. He no longer saw the silly child that made him laugh. He saw the outline of her breasts under her deerskin dress, the curve of her hips. Once, when she squatted at the fire, he caught a glimpse of the pale, delicate skin of the inside of her thigh. He had ducked around a nearby tent to hide his sudden yearning.

And now she lay before him. He knelt next to her, brushing her hair from her face and tracing her cheek with the back of his hand. She smiled at him, and as ever, he could not help but smile back.
    "Are you frightened, átawit?"
    "Ha! Of you?" she snorted.
    For whatever reason, Ayashe may have needed him, but he and his people needed her more than she knew.

The ceremony began as the sun set that night. Asku turned once Toward the Great Mountains and the Setting Sun, where Pahto watched in all his majesty. The sky, bright pink on the horizon, illuminated the mountain in a bluish hue. The fluffy clouds above Pahto's peak looked like pink smoke spilling from the mountain's core. Up higher, the clouds swirled in darker blues and grays. He made almost a game of closing his eyes for a few moments, then opening them to see how the colors had changed. *Pahto seems to call out to me on this special day, lighting the path ahead. My spirit is content.*
    Too bad I cannot eat a thing, in spite of the enormous amounts of food the women have made. He pretended to try everything, but all he really wanted was the tea the Grandfather made to settle jumpy stomachs. Unfortunately, none was set before him. Noting Asku's discomfort, Pajackok poked Sunu in the side and snorted.
    The mating tent seemed to loom over the firepit. Handprints covered the lower section, some big and some very small. He knew where Matahnu and Susannawa's were, for they had proudly showed him that morning. But now a section above them caught Asku's eye: a bright sun, a horse, and a bison in stick figures. He thought of his losses, the losses of those present, and for a moment, pain washed over his heart. Then the Teacher spoke.
    "It is time."
    A hush fell about the busy firepit. At some emotional remove, Asku felt their excitement and anticipation, a sense of being at the beginning of healing times.

Chitsa and Huyana led Kaliskah through the door of the tent, wrapped in the most beautiful white fur Asku had ever seen. The women had made sure the fur showed off Kaliskah's shape to best advantage. Atop her elaborate braid sat a hide crown, stained black, with short vibrant feathers poking out the top. On the belt that cinched the robe at her waist, Asku saw the exquisite dagger he had made for her and understood why she wore it today. It was not there as a tool, nor as a weapon. It was the symbol of a strong young woman who had killed in defense of the people into whom she would mate.

Asku was not sure how things were done at the Wanuukshiłáma, but he had seen enough mating ceremonies within his tribe. Among the Patisapatisháma, the woman was usually led by her father and mother. The two always walked her from the tent to the ceremonial fire, where her intended mate stood waiting with the Chief, the Teacher, and the Mating Cord. There the woman's parents would guide her into the arms of her new love.

But here, now, there were neither chiefs nor fathers present. Asku thought of the pain that must cause her now. *Now I am her chief. And her mate. How can I be both to her?*

The women had solved the procedural question in their own way. Kaliskah had mothers on either side: Chitsa and Huyana, looking proud and decorous.

Asku stood, forgot the weight of the *tamáawish*, nearly fell backward, then managed to adjust. There were chuckles, but they bespoke good nature. The Teacher unrolled the long, twisted Mating Cord as Asku walked forward. They had looked at it together that morning, when the Teacher had explained that it was the same cord with which he had united Asku's mother and father. He had studied the rough, antiquated weave, something he had not done in all the times he had seen it wrapped around other couples. In his mind, he saw only one couple: *a young chief with a heavy awkward headdress on his head, and a small, quiet girl with dirt from the Elk Plains still on her feet.*

The vision had made him sad and happy at the same time, like now.

The Teacher and Pajackok each took an end of the cord. When Chitsa and Huyana stepped back, the two men wrapped the cord around

Asku's shoulders and then around Kaliskah's. They tied it tightly in front of them in a big, thick knot.

A drum began to beat softly from around the fire, very softly. The Teacher sang words that Asku had heard before: *"Inmíma átawitma tíinma…*Great Spirits, unite our tribes once again. Bless our young Chief with many sons and daughters. Unite these two—Askuwa'tu Haylaku, our young chief, and Kaliskah Sayen, the beautiful Great Sea daughter."

The people softly chanted to the quiet tapping of the big drums. *"Watwáa naknúwim…"*

The Teacher smiled and said, *"Áwpam txána paláxs*…now you have become one."

Asku looked into Kaliskah's eyes. He could see the fire's flames dancing in their depths, and he found hope and joy again. He reached for her hands and pulled her to his chest.

He had no words, but her smile said he didn't need them.

＞—→

Asku awoke to the crispness of early morning. Kaliskah's arm was across his chest, her face nestled against his shoulder, chest rising and falling in slow rhythm.

I could gladly stay here a long time. But I can't. Without waking Kaliskah up, he disengaged from her arm and rearranged the furs over her. She would need them; even inside the tent and near the fire, he could feel the morning chill.

With one last longing look, Asku stepped from the tent. He sat down next to the Teacher, pulled his legs under his wrap, closed his eyes, and began to take slow, deep breaths.

But Saigwan did not speak to him this time. No vision overtook him, no sorrow, no pain, not even joy filled his heart as he stepped into that other time. There was only the cool, fresh morning air.

"Askuwa'tu," the Teacher began, "how are you, my *tita*?"

Asku looked into the old man's eyes before responding. "I will be fine."

"Yes. But with me, it will be okay, if you are not."

"*Kw'atá, Sapsikw'atá*. That is a comfort. Can we talk after my rounds this morning? There are preparations to make."

➤—→

All was still quiet at his home. He looked out toward Pahto, past the drying tree and the new tent and firepit the tribe had begun. Asku bent over his family firepit, re-stoking the fire and moving the hot rocks back into the flames. He heard the little ones beginning to stir inside the tent. Soon enough, his mother stepped out, tying her hair behind her. She looked like she had not slept much again.

"Blessings on this cold day, *ita*," he said, smiling.

She did not smile back. "And to you, *isha*. Thank you for starting the fire again. How was your night?"

"Oh, you know," he mumbled in embarrassment, "very uneventful."

"I am sure it was." Chitsa sounded as if she had aged ten winters in ten days.

His aunt soon stepped from the tent, then Nayhali and then a couple of sleepy little ones, hair all messy, rubbing their eyes. He stood up, greeted everyone, and went back toward the tent where he had spent the night. As he checked the ceremonial firepit, Kaliskah stepped out into the rising sun's light, hair combed and pulled back in a neat long braid, feet bare as usual.

He wrapped his arms around her waist, lifted her off the ground and held her tightly. *And now, I say this for the first time, what I will say each morning for all my life.* "Blessings today, *átawit*," he whispered in her ear.

"And to you, *Wyánch'i*. I missed you."

He took a step back and smiled. "As you know, *átawit*, my father taught me that each morning I ought to walk around, check on dwellings, greet people, look in on those in need. My mother did not accompany him on those walks, and probably most of the time you will be too busy, but today you are not. I think many of our people would like to welcome you personally. Will you join me?"

Kaliskah's smile lit up the morning like a second sunrise. "I would be glad. I was so worried you would have to do it without me; I know customs are different. But I will make my home here, and I wish to know everyone from the newest baby to the most ancient grandfather."

"Then let's go."

At each home they were greeted with a blessing for the new couple, and at each home they responded similarly. They looked at tents, and for signs of anything amiss. They checked the garden, then they walked hand in hand down to the bluff, meeting mothers and children along the way.

They stood at the bluff for a while, in silence, just looking at the great expanse. From the Rising Sun to the Setting Sun, Nch'i-Wána flowed as it always had—as it always would. Nothing could or would ever stop the flow of the mighty River.

Chapter 38

Asku sat with the Teacher all morning, making preparations for the voyage to Apenimon's funeral: who should go, who should stay, what gifts to send, how the Patisapatisháma should honor the Wanuukshiłáma chief. Then they talked about his father.

"You know, Askuwa'tu, your father sat in that very spot. We discussed his trip to the Elk Plains to seek the hand of the chief's daughter, and then of his journey to honor the Sea Chief with his sister. He was younger than you are now."

"I remember the story well. Only days after he put on the *tamáawish*, he mated his sister to the Wanuukshiłáma chief, then went and got my mother from the Wawyukyáma."

"It was a very difficult time for him," the old man continued, walking about the Story House, smudging it with sage and lemongrass.

It cleared Asku's mind. He closed his eyes.

In his mind he saw Saigwan, standing at the mouth of the cave, his hand held high in blessing, the bison head at the back of his neck.

Saigwan is calling to me.

"*Sapsikw'ałá*, I think I will visit the cave before we go. There is something I am to see."

"Then you must," said the elder. "Best that you do not delay."

He told Kaliskah, and she understood.

———

Asku had no trouble getting up before the sun; of late, sleep had become a stranger. He let Kaliskah sleep, stoked up the fire a bit, and soon met Kitchi and Hawiłish. All were equipped for a short journey.

Other than the newly tightened watch system, the only other person up at that hour was the Teacher.

"*Watwáa naknúwim,*" the old man said, keeping his voice low. "May the Great Spirits protect you and return you to us safely to us."

They pushed the little canoe into Nch'i-Wána just the as sun began to rise. Asku could not look away as the very tip of the sun crested the plateau out toward the Elk Plains. Toward the Great Mountains, the sun illuminated Pahto in bright pinks with little streaks of white clouds. The rest of the sky became the lightest of blues as light crossed the land once again.

Asku breathed in the new day.

After a quick crossing, there was a brief debate as they tried to rediscover the trail up the bluff. The hike was easier than Asku remembered and posed little challenge even for Kitchi. That, of course, did not prevent Kitchi from sharing sporadic complaints all the way up. As they sat around the fire in the same rock-sheltered campsite as before, Asku watched him rubbing his knee. "*Mishnam wá, pásiks?*"

Kitchi pulled his trouser leg up past his knee. In the light of the fire, the long, thick scar looked red and sore. "Good, man," he replied, rubbing at it. "It feels good today."

Hawilish and Asku traded the faintest of smiles. "Hopefully tomorrow will be easier," said Hawilish.

"So," Kitchi began, his trouser leg still pulled up, "will you tell us now, please?"

Hawilish rolled his eyes. "Kitchi, leave it be."

"*Kúu mish,*" Asku said, amused to see Hawilish's eyes go up. "Okay. What do you want to know?"

"All of it, of course." Even Hawilish seemed to lean forward a bit. "What is it like? Did you figure it out? How did you know what to do?"

Asku laughed, a deeper laugh than he had enjoyed in some time. "Yes, I figured it out. I mean, once you spend some time with each other, it just makes sense."

Hawilish looked confused. "That doesn't explain anything," Kitchi sighed dramatically.

"Well, neither of us knew exactly what to do. But we just, well, figured it out together."

"Uh-huh," Kitchi encouraged. "I am listening."

"I mean, you just have to take your time and not be…rushed, I guess."

"What? That explanation is not worth a leaky basket," protested Kitchi. Hawilish just laughed.

"It happens to be the truth, *pásiks*."

"That's it? That's all you are gonna tell us?" Kitchi's voice rose. "Okay, chief or no chief, I am about to kick your…"

"We are hunting after we get home from the sea," Asku interjected.

Hawilish snickered. Kitchi jumped to his feet and knocked Asku backward off the log. They rolled on the ground for a while until all three were laughing.

When that was as resolved as it was going to be, Asku tossed another couple of pieces of wood onto the fire. "So, Kitchi, when we go on the hunt, will you take care of the village while we are gone?"

"What?" Hawilish asked. "You are going?"

"So are you." *And now, I have to hope this is enough.* "Kitchi, I need you and Liwanu to take care of the village while I am gone. I am setting you two in charge of the watch. You both are hotheads, but there is no one else I trust more. I need you to do this for me."

Kitchi's eyes clouded over. "I can do that."

"I mean it, Kitchi." Asku narrowed his stare and waited until Kitchi looked at him. "We cannot be caught unaware again. I won't let that happen. Things need to change. Do you understand me?"

Kitchi nodded and ran a hand over his face. Then he took a deep breath. "*Máalnam winata*? How far will you go?"

"As far as we need to in order to get goats, elk, deer, whatever we can find. Winter is coming."

Since they were little boys, they had dreamed of the day they would leave on a real hunting trip—not just as their fathers' helpers, but as hunters on a necessary mission. It was the dream of every little boy and every young man. That included Kitchi, who just stared into the fire.

Please, Spirits. He must have something, and this is the best thing he can do. I have lost too much, and I cannot lose this friend. "Kitchi, I need your help, man. I cannot be both at Pahto and at Nch'i-Wána; you know that is impossible. Will you help me, *pásiks?*"

Something strange crossed Kitchi's eyes. "Yes, little *Wyánch'i,*" he nodded and smirked. "Liwanu and I will handle it."

"Good. Thank you." Asku turned to get the stick they were using as a poker. *Spirits, thank you.*

Kitchi cleared his throat noisily behind him. "If..."

Asku turned to look at him, narrowing his eyes. *Here it comes.*

"...you tell us more. And this time...details."

➤—→

The light of dawn crept over the mountains Toward the Rising Sun as they climbed the jagged rock to the cave. Asku yearned for the cave, for the paintings and the memories, for the voices. He needed this cave.

It was just as he remembered it. Asku walked the perimeter, examining Yiska's ancient artwork. He found the painting of Saigwan's father, the chief, when they had first found the cave. There was the image of Saigwan's birth, and then the heart-wrenching scene of his father's death. Asku laid his hand upon the image of a boy of fourteen winters, blood dripping from his back, as he stumbled carrying the body of his father. Hawɨlish rested a hand on Asku's shoulder.

He lingered in front of the pictures Manneha had drawn of his family and his people, the great mammoth bear's vengeance, and then of his own. Next came the added picture of Manneha's death, and the story the bear had told Saigwan. Parts of the paint had crumbled away, but one who had felt the stories happen still knew.

"*Áwnam wá wishúwani?*" he asked as they stood before the dark back tunnel.

"Sure." Kitchi pulled his knife from his belt, shifted the cane to his other hand, and started down the tunnel.

"Just be careful. The air could be worse now," Hawɨlish reminded him.

They stopped from time to time to listen, but there were no noises. No chanting, no drums, no echoed screams. All Asku could feel coming from the ancient hallway to the ritual chamber was the movement of cool, stale air.

"It stinks," Kitchi whispered as he held his torch high, the light casting an eerie glow across the room.

Asku walked the perimeter of the chamber. Not long ago, the pictures had frightened him, but not now. He stopped at the scene of Saigwan's manhood ceremony. The drawings were sharper and better preserved in this chamber. He saw the scene in his mind again: the boy lifted onto the altar, the bear claws carving scars into his flesh, the masks, the shadows, the words...

The ancient firepit still had enough wood for a small fire, and it took Hawilish and Kitchi little time to get one going. Asku sat down at the fire, watching the flames dance in the weird breeze of the cave's inner chamber, and closed his eyes. The ancient memory washed over him...

It was still dark inside his tent home, and so very cold. He edged out from under Ayashe's arm and tucked her back in. She held his infant son, Moema's second living son, nestled in the crook of her other arm. Saigwan paused to look at his older two where they lay snuggled together under a thick bearskin and smiled.

He took a moment to breathe the early morning air of the cave. He stretched his back and legs, then stoked up the embers of yesterday's fire. When it was hot enough, he added two pieces of reindeer bone; they would take a while to burn. He warmed his icy hands at the fire's edge.

The night lookout carved on a piece of elk antler. He looked up at the sound of Saigwan's footsteps. "Blessings this morning, Wyánch'i," said the tired-looking man.

"And to you," Saigwan replied. "How goes the watch?"

"Nothing amiss, Wyánch'i." He sniffed, wiping his nose on the back of his hand.

"Go get some rest. You look tired and cold."

Niyol soon found him there. They sat quietly at the cliff's edge.

"We must hunt, Niyol." Saigwan poked at the fire with a long stick. "We are running very low on everything."

"The wák'amu flour will sustain."

"Not for long, Niyol," Saigwan sighed. "We must hunt again. We need meat."

Niyol nodded. They sat in silence until the tribe began to stir with the morning's activities behind them.

After a time, a group of mothers arrived at the cave entrance. Saigwan stood to greet each of them and wish them luck on their gathering. "Máalnam wínata, lamyáy?" he asked one.

"Only as far as the river, Wyánch'i," she replied, tying her wrap. "It is too cold to go far with the little ones."

Saigwan and Niyol stood at the mouth of the cave watching the trail of mothers make their way out toward the frozen river. Saigwan prayed to the Great Spirits for their safe return.

Things have to get better, or we will never survive.

"Should we move on, yawtii?"

"I do not know, Wyánch'i. I do not know where would be better. We just have to keep trying."

They stood there for a long time watching the still-dusky sky's colors change and brighten. Aanyáy did not appear, though the day dawned like every other day. "Please," he whispered into the morning sky. "Please come back. We need you."

Niyol pointed into the distance. "Look there."

A young mother was shouting up and waving from the foot of the cliff. Saigwan moved toward her as fast as the jagged rocks would permit, fearing the worst, Niyol right behind him.

Only when he reached the base of the cliff did he realize that she was smiling. Tears coursed down her cheeks. Her hood was off, the icy wind whipping her hair into a tangle.

"What is it?" he asked, drawing his knife. Niyol skidded to a stop behind him, knife already drawn.

"Wyánch'i!" The words came out in gasps. "Núsux...in the river...they swim! They are here!"

"What?"

"The salmon swim! Many of them. We can see them under the ice!"

He turned to look at Niyol. Could it really be true? Have the salmon returned under the ice?

"Niyol, assemble the others—kitu!"

Niyol scrambled back up the cliff, shouting the life-sustaining news. It would worry everyone at first, but Saigwan dared not wait. The fishing opportunity could pass. All hands were needed at once.

"Come see, Wyánch'i!" He ran after the young mother, too excited to do anything else. Soon they passed through the trees that lived at the river's edge. To the casual observer, Nch'i-Wána was iced over, a thin layer of snow atop the ice. The women were gathered at the edge; some were laughing and singing, others were sobbing and holding one another. Numerous babies protested the commotion by joining it at the tops of their miniature lungs.

Saigwan walked toward where the water used to be. At the bank, he dropped to his knees and laid a hand on the ice. He could see through it!

And there under the ice, beneath his hand, swam hundreds of fish, many of them longer than his forearm. No one could mistake their red and black spots, nor the hook end of their noses. They swam upstream, and as he watched them swim, more came.

Then he felt sudden warmth on his face. Saigwan tore his eyes away from the incredible sight and looked up. A sliver of Aanyáy shone down upon him, her warmth a reassurance of better times to come.

"Kw'alá," he whispered. The women echoed his words. "Thank you, Great Spirits, may you find gladness in this people."

Asku opened his eyes. There in the inner chamber of the cave, of these things he was certain:

…he would love, and he would lose again…

…he would have fear and pain in his life…

…but he would also have great joy and hope…

"My blood will protect this people. My blood will lead this people. My blood will spill for this people. The blood of my father, the blood of my grandfather, the blood of the great chief Saigwan…for my people," he intoned.

Hawilish nodded.

"We are with you, man," Kitchi added, from across the small fire.

Chapter 39

They left at dawn. Chitsa and Kaliskah sat at the bow, huddled together against the cold morning wind. It felt like winter already. *This would not be the day to mishandle a canoe and dump anyone into Nch'i-Wána.*

Asku had left orders to begin preparations for the winter ahead. He remembered Saigwan's story, in which the babies had died because their mothers did not have enough food for themselves to provide what was needed to nurse them. *We live in such an easy time by comparison, but still, I feel the weight of the world on my shoulders.*

Asku turned one last time to watch as the Teacher and Kitchi disappeared from sight. He prayed to the Great Spirits for his people's safety while he was away. Liwanu and Kitchi had showed him the new plan to guard the village; things would be different from now on. *My people will not live in fear of another tragedy.* He had also asked Hatayah to stay with Nayhali and the little ones. She seemed glad to help.

The Grandfather had made sure Sunu was propped up comfortably in the canoe, with enough healing teas and poultices to doctor him all the way home, and strict instructions for his care. Both Sunu and Pajackok had bidden the old man farewell with fervent thanks. Now Pajackok steered their canoe. Huyana looked after Sunu, who was patient with all of them.

Hawilish and Takoda rode another canoe, talking and arguing at times about the proper way of paddling a canoe down river. Another boat followed them, loaded down with gifts for the Wanuukshiłáma.

Other than the cold breeze, the weather held fair the entire way. The only headaches were the inevitable portages. That at Wayám was easiest, for many who were present wanted to offer condolences and support for both families and tribes.

Kohana and a crew of Wanuukshiłáma met them at the water's edge in the small cove where the trail began off Skip-pi-náu-in. He walked with a cane now but was not so lamed as to refrain from hurrying forward to help Sunu. There was much rejoicing to see Sunu on the mend, and four men hoisted him onto their shoulders on a woven *tk'ú* mat with two long poles on either side. Others carried all of the gear and gifts.

The entire party stopped at the bluff where the sand began, and the winding trail passed the poking plants and grasses. Here Pajackok raised his hands in blessing.

"*T'k-tók-te Tl'ka-ná-a Wé-ko-wa*...Good Mother Sea," he chanted, "we thank you. May you be glad with this people."

Further down, Asku laughed at the antics of the little gray birds hovering over the sand, and the funny white birds with long legs and smiling orange beaks. He had forgotten how refreshing he found the sea. The tall dune grass whistled all around him. The dry, prickly plants now seemed to line the entire length of the trail.

The roar and crash of the moving sea caught his ear, and he shielded his eyes to look out beyond the fingers of white water. Kohana was also looking. "Ah, yes. Paj, there is something you should see. Look."

Asku also did so. Off in the distance and barely visible on the horizon was—something.

Pajackok stopped to look where he pointed. "How long has it been there?"

"Two or three days." Kohana replied. "It floats Toward the Great Mountains and the mouth, then back again. The second time it reappeared, I sent scouts to follow. They reported that it seemed to attempt entering Nch'i-Wána, but then backed away. Here it sits."

"What is it?" inquired Asku.

"A Floating House," Kohana replied. "It looks like...we need to prepare." He looked back at Asku.

Asku nodded his head. "Of course, but what for, brother?"

Pajackok narrowed his eyes and gazed back out over the horizon. "I fear a flood is coming."

ʼAWACHA NÁY

Tribal Kinships

Patisapatisháma *"the people like branches of a tree"*—
The River Tribe
Languages: Sahaptin, Chinook Jargon

Napayshni Hianayi—Asku's father, Chief or current head elder of the
River Tribe
Chitsa—Asku's mother, daughter of Kalataka of the Elk Plains Tribe
     Nayhali—Asku's older sister
     Askuwa'tu Haylaku (Asku)
    Susannawa (Sus)—Asku's younger brother
    Nis'hani (Nisy)—Asku's younger sister
   Mininaywah (Mini)—Asku's youngest sister
Amitola—Asku's grandmother, Napayshni's stepmother
Anamy—Tribal Elder
Ashkii—Patisapatisháma warrior, elder brother of Haysutu and Maska
Chaytan—Napayshni's adopted brother, Asku's adopted uncle
Hatayah—Asku's friend, neighbor
Hawilish—Asku's best friend
Haymawihiu—Teacher/*Sapsikw'alá*; most respected elder & learned man
within the Patisapatisháma
Haysutu—young Patisapatisháma warrior, brother of Ashkii and Maska
Huwahkan—neighbor, Hatayah's brother
Ituha—Kitchi's mother
Kitchi—Asku's best friend
Kiyiya—Grandfather; Healer, medicine man
Laytiah—Hatayah's mother
Nayati—Kitchi's father, Tribal Elder
Liwanu—Patisapatisháma warrior
Maska—teenage boy in tribe, brother of Ashkii and Haysutu

Matahnu (Mat)—neighbor, Susannawa's best friend
Sahkantiak—Patisapatisháma warrior
Sunsaa—Asku's grandfather's best friend, Tribal Elder
U'taktay—Tribal Elder
Wahkan—Tribal Elder

Wawyukyáma *"the people of the Elk Plains"*
Languages: Sahaptin, Chinook Jargon

Kalataka Wahchinksapa—Chief or current head elder, Asku's maternal grandfather
Hay'wii—Asku's maternal grandmother, Healer, medicine woman
      U'hitaykah—Asku's maternal uncle
      Chitsa—Asku's mother
Aanapay—the chief's nephew, village messenger & horse keeper
Mach'ni—Wawyukyáma warrior

Wanuukshiłáma or Wé-ko-wa Til'lig-hum
"the people where the river meets the sea"
Languages: Lower Chinookan, Chinook Jargon

Apenimon—Chief
Huyana—Asku's paternal aunt, second wife of Apenimon
      Pajackok—eldest son of Apenimon's first wife
      Sunukkuhkau—second son of Apenimon's first wife
      Kaliskah—only daughter born of Apenimon's first wife
      Takoda—Huyana's eldest son, Asku's cousin
Kohana—Wanuukshiłáma warrior & messenger, speaks Sahaptin

Pyúsh P'ushtáayama "the people below the Snake Hills"
Languages: Northern Paiute, Chinook Jargon

Matunaaga (Matchitehew "with an evil heart")—self-proclaimed chief
Keme—young outcast
Mahkah—grandson of powerful Southern Pyúsh chief

Ancient Tribal Kinships

Nch'i-Wána Tánawit *"the people of the river cave"*

Saigwan—Chief
Una—Saigwan's first wife
Moema—Saigwan's second wife
        Isi—Saigwan & Moema's daughter
        Manneha—Saigwan & Moema's son
Achak— Teacher/*Sapsikw'atá*, most respected elder within tribe
Kaga—Saigwan's father, chief
Kasa—Saigwan's younger sister
Manneha—young chief from another Blue Mountain tribe
Niyol—Saigwan's best friend
Yiska—Elder, gifted storyteller & painter

Pítxanuk Lawilat-łá
"the people below the trees of Fire Mountain"

Sahale—Saigwan's maternal grandfather, chief
Ayashe—daughter of the tribe's greatest warrior

Glossary of Words and Phrases

Father: Túta
Mother: Íła
Son: Tɨta (man's) Ɨsha (woman's)
Daughter: Ɨsha (man or woman's)
Grandfather: Púsha (paternal), Tíla (maternal)
Grandmother: Ála (paternal) Káła (maternal)
Brother (or male cousin):

> yáya (man's older)
> nɨka (man's younger)
> yáya (woman's older)
> nɨpa (woman's younger)

Sister (or female cousin):

> nána (man's older)
> lítsa (man's younger)
> nɨsha (woman's older)
> níya (woman's younger)

Uncle: Mɨxa (paternal) Káka (maternal)
Aunt: Shísha (paternal) Xáxa (maternal)
Nephew:

> Páya (man's brother son)
> Píti (man's sister son)
> Pámta (woman's brother son)
> Íti (woman's sister son)

Niece:

> Páya (man's brother daughter)
> Píti (man's sister daughter)
> Páway (woman's brother daughter)
> Písi (woman's sister daughter)

Grandchild:

> Púsha (man's son's child)
> Ála (woman's son's child)
> íla (man's daughter's child)
> áła (woman's daughter's child)

A̓

A̓mash wáchuk—Quiet down now
Átawishamash—I love you
Átawit—sweetheart, beloved
A̓wacha náy—This is the way it was (storyteller question to listeners).
Children would reply loudly "Íi" (yes).
A̓w icháawi—Now he is gone; He died
A̓wnam wá wishúwani—Are you ready now?
A̓wna náwnak̲'i—Now we are finished
A̓wna túx̲sha—Let's go home now
A̓wna wínasha—Let's go
A̓wpam tx̲ána paláxs—Now you have become one
Áx̲sh'ax̲sh—tusk shell, dentalium
Áypx̲—plain, plateau

A

Al'-ta—now (Chinook Jargon)
Al-tákh—now (Lower Chinook)
Anahúy—black bear
Aputaput—Palouse Falls
Ashwaníya—slave
As-sin-wati—Cree word for the Rocky Mountain Range
Ats—younger sister (Chinook Jargon & Lower Chinook)
Awkɫáw áw—Stop now, that's enough

Aa

Aanyáy—Sun of legends

B

Buha—balance, the fundamental aspect of Paiute religion (Northern Paiute)

C

Chalámat—ceremonial clay pipe
Chcháya—juneberry, serviceberry
Chchúu tx̲ának—Be quiet

Cheechako—tenderfoot; newcomer (Chinook Jargon)
Chiskíin—Sahaptin, "Our way of speaking"
Chú'—hush (historically derived)
Chúksh—obsidian

Ch'
Ch'láy—salmon flour

E
Eh'-ko-lie—whale (Chinook Jargon)

H
Hiqua—tusk shell, dentalium (Chinook Jargon)
Hy-ak—fast, swift (Chinook Jargon)

I
Iksíks Wána—Yakima River
Ilksáas wínasha—I am going alone
Ikwá-na—salmon (Lower Chinook)
Inmíma átawitma tíinma—My beloved people (heard at meetings)
Ipáyknɨm—Pay attention to me

Íi
Íi—Yes

Ii
Iiooie—I am well (Northern Paiute)

K
Káhp-ho—older brother (Chinook Jargon)
Ká'uyt—celebration of first foods
Kimooenim—Tucannon River (Nez Perce)
K'ɨplach—tomahawk
Kɨtu—hurry
Kla'-how-ya—How do you do or Goodbye; ordinary salutation meeting or parting (Chinook Jargon)

Ko-pet'—Stop (Chinook Jargon)
Kúu mísh—Okay; Alright; I don't know

K'
K'súyaas—lamprey

Kw'
Kw'ałá—Thank you
Kw'ayawí—cougar
Kw'sís—village just west of the confluence of the Snake and Columbia

<u>K</u>'
<u>K</u>'a'áay—No way, BS
<u>K</u>'mił—Rock Creek

L
Lalíik—Rattlesnake Ridge
Lamyáy—female elder (respectful)
Lawilat-łá—Mt. St. Helens

Ł
Łáta<u>x</u>at Wána—Klickitat River
Łík—Go away; Get out

M
Máalnam wínata—How long will you be away? How far will you go?
Máh-sie—Thank you (Chinook Jargon)
Małáwitash—1st time menstruation
Mamook kloshe tumtum—To make peace, to make friends (Chinook Jargon)
Mem'-a-loost—dead (Chinook Jargon)
Mɨnán—Where? In which direction?
Mi-sái-ka klim-sá-mama—your father (Lower Chinook)
Míshnam wá—How are you?
Míshnam pamshtk'úksha'—Do you understand me?
Míshpam míshana—What have you been doing?

Misht'ipni—stupid, senseless, out of one's mind
Myánash—child

N
Nak-i-kláu-a-nak—1st fork of Youngs River (Lower Chinook)
Nakst—no (Lower Chinook)
Náy—Okay? Alright?
Nch'ínch'ima—elders
Nch'i-Wána—The Big River, The Columbia River
Nch'i-Wána Tánawit—Saigwan's people, the Ancient Ones, "the people of the river cave"
Nixanásh—fish weir
Noonie-tu-cubin—You are my friend (Northern Paiute)
Nuksháy—Otter
Núsux—salmon (general)

O
Ok-ó-la—waves (Lower Chinook)
Ow—little brother, younger male cousin (Chinook Jargon)

P
Pahto—Mt. Adams
Pa'iwáxim—Wait for me
Pák'u—council meeting
Pa-lús—Palouse River
Patisapatisháma—Asku's people, the River People, "the people like branches of a tree"
Pásiks—lifetime friend
Pawaat-łá—Spirit Guide
Páwanikt—name giving ceremony
Pe kahta—Why so? (Chinook Jargon)
Pik'ú-nen—Snake River (Nez Perce)
Pináwaachik—Watch out
Pítxanuk Lawilat-łá—Saigwan's grandfather's tribe, the Ancient Ones, "the people below the trees of Fire Mountain"
Pt'íniks—girl; Pt'ilíyin (du); Pt'ilíma (pl)

Pyúsh P'ushtáayama—renegade Pyúsh, the Snake People, "the people below the Snake Hills"

S
Sapsikw'ałá—Teacher
Síks—friend
Skip-pi-náu-in—Skipanoun Creek (Lower Chinook)
Spilyáy—Coyote of legends
Sts'áat—dark, darkness
Sut'x̱włá—whale
Sut'x̱włayáy—Whale of legends
Sx̱íx̱tama—mercenaries/renegades from the Angry Hills

Sh
Shikhs—friend (Chinook Jargon)
Shínmash wá wanícht—What is your name?
Shín pawá imák—Who are you?
Shín pawá piiník—Who are they?
Shíx máytsk̲i—Good morning
Shwúyi—moose

T
Táaminwa—always, at all times, forever
Talápas—pouch, wallet or purse
Tamáawish—eagle feather headdress
Tax̱úma—Mt. Rainier
Ten'-as—child (Chinook Jargon)
Tɨmná—heart, seed
Tíshpun—black widow spider
Ti-tum-má-ma—my father (Lower Chinook)
Tk'í—vision
Tk'ú—tule
Tkwínat—Chinook salmon
Tlakluit—seminomadic tribe across the river from Wayám
Tl-ka-má-ma—father (Lower Chinook)
Tl'ka-ná-a—mother (Lower Chinook)

Tu-cubin-noonie—I am your friend (Northern Paiute)
Tûkspûsh—John Day River
Túnmash wá shapyáwit—What's bothering you?
Túnmash wá táymun—What's new? What news do you have?
Tu-se—Touchet River
Twaluutpamá—fishing platform or scaffolding
Twáytash—smoke house, drying shed
Ty-ee'—chief (Chinook Jargon)

T'
T'at'aɫíya—Witch Woman of legends
T'k-tók-te—Good (Lower Chinook)

U
Ul-há-i-pa—demon race (Lower Chinook)
Uyt-ɫáma—the First People, ancestors

W
Wák̲'amu—camas
Walawála—Walla Walla River
Waluulapam—people living near the Walla Walla River
Wanuukshiɫáma—Sea People, near Astoria, "the people where the river meets the sea"
Watwáa naknúwim—Protect and take care of us
Wawachí—acorn
Wawyukyáma—Asku's grandfather's people, above Palouse Falls, "the people of the Elk Plains"
Wáx̲push—rattlesnake
Wé-ko-wa—the sea (Lower Chinook)
Wisík—Blackberry
Wyá'ayat—female head of household
Wayám—"Echo of Falling Water," Celilo
Wílaps—sturgeon
Wínak—Go
Wíshpush—large beaver
Wyanawiɫá—stranger, visitor

Wyánch'i—leader, chief or oldest living member of a family tree, subject to people
Wyanúukɨm íchɨn—Come this way
Wy-east—Mt. Hood

Xw
Xwayátsh—sweatlodge

X̲
X̲álish—wolf
X̲átxat—mallard duck
X̲ɨtway—friend, relative
X̲uxuxyáy—Raven of legends

Y
Yawtíi—companion (historically derived)
Yɨx̲a X̲ápaawish—Asku's waterfall, named after the beaver dam

MAPS

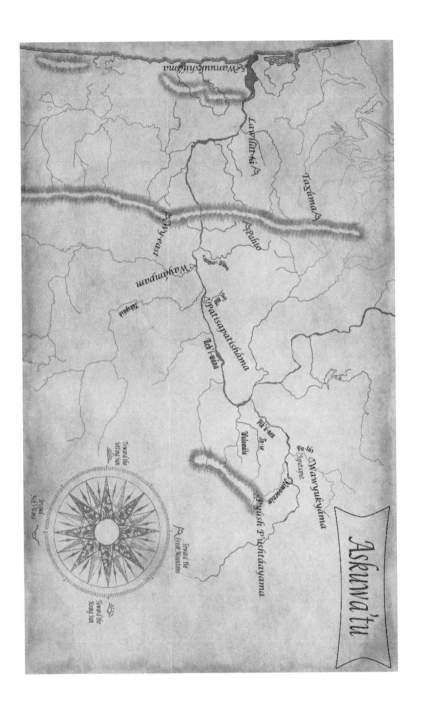

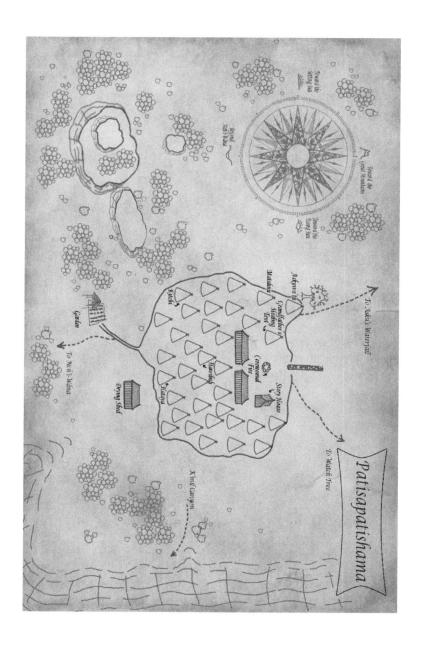

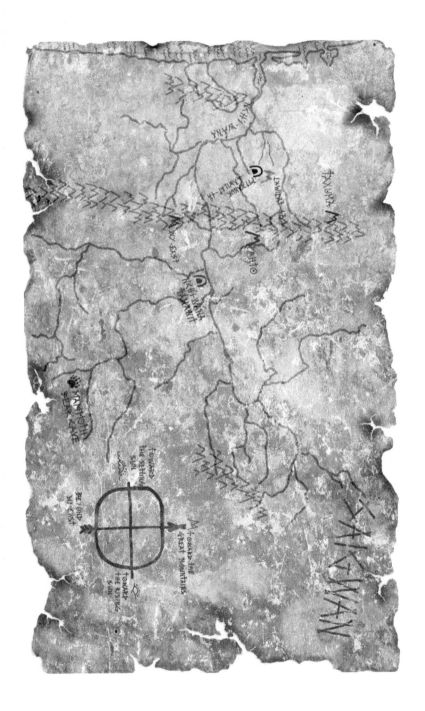

Made in the USA
Middletown, DE
15 February 2022